Bird on a Wire

Mark Richardson

The characters and events portrayed in this book are fictitious.
Any similarity to real persons, living or dead,
is coincidental and not intended by the author.

No part of this book may be reproduced, or stored in a retrieval system, or transmitted in any form or by any means, electronic, mechanical, photocopying, recording, or otherwise, without express written permission of the publisher.

Cover design by Eric Sweet

www.markrichardson.ca

First published 2021, Second edition 2025

Copyright © 2021, 2025 Mark Richardson
Jackie Blue Bike Press
All rights reserved.
ISBN: 978-1-7777590-2-5

Like a bird on the wire,
Like a drunk in a midnight choir,
I have tried in my way to be free.

- Leonard Cohen

CONTENTS

	Prologue	Pg. 1

PART ONE

1	Claire	Pg. 7
2	Jon	Pg. 15
3	Claire	Pg. 25
4	Jon	Pg. 33
5	Claire	Pg. 45
6	Jon	Pg. 55
7	Claire	Pg. 65

PART TWO

8	Jon	Pg. 77
9	Claire	Pg. 87
10	Jon	Pg. 101
11	Claire	Pg. 109
12	Jon	Pg. 115
13	Claire	Pg. 123
14	Jon	Pg. 129
15	Claire	Pg. 137
16	Jon	Pg. 143
17	Claire	Pg. 149
18	Vivian	Pg. 153
19	Jon	Pg. 155
20	Vivian	Pg. 161
21	Jon	Pg. 169
22	Vivian	Pg. 175
23	Jon	Pg. 177
24	Claire	Pg. 183

PART THREE

25	Jon	Pg. 191
26	Grant	Pg. 201
27	Jon	Pg. 207
28	Claire	Pg. 217
29	Grant	Pg. 219
30	Jon	Pg. 225
31	Claire	Pg. 233
32	Vivian	Pg. 235
33	Jon	Pg. 237
34	Grant	Pg. 247
35	Jon	Pg. 253
36	Vivian	Pg. 265
37	Jon	Pg. 267
38	Vivian	Pg. 275
	Acknowledgements	Pg. 281
	About the author	Pg. 283

Bird on a Wire

Prologue

Tampa, 2004

The mall was busy, even for a Monday in December. Two floors and people everywhere, surging and shuffling in and out of the doors and between the kiosks, every which way, bumping against each other in their push to get through to a couple of hundred stores.

Up by Santa's Grotto, the lineup stretched right over to the food court, where the lineups for McDonald's and Starbucks and Popeye's reached far beyond the tables. Shoppers pressed in under the Sunlight Dome, striding and pressing, ducking and deking in the last few days before Christmas.

The red-haired woman was no different from the other young mothers, pushing a three-wheeled stroller, guiding a small girl in a green summer dress who held tight to the stroller's arm. She was talking to her children, of course, and the security guard who watched through the cameras couldn't hear what she was saying but he zoomed in anyway. She had great legs, well toned, and they were well displayed in blue denim shorts.

Most of the cameras in the mall had fixed viewpoints, capable of zooming in and out but too simple to move from side to side. They were set to capture and record a high-resolution digital frame grab every ten seconds, and the videos were constantly playing out on two of the three large TV screens in the security office, half-hidden over by the restrooms. There were also some new, moveable video cameras near the food court and the watching guard could slide them around with a joystick, roaming the floor, looking for women with good legs.

The guards called the TV screens "the Fly" because it looked like something a housefly would see through its multi-lensed eyes. There were 48 color video feeds displayed on a grid across the two large screens, but the guards rarely watched them – there were too many images in one place and they'd give a headache if watched for too long. They were really just there as a record for checking back on anything that had already happened, and to look impressive to the unfortunate visitors to the office, those caught with light fingers in the mall's smaller stores and brought in for processing at the outer desk.

Instead, whoever was the guard on camera duty would watch the third big screen, which showed the images from the four video cameras that could be moved around. The pictures weren't great resolution, especially when they zoomed up close to capture some enticing cleavage or promising ass, but you could sweep most every inch of the mall like a drone over a battlefield and, with a bit of imagination, it was almost like flying.

There was only room for one guard, usually the Supervisor, to watch the Fly while the other three were out on patrol duty. Only one person needed to be there, anyway. If the Super saw anything that caught his eye, he'd radio through to the floor and the patrol guards would hear his words in their ear pieces and talk into their wrists to acknowledge and head on over.

Nobody monitored their conversations and outsiders couldn't hear the spoken words, but they kept up a special code anyway. A 10-44 was a large pair of breasts and the code ranged all the way up to a 10-48, depending on the Supervisor's estimate. Occasionally, he would call in a 10-49 over by Millie's Shoes or the Sears and all three guards would wander over to offer their own assessment. A 10-55 was a spectacular ass. A 10-69 was athletic. Didn't have to be pretty.

The Supervisor was a fleshy man with shaved hair that only accentuated his fleshy face and jowls. He was chewing on a toothpick and watching the red-haired woman – had been, off and on, for 20 minutes since she walked in with the kids out of the heat. He was watching a half-dozen other women too, though he hadn't radioed any of them in. He was darting around with his video cameras more like a mosquito than a housefly, zooming right in for a poke, a prod, then out again to take in more and more of the shoppers, swarming just outside his patch. It was tedious, boring work, watching silent people living noisy lives, but at least it could pick right up when a 10-55 came into view.

The redhead paused outside the Pens'n'Ink stationery store and bent over to look into the stroller, probably to tend to the child inside. Her back was to the camera and when she bent right over, her butt was right there in those tight blue shorts.

The Super zoomed in, sucking on his toothpick, rolling his thumb over the wheel on the joystick, *waaaaay in*, so the grain on her denim was clear and filled the camera's lens. He raised the camera slightly and could see some blue and black ink swirling above the shorts on the woman's back, but her shirt wasn't raised enough to get a good look at the tattoo. There would be no recording of this video unless he pressed the Record button. Video used far too much digital storage, which is why the cameras recorded still photographs only once every 10 seconds, and their repetitive, inconsequential images were erased every two days.

The ass disappeared suddenly when the woman moved, and instead, the Super saw the child inside the stroller, a big kid, a boy, fully dressed, probably three or four years old and too big, surely, to be pushed around like this, sitting back on a light blue blanket with his eyes closed. *Lazy*, thought the Super.

He rolled his thumb back to pull the camera out from the tight shot and saw the woman had turned to look back the way she'd come. She was attractive, all right. Short hair in a bob, small features in a slim frame, a white designer T-shirt that, if she twisted to one side, showed a tan, flat stomach. And she was twisting. A lot.

Something wasn't right. She was looking into the mall, at the throng of strangers, her head turning left and right. Now she was calling something, her mouth opening and closing in the silent video on the screen.

The Super stopped chewing on his toothpick and rolled his thumb some more on the joystick to pull out from the woman. He hit the button on his keyboard that expanded the image on the screen, pushing the other three video feeds into a small vertical grid to the left, and he saw the groups of people near the stationery store slow down and look at the woman and her stroller. He pressed Record.

He saw an older woman approach her, say something to her, then turn and look around. He squinted at the screen as he reached for his radio to call for a guard on the ground, then realized the cause: the little girl in the green summer dress was nowhere to be seen.

The images on the Fly changed in a constant rotation of flickering color. They showed the unending rivers and streams of Christmas shoppers moving, eddying, swirling through the mall, and the red-haired woman ran between them from camera image to camera image, parting the people with the stroller's chunky tires, calling, yelling, shouting through the mall, silent on the screen. They showed the guards approach her and they showed her flail her arms and twist her head every which way.

In the security office, the radio was crackling with calls from the guards. The Supervisor was scanning the Fly, looking for a green dress, looking for anything. He flew through the mall as best the cameras would let him, but finally settled back for one last look at the red-haired woman, and he reached for his phone to call the police.

He saw her look directly at his camera and he couldn't help but roll his thumb over the joystick wheel, zooming up tight, letting her face fill the screen. And he watched her eyes close and her mouth open, and even so far away, over by the restrooms on the other side of a locked door, he could hear her scream.

PART ONE

BIRD ON A WIRE

Chapter 1

CLAIRE, Toronto, 2023

My daughter's father was an asshole. Is an asshole. I know he's still alive because I creep him online, which is as much as I want anything to do with him. I doubt he creeps me. I doubt he even thinks about me these days, but I think about him, not in a good way.

He's not on any social media because he's low-life trash, but he sells cars and so his name comes up in the advertising for his dealership down in Florida. I'm really curious to know more – wouldn't you be? – but not so much that I'll do more than Google his name every week or so, just to see if anything's changed.

He could find out more about me if he wanted to and maybe he does, but I really doubt it. My life's not very interesting: I go to work on the ward at the hospital, I visit with my mom, I go out for a drink every now and again with friends, and I knit sweaters and put photos of them on Instagram. Knitting keeps me sane; it keeps me busy. I've turned into a homebody over the last decade though my apartment's nothing to speak of. Dull, huh?

I started knitting back when I was with John because that's what I thought new mothers were supposed to do. Baby socks and baby hats. The only ones I could find in the stores then were either pink or blue and I've never bought into that, so I made them myself in yellow, red, green, purple, whatever looked good. Not that Jess really needed woolen socks or hats because it never gets cold down there in Florida, but they looked nice and the knitting gave me something to do while I couldn't work and John was away.

John was away a lot. Asshole.

. . .

Jess. I think about her all the time. I hear a baby cry and I'm looking down into her cot, reaching in to let her hold my finger in her bunched fist. I can smell her clean hair after her warm bath and feel her pressure on my breast. I don't smell the bad things but I smile at the thought of the diapers and the towel on my shoulder.

I hear a little girl's voice and immediately, I picture her looking up at me at three years old, asking about her shoes, asking for a cookie, asking about our dog. She's talking constantly, catching up on lost time. So many questions.

I hear a young girl's voice and I see her ready for school, and I imagine myself packing her a lunch, no peanut butter. Even when I hear a teenage girl, just calling to a friend, I see Jess. But it's never Jess. I've not seen Jess since the day she turned four years old, that day at the mall.

I've put it all to one side, tried to concentrate on other stuff, but the smallest things will set me off. If I hear a girl on the street calling for her mother – *Mom!* – then I'll be a wreck for hours. If I see a girl with red hair like mine, I'll want to look away but I can't look away, in case it's her. Which is ridiculous, I know, because Jess will be a woman now. She'll be fully grown, with hips and breasts and a life of her own. I like to think so, anyway. Maybe even a child of her own. I was young when she was born, and maybe it runs in the genes.

I like to think that Jess was taken and raised by a nice family that really, really wanted a daughter, and when she came along, she completed them. She just moved from my house to another house, perhaps a bigger house, and she had her own room and she went to school and now she's studying law and she has no idea that the person she thinks is her mother is not her mother. Because I'm her fucking mother. But that's the best-case scenario and it's possible and that's what keeps me going. I like to think that. It's quite possible, isn't it?

The truth is, I think I know who took her. I think I've always known, and maybe it's what kept me alive. I think it was her father. I think it was John, or Jonathan, or whatever he calls himself now. The police thought so too at the time and I didn't want to believe them, but I could never get it out of my mind.

. . .

John and I were together for five years. I thought it was a good relationship. John was rough, but a loveable rough, you know? Marlon Brando in *A Streetcar Named Desire*. I've never seen the movie, but I've seen the photos in that white singlet. That's just the kind of guy who would click for me, like Jack Sparrow or Han Solo, that sort of thing. They weren't junkies and although John wasn't that clean when we first met, he had a streak of decency in him and he had a conscience. He came from a hell of a family but he kept away from them when he was with me and I thought we were solid. And then I realized we weren't.

That was back when I was living in Florida, of course. I hate Florida now, but back then, I loved it. No snow! Tans in the wintertime; pelicans on the beach; mimosas for breakfast; do your own thing. What's not to love, right? I'd gone down to stay over Christmas with a friend who had a place on the beach at Clearwater, and then I met John on the third day and that was it. He was so *magnetic*! He pulled me in like catching one of those big deepwater marlins on the lines out in the bay, and I never even put up a fight. I was pretty confident back then.

At the end of the two weeks, I moved into his place and blew off my second semester of school; it was only the first year of Liberal Arts at York, but I didn't want to go back. I'd ended a pretty intense relationship with a guy in Philosophy and was happy to never see him again. I pulled all the cash out of my bank that was supposed to pay for school, told mom I was taking a break, moved in with John, and then just stayed down there in Florida's endless summer. I'm a Canadian with red hair and freckles, so everyone just assumed I was a snowbird, hiding from the winter. Which I was.

Mom was surprisingly okay with it. I told her I was living with my friend on the beach at Clearwater and she'd send my mail to her. John worked for his uncle at a car repair place, which was good for him because he spent more time playing hooky from the shop than he ever spent fixing cars. He sold some drugs on the side but not the bad stuff, just weed and hash and some coke, and he was away a lot but in those early days, I didn't mind.

The guy at York, his name was Jerry, he'd been intense but he was a jerk, Jerry the Jerk, and John was as far removed from him as a real man could be. John was laid back and he was smart. He had lots of friends – everyone liked John, and he looked really good in a wife-beater. Don't get me wrong, he never hit me, though a few times I thought he was going to, but those firm tan biceps and that sculpted chest, and that treasure trail leading down into his jeans, well, I just couldn't resist.

I was 19 years old while he was 20. He was Mr. Perfect, if only for a winter. A winter with palm trees and hot sunshine and Mr. Perfect and warm sand between my toes.

"I love you so much," he used to say, of course, and I told him I loved him, of course, and we probably both did, and then in just three months, I was pregnant. I wasn't ready for it – I was 19, for chrissake – but I didn't really mind. It helped make the decision that I should stay down there with him.

"You want to keep it?" he asked.

"Of course I goddamn do!" What a question! "And don't say 'it'," I told him – "this is a baby, a he or a she, a boy or a girl. John, this could be your son! Or she could be my daughter!"

"Or it could be some other guy's kid," he said.

Wrong thing to say!

I smacked him hard across the face.

"Whoa! Kidding, baby! Take it easy!"

He used to wear a little gold ring through his eyebrow, and when I hit him, my hand ripped it out. I didn't mean to, but it just tore away. There was a smudge of blood in his hair and he looked like it hurt. He'd have a scar forever and I didn't care – that was such a hurtful thing to say. He told me he didn't mean it, said sorry a hundred times, and I ended up believing him because John was always one to speak first and think about it later. Back then, neither of us really understood what we were getting into.

We'd been using protection but we were passionate and we were reckless. The rubber came off a few times, so I'm not sure exactly which occasion it was, but I like to think it was the middle of the night in our bedroom. It could have been the back of his truck, and it could have been on the kitchen table, but in the bedroom would have been best: the air-conditioner in the window shut off and the overhead fan churning slowly through the thick, humid air; the sheers willowing a little in the breeze; shadows on the wall from the trees outside and no traffic on the road. Perhaps an owl hooting quietly, or a dog in the distance, barking at the moon.

Who am I kidding? It was the back of his truck. That's where the rubber came off for Jess.

. . .

CLAIRE - Toronto

I had to come back up to Canada in the summer to apply for a visa to remain in the U.S., and I stayed with Mom and Lex, who was my step-dad back then. I was five months pregnant and I hadn't told them. I wanted John to come with me, meet the family, smoke cigars with Lex and flirt playfully with Mom or whatever it is potential husbands do, but he wouldn't do it and I didn't press the point. I never thought of him as a potential husband anyway because that was way too formal, too conventional, too middle-class. I thought of him as the father of my child and didn't like to start imagining too far into the future about anything else.

So I stepped off the big dieselly bus in Toronto and Mom and Lex were there at the terminal to see my five-months-pregnant belly and Mom's eyes widened and Lex just seemed to sag, and that's the way it was. Too late for an abortion, not that they'd have wanted that, but too late to do anything except just accept it and be supportive.

I told them in the car that we'd been together for most of the year. What could they do now? "John so wanted to come up to meet you both, but he couldn't take the time from work," I lied to them. "He's going to be such a great father. I hope you can come down to meet him."

They tried to persuade me to stay in Canada, with free health care from both the government and my mom, but it was never going to happen. I'd applied for college in Tampa to study nursing, I told them, which was true. I expected to get a generous scholarship from the school, I told them, which was a lie. I said John really wanted to move up to Canada with me and open his own repair shop, which was a huge lie on both counts, but it sounded good and helped swing them to support my return to Florida. I wanted my baby born in the States, I told Mom, so he or she would have a right to American citizenship, just open up the options for later in life. That same month, I got the year's visa, which didn't allow me to work, and Lex even paid for health insurance.

I flew back south and landed at the airport. I remember all the people who were at the gate in the terminal to meet their families, their friends, off the plane. They all had super-tan legs in primary-coloured shorts and deeply brown arms in matching pastel Tees, and white teeth, and sunglasses on the tops of their super-tan heads.

I walked through into the chill of the air-conditioning that was even colder than the plane and saw all these smiling faces and I just felt *triumphant* – I'd won this one – and waited for John. He wasn't there. He'd said he would be there but he didn't come. I called his phone and got his machine, with its curt, all-business message: *You got John. It's your dime, so speak.* I called again, and again, and again.

After an hour, all the passengers in the terminal who'd been waiting to file onto the plane for its return flight to Canada had boarded, and the plane pulled away, and I was sitting there on a grey vinyl seat, linked to a dozen other grey vinyl seats, all empty now, and I felt a kick inside me. It was the first time I ever felt her move. I sat there with one hand cupped below my belly and the other on top of it, as pregnant moms are supposed to do but which just comes naturally, and I realized for the first time that there really was somebody inside me. A real person, moving around, making contact at last. Before then, it had been John and me, but there in the terminal, it was her and me, Jessica and me, together against the world.

The airline hostess was still at the counter and we made eye contact when I got up and reached for my carry-on. She looked concerned. "Do you need a ride to the luggage carousel, hon?" she asked. No, I said, I need a ride to Northview Hills. I didn't have any checked luggage. My old bedroom in Toronto was still full of clothes.

I took a taxi to John's house, to the little blue single-storey stucco house we shared together. There were bars on the windows, but everyone had bars on the windows around there. All the way over, I hoped the cab would pull up and he'd fling open the front door, run down the short driveway to the road, hopping shirtless with bare feet on the sharp gravel of the driveway, his long hair flapping over his face. *Babe!* he'd call out. *Oh my god, I'm sorry – I fell asleep waiting to go get you!* But there was none of that.

I paid the cab, lugged my carry-on over the gravel, and felt the baby kick again. *We're home, Lovely,* I said, but I wasn't sure I believed it. The shades were across all the windows, shielding the inside from the hot sun like a phalanx of shields. The air-conditioner in the bedroom window hummed and dripped water onto the grass, a small patch of green in a crisp lattice of dead brown. I remember a dove cooing for its mate in the sugarberry to the side.

I tried the handle on the door and it was locked, and I remember pausing for just a moment before sliding my key into the lock, wondering if it would still fit.

The key worked, the door opened, and inside was pretty much just as I'd left it, though messier: the couch in front of the TV, with the open kitchen at the back and the doors open to the two bedrooms. There were plates on the counter and pans in the sink. I stepped into the cool, into the quiet, into the dark, and put my case down beside the couch. My hand went straight to my belly and cupped it from beneath.

Welcome home, Lovely, I whispered. There was no movement inside me and the only sound was from the air-conditioner, just a low *thrumm* that underlaid everything. I thought about leaving, getting a hotel room and making him run around town to find me, but I was too tired for that. I fell asleep on the couch. It would have been 4 pm. I was still asleep when John came in at 6:30. He woke me by squatting down and taking my face in his hands and stroking my hair away from my eyes.

"Baby, I'm sorry. I should have come get you," he said.

It wasn't his touch that I noticed, but the smell on his fingers of the other woman.

BIRD ON A WIRE

Chapter 2

JON, Tampa, 2023

My name is Jonathan Anthony Morgan. People call me Jon, unless they're pissed at me and then they call me Jonathan, usually with a bit of a sneer and pronouncing each vowel. *Jon-A-Thon*. It doesn't matter to me. Just don't call me late for biscuits and gravy. Or a beer. Or biscuits and gravy with a beer. Best meal of the day!

I used to be just plain John, but I didn't like that and changed my name legally a decade back. You should know that. Most of it's fake news, of course. Fake info told to the cops who just want to hear a good story from a dozen snitches, a hundred people with axes to grind, but that's okay. I'll tell you the real story now, since I'm here and I'm drinking a beer.

I changed my name because my dad was a john. Not a John – his name was Carl – but a john who used prostitutes all the time. It was a weakness of his. He had a lot of weaknesses, all laid out in a thick file somewhere, getting dusty, I hope, since his death. It's all in there about my dad and his record and his FBI files and his psychiatric reports. I'm sure it was my dad's idea to name me John so eventually I bucked against that and became Jon, or Jonathan. I know the difference, and that's what's important. Far more clean-cut, if a bit Ivy League, and I've done okay by it.

It was Claire who got me to strike out on my own, get away from the family. Anywhere else, I'd be the black sheep but with my lot, I was the good one, the one with the conscience and the morals. I saw her when I stopped at a 7-11 to buy Marlboros and she stood out with her smooth pale skin in a halter top and short shorts. She has red hair, but it was hidden away under a big straw hat. All the women down here have dark hair or they're fake blond, and they're brown as turds. British, I figured, but then she spoke to the clerk while we were both at the counter and I couldn't quite fix her. New York? Chicago?

"You from up north?" I asked her, which is a stupid question in Florida because every English-speaking out-of-stater is from up north. She turned to me, looked me up and down, and just said, "sure," then turned away again. Cheeky bitch. She had a tramp stamp on the small of her back, just a pattern of swirls but it was enough to lure me in. I had to follow that, didn't I?

I bought the smokes and caught up to her at the door. "Hey!" I said. "I want to know where you're from!"

"What do you care?" she asked. She has blue eyes and they looked straight at me, not blinking. Confident. A great body too, but it was the blue eyes that hooked me in. Light red eyebrows as well, and this close, I could see her hair under that big straw hat. I've always had a thing for red-heads.

"I just do. You look kind of interesting. I want to know if you really are interesting. I want to know if I should buy you a drink."

She looked me up and down again and, I've gotta say, in those days I was in pretty good shape. Fifty pounds less than now, anyway. A hundred and seventy pounds with not an ounce of fat, and long hair that I thought turned me into Jesus. Women would say *Jesus!* around me a lot. Usually a few days' growth of beard, but I don't remember if I'd shaved that day. Her mouth curled up at the ends – she does that when she smiles, just the ends of her mouth – and she said to me, there in the doorway of the 7-11, that she'd make me a deal. Like I said, confident.

"You've got three guesses to figure which city I'm from," she said. "It's a big city, there's a clue. If you get it right, you can buy me that drink. If you get it wrong, you have to throw away those cigarettes and quit smoking."

Hell of a deal. I hadn't unwrapped the pack. I could come back later and pull it from the trash.

"New York." She shook her head and showed me her index finger. I remember she had pale blue nail polish and long fingernails. Good for digging into my back.

"Philadelphia." It was a wild guess based on nothing, and she showed me the finger and her thumb, turning them to point at me like a gun. I pictured them sliding down into my jeans.

"This ain't fair!" I said. "You could be from anywhere! I need a clue!"

It was a pretty good clue. Later, she told me she'd wanted me as bad as I wanted her. "It's not in the States," she said. "Think farther north." And I realized she was Canadian. I blurted out the only Canadian city I knew.

"Montreal!"

"Close enough," she said. "Where are we getting that drink?"

Montreal is 300 miles from where she lived in Toronto, different province, different language even, but that wasn't going to stop her hooking up with me. She even got me to quit cigarettes, for a while, anyway.

. . .

We did okay, the two of us. Getting knocked up was a surprise and we were really young, the ink still fresh on our fake IDs, but I had my own place and she moved in and we had a good time. I made no promises for marriage or anything like that but she never asked. I didn't want to meet the family up north in their big house and I sure as shit didn't want her to meet mine. My brother was in a Big House of his own, *know what I mean*?

I was working for my Uncle Luis at his chop shop, cutting up cars and trucks and bikes and running errands, and I sold some weed on the side, like we all did. There was always cash to pay the bills. Not cartel cash in thick rolls of C-notes, but enough that we ate better than wieners and beans. Steak for us! Fish on the grill, always fresh.

Claire liked the weather down here that winter, and she waited till the summer to go back up to Canada and sort herself a visa. She told her folks about the baby too, and they went along with it. Her mom, Vivian, can be a tyrant, but she was okay with being a grandmother. Claire wanted to go to school here to be a nurse but there wasn't any time for that – Jessica was born just before Christmas.

You know how people say their lives change when they have a kid? It was like that for me. I took Claire to the hospital and it was no big deal – she wasn't that fat, just a big bump where her stomach should be. She wanted me there for the birth and I said sure, why not, but I really wasn't bothered.

There were problems, though, when the time came and she was in the birthing room. The doctors started calling to each other and nobody would speak to me. I kept my hand on Claire's shoulder and she was sweating and cussing and suddenly this all started to really *matter*. I thought we might lose the baby and I didn't want that to happen, not if it had come this far. All I'd been thinking about was how this baby was going to tear up my girlfriend's snatch, but now I started thinking about the baby in there fighting to get out and it really *mattered*, you know?

When she did come out, it was really quick and suddenly she was there and I saw her little crotch and I squatted down so my head was close to Claire. "It's a girl, just like you," I told her, and she smiled and at that moment, all was right.

For me, it was like a bolt of lightning, a shaft of sunlight, a blinding fucking spotlight onto the stage in the room, and suddenly everything was different.

If I hadn't been there, if I'd been out in the waiting room or at work, waiting for a call or something, it would just have been a hassle, another thing to deal with, but because I was in there, it was all okay. She was so delicate, so vulnerable, her tiny fingers so wrinkled and her soft fingernails torn from padding around inside and never getting chewed, and when they let me hold her, I whispered to her and made her a promise. *You'll be okay, kid*, I said. *I'll always be here for you.* And that was the first lie I ever told her.

. . .

Claire's mom flew down to look after her in that final month and she stayed through Christmas. Tampa's a great place to be in December. There's sunshine and warm evenings and energy everywhere, and she stayed at a hotel near our place. It was a fancy hotel, too, the Hilton, and I wondered how she got to pay for it, but when I saw Vivian on the day she arrived, it was obvious she had money. Nice clothes. Designer clothes.

She looked good for a woman in her fifties, too. I figured she'd married well but Claire told me her dad was an engineer or something and the two of them had done okay with a business they'd started and they were "comfortable." That's middle-class talk for rich. It didn't matter to me, though. I figured I was comfortable already and I'd be rich soon enough.

"Claire says you'd like to come visit Canada," Vivian said to me back then. "She says you'd like to open your own shop, maybe in Toronto."

Now why in hell would I want to do that? So I could sell snowmobiles? I was doing just fine down here. I get to watch the weather reports and laugh at all the Northerners in the cold. They're shoveling their sidewalks and sliding into ditches and wishing they're in Florida, so why would I ever want to trade places? Even so, I knew what to say to Vivian.

"Yeah, that would be a dream. Canada looks like a really cool place."

She smiled at that, and I smiled back, and we moved right along.

The money kept coming in, but it started getting stretched. Claire was stretched, too – *know what I mean*? I loved my baby girl, but my relationship with Claire just wasn't the same. I wasn't the Number One person in her life any more. That was okay, though. I hung out with my friends like any guy in his twenties and I came home to play with my baby and make sure her mother was looking after her right, and we'd take walks in the park and all that family stuff.

We really did try. We even got a puppy from the pound and it grew up to be like a guard dog, protective of its women. We called it Rags because it looked like its pen at the pound was full of rags, and it was like a big pit bull, some kind of mastiff. Scary-looking dog with yellow teeth and drool and pale eyes that never quite closed, always watching you.

I got him to protect Claire and Jess, and Jess was scared of him at first, but she quickly came to love him. The dog growled at me a few times when I moved too sudden but I showed him who was boss. He even bit my sister Tammy's boyfriend one time when they were over to visit and the guy had to get a shot, and I was kinda proud. I never liked that asshole. I think there was way more chance of him infecting the dog with something disgusting than the other way around.

I tried to leave my own family alone in those years, but my sister would visit sometimes, usually to pick up some weed or borrow some money. My dad was dead and my twin sister too, she died as a child, and my brother Mike was in prison, and my mom moved to Texas with some guy, so they were all out of the picture, and there was Uncle Luis of course, but Tammy was still around, for a couple of years anyway. She was a meth-head. Claire hated her and her loser boyfriend Billy and wanted me to have nothing to do with them, and for the most part I didn't, but they lived nearby so we'd catch up every now and again. She died of an overdose, heroin, when Jess was still with us.

Brother Mike's still alive, kind of. Depends if you think rotting away upstate on Death Row is still alive. In any case, his heart's pumping for now but he's dead to me.

. . .

Where was I? Drinking a beer and filling you in on all this background shit, that's right. You holding up okay? You need some context up front if you're going to understand, right?

Anyway, you want to know about the snatching. The abduction. The *disappearance*, and that's what it was – just a complete, total fucking disappearance into thin air that nobody's ever explained. She was there and then she was a ghost, just a memory, like smoke off a cigarette. Pixels on a screen before it shuts down. A pencil rubbed from a thin sheet of paper.

We still had her things, the clothes she would wear and the toys she would touch, but Jess herself was gone. No idea where. It was her birthday, too. She was four years old that day, and Claire took her to the mall as a treat.

I don't think she's still alive, but it's taken a long time to come to terms with that. I hope she didn't suffer too long. Sometimes, I'll think of her as she would be now, a young woman with red hair like her mother but green eyes, and that's a comforting thought right up until I imagine her locked away in some room, captive to some perv, shut away from society like my asshole brother. The only thing that settles my thoughts when that happens is Jack Daniels and lots of it.

It's been happening more recently that I've been thinking about her. If there was a body, I could live with that. If there was even a photo from one of the mall cameras that showed her being led away somewhere, I could even live with that because it wouldn't be such a mystery, but there's nothing, nothing at all.

After she wandered away from Claire at the mall, there's only one photo that shows her clearly, and she's looking up at the camera near a cookie booth and smiling, like she's smiling straight at you. People everywhere and she only comes up to their waists, but she's the only one looking at you and she's smiling like she's just recognized you. That's the picture they used in all the newscasts. That's the one people remember. But after that, nothing. Just … *poof*.

The press wanted to know how a little girl can vanish in a crowded shopping mall. The cheap bastards who owned the place had plenty of cameras but their hard drives only stored photos, not video, because video used too much memory and their hard drives weren't big enough to store that much memory. These days, I have more memory on my friggin' iPhone than that shopping mall back then, but that's the way it was, cheap bastards, and there's no point dwelling on it. There are thousands of photos from the day, all filled with people but only one with Jess in it after that moment, 12:17 pm on December 20th, when she walked away from her mom and looked up at the camera.

Claire was looking after our friend's kid that day. Kim. She had a son called Jason, who was a gimpy little boy with a bad foot. She lived a couple of streets over and was married to a guy who worked on a rig in the Gulf, so for three weeks every month she was a single mom. That was hard work for her with Jason, who was a live wire, either full on or asleep with no middle switch.

Kim had an arrangement with Claire where she'd pay Claire to look after him every Monday, so she could run errands and just get a break. Claire didn't mind. She wasn't working and it was some cash of her own and Jason and Jess were about the same age, and they were friends.

Of course, that day, Kim was getting a break with me. We had our twice-a-month nooner and I'm not too proud of that, but again, it's just the way it was and there's no changing anything now. I told you I'll tell you the real story. There'll be no fake news with me.

I never made Claire any promises that I would be faithful to her alone, and I never said I'd be monogamous – *monotonous*, more like – now I was the father of our child, but I knew well enough that she expected it. I might even have done it too if she'd paid me some more attention, not fallen asleep every night just as I was getting going. This way, with Kim and with all the others, I made sure I was okay but that Jess and Claire were also okay. I just didn't talk about it, that's all, and she didn't ask about it.

She called me when I was in Kim's bedroom – *in Kim*, since I'm trying to be precise – to tell me Jess was gone. I remember, I had one of those silver flip phones that showed the name of the caller on the little screen at the front, and I saw it light up on the bedside table and start buzzing around on the polished oak, and then the name came up, CLAIRE, and I didn't answer. Would you? I was right in the middle of it with Kim. She was a great lay, too. Claire called back a few times over the next 20 minutes or so. CLAIRE. CLAIRE. CLAIRE. CLAIRE. Eventually it got annoying, so I pulled out of what I was doing – *who* I was doing – and answered the phone, CLAIRE, and for the second time in four years, my life changed with a bolt of lightning.

John, I'm at the Fairfield Mall and Jess is gone! I could barely understand her, she was crying so much, gasping for air. Big wet gulps I could hear through the phone. *The cops are here. No-one can find her. I need you here now!*

I pulled on my pants and shirt and told Kim and she was pissed and horrified at the same time, then I ran out to my truck that was parked in the back alley and rolled coal all the way over to the mall, maybe 15 minutes away, feeling really shit for not answering the calls.

The cops had already closed off the mall and they were talking to all the shoppers who were trying to leave. I told them I was Jess's dad and they let me go in and find Claire. I had to phone her again to find her because she was still running all over the place, pushing Jason in his stroller. The cops had told her to wait over by where she'd last been with Jess and eventually she did that, and I waited with her, sitting on a wooden bench, holding her hand. I don't think she looked at me once.

"Where the hell were you?" She spat the question at me.

"I was at work, baby. I left my phone out in the truck."

"I called Luis. He didn't know where you were."

"I was out in the yard. I was taking inventory."

Claire didn't question me any more on that. She kept running her fingers through her hair, pulling on it, hard, and she kept breaking down, sobbing, loud. She called Kim to come collect Jason, and when Kim got there and looked me in the eye, I felt like a total shit. Claire never noticed. She only cared about where Jess was.

"I should be searching for her," she said. "She might be frightened by all these cops. She might be hiding. She'll come to my voice."

"She'll come to where she last saw you," I said, and we waited, helpless, useless, as she cried and held onto my hand.

The cops said they wanted to talk to me but I had to wait till things slowed down. That was at least an hour, maybe two hours, while they searched the mall and looked over the photos from the cameras. It wasn't easy for them with all those people around. They could only close the mall to really search it properly for two hours, and then some lawyer from the mall owners made them reopen and people poured back in like nothing had happened. Assholes, all of them.

Finally, some young cop in a uniform came over and said the lead detective wanted to speak with me. He took me over to where there was a fat guy in a tartan sport jacket talking to another fat guy in another tartan sport jacket, and he told me to wait there, and then left. I stood there impatiently and I could hear what they were saying, these two fat guys. They were the detectives, and they were talking about Jess, and I can remember every word. Every. Single. Word.

"Little girls like that, they don't last long," said the fat guy with his back closest to me, talking to his fat pal. "That red hair and that cute smile with those little white teeth – every pedo wants a mouth like that on his cock, even if he has to keep the head in his fridge."

That was my introduction to Detective Sergeant Cocksucker Floyd Woods. His introduction to me was when I cocksucker-punched him in the back of the head, knocking him to the shiny ground right in front of all his cop friends and hundreds of shoppers, as well as a photographer from the *Tribune*.

That caused a scene, I can tell you, all those uniforms and suits and me rolling around on the floor. And when the photo was published the next day in the paper, that's when the squad cars came to the house and Cocksucker Woods himself met me with a smirk on my doorstep in front of Claire and a bunch of cameras and took me in to the station to ask why I would steal my own daughter.

BIRD ON A WIRE

Chapter 3

CLAIRE, Toronto

I'm home now, still churning over introducing you to my story, and I'm sorry but I need a break from this. I can only rehash it for so long before I have to flush my head clear.

I pushed my bicycle from the hallway and out to the elevator, then down the three floors to the lobby and the sunshine. Mom lives 15 minutes away if I cycle over there, though she's at least 20 minutes by car and twice that by bus; Toronto has a great network of bicycle lanes that helps avoid the cars and the old-style tracks in the road for the streetcars, and I use my bicycle every chance I can. It's a Mary Poppins bike with three gears and handlebars straight across and a wire-frame shopping basket for my purse. One day, maybe I'll get a little handbag dog that can ride along in the basket, but not just yet. I need to sort myself out first.

Mom was filling the hummingbird feeder in the front garden. It's a small house with a small garden, but it suits her fine and it's got to be worth a million dollars these days, or probably more like two million with house prices as they are. It's really narrow, on two floors with two bedrooms and two bathrooms and an unfinished basement. She says I'll inherit it when she goes but that won't be for a long time yet.

Mom speaks a lot about *when I go, this will be yours* and *that will be yours*, which is really just an invitation for me to say *Oh Mom!* and then she can start telling me about her health. I think all people in their 70s like to talk about their health, almost as much as they like to talk about their friends' health, and especially these days, still coming off Covid. Mom and I are front and centre in each other's social bubbles, though her bubble's bigger than mine; she has more friends, but I have more sick patients at the hospital, so I still need to be very cautious with her.

I swung my leg through the bicycle frame while it was still coasting on the road, then jumped off and pushed it across the sidewalk to her little front gate.

"How are you doing today, Mom?" It's the standard opener, and I knew the standard reply.

"Oh, I'm okay," and I waited a beat for it. Then, "considering."

I never take the bait. "Glad to hear it. Any chance of a cup of tea?"

There's always tea at my mother's house – it's her Irish pedigree. She smiled because she knew it's a stupid question, and I wheeled the bicycle through the gate and up onto the porch, padlocking it to the rail with the cable and guaranteed-unbreakable lock that's already there, just for me, and I followed her in.

I was feeling a lot better now from the exercise. The ride over did me good, warm but not hot with the leaves starting to turn but still on the trees. I cycle here most days though I should do more of it, because I don't get enough exercise and it shows in my face, in my bum.

I followed Mom into the kitchen where she ticked through the checklist of making the tea: kettle on, warm the pot, find the teabags (no time for loose-leaf here), pour the boiling water, then wait five minutes to brew. On her last birthday, the two of us worked out that she'd probably made 100,000 cups of tea in her lifetime, with about 4,000 gallons of water. That's not enough to fill a proper swimming pool, but it's still a lot of tea.

"How are *you* doing, dear?" asked Mom when I leaned back against the counter while the tea brewed, and she fussed into one of the cupboards, looking for cookies. She knows I won't turn down a cookie, except she didn't have any cookies; her weekly grocery shop is on the weekend, with me, and she was running low. "Feeling any better?"

She's straight to the point, my mom. No niceties with Vivian.

"Not really," I admitted. "It's all just more of the same, you know? Starts out well enough, but then it spirals off into the void." This is getting deep, fast, and Mom knows it. She's found some carrot cake in the fridge and pulls it victoriously off the shelf.

"I got this in just for you!" It's a family joke. My dad used to call me his *cutie carrot* when I was six years old, because of my red hair, and it's always stuck. Here it was again, 33 years later, and Mom put a couple of slices on a plate.

She poured the tea, handed me my mug, and we moved to the sitting room with me balancing the cake and a small silver fork on my plate. This is the room with the family photos on the walls and on the mantle and although I know every one of the pictures intimately, it always gives a moment of pause to see Jess there, on the glass table beside the window. Mom's offered to remove the photo, or put it upstairs, but I won't hear of it. Jess is still a member of the family and while she's here in this picture, she's still alive.

I sat down and Mom saw me looking at Jess's photo. In the frame, she's three years old and sitting on a red blanket that's on the warm green grass, having a picnic in the park with me and her father. I took the picture and I zoomed right in so it's only her, holding a teacup just as I'm doing now. She's looking around on the blanket for the Tupperware sugar bowl. It's a regular tea party.

"I should put that picture away," Mom said. "You don't need to be reminded of her every time you visit. Whether she's alive and well, or long since passed, you should be able to sit and enjoy a cup of tea without having to think about her and start up all the *what ifs?* over and over and over."

"I do it anyway, Mom. It doesn't matter if I see her picture or not. I think about her every hour of every day, and nothing's changed since she left us."

Mom's used to this. She hears it from me all the time.

"Just enjoy your tea, dear. How is it at the hospital?"

"It's the same as it always is."

That's not quite true. There's still Covid, but at least I'm not one of those frontline workers in Emergency, or a paramedic in the streets. People treat me like I'm a hero but I don't deserve it as those people do. Sure, we're all exhausted from long hours and too many patients needing attention – that's always been the way. It's bad up here, but it's bad down in Florida too, where I began training as a nurse and where I might still be if Jess was with me. Back then, I stuck around for another year, hoping there was something I could do, hoping I'd hear something or see something, but there was nothing and eventually I just couldn't stand the silence any longer. I'd moved out of John's house pretty quickly and got my own place, but Mom and Lex persuaded me to come back up for the next Christmas and I've been here ever since. I hated to leave my little girl, but I couldn't be anywhere near John.

. . .

I think it was him. I don't know how he did it, but I know it was him. I'm sure it was him. It's that feeling a mother has that something isn't quite right and it doesn't add up, and I've spent so long trying to add things up and it always comes back to John. He knew I was thinking of moving back up to Canada and taking Jess with me, and he didn't want to lose her, so he took her and hid her away somewhere.

At the time, the police said they were sure that Jess would only have gone with somebody she knew. A total stranger could have literally picked her up and carried her out of there because she was small enough, all 35 pounds of her, less than a bag of dog food, but people would have noticed and it would have been seen on the cameras. Somebody she knew, though, could have told her to hide, or duck down, or whatever, and Jess would have gone along with it and probably turned it into a game. It was her birthday and she knew there'd be games on her birthday. So that's Strike One against John. He was trusted. He was her father, for God's sake.

I don't know where he was at the time, at 12:17 pm on Monday, December 20, 2004. He sure as hell wasn't with me and he didn't show up till at least an hour after that. He told the police in the mall that he'd come straight from work, but his uncle who owned the car repair business refused to lie for him and the police realized quickly he was already grasping.

There were some men in the security photos from the mall that could have been John, before it happened, but the pictures weren't clear – just young guys in ball caps and sunglasses, seen from above, same strong build. It wasn't till they took him in the next day that he came up with an alibi, that he was screwing our friend Kim at her home. My ex-friend Kim, that is. The woman was a slut. Her husband was away at work and apparently it was the first time they'd ever done this. It ended her marriage to tell this to the police and it sure as hell ended our friendship, but I think she was looking for a way out anyway because her husband was just never around. I'm not surprised she pulled in John.

She got me to look after her son Jason for the day, which I used to do every Monday to give her a break. Jason had a club foot and he could be a handful and probably on the spectrum too, so she paid me to look after him on Mondays and that would give her a break after the weekend. I didn't mind – he was a good kid and good company for Jess. He was just a few months younger than her, so Kim would drop him off after breakfast and give me 40 dollars, and I'd take him off her hands for the rest of the day. I was saving that money too, which was literally cash under the mattress for just in case. Of course, that all ended when she said she'd been screwing John.

To be honest, I wouldn't be surprised if they *weren't* having sex. John's always had this charm about him, with women and men the same, and he can convince you to like him even when you know he's messing you over. It was only Kim's word for it with the police that he was with her. There were no photos or witnesses or anything, and the cops went for it because they thought it was such a huge, marriage-ending admission that it must be true. But if she didn't care about her marriage, and John was somewhere else, into the really bad stuff – I don't know, running heroin or killing somebody or stealing our daughter, whatever he wouldn't want to admit to the police – then I'm sure he could persuade her to give him the alibi he needed. Maybe he told her he was delivering drugs or something. That's Strike Two against John. He really didn't have an alibi.

And then there's the question of *Why*? Why would John abduct his own daughter? It's no secret we were having a rough time as a couple. I was a stay-at-home mom, not working and not making any money, and we weren't having much sex any more. And he adored Jess. My mom thinks he was worried I would move back up to Canada when I graduated and take her with me and he'd lose her, so maybe he took her while he still could and he kept her safe somewhere nearby. Maybe he stole her away to give her to some childless couple he knew, so she would stay in Florida and he'd still be a part of her life, without me fighting for custody. That would just be so cold, and it's hard to believe that John could do that to me, but I'm sure he took her. I just know it.

Mom's had people keep a watch on him sometimes, off and on, though not for a few years now. Private investigators followed him for a week, several times, and they struck up conversations with him in bars, and sometimes even played pool with him. Once, Mom got a woman investigator to flirt with him and go on a couple of dates, hanging her boobs out over the restaurant table and saying how much she regretted never having kids and how she wished she could meet a single dad – that sort of thing. If he had confessed to her that he had a teenage daughter hidden away, I would be so relieved. He'd be the family that really, really wanted a daughter. I wouldn't forgive him, ever, but I'd be so relieved for Jess.

That's because the alternative is just too horrific. It's the worst of them all, where John somehow gets Jess out of the mall and takes her away somewhere and rapes her, his own daughter. Finally, he gets her alone without me, because I was always, always there with her. You remember that picnic in the park? While we were sitting there after the lunch, John lying back with his ball-cap over his eyes and resting his hand on Jess's foot, a young guy cycled past on the pathway a hundred metres away with one of those ice-cream vendor tricycles. Jess heard him ring the bell and she looked at me, wanting an ice-cream.

"John, why don't you get us all ice-creams?" I asked.

"I'm okay, baby," he said. "I just closed my eyes. You go if you want."

And I didn't go. I just left it. I told myself at the time it was because I didn't really need an ice-cream to go straight to my hips and Jess would forget about it quickly, and she did, but thinking about it after, it was really because I didn't want to leave her on the blanket sitting next to John, touching her as he was. Totally innocent to anyone else, but I could never quite accept that.

I would never leave him alone with her, because of his family. He told me once, after his druggie sister died, that there was a rumour the two of them used to screw each other when they were teenagers. I didn't believe it then but I never forgot it, and for all I know, it was true. He was from a family of sexual predators, which makes him a sexual predator too. It's what the police thought when they questioned him, and it's what the rest of the city thought when the story against him came out in the local press. It didn't take the media long to realize who his dad was, and his brother: men who liked sex with young girls, and who wouldn't listen to No.

I saw it on the six o'clock news the next day, almost 30 hours after she was taken. John had been gone half the night, when he said he was with Luis looking for her, and then he was taken to the police station later in the morning and they held him there overnight. I was shut in alone at our house, though there were TV trucks humming out on the road and the reporters had talked with all the neighbours. Mom and Lex were coming down, but they couldn't get a flight till the next day so they hadn't arrived yet.

I was alone that Tuesday night with our dog, Rags, down by my feet. John hated dogs but our neighbourhood wasn't the safest and I'd persuaded him to get us a puppy for protection. Rags grew really big, really fast. He knew something was wrong and he was missing Jess, crying and chewing on his feet, but there was no Jess, and there was no John.

I sat on the couch and watched the TV and heard the words and saw the pictures and didn't quite believe any of it.

Tampa police today took in for questioning the father of little Jessica Morgan, who disappeared yesterday on her fourth birthday from the Fairfield Mall while on a shopping trip with her mother.

John Morgan is the son of Carl Morgan, who was convicted of raping and killing his nine-year-old daughter Kelly in 1986 and was executed six years ago. He is also the brother of Mike Morgan, who is on Death Row after being convicted of the murders of the Cooper family at their home in Clearwater Beach in 1998. Teenagers Susan and Sarah Cooper were raped and killed, and their parents killed, during the home invasion.

The TV showed the mugshot photos of the two Morgans as they were mentioned, father and son. I'd never seen their pictures before, but in the mugshots they looked guilty as hell, which they were, of course. I could see John's eyes in his father, brown and a little too close together, and his lips, fuller than most, but that was it. His brother shared the same lips too. But those two men looked hard and weather-beaten, like they'd been dragged from garbage-filled cars in the parking lot after sleeping in them overnight; they had wrinkled foreheads and blotchy coffee-stain sunspots while John's face was fresher, younger, more innocent. John needed his fake ID, but those guys had been propping up bars since they started shaving.

A murderous pedophile family – that's a big Strike Three against John. Three strikes and he's out.

. . .

"Another slice of cake, dear?" Mom is always concerned for my appetite. We'd been chatting for only a short while, but I needed to go home to get my things before heading into the hospital for the night's shift, so no more cake for me, thank you. Normally, I work 10 hours at a time, four days a week, but there's been a lot of overtime in the last few months, both paid and unpaid. I've been happy to take what I can get. Well, not *happy*, but you know what I mean.

"Before you go, dear," said Mom, "I want to show you this." She picked up her iPad and brought it to life, and I could see a web page open up on the screen. She handed me the tablet to read the news story on the page, which was a local blog in Florida, in Tampa, and as soon as I saw it I bit the inside of my cheek, hard. *Forty-year veteran retires from the force*, read the headline, and there was a photo of Detective Floyd Woods, fatter than ever in a Hawaiian shirt, his stupid little moustache still in place on his pudgy upper lip, smiling at the camera.

"Why should I care about this guy, Mom?"

"I saw it this morning. I keep up with the news down there, you know, just in case. He's the detective in charge of looking for Jessica, right?"

"Well, he was. He'll have forgotten her name. He'll definitely forget it when he's on the golf course. Beaching himself at some swimming pool."

"It's just an idea – maybe he's got some time on his hands now. You know how Americans are with private enterprise. He retired last week. Perhaps if we wave some money at him, he can make things happen that he couldn't make happen before. It's just a thought."

"What kind of money? What kind of things?"

"I don't know if he can discover anything else. I don't know if there's anything even to be discovered. But if he's up for it, five or 10 thousand dollars should be plenty, and if he can find just one thing that's been hidden so far, that might help us answer a lot of questions. I'm happy to pay for it, if you agree."

I'll think about it, I tell her. I'll think about it every hour of every day until something finally gives.

Chapter 4

JON, Tampa

This is my favorite bar. I come here a couple of times a month. There's no point in coming more often because it's just a small place and they don't change the girls around that much, and most of them aren't that great. That's why I limit the visits to every two weeks or so, when there's usually somebody new who might be worth checking out. The beer and the liquor is overpriced thanks to the entertainment, but I don't mind paying for it. *Drinking with benefits,* that's what it is.

I'd have more money if I worked harder. My legitimate job is selling cars, used cars, and I could make more if I worked longer hours at the dealership and spent more time promoting myself, but I make plenty enough already to pay the bills and that's fine with me. There's cash from Uncle Luis when I run his errands and if I made much more, I'd just get myself into trouble, especially in a bar like this.

They closed the place down during the Covid virus, but then it called itself a restaurant to skirt the ban on bars and it's been back up and running for a few years now in its own shabby way. I wouldn't want to eat here, that's for sure. At least, nothing that's on the menu.

Amy came over to take my order and I asked for a Michelob, no surprise there, and read the text on my phone again. It's from Uncle Luis. *Might have something. Be here at 6.* That wasn't for another four hours. No point going back to the dealership. Besides, it was cool in there and dark, all dim lights and cheap wood panels, and the music was playing, classic rock. Most of the music is older than the girls, but the customers grew up with vinyl and it's what we like.

Amy came back with the bottle, swiped at the table with a Clorox, and nodded when I asked to run a tab. She knows I'm a regular. If it had been

Katie, who's older, she'd have brought the Michelob without needing to take the order or ask about a tab. Don't know if she'd have wiped the table.

There were maybe four girls on the floor this afternoon. Business never really caught back up when they reopened after the virus. The place used to fit 150 people with 20 girls at least but now it's lucky to get a third of that, and that's on a Friday night. It makes the girls a little hungrier, more anxious to please, and that's okay with me.

They start out sitting over to the side at their own tables. Two of them were sitting there when I came in, trying to make eye contact without being too pushy. I knew whoever I'd smile at, she'd come over, carrying her little white towel and her spray-bottle of sanitizer. She'd clean off the seat next to me with a squirt and a swipe, then enter my personal space in any which way I let her in.

I knew all these girls, and they all knew me. I'm a nice guy, respectful, and I rarely leave without dropping a hundred bucks in an afternoon, or a couple of hundred in an evening. They know that, so the first girl I looked at was quick to join me. It was a slow Wednesday afternoon for her anyway. Just a half-dozen guys in the bar.

"What's up, Jon?" said Savanah, and raised an eyebrow before looking down at my crotch. I shrugged and smiled. *That's* not up, not yet.

"Not much," I told her. "Killing time before a business meeting. How you doing? You keeping busy?"

"No, not really. It's difficult now. And I'm being straight with you, because I know you like to be real straight with me" – another raised eyebrow and another glance at my crotch – "but I don't get by anymore on the money I make here. I got bills, you know?"

Savanah was older, maybe 30 already. She had long blond hair down to the small of her back and thin painted eyebrows. I don't know if the carpet matched the drapes because she's shaved down there, but I'm guessing it most certainly did not. Today, she was wearing the standard stripper outfit of a gold bikini with a red lace shawl, with red high heels laced up to her knees. Her tits were too big for me though, and she'd got a large rump. Not really my type, but she worked it all the same. She danced for me last month and she was clearly looking to do the same again today.

"That's too bad, honey. I hope it picks up for you."

"You could help it pick up. Want a private dance? Want to have some fun?"

I just got here and I was only two sips into my beer. "Maybe later, honey," I told her. I'll drink my beer first.

She looked pissed because she knew full well that the other girl could seduce me while she was away, almost certainly, but there was nothing she could do with her rejection except smile. *That's the way it is, honey.*

Savanah got up and collected her little towel, and the other girl off to the side, short brown hair, can't remember her name, saw the opportunity and started walking toward me, but when she did, the music ended and the DJ – every strip-joint has its own DJ, to play the girls' own songs – came onto the speakers. *Gentlemen, please give a warm Florida Angels welcome to Cherie!*

ZZ Tops' *Legs* started up, real loud. A new girl, tall and slim, someone I've not seen before, walked out from behind a silver curtain strung across a gap in the wood paneling and onto the stage. I swivelled my chair around for a better look and I was captivated. Short Brown Hair said hello but I gave her only a cursory nod and she took the hint to totter back to her table on her stripper heels. I watched the new girl begin her three-song routine.

You can't blame me. She had wavy, fiery hair half-way down her back. I love fiery hair.

. . .

"Why'd you do it, John?" Woods was in the front of the cruiser while I sprawled across the back seat. A patrolman did the driving. "Where did you take her? If she's still alive, you can save yourself now, but if she's dead, then we'll find her and you're fucked. You might as well just go join your brother."

I stayed silent and closed my eyes. I'd spent plenty of time talking to cops, and not talking to cops, and I knew my rights. This wasn't an arrest – I'd not been charged with anything. I knew Claire would have already called Luis, and Luis would have already called his lawyer, and guilty or innocent, it didn't matter, I shouldn't say a word until the lawyer showed up.

The press chased us down to the station, though we went into the underground parking lot and nobody could follow in there. As soon as we were through the gate, Woods grew very businesslike. He knew this had to be by the book whenever there might be a witness, because Luis would have a very good lawyer, probably Thurston Bell, who would exploit any and every loophole he could find. So no loopholes.

I was taken into an interview room with some wooden chairs and a big metal table and left there to stew a while. They'd be looking at me through the one-way glass. I closed my eyes again and sat them out. I knew I needed an alibi but I didn't know if Luis would back me up on this, like I'd asked the night before. He'd said he'd think about it. I didn't want to tell them the story about Kim, get her involved.

When they came in, Woods and the other fat detective he'd been talking to in the mall, Fric and Frac, the whole atmosphere changed. Probably somebody was watching *them* through the window. Woods carried a coffee in a styrofoam cup and the other guy held onto a plastic bottle of water. They asked if I wanted anything and I shook my head. There was no ashtray on the table so I figured a smoke wasn't happening. They turned on a tape recorder, introduced themselves, and we got started.

The other guy, Detective Crocker, sat in front of me and began the talking.

"John Anthony Morgan, where were you yesterday at 12:17 pm?"

I stayed silent. No lawyer, no comment.

"John, when we spoke to you at the mall yesterday, you told us you had come straight from your work, but your uncle, Luis Lopez, says you left for an early lunch. Where did you go for lunch?"

Fuck Luis! It would have been so simple for him to back me up, but I guess even he thought I might be guilty. I stayed silent, waiting for the lawyer.

"John, your lawyer is on his way over and, legally, that's okay if you want to wait for him. But your daughter is missing and I'm sure you know that in a time like this, every minute counts. Every second counts. If she's still alive, anything you can tell us right now could help save her life."

Bullshit. I stayed silent.

Woods was standing behind Crocker and now he stepped up and placed a meaty hand on the guy's shoulder.

"John," said Woods, "we know who you are. We have a file on you as thick as my fucking fist. We know who your dad is, or at least, who he was until the state executed him. We know who your brother is, and the state is going to execute him, too. We also know that with families like yours, the apple don't fall too far from the tree. We know you like sex, and who doesn't? Maybe even with your own sister, like your brother says – it's in your file.

But right now, there's a pretty little girl missing and you have no alibi, and that makes you the prime suspect. You should talk to us now, while you're still just a suspect, before this goes too far and Florida goes three for three on the Morgans."

I knew my rights. I stayed silent and waited for the lawyer.

. . .

Cherie wore a mask throughout her set, unusual in Florida, and it must have been difficult because it was a real workout. It was a black satin mask with a design of a cat's mouth and nose on it, like maybe something they'd wear in *Cats*, if they did musicals with masks. Her white halter-top showed off her lightly tan skin, and short black denim shorts with short white leather boots showed off her long, smooth legs. Not the usual stripper getup at all.

The top came off in the first song, showing a perfect pair of titties, no tan lines or tattoos, and when she got close on the stage, I saw the light dusting of freckles that ran along her chest and over her shoulders. Her shorts came off in the second song, Lenny Kravitz singing *American Woman*, and then her panties right at the end of the third song, that one about *When I think about you, I touch myself.* I don't know who sang it, but Cherie was a real tease. Most women at this joint just rip everything off right at the beginning and then strut around looking bored, especially for six old white guys on a Wednesday afternoon, but Cherie put on a real energetic show, up the pole, around the pole, up the pole some more, for all three songs.

I moved to a chair closer to the stage and made a point of folding dollar bills to tuck into her G-string, but she didn't come any nearer. In the end, I threw the bills onto the stage, making it rain with maybe 20 bucks, and when the song ended, she looked at me when she stooped down to gather them up. Her whole body below the neck was on display, but all I could see were her eyes above the cat's mouth and whiskery nose, round and green and seductive.

. . .

When the lawyer arrived, Thurston Bell as I'd hoped, he made it damn clear that if I was innocent – even if I was guilty – I needed an alibi and Uncle Luis wasn't going to give it. Luis had too much to lose if the cops started leaning hard on him. I told the lawyer I'd been screwing Kim and I didn't want to get her into trouble with her husband, and the guy just shrugged. *We've all got to pay the piper*, he said, which didn't make a lot of sense at the time, but I took it as sound legal advice that I should tell Cocksucker Woods and Crockofshit Crocker to give Kim a call.

More than that, he told me that he'd applied to have Woods removed from the case. Apparently, back when my brother was arrested a few years before, Tampa police sent four patrolmen into his house to bring him out and Mike put up quite a struggle before the cuffs went on. One of the cops was kicked in the head so bad he was taken out of there on a stretcher and he's never been the same since. That guy was the son of another Tampa cop, I don't remember his name, and that older cop was Woods' best buddy. The lawyer tried to make the case that Woods was compromised against me because of my brother hurting his friend's son, which he probably was, but the judge would have none of it and Woods stayed as the lead detective. Another sound legal decision, my ass.

They kept me in overnight, which Thurston said would look good on me – it would show I wanted to help solve the case despite being free to leave at any time. When I finally left late the next morning, I took a taxi home. There were two TV trucks outside on the road but I got in before the reporters saw me.

Claire was sitting on the couch, reading *Vanity Fair*. I remember the magazine because Leonardo DiCaprio was on the cover and she used to say he looked like me. It was noon and it was now 48 hours since Jess disappeared. Luis had already gotten the update from Thurston and told Claire about me screwing Kim. Her bags were packed and waiting beside the bedroom door. When I walked in, she didn't say hi, but she did put down the magazine and looked at me.

"John, do you know where Jess is?" she asked, real casual, as if she thought she might catch me out. "Anything at all?"

"Nothing, honey," I said. "How can you ask that? This is tearing me up too. There's a huge part of me that's missing with our little girl."

"So you don't know where she is? You swear that to me?"

"I swear it, honey! I swear it on all my family's graves!"

That was probably the wrong thing to say.

"Our daughter's coming home John, and her home is with me," said Claire. Her eyes were red and wet – she'd been crying a lot, and there were tears on her flushed cheeks when she spoke to me, but her voice was low and steady. She met my look for a long time, then stooped to pick up her two bags and turned toward the door.

"My parents are flying in. I'm going to collect them at the airport," she said, and stepped outside. The TV reporters, alert now, were in a pack on the sidewalk and called to her: *Claire, where are you going? Claire, are you leaving John? Did John take Jessica?* She ignored them and drove away in my truck.

Later, her mother phoned to say Claire had met them and they'd taken a taxi together to their hotel, where she'd be staying for the next few days. She didn't tell me which hotel, but she did say my truck was parked at the airport's valet parking lot, and it was costing 60 bucks a day.

. . .

Cherie came out onto the floor from behind the paneling, dressed again in the halter top and shorts, still wearing a mask though she'd changed it: it was still a cat's face, this time on a dark blue background. She didn't sit at her own little table with a Perrier but came directly over to me. I still had a hard-on.

"You liked my dance?" she asked.

I was expecting a French accent, or Boston at least, but she sounded just like girl-next-door. She looked like girl-next-door too, if you live next door to the Playboy Mansion.

"I loved your dance," I said. "It was really something. It must keep you in shape."

"Would you like your own dance? In a booth? Just you and me for a party?"

No messing around with this one!

Of course I would, and she led the way over to the Champagne Rooms, me following with my Michelob. I've been there many times – I know the routine.

The "Champagne Room" has never seen a glass of champagne in its life. Cherie led the way into the small, windowless room, one of several in the back that's barely big enough to swing a pussy, and she took a few moments with a bottle of sanitizer to spray the cushioned easy chair, the side table, and the small stool. It's not easy to see – the red-tinted light was maybe 25 watts, probably 10, and the paneling was very dark. There was a security camera up by the ceiling, behind where I'd sit. When she'd sprayed everything, she wiped it all down with a Lysol towel. Then she squirted some Febreze into the air and invited me in.

"This room is the best because the camera doesn't work," she said. "It's the only one that's broken. More fun for us."

None of the strippers ever told me that before.

It was "full contact" back there, which meant she can touch you all she likes but only on top of your pants. It also meant she can put her little towel on your lap, sit on your crotch, and grind away on your chubby till the cows come home. You pay 20 bucks a song, so the girls who are really good grind away and get you almost to the point of no return when the song ends, and then they pause and start all over again, song after song after song.

I thought, *I hoped,* that Cherie was really, really good. There's nothing quite like running your fingers over the warm, firm skin of a girl barely out of her teens, one of her hard nipples in your mouth, while she rubs her smooth nakedness against you, slides her hand under your shirt and toys with your chest hair. In the dim light, you're only as old as you feel, not as old as you look.

There was still a song playing, Britney Spears, when I settled into the laid-back chair, so there was time for some small talk.

"Are you from here?" I asked. That's the standard starter.

"No," she said, sitting on the little stool. She was still wearing the mask. "I was born here, but moved upstate a long time ago. I'm back in Tampa now to go to school. This pays for tuition."

Still with the girl-next-door, and that was fine with me. Then she leaned forward.

"You know, I can dance for you if you like, and that'll cost you 20 a song. Then you can go home and jerk off. But we're alone here in a room with a camera that's broken. If you want me to blow you, I can do that for 200 dollars and I won't even charge you separate for the songs."

God damn! How could any red-blooded male resist that? I smiled and nodded. "If you do that, you'll have to take off your mask," I said. "Is that allowed under government guidelines?" It was a joke. Like I cared.

"I keep it on till I know I'm with somebody I want to be close with," she said, and took it off, slowly, right side and then left side, and she was smiling. She was beautiful, as I expected, with a small, lightly freckled nose and a rosebud mouth, very white teeth, but without the hidden suggestion of the mask, she was slightly less erotic. Don't get me wrong, I'm not complaining, but the mask just added a certain *coyness* that was no longer there. Didn't slow me down any, though.

"You're very beautiful," I said. The song on the speakers ended and the show was about to begin. The next song was that one by the woman who used to live in her car. *Wake up in the morning feeling like P. Diddy*, she sang, and Cherie leaned forward right away to unhook my belt and unzip my fly.

"You know, I thought you were French with a name like Cherie," I said.

"Yeah? Nobody here uses their real name. That's just a name I like."

Before I leave, brush my teeth with a bottle of Jack.

"What's your real name? For 200 bucks, you should tell me."

She pulled open my pants and found what's important. It wasn't difficult to locate.

'Cause when I leave for the night, I ain't comin' back.

"Sure. My real name is Jessica. Very girl next door, huh?"

. . .

It wasn't good after I left the Champagne Room. At the beginning, while Cherie/Jessica was putting my cock in her mouth, my head was swirling. Was this my daughter, all grown up now into a woman, so many years since I'd seen her last? My imagination was all over the place, turned off, turned on, turned every which way. Very *Game of Thrones*. She's probably the right age. Dammit, she's the right everything!

Her mouth knew what it was doing. I didn't, but I sure as hell stayed hard. She'd have finished the job in record time, too, except the door opened suddenly and the security guard was there, standing in the light with the DJ. Caught in the act. Cherie/Jessica rose off me, all the evidence on display. She looked startled. The two guys in the doorway looked pissed.

"We fixed the camera, Cherie," said the DJ, a wiry little guy.

"You gotta go," said the guard, a huge black guy with no neck who surely played a lot of football. "You both gotta go before you get us closed down. And you don't come back. Never."

It was still mid-afternoon outside and I waited in my truck, trying to enjoy a smoke. Cherie/Jessica finally left from a side door and walked toward a little silver-colored Hyundai hatch in the mostly empty lot. She looked athletic in blue jeans, a yellow T-shirt, and runners, with a baseball cap and her red hair poked through the back of it in a ponytail. I thought the Hyundai might be her car and so I drove over earlier to park closer to it. I leaned out the window and called to her. *Jessica!*

She looked over, tipped her head to one side, then walked up to my truck. "You owe me 200 bucks," she said. She was still attractive, fresh-faced beneath the cap, even in the harsh sunlight.

I thought about saying that she never finished the job. I thought about asking her to finish the job right there in my truck, and she probably would have. I could have held onto that ponytail while she went down. But more important, I needed to know if she's my little lost girl. Blow-jobs and reunions don't go together, at least not in that order.

"Of course," I said, and gave her 200 bucks, two fresh Benjamins, right there with no argument. She was clearly surprised to get the money so easy, and she warmed to me a little. I'm straight up, an honest guy. I paid Amy inside too as I left, a 20 for one beer. I'm not cheap.

"Can I ask you a question?" I said. I'd ask whatever, even if I'd have to yell it across the lot. She nodded. The cash softened her up. I wouldn't need to yell.

"I was going to stop you in there anyway" – *like hell I was* – "because I had a daughter named Jessica, years ago. She had red hair like you. Green eyes like you. She was taken from me, and I …"

Jessica's face was frozen. Something was wrong. Something turned. When I paused, it cracked to life in disgust. In rage.

"You thought you were getting sucked off by your daughter? What kind of sick old fuck are you? You weren't trying to stop me, were you? *Oh my god!* Get away from me!"

"Please – if you're her, I need to know."

"*Fuck off, mister! I'm not her!* My name's not even Jessica – I use that name for old perverts like you. There's no way I'm telling you my real name. Just fuck off home to your wife. No wonder your daughter left – you're disgusting! *Oh my god.*"

She turned and ran – *ran!* – to her car three spaces over. I wondered if she'd toss the money I gave her on the ground in a demonstration of disgust, to show she wanted nothing to do with me, but it was safe in her purse and staying put. She got in the car, slammed the door, started the engine and stomped on the gas, squealing the front tires a little as she sped off.

I already had a photo of her license plate number saved on my phone, just in case. I don't think I'll do anything with it, but you never know.

BIRD ON A WIRE

Chapter 5

CLAIRE, Toronto

I met Floyd Woods exactly three times back when I was living in Florida. The first time was at the Fairfield Mall on the day Jess was taken, when he took a statement from me. The second time was the next day, when he came to the door, media in tow, to take John to the station for questioning. The third time was a week later when I called on him with my parents at the station to find out how the investigation was going, and he talked to me in the lobby for a couple of minutes and that was it.

Outside of that, I spoke to him on the phone every week, and then every month, always me calling him in the hope of some kind of update, some kind of anything, but there was never anything he could tell me, or that he *would* tell me. He was polite but I always felt I was intruding and my call was not welcome, a disruption to a busy day.

"Miss Copeland," he'd say, "I wish I had something to tell you. We're checking everything, every lead, every possibility, but there's nothing new to add today. When we do have something, you're the first person I'll call." And a couple of times, maybe a bit exasperated with me, he'd add, "You know, you should be prepared for bad news. We have no reason to believe Jessica is still alive. We just don't know yet. But we're going to find out, you can be sure of that."

Like I hadn't spent every waking moment preparing myself for bad news.

I phoned him a few times after I left and moved up here to Toronto, but it was the same thing, and then the last couple of times, I called and left a message and he never phoned back. I can take a hint.

Now, though, it's time to talk again. Mom convinced me of it. I called the station a couple of days ago and asked somebody there in the personnel department to pass along a message: "Please tell him I have a potential job for him, and since he's retired, I can pay him for his time." Now, at home in my apartment, not long after lunch, and my phone rang; the name came up as "Unknown" but I hoped it was him and took the call. Right away, I recognized his deep smoker's voice. Even after more than a dozen years, even expecting the call, it was disturbing to hear him. It was a nudge into another life.

"Ms. Copeland, this is Floyd Woods calling you back," he said. "It's been a long time since we've talked."

I gulped, paused, gathered my thoughts. "It's been a very long time, yes, more than a decade," I said. "Thank you for calling back. I didn't know if I'd be able to find you now you've retired." I'm not sure what else to say. My speech, rehearsed all yesterday evening, was forgotten.

"How can I help you, Ms. Copeland?"

I just waded right in, though I assumed he already knew what I'd say. "I haven't given up hope that Jessica is still alive, Mr. Woods." *He's not Detective, anymore.* "I don't know – is there anything you can do there now as a private citizen, as a private investigator, that you couldn't do before? I just thought that if you're retired now, you might have some available time, and if you have the time for a private investigation, I can pay you for that."

"Ms. Copeland, you should know that I do not believe your daughter is still alive. If I do this for you, I don't know what I'll find. Frankly, I'll probably find nothing."

"I understand that, but at least you're familiar with her case. I don't know – maybe there's something now to be checked out that you didn't have the time, or the approval, to check out before." *Because you were too damn lazy!* "Whether Jess is alive or dead, I just want some closure to all this." I had to pause and let him speak because I was starting to choke up. Surely, he could hear it in my voice.

It was a long pause and I heard him cough. It made me think of gravel being rolled around between his palms. Probably felt the same for him, too.

"Can I call you back on this, Ms. Copeland?" he asked. "It's not something I thought of doing and I don't want to waste your time if it doesn't work out."

Of course, I told him. He said he'd call back tomorrow and when he hung up, it was a relief. Maybe something might actually happen! Maybe John will go to jail! God, I hope so. I went to put his number in my phone's Contacts list, but his number was Unknown too.

. . .

Woods was a lot more considerate when he called back than he was when this all began. I was in my kitchen now listening to him, but my mind was stuck in the mall, 19 years ago. I suppose there wasn't really much back then to ask me, Jess's mother, except for what she was wearing. I remember giving them a photograph of her from my purse, then the police closed the mall for an hour or so, asked everyone to leave, and questioned everybody as they went out through the doors. Most of the shoppers just sat in their cars and waited to be allowed back in.

While the mall was emptying out, maybe 20 patrol officers went through all the stores and all the back rooms to search for Jessica, and the store workers were asked to help, but nobody found anything. There were other police officers in the parking lots and they kept searching after people were allowed back in, but nothing. There was not a thing, except for the photo.

It didn't take them long to find that photograph of Jess by the Mrs. French's Cookies booth. She's looking up at the mall surveillance camera and smiling, though the camera was way up near the roof two storeys above her, so she was just smiling for herself, because she was happy. Sometimes, I wonder if that was the last time she was ever happy.

"I'll see what I can find for you, Ms. Copeland," Woods said over the phone, "but I can offer no guarantees of anything. There are some leads I can follow up that may have been, perhaps, *abbreviated* before."

I took that to mean that maybe they made a phone call and left a message, before heading out to some bar and forgetting about it, or maybe they skipped the phone call and message completely to just go straight to the bar.

"Thank you," I said.

"My fee is $100 an hour, or $600 a day for the days I spend actually investigating the case, plus whatever expenses are necessary. I'll ask you for approval beforehand if the expenses exceed $200 dollars a day."

"Thank you," I said. "That sounds fine."

"You need to set a cap on the final fee. This could get expensive for you very quickly."

I felt like the person looking at a car in a showroom, when the salesperson asks how much you want to spend, and whatever price you say, you won't spend less. I know Mom was offering to cover $10,000 from her savings, maybe more, but I didn't want to tell him that.

"I think we should evaluate this after a week, just to see where we're at. I'm not a wealthy woman, Mr. Woods, and a week of your time will probably be around four or five thousand dollars."

"I don't work every day. I work the hours and the days that need to be worked. Sometimes, I need to wait to make the next move, and in a week, I may not be able to devote more than 10 hours, or two or three days, to this investigation. Or I may be on it every day, all day. Each case is different and I just can't predict how this will be. I'm happy to speak to you after a week, though, and we can decide where to go from there."

Woods sounded like he's been doing private investigations for years, though he was only retired a week from the force. I wondered if he's been doing this on the side all along, and I wondered if I missed any hints from him all those years ago, and if he would have done this at the time, made the extra effort, if the money was offered then. That would have been bribery, surely?

"Yes, that sounds fine." His spiel was supposed to be reassuring, but I'm prepared for him to bill me for seven days straight and then say he's turned up nothing. Probably, he'll play golf on those seven days and I'll be none the wiser. Whatever, he's still the best choice I have and it's him or it's nothing.

"I'll need a down-payment, too. An advance before I can get started. It's a standard thing I have to ask for."

"How much do you need?"

There was a pause. The pause told me the down-payment is definitely *not* a standard thing.

"Three thousand dollars. You can make the payment by direct deposit."

I paused too. Frankly, I was expecting him to ask for five thousand up front, and Mom gave me the go-ahead to throw away twice that on the off-chance of something, anything. But I paused, just to show this is a weighty figure that I need to consider carefully and that he shouldn't be too greedy. Then, "Sure, I can do that."

"Okay, if you give me your e-mail, I'll send you a contract. When you've signed it and sent through the initial funds, I can get started right away."

"Sure." And then I added: "You should start by checking into her father. I'm certain it was him who took her."

"Why do you think that?"

"I just know it, Mr. Woods. John knew I might leave with Jess to live in Canada, and I think he took her, or arranged for somebody to take her, so that she'd stay in Florida without having a custody fight. It's why I think she's still alive."

"You may be right. Anything is possible. Do you have a contact number or address for John Morgan?"

"Actually, no, not for his home, but he still works at the Triple-A car dealership." He used to joke about moving up to Canada with me, when Jessica was still with us, and opening his own dealership called the Triple-Eh. It was always only a joke. It was never going to happen. "His uncle Luis owned it and probably still does. Are you going to talk to him?"

"Can I be straight with you, Ms. Copeland?"

Uh-oh.

"Yes. Please do."

"We always thought the same thing – that it was her father, your boyfriend, John, who took Jessica. It was in his genes to want to have her to himself. You told me on the first day that you rarely let her out of your sight, and we thought he wanted her without you around. Our behavioural psychologist at the time thought so too, and all the other profilers we consult for things like this."

I asked the obvious question, though I knew his obvious answer.

"Do you think he took her because he wanted to be her father, away from me, or because…"

I had to pause, to swallow. The word wouldn't come easily, but Woods waited. He made me say it.

"… because he wanted to molest her?"

"We were sure he wanted her for sexual gratification," he said. A sudden weight thudded down on me, a darkness. My eyes were closed as I listened to his slow rasping drawl, picturing my daughter's beautiful face screaming in pain and surprise and betrayal.

"Can I ask you a personal question, Ms. Copeland?"

"I guess so."

"Was he aggressive with you, sexually? Was he a man who took charge and wouldn't accept no for an answer? Did he ever hit you?"

I knew what Woods wanted to know here. I hate thinking of it, but the question needed an answer.

"He never hit me, Mr. Woods, but in bed, yes, he could be forceful. He knew what he wanted and he'd make sure he got it. Nothing too weird, but aggressive? Yes, I suppose so."

Surely Woods would want details, all the juicy, kinky stuff about me and John the Asshole, but he didn't ask. I didn't want to tell him and I'm not proud of those days. For the first year or so, I thought we were a well-matched couple, physically at least. I wanted John as much as John wanted me, and I didn't believe the story about him and his sister, but as Jess developed from being a toddler to being a little girl, I became more protective of her. I was more wary of her father's DNA.

"Please excuse the blunt talk, but I have to be straight with you here. We followed him for several weeks and he actively evaded us. There were periods of a day, or a couple of days, when we lost him and we had no idea where he was. We assumed he was with Jessica, wherever he was keeping her. And then, after a month or so, he stopped evading us. Stayed at home or went to work. Settled down."

I remember that well. He would go away like that throughout the time we were together and he'd never say where, just that he was doing some work for his uncle. I always assumed he was delivering drugs or something else illegal. Later, I thought he was probably screwing around. I moved out when my parents came down after the abduction and I never moved back, but John told me he was trying to go straight and had stopped helping out his uncle on those mysterious disappearances. It didn't matter to me because I hated him no less. Our daughter was gone from my life because of him.

"What we thought at the time, Ms. Copeland, is that after that month or two, Jessica finally died at whatever place he'd been keeping her. Though there is another possibility."

Uh-oh.

"It's always possible that he sold her on to somebody. I'm sorry to say it, but he's one of the Morgan boys, and those apples don't fall too far from the tree."

That hit me like a smack across the face. I never thought of that. John sold our daughter to some pervert? *Sold her?* Do people really do that? I always hoped he gave her to another couple, a childless couple, so she'd stay close to home and he could be a part of her life without me taking her far away. I suggested that again to Woods, but he said it's unlikely because there was too much chance of it coming back on him in some way. He said the overwhelming probability was that if he had taken her, he'd raped her and then she'd died, but if she'd lived, he'd have moved her on to someone else with a lust for little girls.

That thought just numbed me and kept my mind distracted long after our call ends. The darkness that thudded down when he began speaking so matter-of-factly about Jess's rape and murder didn't lift. I'd hoped he was somehow raising her himself, even if she was soiled goods, and if not that, I'd hoped she'd died quickly, the same afternoon. It would be the worst thing of all for her to be with somebody else like him.

. . .

Woods e-mailed me a two-page contract that looked as if he'd typed it up that morning. It mostly stated that his service costs $100 an hour, or $600 a day, plus expenses, and that he must be paid even if he comes up with nothing at all. It was a cover-his-fat-ass contract. Later in the day, I signed it and sent it back with an Interac transfer of $3,000 American, then I finally called Mom and told her about the call. She agreed I did the right thing in hiring Woods with her money. With all that done, I closed all the drapes and my black-out blind, startling some pigeons outside on the sill, took another Ambien, and went to bed.

In the dark room, I flashed through all the time I ever spent with Jessica, and with John. There were the confident days of the pregnancy; the tiring days and nights of her first two years; the protective days of her coming in to her own as a little girl, learning to walk and to speak and to be her own person.

Jess and I were always together because I wasn't working. John had money, so I made the choice – *we* made the choice – to be the best mom I could be and stay at home to raise my daughter. My visa let me live in the U.S. because my daughter was born there, but I still wasn't allowed to work. We talked about getting married to help me qualify for a Green Card, but I wasn't that concerned about it, as long as they kept giving me papers that wouldn't throw me out of the country. Part of me always thought that I'd return north to Canada once Jessica was ready for kindergarten and that would have been the next year. John never wanted to talk about it, so I didn't mention it much. I just kept my thoughts to myself, and he would find out for himself when the time came.

We were happy, but we weren't a traditional mom-and-pop American family. We were too young for that, I guess. I really did think of the three of us as being me and Jess, and then John. And no, deep down, I never completely trusted him to be alone with her, so yes, I was always there, knitting socks and sweaters and hats with Rags to protect us.

He'd told me about his father raping his twin sister Kelly, for a while apparently until one afternoon when she was around nine years old, when she didn't give herself up to him so easily and he strangled her. He'd started molesting her younger sister, Tammy, too, and John was glad his dad was sent to the chair. *Good riddance*, he'd say, though sometimes I wondered if he was laying it on a little too thick, for effect. He also told me about his brother Mike breaking into a house in Clearwater and killing the whole family but not until after raping the two teenage girls. It was all just horrific.

I'm not Mike, he said. *I don't even know who he is*. Even so, I never left him alone with Jess.

On the night of the day she was taken, the police told us to go home and stay near a phone. We drove back to the house after dark, past all the Christmas decorations on the lawns, all the candy canes and inflatable Santas and the wire reindeer, everything lit up with spotlights and sparkling lights in the windows and on the roofs. That was my fifth Christmas down there and it still seemed bizarre to have plastic snowmen illuminated on the grass, under the palm trees.

Kim had come to the mall hours earlier to fetch Jason – I didn't know yet that she'd been screwing my stolen daughter's father – and John drove me home in my car, both of us barely speaking. We stopped on the way to get some take-out KFC but I don't think I ate any of it.

Not long after we got back, me a wreck and Rags knowing something was up and whimpering and searching the house for Jess, John said he had to go back to the mall to get his truck. I offered to drive him but he said no, I should stay at the house to be near the phone. We never had a land-line. I had my cell phone but the battery was almost dead and it needed to be plugged in and there was no way back then to recharge it in the car. Besides, he said, I'd taken a Valium and he didn't want me driving. I didn't want the Valium, but he'd urged me to take it, to calm my nerves, so I did. And then he called a taxi and went over to get the truck and he didn't come home again until three in the morning. Our daughter was stolen and he left me alone for six hours. Alone. For six hours.

He found me on the couch. There was an infomercial on the TV for something like a ShamWow. I wasn't watching; I wasn't listening; I wasn't doing anything except sitting there catatonic, praying for a phone call from the police, from the abductor, from somebody who'd found my little girl wandering on the road, but there was no phone call and never would be.

"Where have you been?" I asked, quietly, the moment he walked in. "Why didn't you call me?"

"Baby, I was with Luis. We were putting out calls to find Jess," he said. "You know Luis is the best person to help with this, right? Not the cops. Luis is family and he knows a lot of people who can help us. Direct action with no red tape. Jess will be fine, but somebody's taken her to get at Luis and me. They want money, or something else Luis has. That's the motive. It's got to be."

"You didn't call me."

"I didn't want to tie up the phone. The kidnapper might have called you and not me."

This was 2004, don't forget, and cell phones didn't let you put calls on hold like they do now. He always had an answer, but it's why I hadn't tried to call him.

John sat with me on the couch. I remember lifting his hand to my face to let him stroke my cheek, then moving it over to my mouth so I could kiss his fingertips. Maybe he thought it was a tender moment, but I was breathing in deeply, smelling for anything on his skin that might betray his story. There was no scent – nothing except tobacco. I brushed my mouth against his hand instead of kissing him and from then on, I would never kiss him again.

He fell asleep beside me on the couch as I waited for the daylight and the start of the first full day of the end of my life.

John was lucky the police didn't arrest him when he punched Floyd Woods at the mall and knocked him to the ground. Somebody convinced Woods to not press charges because they knew I had no family in Tampa, and I didn't even have any real friends. My parents wouldn't arrive until the next day and I shouldn't be alone that night, but all the same, I was alone for most of that night.

Ever since then, I've wondered: *Where was he?*

BIRD ON A WIRE

Chapter 6

JON, Tampa

Uncle Luis keeps an office behind the car wreckers. I love Luis, though it's a love-hate relationship. I love him until I hate him, and then after a while, I love him again. In the end, he's family. They say the only people you can really trust are family, but then, they've never met *my* family. Bunch of losers, all of them. All of them except Luis.

Luis Lopez is my mother's brother so he's not a Morgan. Puerto Rican, but he's been in Florida since he was a kid. There are no sex crimes in his past – or none that I know about. He's a fag anyway and always has been. Doesn't bother me none. He doesn't drink, and he doesn't use any of the drugs he sells. He still does things his way and skirts around the law to get stuff done, and I'm sure the cops have a thick file on him, but nothing ever sticks. He covers his tracks, and his lawyer, Thurston Bell, knows his way around a courtroom. He earns his retainer, does Thurston.

After my dad was arrested and put away, Luis stepped in to help Mom look after us three kids. We were a handful: Mike was ten when Dad left and I was just a year behind him, while Tammy was only seven. She told us Dad had started fucking her too, so she was already pretty screwed up. Mom hung in for a few years and went through a bunch of guys, but Luis was protective of her and none of them stuck around for long. Eventually, Mom moved out to Louisiana with somebody and left us behind with Luis.

Like I said, Luis is gay and while he doesn't parade it, he doesn't hide it. He's always lived alone, but there were other fags who would come over to the house and they'd get it on. I never walked in on anything, but Mike did when he was 12 years old. Mike saw them at it, went crazy, tried to stab the guy and tried to stab Luis. They got the knife off him and threw him out of the room and got dressed. By the time they came out, Mike was gone. He lived on the streets or in squats from that day on. I'd see him often enough and sometimes he'd ask me to come join him, but I was happy at Luis's place.

Luis knows all kinds of people. He'd keep an eye on Mike through his friends, and he'd try to help him when he could, get people to offer him work, that sort of thing, but Mike would have nothing to do with him. Luis did that for Mom, too. He told me she's with another guy now, in Texas, and he knows where she lives, but he won't tell me more than that. I don't care. I don't ask. I don't need her.

In the Bay region here, Luis Lopez is known as The Car Guy. He owns a Ford dealership and three used vehicle dealerships, one of which I work at and all of which are completely legitimate. He also owns a parts supply and delivery business and two wrecker's yards. One of the yards won the 2018 Green Pyramid Award for Excellence in Environmental Automotive Recycling, which we all thought was pretty cool. Pretty funny too, considering the shit that goes on at the other yard, the one I'm pulling into. Let's just say that not everything in those cubes of compressed metal is automotive, *know what I mean?*

Luis has a respectable office upstairs at the Ford dealership, but the real work gets done in his office here at the wreckers. They knew me at the gate, of course, so I drove my truck in and past the rows upon rows of rusted hulks – more than 3,000 of them on the books – toward the metal warehouse buildings at the back. Past the cameras. Past the sleeping dogs on chains. Past the second fence and the second controlled metal gate, which slid open to welcome me in, then shut to keep me safe inside.

I parked beside Luis's Mercedes SUV and a handful of other cars, all of them underneath a corrugated roof to protect them from both sun and satellites, and walked in through a nondescript side door.

This was the chop shop. Don't confuse it with the process next door, where the wrecked vehicles from the yard get drained of fluids, pulled apart and sorted into scrap or sale or recycling. No, this is where luxurious and powerful vehicles, freshly located in the Bay area, get pulled apart, recycled and sometimes rebuilt. There are only one or two here this afternoon. Business isn't what it used to be with the hassle of finding and removing the tracking devices before they arrive.

Take it from me: if you want to keep your expensive wheels, fit a tracking device. It catches the amateur thieves and it helps out Luis – he owns the franchise in Central Florida for installing a couple of the brands.

The shop was fairly quiet at six o'clock, just four guys shooting the shit before leaving, and we all knew each other. Domingo gave me a chin-up nod and pointed toward another door to the side, which is where I'd find Luis in his office. He was waiting for me. Gary was here too, leaning against the far wall.

"Jonny-Boy!" said Luis when I walked into the tidy office, shop manuals in alphabetical order on neat bookshelves, modern furniture that cost somebody a lot of money. A couple of large and heavy scale-model cars sat on his big oak desk: a '60s T-Bird and a '50s Corvette. He was sitting at the desk so I strode straight up to shake his hand with a firm grip. Luis isn't that tall so he didn't get up, but reached across to grasp my hand with his smooth, fleshy palm, as smooth as his head. I nodded over his shoulder at Gary. I've known Gary Richards for years but I don't like him. He wears what's left of his stringy hair in a ponytail and I'm sure if Luis pulls on it, he'll make a noise like a bell. Yes, Luis. You're right, Luis. Great idea, Luis. I wish I was gay like you, Luis. Fucking sycophant. He's the heir to the throne and he just rubs me the wrong way.

"Jon, there's a drive to Miami for you, leaving now," said Luis. "You okay with that?"

Like I have a choice. I nodded. Of course!

"Good. It's the shop by the docks. They'll wait for you till midnight. Your car's at the Sunset. Get back to the Bayshore by six and we're golden."

It would be eight hours of driving in the next 12 hours, and it would be through the night on some of the most boring highway in America. I was fine with that. Set the cruise control, play some podcasts, all good.

"Julio will run you over now to your car. When you get back, go to bed! You don't need to go into the dealership."

Like I'd be able to sell anyone a used car on two hours of sleep. That was fine with me.

I was leaving the office to go find Julio when Gary spoke for the first time.

"Jon," he said, "watch your back out there. One eye on the mirror."

Always, asshole. *Always.*

. . .

I didn't know why I was going to Miami and I didn't want to know. Every run is different. I assume it's either guns or drugs in the trunk, or in some hidden compartment, though sometimes I'll drive a cube van and I feel movement and I wonder if there are people back there. I don't know if I'm delivering, or collecting, or both.

The drop sites change around though I've never been west of Houston or north of Milwaukee. For those longer runs, Luis gives me a heads-up so I can get some rest beforehand. Most often, it's somewhere in Florida and most often of all, it's Miami. I can do that run with my eyes closed, and when I'm going on no sleep, the challenge is to *not* do that.

Julio took me over to the Sunset Motel near the airport, where there was a late-model brown Chevy Malibu waiting. One of the advantages of owning car dealerships is there's always a bunch of new, clean cars coming in and going out, so it's easy to borrow one for a while, especially a boring, forgettable one.

When I get to the shop in Miami, I'll hand over the Malibu and drive away in whatever they have waiting for me. It'll be running well and full of gas. It'll probably even have one of Luis's trackers in it, though I've been doing this so long he knows he can trust me. The danger comes from getting jacked along the way by one of Luis's rivals, and there's no shortage of them in South Florida.

The Malibu was comfortable enough, with leather seats and a USB charger for my phone. Luis gave me this phone last year. There's no GPS in it, which is why I keep my own iPhone that I just switch off, but it does let me store music and podcasts for the long, boring drives, and it has an automatic encryption system for texts, to stay in touch. I don't want to stop if I don't have to. Earlier, I picked up some teriyaki jerky and peanut M&Ms for road snacks, and some red and blue Gatorade. I wouldn't need to piss till I hand over in Miami.

. . .

I was through the toll booth just past Naples and heading east on Alligator Alley, driving through the dark with the cruise control at a tick under the 70 limit. There was nothing to raise any attention: brown sedan, legal speed, all the lights worked. At the toll booth, I paid the $3.25 charge in cash. This is a straight, flat, four-lane highway with wide grass verges and a wide grass median, low trees on each side of a fence that's there to keep wildlife off the road, so it's as boring as can be.

I still couldn't relax: two years ago, right at dusk, I hit a panther on this stretch of road. A fucking *panther*. Just ran out in front of me – a blur to the right and then it was into my grille and under my wheels. A hundred-and-something pounds of endangered reddy-brown fur and blood, suddenly a lot more red than brown, just destroyed the front end and smashed out both lights. I pulled over and other drivers pulled over, and people started taking photos of the carcass and the ripped-off limbs and the damage, and somebody called the cops.

Panthers are protected here so it was a big deal. I was driving a Ford Edge over to Miami and the cops wanted to know everything about why I was there, but they never searched the vehicle. I had legal papers and told them I was heading over to visit a girlfriend in Lauderdale for the night, which seemed fine. Fortunately, I really did have a girlfriend in Lauderdale who would have vouched for me if they'd called. Also fortunately, Luis told me to let the cops tow the vehicle and he'd send somebody down to collect me. I must have been running empty.

This was still a safer road than any of the alternatives. I'm not really worried about cops – I watch for the low-lifes who might have heard I'm out on the highway and who want whatever it is I've got. The turnpike is too public for them. The main danger is in the first few blocks from the shop to the interstate, or out on some lonely road that no-one else travels. So I drive the well-covered routes, protected by the unaware cops and the speeders who attract their attention, slipping through in comfortable anonymity.

Normally, this straight stretch is where I listen to a podcast – spoken-word stuff helps keep me alert. I like all kinds, mostly news shows. Joe Rogan's good. Car history. True crime. Sometimes, when I'm mellow in the middle of the day, I'll listen to *This American Life* and think about how *this* American life came to be driving across the country, minding his business, against all the odds.

. . .

The police don't bother me much these days. I was in and out of trouble all the time before I met Claire and I'll give her her due, she helped me clean up my life and appreciate what I had. I'd spent some time in juvie for jacking cars, which was supposed to scare me straight, but when you're hanging around Luis's yard, you don't realize there's an alternative. My little sister Tammy got herself too deep into drugs and never left. Then I met Claire. Even so, it was Jess, not Claire, who stopped me using coke because I wanted to be a better dad. For a few years there, I cut back on drinking, no smoking, ate well, worked out. Less coke, more Diet Coke, I used to say.

After I lost Jess, after she left and I accepted she wasn't coming back, it was really hard for me. I thought about leaving Tampa and just going somewhere else, anywhere. I had money saved from Luis's errands and I figured I could maybe move to California for a few years just to hang out. I thought about Mexico, living on the beach and running a bar, sleeping warm, naked nights in a hammock. I thought about a lot of places. I even thought about Alaska and learning to live with snow, but that lasted about a minute. In the end, I just stayed home, told Luis I needed a break from everything and he understood. We're family, don't forget.

A big reason I wanted to run away was because Claire was still down here. She said she wouldn't leave – Jess needed a home to return to. She'd moved out of my place before Christmas when her parents flew down and she never came back, but I still saw her enough.

She blamed me for losing Jess, though even if I hadn't been screwing Kim, I'd have been away at work. She blamed me for souring the cops, and for not supporting her enough, and for being a lousy dad, and for being an asshole. She'd have blamed me for Pearl Harbor and Watergate if she could. She's probably blaming me now for the China virus. So what could I do? I started drinking more, smoking of course, and taking the edge off with a few lines, and I never did try to win her back. I think that's what pissed her off the most.

Her family always had money and they paid for her to get a place in a nicer part of town, near the college where she enrolled in nursing school. I'd have given her the money too, if she'd asked, but she never asked. At the end of the year, after a semester of school, she moved back up to Canada to be with them. She told me she wouldn't be able to handle another Christmas down here on her own. Fine, I said – I owed her nothing. *Merry fucking Christmas!*

We kind of stayed in touch for a while but that slipped pretty quick. She went back to school and I think she's a nurse now, up in Canada. I don't know if she's married, or what. It's funny – I shouldn't really care but I still do care, *know what I mean*? We were pretty good for a time, the best even, and you can't just shrug that off like it was nothing. After all, she's still the mother of my child.

. . .

It was an easy swap in Miami, at the shop four blocks off the interstate. I sent a text from a couple of minutes away and they were watching for me, sliding the garage door half-open as I drove up, closing it again as soon as I was in.

"Good to see you, Captain Morgan!" That's Mateo, flashing his silver-tooth smile. He always looks like a pirate in his dreadlocks and wide bandana, and when I told him this, that was when he coined his name for me. I don't mind but it stays between us. Nobody I work with outside of Florida knows my last name. Fuck, hardly anyone *inside* Florida does either, or even my first name. There's just no need for it.

I took my stuff from the Malibu, gave the keys to one of the other three guys there, and headed into the back for a piss and a smoke. When I came back, Mateo handed me the keys to a silver Ford Escape that was waiting on the polished floor. We like Fords, especially for the return run. They're easier to explain with Luis's dealership. We don't like Lincolns though, not after that old guy from the Clint Eastwood movie got busted in his Lincoln pickup truck.

I got in the Escape with my shit, checked the glove box for the legal papers, the door opened again and I drove back out onto the quiet road. It was 11 pm. The road was lit by street lamps but there were dark shadows everywhere pooling on the sidewalks, in the alleys to the side. Everything was still and the palm fronds weren't moving at all. If anything will happen, it'd probably be here.

Two of the guys from the shop followed me out, close behind, driving a Dodge Charger, and we stayed in convoy till we reached the turnpike. They followed me up, then peeled off at the next exit and I was back on my own again, headed home to Tampa.

This time, though, I wasn't quite so comfortable. I was jittery. Maybe it was seeing that Jessica stripper earlier, or maybe it was Gary's words, *one eye on the mirror*! I kept both eyes on the mirrors. All I could see were headlamps across all four lanes as the turnpike rolled north to the 595, and when the exit took me off to the west, to pick up I-75 again, there was still a cluster of lights bobbing behind, too many to know if any were just sitting on my tail.

At the toll station, I stayed in the right lane for the SunPass, and then, at the last moment before the booths, I swerved hard to the left. Tires squealed, traffic lurched to a halt behind, horns honked. At the booth, the attendant looked unimpressed.

"What the hell was that?" she said.

"Sorry – I forgot my transponder's in the other car."

It took a while to fish for change in my pants pocket, stalling for time to let all the other lanes get well ahead. Horns started honking again behind me and finally, I handed over a five-dollar bill. The bar flipped up and the attendant gave me change with a latex-gloved hand, and waved me through.

On the other side, there was a dark red Mazda sedan parked on the right shoulder. The windows were completely blacked out. After I drove past, the Mazda pulled off the shoulder and tucked in, a hundred yards behind.

Past the tollbooths and out onto Alligator Alley proper, the road got real dark, real quick. It was cloudy – no stars. My rearview mirror automatically dimmed the lights of the Mazda but I reached up and switched the dimmer off. I wanted those lights tickling my eyeballs. If they start to move to the side, move closer, move farther away, I needed to know.

What I really, *really* wanted was a patrol cruiser to tuck in behind for the next 80 miles, but they don't drive back and forth, they just hide over by the fence in the darkness, eating donuts, waiting to pull out with the cherries flashing when a speeder whips by. Then they'll write their ticket and go back into hiding again and eat more donuts.

Next best is a transport to pull alongside. He wouldn't want to stop, but he'd have a radio and he might block things off if he sees there's trouble.

And if there's nothing else around? My Glock's in the glovebox. Shoot first, don't bother asking questions.

. . .

Now I really needed to piss. It was nerves, got to be. I tailed an 18-wheeler for a while and then, when it was clear he was on cruise at 72, I pulled past him and sat in the left lane at 72, about 50 yards ahead of his front bumper. Florida's full of left-lane bandits. Maybe this is why. His lights were filling my door mirror but I could see the Mazda's lights in the rear-view. The Mazda stayed behind the truck in the right lane, not trying to pass, not even able to pass. And I could take it like this all the way to Fort Myers except I had to piss.

There was no fucking way, however, that I was pulling over. Not beside the road. Not at a rest area. Not at a service center. I'd just piss myself if I had to, all over the 12-way-adjustable faux-leather seat, and then I realized I still had the plastic bottle from the blue Gatorade, empty now. There was nothing else for it. I set the cruise and let the SUV's automatic steering keep me in the center of the lane, hands off the wheel, then I fumbled with my zip to pull out my dick like I'm on a date with some high-school cheerleader. The trucker was probably watching it all through my rear window. Can't be helped.

I was a bit too big to fit inside the wide-mouth neck of the bottle, which is both good and bad. Good, because, well, I'm a bit too big. Bad, because I had to hold both the bottle and my dick. I also had to stand up a bit so I could shoot down into the bottle, not up. But I did it, hands off the wheel, feet off the pedals, thank God for modern cars, and the relief was massive when my bladder drained and the bottle filled. For a while, I wondered if it might overflow but it started to taper off around the half-way mark.

The automatic steering, however, is only designed to work for 15 seconds at a time. I know this because I fucking sell cars for a living. And when the time's up, if I don't get my hands back on the wheel, it will eventually assume I've had a heart attack and will put on the brakes and the flashers, and that's the last thing I wanted.

Damn! I was still pissing, draining out, and the warning light came on the dash. *Place hands on the steering wheel!* I wished I could, but my right hand was holding my dick and my left hand was holding a half-full bottle of warm piss. The cruise control turned off and the car started to slow and the light flashed more insistent now. *Place hands on the steering wheel!* There was nothing for it before the brakes came on except to shut off the flow and maybe get back to it later.

I let go of my cock, reached for the wheel, drops of piss flew off me, and the transport that was 50 yards back was now almost alongside. Great. I let go of the wheel again to reach for the bottle cap that was loose on the seat beside me, steering with my left elbow, and as I lurched back to fit the cap on the bottle and the truck was now right beside me, I dropped the open fucking bottle into my lap.

By the time I got the cap on the bottle and my dick back in my pants, the transport truck was well ahead, still in the right lane. There was no other traffic nearby. The Mazda was nowhere to be seen.

I'm getting too old for this shit.

. . .

It was three in the morning when I pulled into the Bayshore Motel. My truck was sitting there. I parked and locked the Escape, kept the key in my pocket, then opened my truck with its spare key and fired it up. Fortunately, my pants had dried off but they still stank.

In the center console, there was a large brown envelope. I didn't need to open it to check it – it'd be 10,000 in 20-dollar bills, the standard cost of a Miami run.

It was a 15-minute drive back to my house, two cigarettes with no traffic, and the place was dark when I let myself in. Normally, I'd crack a beer now and finally relax with some mindless TV, but this time, I headed straight for the shower, stripping off on the way and throwing everything into the laundry basket in the hall closet. The shower was hot, great pressure, and eventually, with enough soap and shampoo, I felt clean again. Clean enough to go to bed.

I left the lights off in the bedroom and slid in naked between the sheets. The cotton was cool and slightly stiff. It's a wonderful feeling against my clean skin. I could see the shadow against the ceiling of the overhead fan turning slowly.

The voice beside me was quiet, half asleep.

"What time is it? Molly wants you to take her to school in the morning with your truck. She has to hand in her volcano project. Can you do that?"

"Sure honey," I said. "I'll get up with you in the morning."

We pressed into each other, Maria resting her head on my shoulder and sliding her hand across me, toying sleepily with the hair on my chest.

Chapter 7

CLAIRE, Toronto

Floyd Woods called back a week later, soon after I got home from my night shift and at the start of three days off. It was not good news, but it could have been worse.

"I want to update you on what I've found so far, as we agreed," he said over the phone. "I don't think I'm any farther ahead with locating Jessica, but we can never be sure if something's important till we get to look back on everything."

"Okay," I said. He coughed, that gravelly hawk of his. This time, I thought of him rubbing his fat banana fingers together at the thought of the easy money coming his way.

"You're right that John Morgan is still working at the Triple-A dealership. I've kept an eye on him. He's changed his first name to Jonathan now. He changed it legally in 2007. There's no record of any money troubles or even legal troubles, so I don't know why he would have done that."

No legal troubles? Really?

"He's had no charges against him for anything at all except parking tickets – he gets quite a few of them. He must bring in money from somewhere else, because he bought a house in 2017 that he paid for with cash, 2.3 million dollars, but he keeps himself clean. Same as his uncle, Luis Lopez. We know Lopez has his hands in all kinds of shady business, but we've never been able to pin anything on him. At least, nothing substantial."

Two million dollars? Jesus – crime really does pay! But aside from John buying a nice house, none of this was news.

"That same year, in 2017, he married a woman named Maria Martinez. Does that name mean anything to you? Do you know of her?"

Now that's news!

"No, not at all," I tell him. *Poor Maria!* "Are they still married?"

"They are, and Maria has a daughter, Molly. Now, she'll be twelve years old. She's in Grade 7 and it looks like everything's just fine. They're a happy little American family."

My heart skipped a beat. "Does the school board know about John?" I asked. *Poor Molly!*

"There's nothing for them to know. John Morgan has never been accused of improper behaviour with a minor, despite his family. When we took him in, we never arrested him, just questioned him. The point is, he may have gotten a bad rap from us before because of his family ties, or he may just be smart. I wanted to ask you for your gut feeling on this. If you look back on everything now, do you still think he had anything to do with Jessica's disappearance? Honestly?"

Yes! Yes I do! YesYesYES!

"I do, Mr. Woods, but I have no proof. None at all. While we were together, he never did anything overtly wrong with Jess. I never caught him at anything. In fact, he was a devoted father, at least as devoted as he could be. But my gut always told me I should never leave him alone with her."

"She was your only child, is that correct? There've been no other children, before or since?"

"No."

"Not even a miscarriage? Or an abortion?"

Why does he need to know that?

I paused a long time before answering. Woods, down in Florida, stayed silent at the other end of the phone. I could hear him breathing. He probably knew the answer already. I closed my eyes.

"A year after Jess was born, I had a miscarriage. I don't know why. Sometimes, these things just happen. I was three months along, the end of the first trimester. He was a little boy. We called him Patrick, after my father."

I was speaking steadily, holding it together for this fat, lazy ex-cop who never found reason to ask such a question 16 years ago.

"At the hospital, they had to take precautions against infection and they gave me a D-and-C, a dilation and curettage, a scraping-out if you will, and since then, I've not been able to have children of my own."

I had to stop. I was angry now for being made to bring this up, to rehash it all back into the open and to bring it to life.

"Why do you need to know this?"

"I'm sorry, Ms. Copeland. I don't want to upset you. I'm just trying to assess John Morgan as a father – what kind of father he was. I'm also concerned for this young girl Molly, and what kind of a father he may now be. I'm hoping you can give me an idea of that."

Oh, Woods was good, turning it back on me! Now I stayed silent. He could smooth-talk his way out of this.

"What was John's reaction to the miscarriage?" Woods asked.

"He was as devastated as I was. We both went into depression, we became less intimate, but I had to keep it together for Jess's sake. I suppose he did too. I think it was harder for him because Patrick was his son, and every man wants a son, somebody to be like them. Do you have children, Mr. Woods?"

"No. My wife and I were never blessed with children, but we had friends with children that we treated as our own."

This didn't help me warm to him, not at all. If he never had sleepless nights, or financial hardship, or sacrifices, then I have no sympathy.

"There are some other avenues of investigation that are still open," he continued. "Over the years, we'd get reports of girls being seen in circumstances that seemed strange to the people making the reports. Unusual behaviour, just something that didn't come across right, whatever. Those reports would be made to the front desk and not passed along to the detectives unless there was reason to do so. But I want to check them out for girls who might fit Jessica's description. I've already begun – I have friends on the force who don't mind passing me information. To do it properly, though, for a comprehensive list going back 16 years, I'll need to cover some considerations, for the officers' time. Probably about 500 dollars. Is that okay for you?"

So this is how it works. *Considerations.* He was telling me he needed to bribe his police friends to give him information he should have had in the first place, which is information he should have followed up years ago, except he was too busy doing other investigations on the side for people who paid in cash. Most likely, this time around he'll spend 100 dollars on buying drinks for all his friends and pocket the rest. I had no choice but to go along with it; we were still well under the budget. Mom was clear she was prepared to throw away $10,000 on the off-chance *something* might come out of it.

"That's okay, Mr. Woods. Thank you for checking with me."

"And Ms. Copeland, this will bring my charges so far to $2,900. I suggest you commit to another week and then we can check back in with each other."

Money. It's just money. I agreed, ended the call and went to bed.

. . .

I'm used to sleeping in the daytime; I've done it for years. My first job after graduating from nursing school back up here in Toronto was night work and I found it soothing, peaceful on the ward. Most people who die in hospital wards seem to die at night but that's okay. It's a nice time to go, slipping away into the dark.

Woods' call had me thinking as I lay in bed about my other lost child, Patrick, who was gone before he had a chance to know me or know anything at all. He was gone for no reason except God wanted him back – at least, that's what the nurses told me. Goddamn God. He took my little boy and then he took my little girl. Stupid nurses too. They were kind at least, even if they were misguided, fundamentalist zealots. Their kindness reinforced my ambition to become a nurse, and when I did, I never, ever told anybody that God had taken their loved one up to Heaven or over the Rainbow Bridge or wherever the hell Paradise is supposed to be. No, I gave *them* the comfort, not their dead loved one who didn't need it any more.

Little Patrick lives in my heart. Jessica? I don't know where she lives. I just don't know.

Remembering Patrick always brings back my father, too. We named our boy after him and he was the best man I've ever known. He was an engineer who went into the tool-and-die business with a clever friend but his real talent was inventing things, and the two of them made a success of whatever he designed: a better coffee-cup lid, a more efficient tail-gate hinge, a smarter camera tripod.

We lived well enough to have a nice house in Toronto and Daddy would push me on the tire swing that hung from the willow tree on our back lawn. He'd walk with me down along the ravine, telling me the names of the birds we could hear overhead in the branches of the trees. Robins, finches, jays, cardinals, he could name them all. Sometimes, I thought the birdsong sounded different from the last time I'd heard it and I'd call him on his identification but he always claimed he was right.

I didn't care because I just liked to hear him say the names of the birds: waxwings, warblers, chickadees, buntings, kingfishers, cuckoos, doves. In the evening, different varieties of owl: long-eared, horned, snowy, barn and, sometimes, the screech owl that always made me shiver.

And then, when I was 10 years old, he died, just washed away. He was gone as suddenly as Jess years later, and I would never touch him again nor hear his voice, never experience his quiet conversation and delight, but when I hear a bird sing, I think of him, and when I hear a screech owl, it still will make me shiver.

My link with Jess is even stronger, with seeing, hearing, touching, every little girl in the world. In the hospital, Jess is there. Out on the street, Jess is there. In my bedroom, Jess is there. And at the mall in Tampa, Jess was there, until she wasn't.

Jess is still missing and I'm sure she's alive. She's crying for me as I'm crying for her, separated by veils in the dark, somewhere just out of reach.

. . .

I spent the week before Woods' next call trying not to think about it. I worked, doing my tending-to-the-sick thing. I finished knitting a pair of dark-blue mittens for the winter and immediately began a new pair, in green this time. I went out for lunch one day with my friend Nancy and gave her the blue mittens as a gift that made her smile; we ate vegetarian pizza under the propane heater at a sidewalk patio restaurant and talked about Covid, and we second-guessed the politicians as we always do these days. I spoke to Mom every day on FaceTime, and I cycled over there four times – she never comes to my place. It's only a one-bedroom and it doesn't even have a balcony.

Mom had no problem with committing to the money Woods asked for. She doesn't share her finances with me, but she's comfortable enough; Daddy left her with some money and besides, his business partner, Seth, always made sure Mom was okay with investment advice.

It took eight years from Daddy dying before she met Lex. I don't know why she married him, but I'm sure he married her for her money. It was no big deal though, because Lex was a tightwad insurance agent and quite the opposite of her. He didn't even own a car – I think all he really wanted was security. Mom was married to him for nearly a decade and was distraught when he died from lung cancer.

"I'll never marry again," she said to me at his funeral, her black dress and her hair immaculate but her mascara smudged across the top of her cheeks. "I'm bad luck."

She's been dating though. She does well for 75, but she looks after herself and the funeral was the last time she let her appearance slip. At the moment, she's seeing a German guy who is charming, but I don't quite trust him. Then again, I don't quite trust any man. John soured me that way.

. . .

When the week was up, Woods called and told me he was given some leads by his friends at the station – *he'd better have, for 500 dollars*— and he followed them up and found nothing. *Of course.* A little red-haired girl acted strangely at a Burger King years ago: he said he called the person who phoned it in who didn't remember phoning it in. What do you do with that? A red-haired girl of about ten years old was seen walking on the sidewalk outside some stores downtown in 2010, holding hands with an older black man: "That was just a racist call," he said. "Some people will never learn to change."

He did more digging into John but so far had come up short, he said. John, or Jonathan now, which is just pretentious, is far more private than your average used-car salesman and he knows how to cover his tracks. He pays his taxes, he donates to the Republicans and a handful of local police associations, and aside from all those parking tickets, he keeps his nose clean.

"Ms. Copeland, is there anybody else from that time who you felt uneasy around?" Woods asked over the phone. "Anybody at all? A neighbour, perhaps, or a friend of a friend who might have had an interest in Jessica? You said back then that you could think of nobody who might have been watching Jessica, or who may have targeted her, but does anyone else now come to mind?"

There was no one I could think of. My only friends from then in Florida were from a couple of local mother's groups that I'd joined, and I left those people behind long ago. It was difficult to make new friends when I didn't work or even go to school, and besides, Jess already took all my time, and I had John. I didn't need close friends and I've never had any. I thought there'd be time enough for new friendships once Jess started school, either down there or up here. John's sister would visit sometimes with her boyfriend and they were both junkies and I didn't like them at all, but she died the year before Jess was taken.

"Well, Ms. Copeland, I'm happy to earn your money but I don't want you throwing it away on a hopeless cause. My fee so far is $5,700 and I'm very aware that I've given you nothing to show for it as yet. I'll understand if you want me to stop. But there's still more I can look into, if you'd like me to do so. More leads, more shoe leather."

Yes, I told him. Please keep looking. *Don't give up again on my little girl like you did before.*

. . .

He called again four days later. This time, he really did have news.

"Claire," he said, more familiar now, "I located Kim Lee, your old friend, the woman who gave John his alibi."

The "Ms. Copeland" formality was gone. And I know who Kim Lee is. I don't need an explainer.

"She's living in Atlanta," he said. "I'm calling you from Atlanta now – I drove up here to see her. And Claire, she says John was *not* with her that day. She says he forced her to provide the alibi."

What?

"Was this on the record, Floyd?" Now I was anxious. To hell with formalities. My heart was in my mouth.

"No, not on the record. And she patted me down to make sure I wasn't wearing a wire, and she turned on the faucets for background noise. She must have seen it in a movie."

"How did he force her?"

"She told me she'd struck and killed some guy with her car earlier that year, some homeless bum crossing the road at night, and she'd fled the scene because she was frightened. She called John to fix her car and he took it away and dealt with all the damage to it, but he had photos and threatened to send the proof to the police if she didn't support his story. She said John told her he'd been making a drug run somewhere in town on the lunch hour when Jess was taken, but he couldn't tell that to the police. And she said that she never quite believed him."

So I was right? It was John! That bastard!

"Why did she tell you this?"

"I can be very persuasive when I need to be. She said she's a mother and she liked you and it's been a 19-year guilt trip, but she'd have gone to prison for the hit-and-run, which is probably true. And if she turns evidence now and tells the state she lied and perjured herself to protect him, she really will go to prison. So there's nothing else we can do with this. Maybe John really was making a drug run, probably something he didn't want his uncle to know about since Lopez didn't give him an alibi. Maybe he was sneaking Jessica out of the mall. All we really *do* know is that we *don't* know where John was at 12:17 pm when Jessica was taken. He was off the grid. No idea at all."

. . .

It's such a helpless feeling, to rely so completely on a man you believe lazy and incompetent, because there's no other choice than to wait at home for news. I've become more of a shut-in over the years, anyway. I'm not that girl anymore who went to Florida and defied her parents and shacked up with the loveable rogue. I learned to care for my daughter and when she was taken, I learned to care for my patients on my ward. Now I come home and I care for nothing. Not for a cat and not even for a cactus. It's something I turn on and off like a faucet, but nobody knows that. I stay inside. Here in the apartment building there's a small gym and an indoor pool, but I never speak to anyone in there. I keep to myself.

They see me in the hospital and they call me an angel and a Samaritan and all that bullshit, and I go along with it with my demure, saintly smile, but when I cycle home, I don't give to the homeless or to panhandlers or to anyone. Fuck them. I'm done with caring.

Now, I lie in bed more than I need, avoiding the light, waiting for the Effexor and the Ambien to kick in, just waiting for something to happen. *Anything*. And when nothing happens, my mind turns in on itself and questions everything. *Everything*. It roils through my memories, remembering the forks and turns, the things that could have happened, the alternatives that might have been.

What if I'd not gone to the mall that day? What if I'd gone the day before? What if John hadn't been screwing the neighbour? What if I'd never met John Morgan? What if I'd never gone to Florida?

And then, looming like a storm over the dark sea, what if I'd never gone looking for shells on the beach on that Nova Scotia vacation? What if I'd just left the picnic table to go back to the camper, as Mom had asked? What if I'd never walked so far out along the spit, as the fog rolled in and the low tide began to turn?

I'd pouted and puffed out my cheeks when Mom told me to put my paper plate in the fire and go back inside the camper. When Mom wasn't watching, I ran down the steep wooden steps and out onto the beach to find the shells I knew were there. I ran so far that when Daddy finally came onto the beach to look for me, he was just a speck in the distance. I could see him with the tall cliffs behind; he would have seen me with the fog behind, swirling in from the mouth of the bay.

When he reached me, I was already obscured by the fast-moving mist and he had to follow my voice for the final distance. I heard him splash through the water that now covered the lower-lying sand, calling constantly, and then I saw him, his face not stern as I expected but worried. No, not worried – scared. "Claire!" he said. "How could you run so far?" I was too young to know, but the tidal bore in this bay could rise ten feet in an hour. He carried a pair of orange armbands and slipped them onto my arms, inflating them with deep breaths, and then he took me by the hand and led me toward the sound I could now hear of Mom in the distance calling our names: *Patrick! Claire!*

The tide was coming in fast, rising over all the sand and I began to struggle in the water that was quickly to my knees. When it reached my waist, Daddy lifted me and put me on his shoulders where I felt secure, clinging to fistfuls of hair as he worked his way through the thick mist toward the sound of the calls. *Patrick! Claire!* Daddy called back, *Vivian!* But I could see nothing in the fog, and now I felt the water again at my feet as it reached his chest. The water came up so fast. His calls never stopped: *Vivian! Here!* But Mom's calls grew fainter as he twisted and turned, trying to follow them as they bounced off the cliffs, and the sound of the water splashing now against my hips smothered our names in the mist. *Patrick! Claire!* And then I heard my father: *Claire! Stay with me!* And then I was no longer on his shoulders and his hair was no longer in my hands and I was swept away by the still-rising sea.

I remember this and my eyes are open in the darkness, wet, seeing nothing. In the tree outside my bedroom window, I can hear the mournful cooing of a dove, calling for its lost mate.

. . .

There were so many days like this, hiding in the dark, and so many nights, hiding in full sight, masquerading on the ward as Saint Claire. Days. Weeks. Claire the fraud. Months. I called Floyd Woods every week but he produced nothing else and when his bill hits $10,000, I called him off the search. Mom told me it was only money and at least we tried. We know for sure now who took her, though we can still only suspect why he did so. Woods said he'll "keep his eyes and ears open anyway." Christmas came and went and then the shitty year ended and we started a new shitty year, and we all hoped for better and we didn't really believe it.

And now, in early February, in the coldest month of Toronto's cold winter, my phone rang. I was over at Mom's on a day off, baking chocolate-chip cookies with her in the kitchen.

It was Floyd Woods. I hadn't spoken to him in two months.

"Claire?" he said. "Are you sitting down?" His voice was as raspy and growly as before. Once a smoker, always a smoker.

"Claire," he said. "I've found her."

PART TWO

BIRD ON A WIRE

Chapter 8

JON, Tampa, 2024

The last few months, someone's been watching me. I don't know who it is but I think it started with that Mazda out on Alligator Alley. It's just a feeling I have, nothing I can pin down. Maybe I'm getting paranoid. It's one thing to be careful in this business but it's another to be paranoid. It's not something that just switches off, *know what I'm saying*?

The most likely thing is that somebody knows I do these errands for Uncle Luis and they want to intercept me the next time, take whatever it is that's in the car. Let them try. I've been ready for that for years. The only way they stand a chance is to get me on my own then shoot everything up like Bonnie and Clyde, but that's not going to happen. I only stop at places where there are a lot of people around and at nighttime on the road, I don't sleep and I don't stop. And, obviously, I'm armed. There are 19 rounds in the magazine and floor plate of my Glock 17 and another in the chamber, ready to go.

I carry my gun everywhere. This is Florida! I take it to the range most weeks for practice but I also take it out to the farm, just for fun. I call it the farm, but it's more a few acres in the swamp, with trees. I parked a trailer there years ago and when I need some Jon time, some escape away from everything, I head out with a book or a magazine and take as long as I need to set my mind straight. I've got lots of books out there, mystery novels mostly, some American history. It keeps the shelves clear at home.

I'm a loner at heart. It's easier that way. I have a few friends I drink beer with and a few friends I drink bourbon with, but I don't let them in. There's a guy I drink both beer and bourbon with, Grant; he has a YouTube channel and makes car videos and I lend him cool cars from the dealership for some of those videos. He's probably 10 years younger than me, early 30s I guess, and he works at a local news website so I have to be careful around him. My family – well, I've told you about my family, and all Maria's family are in

Cuba, except her sister Benita in Clearwater who got her the papers to stay in America.

There's a bed in the trailer and an easy chair under a shelter where I can sit and read, my feet up on a milk crate, swatting at bugs. There's a propane stove for heating water and cans of food, and a cooler for beer and liquor. I have tin foil on all the windows, to keep the temperature down if I'm inside and the air's on, but mostly to stop anyone looking in, not that anyone would ever come by. It's a 200-yard drive in from the road through the brush, so it's all well hidden.

I can shoot my gun all I want and nobody will ever hear a thing. It's my place and mine alone. I bought the land with a numbered company I'd set up, way back when I first started earning, and it'll never be worth anything to anyone except me. It's only an hour or so out of town. I know all the roads here and I'm usually driving different cars, so nobody can ever follow me out. Nobody knows it's there. Not even Maria.

She's used to me going away on Luis's errands. I don't tell her what she doesn't need to know, like where I'm headed, but I do always tell her when to expect me home. She's not stupid – she knows how I make money and she's fine with that. She's especially fine with the cash it brings home, though I've never told her just how much comes in. Enough for nice clothes anyway, and good restaurants. A decent house. No debt. It's a good thing it pays well because she thinks I work a lot more than I do. Sometimes, I'll tell her I'm going away on an errand and I'll go visit somebody instead, like Jodi, the girlfriend in Lauderdale, or my other girlfriend in Orlando. Her name's also Maria. That sure makes it easier for not screwing up conversations when I'm home.

I learned my lesson with Claire, and Maria knows full well that I see other women when I'm far away from her. She's okay with it but she doesn't want any details. "What happens on the road stays on the road," we've agreed, and she's welcome to screw other guys if she's ever outside of Tampa without me. Which she never is. That's probably a good thing for all of us.

We have a great relationship, me and Maria. I really do love her. Molly can be a handful, but I don't try too much to tell her what to do. That's also a good thing for all of us.

. . .

When I got home from the Triple-A, Maria was out back on a lounger beside the pool. February is a great month to be in Tampa – hot and sunny with the hurricanes just a memory.

Maria was lying in the shade of one of the big umbrellas. She doesn't need her skin to be any darker than the light tan it already is. She looks great in a black bikini that sets off her long black hair. Maria visits the gym every morning and her body is toned and healthy for it. Most people think she's probably 30 years old, but actually, she's 39, just five years younger than me. She's always asking me to go join her at the gym and that used to be my thing, but I don't have the time for it anymore. I'm letting myself age gracefully and besides, none of the other women in my life seem to mind.

"I heard you driving up when you were still a mile away," she said, turning toward me on the lounger and lifting the sunglasses from her eyes. I've always liked her eyes. They're dark, like her hair.

"Yeah – I brought home a Challenger that somebody traded in yesterday. I'll let Grant drive it tomorrow. It's the Hellcat, with a really loud exhaust. It has 700 horsepower. You want to go for a ride?"

"Only if it's to Romano's. I don't want to cook tonight. And you need to get changed. You look like a pimp. And maybe you should shave."

Maria's always criticizing my clothes but I don't care. I was wearing white pants and a baby blue shirt, with white loafers. Actually, I don't think it's the clothes that were at fault so much as my shirt having four buttons open. She doesn't like my beard, either. I started growing it a couple months ago when I first got this feeling of being watched and I kinda like it. I keep it short but it's pretty thick and it's got some gray, like the rest of my hair. I think I'll keep it for now, maybe shave it off for the summer.

"Well, you'd have to get changed too, honey. No shirt, no shoes, no service. But if Romano wants to give us a discount for lusting over you, that's okay with me."

It's not really, but she smiled to show she appreciated the compliment hidden in the joke. I was more concerned that she sounded a little slurry. Over the last few months, Maria's lunchtime cocktails have been extending into the afternoon and hooking up with the pre-dinner drinks. Not every day, but more days than not.

"Would Molly like to come with us?"

"Not if you're gonna drive some loud muscle car," said Maria. "She'd be so embarrass. But there's plenty for her here. She can stay in with her homework."

Again, a couple of little slips in the diction. An enunciation different from her usual Cuban lilt. She wasn't hammered yet, but I wouldn't want her driving my car, and if she was to have another drink before we leave, she'll be pissed and we'll have another embarrassment like we did at the Olive Garden last month.

"Sounds good," I said. "Let's make it a date like the old days."

. . .

The Challenger really is loud and the valets outside Romano's turned to watch the big black car drive up. If it was just me, or if I owned this car, there's no way I'd let any of them behind the wheel and I'd park it myself, but Maria likes the star treatment. They've not scratched any of my cars yet, and I know the odometer reading. I gave a little stomp on the gas so it sounded cool outside the restaurant, then got out and handed over the key.

The doorman had already helped Maria onto the sidewalk. She was wearing trousers but it was still obvious she has great legs, and I felt like a million dollars when we walked in.

We knew the menu – I'm as much of a regular at Romano's as I used to be at the strip joint. I've not been back there since they threw me out for the blow job, but I'm sure I'll go back again soon. Nobody wants to lose a good paying customer, so a few months' penance for being a red-blooded male will be plenty. I'll walk in and Katie or Amy will serve me a Michelob and it'll be like nothing ever happened. I doubt Cherie will get her gig back there so easily, but I'm sure she's keeping busy.

Actually, I know she is. Her real name is Andrea Jackson, very patriotic. Might explain why she liked those 20-dollar bills so much. She lives up at New Port Richey and is enrolled at the University of Tampa where she studies Business Administration and Management. It's a private school, so the stripper cash should help offset the tuition debt. It's where Claire studied nursing for a semester. I could have carried on with all the Internet searching after I tracked her down from her license plate, but to be honest, I had no reason to waste any more hours on her. Just curious, that's all.

Maria ordered the lobster salad, of course, and I ordered the chicken parmesan. She suggested a bottle of pinot and I talked her down to just a nine-ounce glass and a six-ounce glass for myself. She took the hint, though didn't look impressed.

"You think I'm snapped?" she said, almost whispering, once the waiter left.

"No honey, but I don't think we need a full bottle. I have to drive home, so I'll just be having the small glass."

She still didn't look impressed. It doesn't matter. She changed the subject.

"Do you know when you're going away next?"

I rarely know I'm running an errand until a few hours before leaving, and a long road trip to New York or Philly gets less than two days' notice, but I do plan my leisure trips farther out. Those are the overnights to Fort Lauderdale and Orlando. Those girls never get to leave town with me on a vacation, though they're always asking. I only take vacation with Maria. It's one of those things that helps make our marriage work.

"I told you already I'll be away Friday, back Saturday lunchtime," I said. That will be for the other Maria in Orlando. If Uncle Luis comes up with something for that night, I'll make it up to her another time. She's used to it.

Maria just nodded. "Sure," she said, avoiding my eyes. "I'll be home when you get back. I always am these days."

This was building to something and now I could see what it was.

"I need a vacation. I'm bored with Tampa," she said. "I need a change of scenery. There are so many places I want to visit." She held up her slender, manicured left hand, showing off the glitter from her rings, and started counting on her fingers. "There's Brazil. There's Spain. There's Portugal. There's Italy. There's Fiji." She moved to the other hand, also sparkling with rings. "You never want to leave America, but I hate Hawaii. I hate California. Where else?"

"How about Colorado? I could teach you to ski?"

She looked horrified – her nose wrinkled and her eyebrows scrunched. It sounds cute but it's not a good look.

"Jon, if I never ski in my life, it'll be too soon. Maybe water-ski – that's it."

I knew this. Maria's never even seen snow that's not on the TV, let alone tried to slide down it. The only ice she's ever experienced is in her drinks, and fortunately, they're not kicking in from the afternoon. Even so, just the one glass of wine will be plenty this evening.

We talked about travel some more, planned vacations that we'll take in a year or two years' time. The food arrived and we talked comfortably. We might never take those vacations, but you never know. You've got to have something to look forward to. Maria, she's looking forward to going back to Cuba for a triumphant visit with her family. Me, I'm looking forward to Friday night.

. . .

The Challenger wasn't scratched or scuffed when the valet brought it to the sidewalk, and he tried not to grin when I pushed a $20 into his hand. The car was so loud that I'm sure we'd all have heard any joyride through town while we ate dinner. It would probably make the glasses shake on the tables.

The engine was running and the guy told me the key was in the cupholder but I gave him a smile of my own and pulled another key, a red key, from my pocket. He knew what it was and nodded his head in appreciation. This car is so powerful it comes with two different electronic key fobs – a normal black fob that muzzles the power, keeps it limited to a healthy speed for when you let your kids, or a valet, drive it, and a special red fob that unleashes all 700-plus horsepower.

The doorman helped Maria into the passenger seat. I got in behind the wheel and the exhaust note changed, a little more rumbly, when the car's computer detected the red key that was back in my pocket. I brought up the touch-screen display and stabbed at the button to turn off the "valet" setting, then winked at the hapless attendant. He nodded with another grin and closed the door, and I finally got to pull away.

It was only a 10-minute drive to get home but I liked this car and Maria was a captive audience, so we took the scenic route back, just cruising on a couple of the drags. The window was open to better hear the pipes. I'd have liked a smoke, but the only things I'll light up in a shop car are the rear tires, and I don't even do much of that any more. I just like the feel of the power, the warm wind through the window, and the scent of Maria's perfume. She smells like somebody special. Somebody classy, but wild underneath.

The black car attracted all kinds of attention and it didn't take long before a yellow Camaro pulled alongside on the four-lane strip. It had some mods but nothing like the raw power of the Hellcat Dodge. The driver knew it, too. His window was down and his ball cap was turned around, and he looked over and gave just a nod before moving ahead. He could see I was an old white guy out with my wife, so there'd be no dragging tonight.

It wasn't the Camaro I was watching, though. It was the red Mazda sedan that was following, far back, since the restaurant.

"Maria, you want ice cream?" I needed to pull over somewhere with people. Why would the Mazda be following me again? It's not hard to know where I live. Maria looked appalled.

"Ice cream? I didn't just eat salad so I can get fat on ice cream."

"How about a drink? An aperitif. A sangria to compliment the pinot?"

She looked puzzled, and then she smiled. She'd think I want to liquor her up just a bit before getting home. She'd think I'm being nice before we hit the sack, just some added insurance for the evening. I was thinking nothing of the sort, but that would be a side benefit. She nodded, and said, "Sure, if you're buying."

I swung the car slowly off East Palm and down into Historic Ybor, watching the rear-view all the way. The Mazda sedan also signaled left and followed us down past the cigar factories and into the restaurant area, where there are rows of outdoor bars and sidewalk eateries. People were out enjoying the warm evening. It didn't take long before there was a bar with some outside tables and a place to park right alongside.

I tucked the big car in, turned it off, jumped out and hustled around to Maria's door next to the sidewalk. The bar was spilling Cuban mambo into the evening air, not too loud, and half the tables were taken with people enjoying their drinks. They watched when I pulled in, because of the loud pipes, but they lost interest pretty quick.

Maria looked impressed that I'd open the door for her, but I was scanning down the road to where the Mazda was approaching. The car was maybe a hundred yards back and driving real slow. No front plate. I was holding Maria's door handle and signaling to her to just wait a moment, pretending to fumble for something in my pocket with my other hand, just stalling for time. The Mazda's dark black windows were closed, completely hiding its interior. If the passenger window starts to open, that's trouble. That'd be a drive-by, Godfather-style.

Maria was looking at me, wondering what the hold-up was. I was looking at the Mazda. And the Mazda's passenger window started winding down.

I squatted on my haunches at Maria's door, which was still closed, as if I was having trouble opening it. This was to protect myself against slugs with the metal of the car's body. Nobody on the sidewalk noticed anything and Maria was looking at me, puzzled again. Behind, there were at least a dozen people at the restaurant's sidewalk tables. This would be messy.

If I saw a muzzle poke through the Mazda's window, I'd open Maria's door, shove her head down into the seat to clear her of the shattering glass and flying slugs through the windows, open the glovebox for my own gun, then power off all 20 rounds into the side and rear of the Mazda as its tires squeal to try to get away. All I had to see was that barrel poking through.

The Mazda was two car lengths back and still approaching, super slow now. Maria could see I was watching something and started turning to look at what got my attention.

Before it was close enough to see inside, something small got thrown out of the Mazda's window onto the road. Gum? The window wound back up and the car passed, blacked out again so its driver and any passengers were totally hidden. It drove ahead and then the tires chirped, just a bit, as it accelerated away, not fast, just more quickly than before.

I stood back up and opened Maria's door. She got out and stood on the sidewalk, but she was looking directly at me.

"What was that about?" she said. "Was something wrong with that red car? Did you know that guy?"

I didn't answer but excused myself to step around her and out onto the road behind where we were parked. There was a half-smoked cigarette butt there on the street. It was still smoldering, and there was a thick smudge of red lipstick on the filter.

. . .

"Luis," I said to my uncle, in his office at the wreckers the next morning. "I think we have trouble. Somebody's been following me. I don't know who it is, and I don't know why."

Uncle Luis was sitting at his desk and he frowned. Gary, standing at his favorite spot beside the desk, over by the service binders, spoke up for him.

"How long you think this has been happening, Jon?"

I didn't look at him. He's an asshole with a greasy ponytail. I kept looking at Luis.

"A few months. Before Christmas, anyway."

"And you're only telling us now?"

"It was just a feeling. Nothing I was sure of." Still looking at Luis. "But last night, the same car, just a blacked-out shitbox, got real close and I thought there was going to be a drive-by."

"But there wasn't?" said Gary. "Everything was cool?"

This was frustrating! I turned and looked at Gary, who was impassive, blinking, just asking dumb questions.

"Everything was not cool! It scared the crap out of me. I thought I was going to turn into Sonny Corleone right there in Old Ybor!"

Luis grinned, still sitting with his hands on his desk. "Would that make me Don Vito? Now that would be okay!" He didn't seem as upset as he should be, which pissed me off.

"I'm serious! Somebody's watching me, and I'm worried about it. What are we going to do about it?"

"Did you get the car's plate?"

No, I didn't. I shook my head. I was mad with myself for that.

"If someone's coming after you, we'll know about it," said Gary. "Just keep your eyes and ears open and don't do anything stupid."

I nodded and turned to leave. This was not reassuring but I needed to get back to the dealership.

"It'll be fine," said Gary, and he blinked again, the way he does. "Stay alert, stay ready, and zoom-zoom – you'll be fine."

BIRD ON A WIRE

Chapter 9

CLAIRE, Tampa, 2024

I flew down to Tampa with Mom two days later, the first flight we could get and the first time I'd been there in almost 18 years. The hospital agreed to me taking a month off "for compassionate reasons."

I was relieved Mom could come with me, but there was no question she'd do so. I'm the one leaning on her now for support and sitting there on the plane, watching the ground drop away when we finally took off from the snow, I was clutching her hand as tightly as I've ever done. All my happy pills were packed too, just to be safe, or at least the ones legal in Florida, anyway. It's too bad I couldn't bring my cannabis gummies along for the ride because the indica in them really helps me relax, but I could find some down there if I needed to. I had one in my pocket and swallowed it just before we checked in for the flight. I didn't want to forget it was there!

Floyd Woods told me he tracked down Jess from a tip, called in to the Tampa police years ago. An elderly woman named Letitia Something-or-other had noticed a little girl in the spring of 2005 who seemed to be living at a duplex down the road – the girl stood out because of her red hair and pale skin, and she lived with two men who Letitia assumed were gay. This Letitia woman sounded like a piece of work: she'd made a point of walking past the building and saying something to the men when she saw them outside, and she was told the little girl was legally adopted, but she didn't like the sound of that and called the police, who then did nothing except call her back and say everything was legitimate.

Floyd said he doubted the police ever checked into it. He found Letitia now living in a seniors' home and she remembered making the call; it was her introduction to "the new gay thing that's everywhere now," she told him. The two men and the girl moved out a decade ago, but Floyd did a trace and found the property they'd bought in Orient Park, on the east side; when he went to check out the house, sure enough, he saw a red-haired woman in the yard who looked to be about the right age. He didn't talk to her, though. "I didn't want to spook her," he said, "just in case." Just in case of what, I'm not sure, but he's been around long enough that he knows best.

Jess is called Becky now, Becky Hunter, and she's the legal owner of the property. Floyd did a title search and he dug into her background and found her parents died in a car crash just a couple of years ago, Brian and Robin Hunter. I'm guessing those were the two men. And she has a child! A two-year-old named Howard. I might be a grandmother! From nothing to everything, overnight.

I didn't believe Floyd when he told me all this, of course. I really, really didn't want to know that Jess had been living with a pair of men unknown to me, because the thought of what probably happened to her with them is just awful to contemplate. Gay, my ass. But we know she's Jess because Floyd followed her to a coffee shop and pulled her paper mug out of the garbage and got a DNA sample from it. My own DNA is still on record with the Tampa police, as well as John's, so they did the test as a favour to him and it's a 99.99 per cent match. As soon as he got the result, he phoned me. She's Jess!

I thought I was going to faint when he told me. Mom was watching from the other side of the kitchen and she hurried over to put her arm around me, more for support than comfort. She realized from what I was saying into the phone that something big was happening.

"Jess!" she heard, over and over. It was all I could say – I could hardly breathe and my vision was swirling. Then when he told me about the DNA, I just couldn't believe it.

"Floyd, are you shitting me? You'd better not be shitting me!"

"I shit you not," he said. "A 99.99 per cent match. That means only one thing, you know."

I know. I had to sit down and managed to pull up a chair just in time. Mom found a chair for herself too and sat in front of me, her hands squeezing my knees tight, her face glowing with hope.

Then Floyd sent me a photo, taken at the coffee shop just the day before. She's drinking a coffee at a sidewalk table in the sunshine, holding the cup close to her lips, and she's looking toward the camera, but clearly unaware of him parked across the street with a powerful lens. Her long auburn hair is tied back and laid across her right shoulder, which is bare and pale like my own. She's smiling slightly, though not with her eyes – her green eyes seem sad. She's so beautiful, and she's so ruined. When I showed her picture to Mom, there in the kitchen filled with the smell of baking cookies, we didn't speak. I put my phone down on the counter, with the picture still clear on the screen, and the two of us sat and held each other and wept for what seemed like eternity.

. . .

Floyd was still fat and he was waiting in the Arrivals terminal, standing out with red shorts and white sneakers and a Hawaiian shirt, and he recognized us straight away. He still had that silly little moustache.

"Claire, it's been a long time," he said, and looked at Mom. "You must be Vivian." He offered a meaty hand as a greeting and we offered gentle fist taps back. That was enough.

"Is Jess at home, do you know?" I asked. Straight to business.

"I came here direct from watching outside her house. She's still not noticed me. If we head over there now, she should be there. She doesn't seem to get out much."

I couldn't believe he was talking about my daughter, about Jess, living her life right now, getting on with her day like everyone else. He led the way outside the terminal to his Cadillac in the parking garage and my legs felt both strong and weak. My stomach was tight.

As soon as we stepped outside, the early-afternoon heat caressed my northern skin and warmed my face. It was the first heat from the sun I'd felt in months and Mom felt it too. "Ah, this is more like it," she said with a soft smile. "There's got to be some pay-off to living down here."

Mom! I glanced at Floyd but if he noticed the jab, he didn't show it. His skin was very brown, especially on top of his thinly haired head, so I assumed he spends plenty of time outdoors, probably on the golf course, while his knees were the same colour as his round, fleshy face, which was starting to sweat from walking in the heat.

I wanted a gummy for my nerves but I had to be sharp for this. He wasn't walking fast enough; he needed to speed up. This could finally be it – the last lap before the finish.

He found his car, one of those great big four-doors that old people still drive, and it was immaculately clean with plenty of room in its trunk for our bags, at least. It would be just over a half-hour to get to Jess's house and we talked about the best way to make the introduction. There's surely a good way and a bad way after all this time, and poor Jess would be even more shocked than us. It all seemed so surreal.

"I know I suggested you be the person to break the news to her," said Floyd. We were on the stretch of interstate that heads down past the city and out to the eastern suburbs, and he kept looking over at me in the passenger seat and I wished he'd just watch the road. "I strongly urge you, though, to let me be the first person to speak with her. Just scope her out, check out the place. This isn't friendly Canada, and there's no knowing how she'll react. You should wait in the car while I do that. If – when – I feel comfortable, then I'll call you over and you can tell her who you are. You okay with that?"

"Floyd, if this is my daughter, I'm going to talk to her whatever happens. I'm not waiting any longer," I told him. Mom was quiet in the back seat. She was as nervous as me.

"I know you are, and I'm sure it will all be fine. But I don't know what stories those two guys who called themselves her parents might have told her about you. And we're in Florida, and she doesn't live in the greatest neighbourhood. If she tries to blow my balls off with a shotgun, it would probably be best if you're still safe in the car while that's going down."

He had a point and we drove on in silence. I was clutching at my thighs, digging in my fingernails.

I can't believe this is really happening. Breathe, Claire. Breathe.

. . .

The house was in Orient Park, a lush but low-rent neighbourhood out toward the fairgrounds on the east side of town. It was a small white clapboard house, almost more a shack, sitting close to the road and surrounded by overgrown grass. Live oaks and Florida maples gave some privacy from the other single-story houses all around. There was a low wire fence surrounding the property, but the driveway wasn't gated and a small white car, like the house, was parked there, under the shade of a car port. Floyd drove past, then turned around and pulled over just down the road but still within sight. He turned off the Cadillac. "I can leave it running if you like, for the AC," he said, as an afterthought, but I said no – the windows would be open, after all.

"That's the Chevy she was driving yesterday, so it looks like she's home," said Floyd. "I'll just go over and tell her I'm a private investigator looking for a young woman who went missing years ago. I'll tell her that I believe she may be that woman. Depending on how receptive she is, I hope I can call you over. I'll wave, but be ready with your phone in case it's more involved and I have to call to explain anything. And if you see her holding that shotgun and me running to the car, get your heads down!" He could see I looked worried. "Joke!" he said. It wasn't a funny joke. "I'm sure that won't happen. But seriously, be prepared for anything. This is Florida."

Breathe, Claire.

Floyd got out of the car and walked back up the street to the house. He left the windows open and Mom and I could see the front door, even if we couldn't quite hear anything.

Was Jess really in there? Would I know her when she speaks with some southern drawl? Would I recognize her touch, if she even let me touch her? Was this all just some fool's hope? Was this the moment when my life returns?

This is actually happening!

Mom was in the back seat but she reached over to hold my hand. I glanced at her when she took it and she nodded at me, but I didn't want to lose sight of Floyd.

Breathe, Claire.

I watched him climb the two concrete steps and knock on the front door. He waited, then knocked a second time. It opened and I could see him talking to somebody inside, though that person was hidden behind the door frame. I was watching Floyd, in his ridiculous high-riding shorts and flowery shirt, talk some more. It seemed to last an hour. Then he pointed toward us, in the car down the street, and I saw a woman step out from the darkness of the doorway and into the sunshine of the front step. A tall woman with long red hair, who looked directly toward us across the distance. And I saw her collapse on the step as her legs buckled and Floyd caught her, and then I gasped and launched myself against the heavy car door, struggling to unlatch it before it finally swung open, and I ran up the street, wailing and yelling, to the daughter who was stolen from me years ago.

. . .

Mom told me later that following me up to that house was both the longest and the shortest journey she ever made. She said it wasn't so far, maybe a hundred metres, but I had sprinted ahead and thrown myself at Jess as she sat on the step. I held my child tightly and cried, gulping for breath between the sobs as Floyd stood over us, so Mom had to try to slow herself down, striding across the distance, across the years, to meet her grand-daughter and discover the woman she had become.

. . .

In the kitchen of the ramshackle house, sitting at the Formica table and sipping on mis-matched glasses of ice water, we all tried to remain composed as best we could. I was breathing more evenly now but even Floyd was emotional – this was his case years before, after all, and it's entirely due to him that we've reunited.

"I never think about the past. I try only to think about the future," said Jess, speaking softly with the slow drawl I was expecting, and looking down at her little boy. His name was Howie, and he was adorable and innocent with a full shock of blond hair and blue eyes. He was sitting on her lap, half asleep and sucking on a Mickey Mouse soother.

Floyd explained how we found her with the tip from Letitia and, most important of all, about the DNA test. She just shook her head while he spoke. Part of me still doubted all of this and clearly, Jess doubted it too – she was wary and she wanted to see our IDs and we showed her our Canadian passports, which were still sitting on the table. But you can't argue with DNA, and Floyd showed her the letter from the police laboratory that proved it. Once she started talking, her story backed everything up.

"I don't remember anything about being taken," she said. "There was a Before time, and there was an After time. Before, I had friends, I had a mom and a dad, and I lived in a house with a garden and a swing in the tree out front. I think I remember that I fell out of that swing and hurt my ankle. That's my earliest memory."

It's true. She was three years old and we had to take her to the hospital where they put her ankle in a brace for a week.

"But except for those vague things, I really don't remember the Before time. I remember the After time, with Brian and Robbie. Brian told me my parents died and I was adopted. I accepted that, but I never really believed it. The thing is, yes, between the Before time and the After time, I know there was the During time. I don't remember anything about it but I know it was there. It was dark and it was painful and it wasn't just some sadness around my parents' death. I know it happened. I don't know if it was a day or a month or a year, but I know it happened. Maybe I'd remember it if I was hypnotized or something, but I'm not going to do that because I just don't want to remember it."

She looked up at both us.

"I'm not going to do that – okay?"

I coud barely listen to this but I did all the same. *That bastard! That fucking bastard!* Jess was sitting at the table with Howie content and asleep on her knee. I wanted to hold Jess in my own arms the same way, but instead, Mom sat beside me on another cheap kitchen chair and I held her hand and listened to Jess as she cradled her child and stared at a spoon on the table to avoid our eyes. Floyd stood over by the sink, sipping his ice water.

We didn't want to interrupt, but I wanted to know how John found these two men. Were they really just a gay couple, desperate to adopt? That would be wonderful, but it's a bit much to believe, isn't it? Even so, I stayed silent, breathing steady at last, to listen to her story.

"Brian and Robbie didn't let me go to school. They home-schooled me and they were smart, so I think I'm fairly smart too. I enjoyed it. My life was pretty normal. I didn't hide away, but I didn't need friends. I always felt *special*, you know? We lived in town for a few years and then we moved out here. That's my room," and she pointed to a closed door, off to the side, "and that was their room," and she pointed to another door beside it, then looked back down at the table.

"It's empty now. I cleared it out after they passed. They died in 2022. It was a car crash. The cops said Brian was drunk. They were both drunk, and high. They went off the road and into the swamp and the car flipped and they both drowned, held in by their seat belts. It was just horrible. I was at home. They were on their way back from visiting some people and I was supposed to be with them, but I didn't feel too good that day so I'd stayed home. I was in my last year of schooling with them, and I'd planned to go on to college, but that all stopped with the crash. And I was pregnant. I had to look after my baby."

I wanted to ask the question: I couldn't see how Howie came to be if Jess stayed home and had no friends, in what she thought was a normal life. There was silence for a while, and then Mom broke the quiet.

"Jess," she said kindly, and then corrected herself. "Becky, who is Howie's father?"

"Oh," said Jess. "It's Brian. He was my father and then he was my lover. Well, once I bled. I was his girl and Robbie was his man. It wasn't incest – don't think that. He wasn't my biological father. Before he left, he gave me the greatest gift a man can give the person he loves. He gave me a son. And now I have Howie, and I see Brian every time I look in his eyes."

. . .

I didn't know which was worse: to look at Howie and think of Brian, Jess's rapist, or to look at Jess and think of John, her other rapist. This story was killing me, listening to the documentation of abuse that she told so matter-of-fact at the kitchen table. Mom clearly felt the same way and she squeezed my hand more tightly.

I reached out with my other hand and touched Jess, gently on her wrist as she was holding her baby's head, and she flinched. It was just slight but enough for me to notice and take my hand away. "I'm sorry," she said. "I'm not used to another woman touching me. I'm not used to *anyone* touching me, except Brian. I think I'm going to need some time. I mean, I don't even remember your names. And you're calling me Jess but my name is Becky. Becky Hunter. Please excuse me for a moment."

She stood, still holding Howie, and left the table, then left the room out through the back door. I could see her through the window there in her grassy yard, just pacing back and forth, rocking Howie. She needed the break. Mom and I were prepared for this for two days now, but for Jess, it was just an hour since we turned her quiet life upside down.

It sent a chill through me to realize my daughter didn't even know her own mother's name. I was watching her speak, slowly and carefully, and taking in every facet of her. Jess – or Becky – was taller than I expected, not

CLAIRE - Toronto

the petite young woman I've always imagined but at least three inches taller than me. She'd grown into her features: the long nose and small mouth, and the pale skin. Her chin, which once was prominent, had receded as the rest of her face matured. But her eyes, her green eyes, were all the proof I need. I didn't know if I believed it, but I did then. No DNA test was necessary.

Jess came back inside and she placed Howie on his high chair at the table, sat again beside him, and looked around at all of us. Nobody knew what to say to restart the conversation. So I stood and reached over and took my daughter's face in my hands, despite her warning, and kissed her forehead. She stiffened but didn't resist, and I laid my own head against hers, finally united against the odds.

. . .

All afternoon, we spent together in the little ramshackle house. When the late-day sun slipped behind a grove of live oak, Jess put some old lawn chairs in the shade at the back and we moved to sit outside, sipping cool lemonade. There was birdsong all around: in turns, a red-winged blackbird, a grosbeak and a warbler; kingfishers visiting the nearby marsh; a mockingbird, loudest of all, repeating and repeating its rasps and scolds. Howie was with us. He'd just started walking, but he sat a blue blanket Jess laid out for him on the ground and played with a plastic car.

She seemed well educated and well-spoken. She said Brian and Robin had a will that left her the house, and there was $30,000 or so in cash that they kept in a back closet, but she was down to the last few thousand dollars and was looking for work. They taught her to drive, but she didn't know what they did for a living or how they supported themselves. They seemed to have lived far off the social grid, probably selling drugs – Jess said they were always smoking weed in the house, and the smoke would get into her lungs and make her cough, so in the final years they started smoking more out in the back yard, where we were sitting. I must admit, I'd have really liked to smoke a joint there right then.

She had only one photograph of them, pinned to the fridge with a Daytona Beach magnet: two normal looking men standing at a distance on a beach in shorts and T-shirts. It was at Daytona a few years ago, Jess says. Brian was clearly older than Robin, but there was nothing remarkable about them at all. When I studied their faces, a little fuzzy from poor focus, nothing registered.

There was no anger or hatred or bitterness. Nothing at all. Ten seconds later, I could barely remember what they looked like.

Floyd said in the car that the names meant nothing to him, which was a surprise now we thought they were drug dealers. That would be how John knew them. When we were still in the kitchen, Floyd took a photo of the fridge picture with his phone and stepped out to make a call from the front yard to check with a friend at the station, but he came back with a shrug; he said there was nobody with the name Brian or Bryan or Robin or Robbie or Rob Hunter on the records of the Tampa PD or even the Florida State Police, except for a black woman named Robin who lives in Pensacola.

Floyd wanted to know how Jess was taken at the mall, but obviously, there was nothing she can tell him. Even if she hadn't blocked out those memories of the During time, she was only four years old.

Now Jess wanted to know more about me, and she wanted to know about John.

I told her about waiting a year for her in Florida, and about the agonies of that year. Then I told her about moving back to Canada and becoming a nurse. "That's so weird!" she said. "I was thinking about nursing school for next year. I'd love to be able to help people and care for them." But that was about it and there was really not that much else to say. I live in an apartment and I watch TV and I'd spent every day dreaming and fantasizing about this moment now. That was my life.

As for John, I didn't know where to begin, so Mom stepped in.

"Your father, his name is John, and he still lives here in Tampa," said Mom. "He sells cars. We've not had anything to do with him in years. Did Brian or Robbie ever speak of a man named John?"

"No, I never heard of him. Shouldn't he be here? I want to meet him." She seemed invigorated, clear eyed, and she looked at me directly. "I want to meet him *now!*"

"Maybe you will," I said, "but that would be a mistake. He's a ruthless man with no conscience and he could hurt you so badly. You should know – it was your father who took you from the mall, not Brian or Robin. It would have been your father who was with you in the During time. And then your father gave you up, or more likely he sold you, to those two men."

"Wait – my dad *sold* me? That's not... That can't..."

She looked horrified.

"We don't know for sure," I said, "but we suspect so, yes."

Floyd stepped forward.

"I don't think you should have anything to do with him," he said, his voice rasping again like there's gravel in his mouth.

Now Jess was confused and who can blame her? This was all just so much for a woman to take in, after waking that morning to a normal, routine day.

"I don't understand," she said, looking at all three of us in turn and searching our eyes for answers. Howie was playing with another plastic car now, bored with the first. "I don't follow how that would be."

"Jess," said Floyd, and then like Mom, he corrected himself. "Becky, we always suspected that you were taken at the mall by somebody you recognized. Without knowing just how you were removed from there, we have to assume you went willingly, so there was no resistance, no yelling, no grabbing – nothing like that. The mall was a very public place and it was filled with shoppers in that week before Christmas. If a stranger snatched you away, somebody would have seen something. At the least, the cameras would have picked it up. Your father John has always been the prime suspect. We don't know where he was at the time you were taken. He had an alibi that protected him back then, but we've discovered somebody lied for him, and we have no idea where he was for about four hours, and again later that night."

She was still confused, of course.

"Why would he take me? We already lived together, right? This makes no sense at all. Why would he sell me to Brian and Robbie? For the money?"

Floyd just shrugged, but this was starting to make sense now.

"I think he wanted you to stay here in Florida, close by," I said. "He didn't want me to find you and take you away from him. I think he knew he couldn't raise you on his own and hide you from me, so he passed you on to his friends Brian and Robin to raise as their own, where you would stay here and he could still watch you grow up."

This was so comforting for a moment – perhaps there never was a During time. But no, Mom brought me back to reality.

"Jess, your father is from a very bad family," she said. "His father was a criminal and was executed by the state. His brother is also a criminal. He's on death row. His sister was a drug addict. She's dead. She overdosed."

"Sometimes," said Floyd, "the apple don't fall too far from the tree."

Jess looked shocked. No, not shocked, but upset, and she dropped her head, deflated now. We were all quiet and she reached over to stroke Howie's blond hair. Finally, in one of the shade trees, a mockingbird trilled sharply and broke the silence.

"His father, his brother – did they hurt little girls?"

"Yes," said Mom. "They killed them."

"And you think he hurt me. It was him. In the During time."

"Yes," said Mom.

"You think he hurt me and then he passed me on to Brian and Robbie. Then I don't want to know him. I want nothing to do with him."

I couldn't imagine what was going on in her head. She must have been feeling ill. From having an adoptive father who raped her to discovering a biological father who raped her and sold her – this must be all too much.

She stood and excused herself again. "I need some more water," she said. She started walking to the door, then paused, turned, and came back to collect Howie from his blanket.

"It's okay – we can watch him," I said.

"No, that's fine," said Jess, a little too forcefully, and walked him in with her to find some water in the kitchen.

This would take a while.

When she returned to join us, she looked agitated and started talking as soon as she stepped outside.

"Okay, if he sold me to Brian and Robbie, then he knows everything already," she said. "He knows they're dead. He knows where I live. He knows who I am. Maybe he's watching this house right now, and he knows you're all here, and he knows you've found me. Maybe he knows you've told me everything about him. Maybe he knows his time is short. If he's as bad as you say he is, then I'm in danger. Howie is in danger. How can I stay here now? He could come after us tonight! We're not safe! What have you done? I should go into hiding! I need to get out of here!"

We'd never thought of this. She was standing with her back against the house, shifting from foot to foot, obviously upset. It was Floyd who spoke first.

"You're okay, my dear. I have people watching him. He's not here and he doesn't know we're here. Even if he does find out, we're way ahead of him and we'll stop him long before he can do anything. You're quite safe. You can move if you want but I think it's better that you stay here, for a few days more at least, while we get to know each other and prepare for the future."

Floyd had people watching John? He didn't tell us that. We didn't expect to be paying him any more money, though I guess it was all part of the service.

But John will find out sooner than Floyd expects. I was thinking now of the 12-year-old girl who lives with him, Molly, and what might be going on inside that million-dollar house of his, and the thought of it was making my stomach churn. I wanted to make sure he can never hurt another little girl, and I wanted to take him down.

BIRD ON A WIRE

Chapter 10

JON, Tampa

I was in Orlando. I hate Orlando, just a fake theme park surrounded by fake, planned communities filled with snowflakes and Yankees, tooling around their fake manufactured houses in stupid golf carts and one-seater electric cars at 10 miles an hour, everyone 100 years old and waiting to die.

But Maria's in Orlando, so I'd come up here whenever I need a break. Not my wife Maria but my girlfriend Maria. That's probably confusing for you, I know, but it's real simple for me. A wife is entitled and shares your life, but a girlfriend is a woman who keeps you on your toes and never says no when you ask for something, because she knows you can just walk away. That's how it is for me, anyway. I have friends who have girlfriends and those women get whatever they want, because they can always play the blackmail card against the wife. But my Maria up here, she knows my Maria down there is cool with it, so she just takes what she can get. To be honest, I'm not sure my wife really is all that cool with it, but we just don't talk about it so I see that as a Get Out Of Jail.

I'll make it simpler for you, though. Maria up here, I often call her Cindy. That's my little pet name for her, because she lives in Orlando and Cinderella lives here at the Disney park. It was either that or Snowy. Or Minnie. Or Goofy, for fuck's sake. It felt a little weird sometimes calling her Maria when I say the same things to my wife at home – *Oh Maria, can I get you a coffee? Oh Maria, feels so good! Oh, suck on this Maria!* – so I came up with the cute little Cindy pet name, and she liked it. It makes her feel special. But the girlfriend does things that the wife won't do, or won't do any more anyway, and that's when she goes back to being Maria, so it's like being with my wife. *Oh Maria, your ass feels so tight! Oh Maria, swallow it all!* I'm happy to be married but it's great to have a girlfriend.

So, Cindy – I'll call her Cindy for you, so you can follow along – she's a little taller and probably 30 pounds heavier than Maria, the wife. She has short brown hair and she's not that good-looking, but she has beautiful eyes, and when I look into her eyes I don't see anything else. They always seem to be smiling, even when she's not. They're clear and dark and oval, so you might think she has some Asian in her, but she's too big to be Asian. We can throw each other around pretty good.

Since we're on the subject, I mentioned Jodi to you as well. She's the redhead in Fort Lauderdale. She reminds me of Claire when we were first together – slim and small and a ball of fire when she gets going. She's a lot younger, too. She was only 17 when we first met, which made her illegal for what we both did best, but she's 20 now. She's a waitress and wants to be an actress, and I let her stay in my condo there for free. I bought the place four years ago when I started investing in real estate and Maria knows she's there. She thinks she pays rent though, and at first, she did. The first three months, anyway.

I'd like to have a blonde girlfriend too. Variety's the spice of life! I thought it was happening last year when I hooked up with a woman from Pensacola but that didn't work out and Pensacola is just too far in the wrong direction. I only ever drive through there when I'm running one of Uncle Luis's errands and like I said, when I'm doing that, I don't stop and I don't sleep. There's no time for any fun.

. . .

Cindy – that's Maria the girlfriend – has a regular job as a regular person in the accounting department of a swimming pool installation company. It sounds like death to me, and if I got to know her much better, I'd probably realize she's really dull. When I come to visit, though, which I've been doing for almost a year now, she lights right up. She's in her mid-30s – 36 or 37, around there – and her time-clock's ticking hard for babies. She hopes I'll leave my wife and move in with her, but that's not going to happen and especially not up here in fake Orlando.

Even so, I have my own key and let myself in through the lobby of her low-rise. She's on the second floor, so I'd always take the stairs, and when I got to her door, I knocked and let her answer instead of just walking in like a husband might do.

When the door opened, there was a smell of incense and she was wearing her little black dress. The one that always works for me. I knew she wouldn't be wearing any panties under there, and I did the quick math and realized she's probably ovulating. She's very open that she wants a child of her own and she's been real clear that I don't need to have any responsibility toward it, but I don't believe her. Besides, I don't want to create any more children. I created Jess and I fucked that up, didn't I?

"You hungry?" said Cindy, purring out the words in a way that's clear she wasn't not talking about food.

"I'm always hungry," I said and stepped inside, placing my hands on her waist – more padded than Maria's – and kissed her forcefully, pushing my tongue between her teeth before the door was even closed.

. . .

I don't know what it was. I've had a lot of stress in my life these last couple of months, people following me, people watching me. I thought Cindy's invitation, her insistence, to come visit would do me good, would be a nice break from it all. On the way up here, I was tense that maybe somebody was on my tail, though I was driving a different car from the shop, a Fusion. It was traded in by a smoker which means it already smelled of tobacco so I could smoke in it, which helped a lot. And when I got here, she looked just so fuckable that I all but exploded.

So why couldn't I fuck her? Why didn't I work? Why did nothing happen down there? Am I going to have to take little blue pills? What the hell?

I kind of got things going again this morning but she seemed just so *desperate* that it didn't last long. When I finally, limply, came, she took what she could scoop up and pushed it inside herself and I just wanted to get the fuck out of there. I didn't stick around for breakfast. She wasn't even dressed before I left.

It was an hour and a half to get home, plenty of time to sit behind the wheel, smoke some cigarettes in silence, and think about what just happened.

I think it was guilt. Not guilt that I'm screwing around on Maria, I don't think I care about that, but guilt that I know damn well I'm shooting blanks. I've never told her, of course. She's never asked. Ten years back, I hooked up again with Kim, the neighbor I was seeing when Jess was around. She was a few years older than me. Her kid was a handful and she didn't want any more children and she convinced me to get the snip. I didn't mind. I didn't want any more children either. Jess was the only child for me.

Kim moved in for a while, but it didn't last more than a year. When we weren't screwing around on our spouses, it just wasn't the same for either of us, and we realized the only mutual attraction was the sex. We had what's called an "amicable split" and we even stayed in touch for a couple of years, but I don't know where she is now. I heard she left the state, moved to California.

I think of her sometimes when I shoot blanks, though. If I told Cindy that I'm sterile, she'd leave me right away for a guy who could give her a baby, I'm sure of it. Maybe, if I'm feeling guilty, which I've never felt before, I should let her do that. It would be *the right thing to do*. Maybe I should think about *doing the right thing*, for once in my life.

The car was on cruise as it headed south-east down the interstate. I was watching the vehicles to each side shuffle forward, shuffle back, at 60 miles an hour, all of us lost in our thoughts.

. . .

It was good to get home a little early because Grant was waiting in the driveway, returning the Challenger. He wanted to show me the video he'll post to his YouTube channel after the weekend, and we sat in the big black muscle car to watch it on his phone. It was standard Grant stuff, full of tire smoke and shaky hand-held selfie narrative, and it's the reason his Grant's Garage channel pulls in 100,000 views every month. Plus, he's a young guy who understands the social media. He always gives me a nod in the credits. I don't think I've sold any cars because of it, but it doesn't hurt.

This morning, he could see my mind wAs elsewhere.

"You seem down," he said when the eight-minute video ended. "I thought you'd be pumping your fist now, giving me a high-five. This is a goddamn Hellcat, for chrissakes!"

"It's okay. Just work stuff. That's a great video."

"Come on – what is it? Something's up, I can tell."

Grant Gibson might be younger and clean-cut but he's one of my oldest friends. I've known him since he left school. He's one of the few people who knows me and knows about Jess, thanks to a few nights with Uncle Jack Daniels. After Claire left, I cut off everybody, started again. I couldn't hide anything but I could start fresh. Luis and Gary and the guys at the yard know, of course, but we've all moved on and it really doesn't matter anymore. It was preppy Grant who suggested I change my name and now I'm a new guy. The new Jon.

Even so, I only talk cars with Grant. He understands enough about me to know that he shouldn't want to know too much. It's like when the Special Ops guys take out some ISIS asshole but everyone waits till after it's done before telling the President, in case something goes wrong, so the President can deny it all.

This thing that's getting at me though is eating away. Grant says he's not really a journalist, more just a "news content provider," and maybe he might have some good advice after all.

I waited a long time before answering. Eventually, without looking at him, I spat it out. "I'm just pissed because somebody's been following me and I don't know who it is. I think it's probably an ex, but I just don't know and it's digging at me." I don't think it's an ex, but it sounds plausible.

"What do you mean, 'following' you?"

"Like, they drive a Mazda6 and I keep seeing the car and I don't know why they care about following me. It's not all the time, but it's enough to piss me off."

"Well, why don't you just trace the plate?"

"They don't get close enough for me to be able to read the plate."

"You driven past any stores with security cameras outside? Any traffic cams? If the Mazda's there, you can get a screen grab and blow up the frame to read the plate."

Why didn't I think of that? Maybe Grant's done this before. Maybe he *should* be a journalist. And there was no criticism in his voice, not even curiosity. My mind was already back at the bar in Ybor where I thought I was going to get blown away. That was only three days before, on Wednesday. Surely it had a camera, and if it did, perhaps it still has the footage.

. . .

An hour later, I was at the bar and talking to the manager, a short, stocky guy who seemed like he was only half paying attention. I'd already noticed the two cameras on the outside wall, trained across each other at the sidewalk tables and out onto the road. They were the first thing I saw.

"I was here with my wife on Wednesday evening. We were parked right outside." I pointed out toward the road. It was just the Fusion parked there now, that I drove in from Orlando. "You guys make a mean sangria, by the way – we had a great time."

He nodded, but he was still not really paying attention. I was distracting him from something else, some bar-management thing.

"Somebody scratched the driver's side of my Challenger that night and I didn't see it till the next day. It's a big red scratch. Do your security cameras show the road, and would you still have footage from Wednesday? Can I see if maybe it happened here?"

He looked a little more concerned now, like maybe I'd sue for damages.

"It's okay – I'm not after you guys," I told him, quick. "I know I was on the public street. But if I can see how the scratch happened, I'd really appreciate that."

I turned over my hand and there was a C-note between my fingers. He looked at it and seemed bemused.

"I'm sorry," he said. "I really don't have the time to search through hours of footage."

So he had the footage. If he didn't, he'd have said it didn't exist. All he was telling me here was that it's not worth a hundred bucks for him to go into the back and spin through the recording. There's an answer for that, of course, and I was ready with it. I deal with guys like him all the time. I reached into my breast pocket and pulled out two more $100 bills.

"I understand. You're a busy guy. But that was an expensive scratch for me. It's a red scratch, from a red car. Does this help cover your time?"

He looked around, then took the three bills and pocketed them quickly. "Come with me," he said.

We stepped into a small office at the back. There were hand-written notes pinned to cork boards on the walls, and pride of place was a large calendar with a photo of boats in the harbor at Havana. He sat at the desk and opened a laptop.

"The pictures are all in the cloud," he said. "We have a storage limit where they record over the old stuff, but I'm sure Wednesday is still there. What time was it?"

I told him and leaned over his shoulder to watch the full-color video come up. It didn't take long to scroll back to Wednesday. There were the two outside cameras and three cameras inside, including one trained on the till, which I foud interesting though I said nothing, of course. He clicked on the image from one of the outside cameras to make it fill the screen and, fast-forwarding at 16 times the normal speed, it tool maybe another 10 seconds before I saw my black Challenger pull up and park.

"That's me!" I said.

"Sweet ride," said the manager.

He slowed the video down and, of course, the next vehicle to pass was the red Mazda, driving real slow. When it came into the left of the frame, the passenger window was already wound back up.

"That's a red car. Does he look like he's right up close to my Dodge?" I was asking rhetorically. I didn't care if he was or not, and we really couldn't see the distance between them on the road.

"I don't think so," said the manager.

"Well, I think he might be."

"You okay there?" He was watching me on the video crouching down, ready to lunge inside the car for my gun.

"Yeah, yeah. Just helping out my wife."

There was a problem. This camera was from the right side of the restaurant, and it was shooting the side and front of the vehicles on the road. In Florida, we don't have license plates on the front, and I wanted to see that Mazda's plate.

"Can we see this from the other camera?" I asked. "I think it might be clearer."

The manager double-clicked on a couple of buttons and the other outside camera image filled the screen. My car was still front and center, and there was me crouching down, but this time, we could see the Mazda passing and then driving away to the right. Through the gap between the Challenger and the car parked in front of it, I could see a flash of the Mazda's license plate.

"That's it! That's the bastard!" I said. "It was that car, I'm sure of it!"

"I don't know, but it's your money," said the manager.

"Can I get a screen grab of that, with the red car's license plate?"

"Sorry Dude, I can't do that for you," said the manager. Of course he could. He just wants more money, but I didn't need a photo for evidence of any non-existent scratch. I just wanted to read the license plate.

"Well, can you zoom in so we can see if the car's plate's in focus?"

"Sure," he said, hoping to sweeten the price. He froze the image when the plate was clear between the vehicles, then zoomed right in with his mouse wheel. The Florida tag was quite legible and before he could zoom out again, I snapped a photo of the screen with my phone from over his shoulder.

"Thanks!" I said.

"Hey – you can't do that!" said the manager.

"I just did," I said, and hustled out of the office, leaving him there in his chair with his laptop and his delivery notes and his picture of Havana, and my 300 bucks. "Great sangria, by the way. We'll be back to see you soon!"

. . .

It didn't take long to track the plate. Auto wreckers have direct access to Florida vehicle records, so we can be sure who owns the vehicles we're towing or crushing. Besides, I knew who owned the plate as soon as I saw it. It was the word "DEALER" along the bottom that gave it away.

Chapter 11

CLAIRE, Tampa

John's house looked nice. It wasn't a monster home, not a mansion, not gaudy, but nice. I might be happy with a house like that. There were tall trees all around, cypress and red maple, with starlings in their branches softly rattling and trilling. Floyd gave us the address yesterday, though he was reluctant to do so; he wanted to know why, and we said we just wanted to take a look. It's white and sort-of-modern, and it seemed well maintained with blue shuttered windows on both floors. It's medium-size but there was a big garage with a black muscle car parked outside – very John. He's such an asshole. The house was behind a tall privacy hedge but the driveway gate was open, so we parked our rental car on the road and Mom and I walked straight up to the double front door and rang the bell.

So much for just taking a look.

I was thinking of pressing the bell button again when the door opened halfway and a woman looked out at us. This had to be Maria, the wife. She had dark, shoulder-length hair and heavy eyebrows, and from what I could see, she looked immaculate, as if she was ready to go designer shopping on Fifth Avenue or Rodeo Drive. I didn't think John cared much about fashion, but he probably wants everyone to appreciate his trophy and the money he can spend on her. That's okay – Mom and I looked immaculate too. We were both wearing paper Covid masks to help obscure our faces, just in case, though they're unusual here in Florida and we were standing well back from the door. The woman seemed suspicious, of course, and she was cautious. I didn't blame her, but Mom and I were practicing for this all morning.

"Yes?" asked the woman.

Mom spoke first. "Good morning!" she said brightly. "We're new to the neighbourhood and just want to introduce ourselves. I'm Vivian, and this is my daughter Claire."

We were both watching her expression to see if there was any recognition there of our names, to see just how much she might know of John's past, but there was nothing.

"Okay," said the woman.

"We just want to say hello," said Mom, not fazed in the least. "I sell real estate and I know how important it is to have good neighbours. Have you lived here for long?"

"*Lo siento, no hablo ingles,*" said the woman, which I knew was bullshit because John would never speak Spanish, but was the one thing we were hoping she would *not* say. Neither Mom nor I have more than a dozen words of Spanish between us. But we were prepared.

"*Entonces nosotras podemos ayudar!*" said Mom with a thick anglo accent – *Then we can help!* – as if this was great news. Those were four of the maybe 12 words we have, which we found that morning on Google Translate. "It's so important to be able to practice speaking English here in the United States, isn't it? And you can practice with us! We should learn some Spanish too, shouldn't we, Claire?"

I looked at Mom as ditzily as I could muster and smiled broadly under my white paper mask. "Sure!" I said. "*Si!*"

"*No hablo ingles,*" said the woman again, but this time, there was another voice that called out from inside the house.

"Who is it, Mom? Is it Amazon? Is it my package?"

The woman ducked inside but she made the mistake of not closing the door and this time, Mom stepped forward and pushed it open slowly with her foot. The woman was in the wide reception area, tiled and mirrored and tacky as hell, trying to shush a girl who could only be Molly, the daughter. Jess was 12 years old too, once. There was a cool chill from the air-conditioning. Molly looked up when the door opened, but when she saw two smartly dressed women standing there, she was curious and not guarded in any way. Mom and I were both smiling like greeters at Walt Disney World, and Mom slid her mask down below her chin to show off her motherly composure.

"Sorry – I thought you'd be the Amazon delivery," the girl said to us, and then turned back to her mother. "You just had to say it wasn't Amazon, you know. It's supposed to come this morning. My phone says the package is on its way. It's those open-toed shoes."

The woman was looking daggers at her daughter. *"Dije, no hablo ingles,"* she said to her, very firmly.

"Oh, lo siento..." said Molly.

"That's okay, my dear, if you can translate for us," said Mom. This was perfect. We wanted to know about Molly, and if she could talk to us herself, all the better.

"Sure," said Molly, who clearly thought it was pretty funny that her mom was still playing the Spanish card.

"We were telling your mom that we're new to this neighbourhood and we're just dropping by to say hello. I'm Vivian and this is my daughter Claire."

"Hi. I'm Molly. This is my mom, Maria." She didn't bother translating that into Spanish. She was also clearly her mother's daughter: dark-haired and clear skinned and pretty. Maybe too pretty. I hated to think what she might have endured up to now.

"Is your father home?" I asked. I knew he's not. Floyd already told us that John met with another guy this morning outside the house, and they sat for a while in the black car that's parked in the driveway, but that he left 15 minutes ago. Apparently, he usually works at the dealership on Saturday mornings, but Floyd was tailing him anyway, just in case. He'd phone us if John started heading home.

"No," said Molly, "but he'll be back soon. You can wave to him on the camera if you like, for when he gets here."

Camera?

Mom and I both looked up and sure enough, there was a small white security camera above the door and its blue light was blinking. *Of course it is.* Mom smiled and waved but I looked down again, quickly. I kept my mask over my mouth and nose and wished I could slide it higher. If he sees this footage, would he recognize me? Would he recognize Mom? Would this be our only visit with any element of surprise?

"We haven't moved in yet," said Mom. "Actually, it's Claire who'll be moving in – the house just up the street with the green garage doors? We're from the other side of town. We just love this neighbourhood."

Molly translated that into Spanish, which was weird because all four women on that step knew full well that Maria could speak fluent English.

"Bueno," said Maria, dryly.

I spoke up now, talking to Molly directly. "Can I ask which school you attend? My daughter's in a private school north of here, but she's not happy and we're thinking of enrolling her locally. We wanted to ask for a recommendation of schools in this area."

Maria started to say something, but then remembered that she couldn't understand what I just asked, so stayed quiet.

"I'm at Lincoln High," said Molly. "It's a good school, I guess."

We thought she would be. This house was in the catchment for Lincoln Junior High School and although most people here can afford private education, Lincoln has a good academic record. But we didn't care about its academic record.

"My daughter – her name is Jessica – she has some issues with school. Some trust issues. Are there good counsellors at Lincoln?"

Mom was looking at me with worried eyes, because I was going into this far more quickly than we'd planned. There were plenty more, inconsequential questions we'd rehearsed to ask first of the mother, just to make her drop her guard, and already I was asking Molly directly about trust. I was rattled by the camera that was watching me. I knew John would see this – *maybe he's seeing it now*. This could be our only chance to scout out Molly and watch her reactions; any comment, any recoil at the possibility of abuse and we'd know John's been at her and it will confirm he went for Jess.

"I dunno – I guess so," said Molly. "I've never spoken to them."

Maria suddenly spoke up, talking to her daughter in a stream of fast, loud Spanish that seemed to startle the young girl. I'd no idea what she was saying. We should have had a hidden voice recorder, to play it back later and maybe Google it or find someone to translate. In any case, it had the right effect and Molly looked chagrined. Now she was concerned about us.

"I'm sorry, but Mom reminded me I have schoolwork that needs finishing." She was very smart and composed for a 12-year-old. "You're welcome to come back later and talk to Dad. He speaks English. He can tell you all about the neighbourhood."

I'd been silenced, but Mom wasn't quitting so easily.

"Thank you my dear, we'll be sure to do that. But can I ask one more question of your mom? I just love her blouse. Can I ask who it is?"

"It's Gucci," said Maria, who then suddenly looked like a deer in the headlights. She spoke some Spanish to Molly, who was trying not to smirk and said something back, then turned to Mom.

"She says it's Gucci," said Molly. "Mom's been practicing her English. She understands some, but speaking the words is still a challenge for her."

"Well, I so hope we can help with that. I'm sure we'll be back soon."

"You're welcome," said Molly. "And hey —" she pointed up at the camera and looked directly at me. "You're safe to take your mask off out there, you know. Don't forget to wave at Dad!"

. . .

We weren't expecting the camera. *Dumb!* Of course a nice house in Florida will be protected with security cameras, and of course, somebody like John will need all the protection he can get, but it doesn't make a difference. John would find out sooner or later that we're down here and that we're onto him, but we just wanted that first assessment of Molly and I guess we got that. She seems smart and well-adjusted. Nothing obvious that would be cause for concern. Which doesn't mean much, I know.

. . .

"That didn't go too badly," said Mom at the Starbucks. "Molly looks to be okay. I don't think we need to be any more worried about her than we already are. Who knows what goes on in that house, but Molly seems smart enough to deal with it."

"Mom, just because she doesn't have bruises and she doesn't hide from us and she's not cowering in a corner, doesn't mean she's okay – it just means she has a good coping mechanism. This doesn't change anything. We need to go back there when John's home and we need to persuade Jess to come with us, convince her it's the right thing, and we need to film it and record it when she tells him that she remembers everything. Whatever his response is, it'll be enough to give to Floyd to take to the police."

"But she doesn't remember everything. I'm sure he'll deny it all. What if he just denies everything? Floyd can't do anything with that, surely."

"Well, we need him to be surprised. If he looks at that camera footage and he recognizes me behind the paper mask, he'll know what's happening and he'll prepare himself. We need to go get Jess and take her over there, and we need to do it now. *Now!*"

We'd only had a couple of sips of our coffees, but they were in to-go cups and we carried them out to the car and drove as fast as we dared to persuade my daughter to confront her father.

Chapter 12

JON, Tampa

Why was I looking at a video of Claire Copeland standing on my doorstep, talking to my wife and daughter? That was her mom with her, too. Why were they wearing masks? Claire lives in Florida now? Why was she saying she's moving here? Why were they asking about schools in the neighborhood? And what was she saying about "my daughter Jessica is having some trust issues"? Did she find Jess? Did she even know who she was talking to?

This doesn't make any sense!

"Dad, you still there?" That was Molly talking to me on the phone, because I'd gone quiet here in my office at the dealership while I looked at the camera images off the cloud. This was the second set of security footage to throw me sideways in the last hour: the license plate being from one of Luis's other dealerships, and now my old girlfriend turning up at my home, asking bizarre questions.

"Dad? You there?"

"Yes sweetie. These look like nice people but you never know these days. You can never tell. I'll be home soon. I'm sure they're fine but if they come back, just don't open the door to them. I'll talk to them if they return."

As soon as I got to my desk, I double-checked the license plate and yes, it's registered to Sunrise Auto Sales over in Plant City, which is one of Luis's two other used-car dealerships. Molly called just as I was about to call Sunrise, but I've got to stay on track here, so I phoned over to George, who sells cars there and always seems to owe me a favor.

George answered after two rings and he knew it was me calling. "*Wassup gringo?*" he said into his phone, not too loud.

"George, can I ask for something? I was driving on Wednesday and I saw this red Mazda6 weaving around on the road and it had one of your dealer plates on it. I don't want to get anyone in trouble, but can you see who it was signed out to on Wednesday? I just want to know who it is."

"Sure," said George, and I told him the number. I could hear him tapping it into the computer on his desk. Sounded like he's not too busy this morning.

"Uh oh," said George.

"Problem?"

"Yeah – that's Winston's plate."

Winston Bradley is the general manager of Sunrise Autos, the most senior guy of the 20 or so people there.

"Does Winston drive a red Mazda6?"

"No, he drives a Porsche. But he has a couple of plates signed out to him – maybe his wife drives the Mazda." More tapping noises. "Huh. We've had a red 2020 Mazda6 here on the books as a trade-in for the last five months, which is at least four months too long for us, but we sent it to auction on Thursday. I wasn't here Thursday, so I didn't see it. There's no record of any damage, if she was weaving around and got into trouble. This was the Signature, 19-inch alloys, aftermarket tint. Sound like the one?"

"That's it. I'd best leave it if it was Brenda's car. Do you know what she's driving now?"

"No. Winston would have signed out something else but it won't show here what vehicle it's on. You want to watch out for her on the road, huh?"

"Oh, I'm sure she's fine. We all have a relapse every now and again." Brenda Bradley used to drink too much, but she claims she's not touched a drop since a month in rehab a couple of years ago. I chit-chatted for a while, then hung up and watched the video again of my ex-girlfriend and her mother talking to my wife and daughter at my home.

None of this makes any sense!

. . .

You know how things happen in threes? There's something else I've not mentioned to you, besides being followed by Brenda Bradley and maybe, maybe not, tracked down by my old girlfriend, talking about our little girl Jess. I've been feeling pretty crappy the last few days. Maybe that's the reason why I had problems with Cindy last night, though it's never been an issue before.

I think I have the virus. The China virus. I had it a couple years ago when it first came out and I thought that gave me immunity, but now I've been tired again, short of breath, coughing a lot. Even just sitting in the car this morning, I could feel myself wheezing, like I'd just run a marathon, not that I've ever run a marathon. Smoking isn't the pleasure it's always been. I was going to check my temperature when I got home but Grant was there and I forgot about it. I really should do something.

I needed to get home, and I think I should take a Covid test. I should see if Luis is around, too. He knows everything that's going on – maybe he knows why Brenda Bradley is following me. I'll ask him before I go knocking on Winston's door.

. . .

I sat in the car after taking the test and Googled "Covid" to remind me of the symptoms and now I'm sure I have it. "Like breathing through a straw," it said. For me, it's more like breathing through a six-foot length of dirty garden hose, but even so, *fuck!* Always something. But maybe not. The test came up negative but Google says these test kits from the pharmacy aren't too accurate, so I'll check it again tomorrow.

I'm not worried about giving this virus to Maria or Molly – they're young enough to beat it easily. I'd better be careful around Luis though, because he's 73, and now that I'm pulling up beside his Benz at the wreckers, I checked if there was a paper mask in my glovebox. There was. It was months old and kinda grimy, but it'd be fine and I stuffed it in my pocket.

He was in the main workshop area when I walked in and he looked surprised to see me, but I wasn't unwelcome.

"How you doing, kid?" Uncle Luis asked when I walked over, and of course I lied to him.

"Doing great!" I said. "But can I talk to you about something?"

"Sure! Here, or in the office?"

"The office would be best." This was nothing unusual. In Luis's line of work, people rarely want others to hear their conversations. He led the way and when I followed him into his office, I shut the door and put on the grubby mask.

"What's with that?" asked Luis, looking bemused as he sat back on the edge of his desk to face me.

"Oh, just being careful. These days, you can't be too careful, right?"

"Sure you can. You look like a prick, especially with that little beard poking out the sides. Only friends come into this office, and friends don't wear masks."

I took it off, stuffed it back in my pocket. So much for being responsible.

"So, what's up?"

I took a deep breath – as best I could, anyway – before starting. Uncle Luis can be unpredictable.

"You remember I told you somebody is following me? You asked if I got the plate? Well, I got the plate."

"And?"

"It's a dealer plate from Sunrise. It's signed out to Winston Bradley. Now why would he be following me?"

"Maybe it's a coincidence," shrugged Luis. "A *co-inky-dink*. You drive around, Winston drives around. You're gonna cross paths sometime, you know."

Now that was just insulting. Luis needed to take this seriously. He takes everything else real serious, so why not this? I could feel my anger rise but I knew to choose my words carefully.

"Luis, you know there aren't any coincidences. Things don't *just happen*."

"Sure they do. Things *just happen* all the time."

"We plan for these things, Luis. We plan for what we expect, and we plan for what we cannot expect. If we didn't, neither of us would be here now."

Suddenly, Luis stood and took two steps forward and slapped me across the face, real hard. *Fuck!*

"Don't tell me how I should do business!"

Luis has a temper, just as I have a temper. It runs in the blood, I suppose. I didn't expect it to bubble up so fast. I wanted to slap him back, no, I wanted to *punch* him back, a right hook into his red round head, bald as a billiard ball, then a left into his paunchy gut. But I didn't. I stood there and tried to look like it didn't hurt.

"That's not what I'm saying, uncle. I'm just saying, I think you should be more concerned if somebody has me in their sights."

"Sit down." Luis pointed at the chair in front of his desk, and then walked around to sit in his own chair on the other side. I didn't sit down.

"I said, *sit down!*" He snarled the words out. He was seriously pissed. Maybe it was the mask.

I sat down where I was told, and it was as if I could see his temper calming, now that he was on his throne and I was in my place as the loyal subject across the desk. He looked at me and I matched his stare as my cheek still stung, but I didn't reach up to touch it as I wanted. I didn't show any pain. He breathed out a big sigh and it was as if he was exhaling the red mist through his fat, punchable nose.

"Listen, Jon. I don't tell you everything. You don't need to know everything. You don't *want* to know everything."

Except I did, but I stayed silent, still matching his stare.

"In our business, we keep an eye on everyone, whether we trust them or not. It's just basic *security*. It's not me. Gary looks after it. When you left last week, I asked him if somebody's been keeping an eye on you recently and he said, yeah. It doesn't mean anything. It doesn't mean we don't trust you, or we do trust you. It's just insurance, that's all. We'd be stupid not to."

"So who keeps an eye on you? Who keeps an eye on Gary?"

Uncle Luis squinted as he kept right on looking at me.

"Don't be fucking smart. You're not me. You're not Gary."

"And why aren't I? I'm your fucking blood, for chrissakes! If you can't trust your fucking blood, you're screwed!"

Uh-oh. I shouldn't have answered back to him. Luis slammed his open palm down on his wooden desk so hard it made his iPhone jump. He shouted back at me.

"You checked out your fucking family recently? Your pervert dad? Your psycho brother? You want that I should trust him, trust Mike?"

He picked up his phone and held it to his ear, pretending to make a call.

"Hello, is this Mike Morgan? Hey Mike – long time! Get your ass down here today so I can trust you to do some business for me and I can put my whole fucking life on the line for you! Oh, what's that? You're on Death Row? I'm so sorry – that slipped my mind! Well, another time, huh? Say hi to the chair for me!"

I thought he was going to hurl the phone across the room, but he stopped short and banged it down on the desk and kept staring at me. I hoped he cracked the screen.

When I answered, after maybe 10 seconds of silence between us, I spoke very calm, very measured.

"You know I'm not my brother. I'm not my dad. They're dead to me. Of all people, you should know that. You're my only family now, you and Maria and Molly. I deserve better than this."

Uncle Luis said nothing but kept matching my stare, so I got up, slid the chair up to his desk, turned my back and walked away without another word. I was hoping to hear him call after me – "Jon, I'm sorry, I over-reacted" – but there was nothing, nothing at all.

. . .

My uncle's always had a quick temper but I thought he would listen to me if I had concerns. I thought I was special. I thought I was family. I guess not.

Maybe I'd have argued it out with him if I was feeling better, but I just didn't have the spirit in me for it. To tell the truth, I'm not sure I have the spirit in me for any of this anymore.

I've never pushed to take over things if he should pass. Gary's the guy to take it all on and that's always been very clear. Gary's maybe 10 years younger than Uncle Luis and he's got a good head for business, so he deserves it. Just because my mom is Luis's sister doesn't make me the obvious heir.

But it should count for something, shouldn't it?

. . .

Twenty-four hours before, life was great. I was getting ready to go get laid in Orlando, and I had no idea my uncle doesn't trust me, my ex-girlfriend is in town and looking for me, and that I have Covid.

When life turns to shit like this, I get through it by heading out to the farm just to resettle everything. It's an hour from the wreckers, a little more from the house, and I used that time in the car to prepare myself. Turn off the phone, no radio, no music, just deep breathing and on-the-go meditation. I drove like a robot, like one of those autonomous cars with a robot at the wheel, and by the time I unlocked the chain, pulled onto the ruts in the grass and drove up past the trees to the trailer, I was already feeling better.

When I reach the trailer, there're always two ways it can go. One way is when I set up my chair, load some beer and bourbon into the cooler, unpack a couple of sandwiches or a sub, and then just nap and read for the afternoon.

Maybe later, put a steak on the grill or a piece of fish. No reading on my phone, no playing any apps. I don't let myself have screen time at the farm, and I don't want anyone locating me through the GPS. It's a getting-away-from-it-all place, *know what I'm saying?*

But that's not the way this was going to go today.

I parked the car outside the trailer, took a moment to finish my cigarette, and stretched over onto the back seat for a can of Coors. It was still cold from the gas-station fridge. Then I reached into the glove box, pulled out the Glock, and with the beer in my left hand and the gun in my right, I kicked the car door closed and started walking into the woods.

There's a patch of wet swampland over there, another hundred yards in, what's left of the mangroves, and it's always good for entertainment.

I was walking quiet, sipping from the beer. The only sound was from the cicadas and frogs. When my shoes started to squelch into the wet ground and the trees cleared to show the edge of the inlet, I paused and looked around and sure enough, there was a small gray-black rise in the water straight ahead, just 10 yards out. Maybe you would think it's a tree root or you might think it's a floating branch, but I knew better than that. I'm not dumb, you know.

The small gray-black rise didn't move but that's because I was being real quiet. I crouched down and put the beer on the warm, damp ground, then slid my finger onto the trigger of the pistol. I stood again, spread my legs like I was at the range, held the gun with my right hand and my right hand with my left, and looked down the short barrel at the dark shape in the water. One deep breath in, which was not easy, then all the way out. I could feel – *feel!* – that red mist exhaling through my nose.

Then I squeezed the trigger again and again and again, the deafening crack of the gunshots bouncing off the trees all around, each shell exploding in anger into the water and against the scaly hide, firing off half the magazine as the big gator thrashed in the water. He had to be nine foot this one, and the water all around him splashed and frothed in white spray as his tail smacked the surface and his huge teeth snapped the air in shock and confusion and fury.

Ten shots in and he was still squirming. I lowered the gun, paused for just a few seconds to watch the throes of pain, then raised it again and aimed directly at his head. Five more shots did it and there was blood everywhere in the shallow water, chunks of flesh and scale floating loose. I was wet from the spray but I did it. I'm in charge. I have the power. I have the power of life and death.

It's so satisfying to kill something so strong, so powerful. I could have waded into the water and hauled the monster out, or pulled some teeth for a token, but I didn't need that. I just needed to remind myself that I'm capable of the act itself. I've always been capable, whatever people say.

I killed Rags, the dog Claire loved so much, and it wasn't the same. He was a big dog, menacing, and he kept pacing the house looking for Claire, whining and slobbering. I thought I'd enjoy it because of his size and strength, but when I took him into the yard and tied him to the tree with a loose length of rope, he just lay on his back and looked up at me, whimpering, submissive, pawing the air. One shot did it through the eye, but I kept firing until his head was blown clean off and it made no difference. No reward there.

In my life, I've only ever killed two people. One was strong and deserved everything I gave, the other was weak and innocent. The strong one raised me up. The weak one almost brought me down.

I turned my back and walked away from the floating carcass of the alligator. It's a $5,000 fine to kill a gator in Florida but the feds will never find it. Something will eat it before the night is over. Something always does.

. . .

It was still daylight when I got home, wearing a fresh shirt and pants from my closet in the trailer and sobered up from the drive back. Part of me expected to see Claire and Vivian sitting on the front porch, drinking iced tea with Maria and Molly, but there was nobody there. Not outside anyway. Everything looked fine. The black Challenger was still parked in front of one of the garage doors and I parked the Fusion beside it.

I was walking toward the porch when I heard a call from behind.

"Hey! Hey Jon! Wait up!"

It was a woman's voice. I recognized it, more than 15 years later.

Sure enough, when I turned it was Claire and Vivian striding through the open gate toward me. But it wasn't just them. There was another woman with them, tall and red-haired. Even after all this time, I thought I knew who she was.

Was this for real? Was this really her? *Is this Jess?*

Chapter 13

CLAIRE, Tampa

John looked truly shocked when I called out and he saw us walking toward him in his driveway. Mom was striding on my right, Jess was a lot more cautious on my left, and Floyd was hanging back, taking photos through the hedge with his long-lens camera and filming with his phone. Howie was safely asleep in the car that was locked and parked out on the road.

"Hey! Hey John! Wait up!"

John didn't say anything. Just turned and waited as we walked up. A little chill ran through me knowing that he was so close, but I pushed it down to where I couldn't feel it so much.

"Hey John. How you doing?"

"Hey Claire. I'm doing okay, thanks." He looked at Mom. "Hi Vivian." And then he looked at Jess. "And you are?"

"This is Jess. Remember Jess? Jessica? Your daughter?"

John looked like he'd seen a ghost. I guess he did.

"How can you be Jess?" he said to her. "Jess was taken. Jess left us years ago."

She looked scared, but she was safe with us and she was doing the right thing by being there.

"Surprised to see her, John?"

And then the house door opened and the girl, Molly, walked out onto the porch. John turned to look at her and raised his hand.

"It's okay, Molly," he said. "I've got this. Stay there." She didn't say a thing.

"Why are you here, Claire?" he asked me. "What is this? What's this about?"

He didn't look too bad for all the years. He'd grown a little beard, close-cut, and was heavier, for sure, and shorter hair, higher on his forehead, but it was unmistakably him. Very tan. Brown eyes, a little too close together. The small scar still cut through his left eyebrow, where I ripped out the ring when I hit him all those years ago. I was pleased to see that. Asshole.

Then Maria was on the step with Molly. "What is this, John?" she called out. No trouble with the English now.

He raised his hand again. "It's okay, Maria. It's no problem."

"Jess has come back, John, and she's told us the truth. This is your chance to tell us the truth, too."

I was holding onto my phone, and although its screen was dark, it was recording this conversation. Mom was doing the same thing with her phone. Floyd was still hidden behind the hedge but shooting video and taking photos through whatever gap he found.

The starlings from the morning had gone now. They'd been replaced in the red maple by a flock of crows, rasping through the branches. No, it's not a flock when they're crows – it's called a murder. A murder of crows.

Jess just stood there, saying nothing, looking at her father for the first time in years. She seemed horrified.

"What truth is it you're looking for, Claire?"

Don't put words into his mouth, Floyd said. If anything he says is to mean something, I couldn't make leading statements or ask leading questions. He had to speak it for himself, dig his own grave.

"The truth about what happened to Jess."

"What's she been saying? This woman can't be Jess." And then he turned to her and asked her the question. "You're not Jess, are you?"

And then, as I was watching him, I saw it: just a flash, the quickest of flickers. *Recognition!* He saw her just as I saw her.

"Jess?"

"Who's Jess?" That was Molly calling out to John, who didn't answer, so I did.

"Jess is his daughter. She's our daughter. I used to live with John and we had a daughter, like you. Has he never mentioned her to you?"

"Dad?" That was Molly again. The poor girl – she must have been so confused. Her mother was standing behind her on the front porch, watching with her head cupped in her hands.

John wasn't responding to Molly, though. He'd walked up to Jessica and was studying her face like a drill sergeant, while poor Jess held back and the crows continued to gather and rasp in the tree to the side. She looked terrified he might try to touch her.

"Dad?" That was Molly again.

"Molly, please, go inside with your mother. I've got this. I'll explain everything, but inside."

I wasn't letting him get off this so easy.

"Why shouldn't she hear what you have to say, John?"

He turned to me and now he looked seriously dangerous.

"You're on my property, and this is my family. I'll talk with you, but don't fuck with my family."

"Dad?"

"*Get inside!*"

Molly and Maria hustled inside, slamming the door behind them. A moment later, they were watching through a ground-floor window.

John looked over at Mom, then me again. Then he looked over my shoulder and yelled so loud it made me jump.

"Floyd – that you? Don't you have enough pictures already?"

I didn't turn, but I could hear Floyd walk up the short driveway toward us. The yell aroused the crows in the red maple and they were rasping more loudly now. They were *cawing* at each other; they were *cawing* at us.

It was a relief to have Floyd come to stand beside me. His phone was in his flowery shirt pocket but the camera lens was pointing out and I knew he was recording this. We shouldn't have cornered John like this. This was a mistake. He's a dangerous man and he'd have a gun somewhere, and he'd use it if he felt like it.

"You can never have too many pictures, John," said Floyd.

"Fuck you, you fat fucker. Still no taste in fashion, I see."

John looked at me again.

"So what is this? A shakedown?"

"It's your reconciliation with your daughter, John," said Mom, the first time she'd spoken.

"Okay. There, we're reconciled. Now fuck off, all of you."

"You don't care about her?" I asked.

"What is it you want?" he asked again. "Is it money?" He pointed at Floyd. "Is this something he's put you up to?"

"John, we want justice," I told him. And then to hell with the leading statements. Whatever he'd say would be drowned out on the recordings by the crows, anyway.

"I know what you did," I said, raising my own voice now. "We all know what you did. We know you lied about where you were when Jess was taken. We know you were at the mall and we know you took Jess away from me. We know you kept her somewhere. It must have been so frustrating for you, eh, never being able to get her alone because I was always there? And then, you had her alone! She was all yours for whatever you wanted, *you sick fuck!* And then, what, you *sold her on?*"

I was spitting out the words now, almost shouting. It felt so good to finally say them to him to his smug face, tanned as an old leather bag. This was such a long time coming.

Jess still hadn't spoken a word, but there was nothing she needed to say.

"She's told us everything, John. We know what you did, and we're going to make sure you pay for it."

He looked over at Mom again, then me. He'd barely even looked at his own daughter after scaring her half to death just now. How can any man be so cold?

The crows were restless in the tree.

"Is this really what you think? You think I'm a sick fucker like my dad? Like my brother?"

Floyd started to speak again: "Well, the apple don't…"

"*Shut the fuck up, fat man!*"

Floyd shut up, mid-sentence.

John turned on his heel, strode back toward his car, reached through the passenger window, and when he stood straight again, he had a gun. *Oh God.* I should have known it was always going to come to this. In the side of my eye, I could see a hundred black wings among the leaves of the maple, moving, flapping, claiming territory, as the birds kept up their *caw! caw!* in the swaying branches.

Floyd reached beneath his loose shirt but John was already pointing his pistol at him.

"Don't start something I have to follow through on," said John.

Floyd put his hands back down by his sides.

John walked back up to us, his gun still trained on Floyd. When he spoke, his voice was very measured, very steady.

"Claire, it's been a long time. I'm sorry it's come to this. Now I'm going to ask you all, very politely, very *Canadian*, to leave my property and not contact me again. You may not like guns up there in Canada, but here in Florida, we love 'em. Here, I have a legal right to protect my family and my property with this gun, and with the other firearms that are in the house, legally registered. And I'll do it. You know that."

He would too. I don't care much for myself, but I won't let him hurt Jess, or Mom.

He looked directly at the phone in Floyd's shirt pocket, the one that was filming all this. Maybe not so discreet as we thought.

"Did you get that, *for the record*?"

The birds had settled. Something calmed them. They were quieter now.

"But before you go, I will tell you this. I did not snatch Jess. I did not take her from the mall. I don't know any more than you about what happened to her. I still think about her every day. That part of my life eats away at me all the time – *all the time* – but I've tried to move on from it because there's nothing else I can do."

He was still pointing the gun at Floyd.

"And now you say that this is Jess." He looked at Jess, who didn't look so scared any more. Instead, she looked – resigned?

"Your tan's faded, but we know each other, don't we?" he said to her. "Or at least, you know the taste of my cock. We don't owe each other nothing. I paid you $200 when we were banned from the club and we're square."

What? Jess had her eyes closed. John turned back to me.

"She can tell you all about it, but not here. Now, get the fuck off my property and don't let me see you again."

He raised the gun and fired a shot toward the sky. It was the first real gunshot I'd heard in years, and it was far louder than I expected. Far, far more violent. It startled the crows and they took flight, the entire murder of them ripping through the branches and leaves in their panic to escape, rasping and cawing in a rushing black cloud of hundreds of wings. Mom gasped. Jessica turned and ran back up the driveway. Floyd spun on his heel and walked fast toward the gate. The gunshot woke Howie, and I could hear him crying in the car up on the road.

I didn't move, which must be one of the bravest things I've ever done. Mom was still beside me. She was brave too.

Everything grew silent, until I spoke up.

"John, you're not going to shoot me."

"No, I'm not, and I'm not going to shoot you either, Vivian."

Mom gave a nod. "Well, thank you," she said.

"But I will shoot that fat fucker, and that bitch. She has you suckered. She's not Jess. And if you don't leave, I'm going to call the cops and have you charged with trespass. In this neighbourhood, they'll be here in less than a minute."

"John, this isn't ending now. Not until we have justice."

"You won't get justice from those two. But you're wrong. This ends now."

We stared at each other a few seconds more, a stand-off.

Then I turned, and Mom and I walked steadily toward the car and the sound of Howie's crying. Our walk may have been steady but my hands were shaking. I held them together tightly in front of me so that John couldn't see, but they were shaking more than I ever knew possible.

Chapter 14

JON, Tampa

It's pretty clear what was happening. Claire's fucked in the head, her mom's not much better, and Floyd and the stripper had them down as an easy mark. I'm not sure where I fit in this, but I don't like it.

Of course, it's possible the stripper really was Jess, but I just can't believe that. Sure, she looks, physically, like the kind of woman Jess might have grown up to be, but there must be thousands of red-heads in Florida, even ones with green eyes like Jess. But I have the advantage here. I know the stripper's real name is probably Andrea Jackson, and I know the address on her vehicle registration in New Port Richey. You never know when information like that will come in useful.

I watched Claire and Vivian walk back up the driveway to their car – *good for them for staying strong!* – and as soon as they were out the gate and gone, Molly and Maria rushed out the front door toward me. Maria knew the story but we'd never told Molly. I've got some explaining to do.

We were always going to tell Molly one day, but always tomorrow. She didn't know about Jess. She didn't know about my dad, and she didn't know about my brother. She didn't know about my twin sister Kelly. She thought my parents are dead from cancer or something years ago, and she knew I had a younger sister, Aunt Tammy, who also died from some illness.

How do you tell a child about the boogeymen when the boogeymen are her family?

Of course, we had no choice now. At 12 years old, Molly is old enough to know about the boogeymen, and about her own half-sister Jessica, so we went inside and we told her.

. . .

People who know I only got married a few years ago assume Molly is my step-daughter, just Maria's child from some guy, but she's my true biological daughter. Maria and I first met 13 years back when she was living with her sister Benita in Clearwater. She was still a refugee from Cuba who'd floated over to Key West the year before to follow her sister on the search for the American Dream. We dated for a couple months and I got her pregnant, but the relationship was over long before Molly was born. I didn't even know I'd put a baby in her.

Those were tough times for Maria. Hell of a Dream. She was a single mom with no income, relying on Benita for everything. She spoke poor English when I first knew her, which didn't help the two of us, but she stuck it out, got her papers, learned the language and learned it well, got some modelling work, clawed her way up and out of the hole. We met again by accident when she came to the dealership looking to buy a car and it was like, this time, it was *supposed* to be. We could finally talk to each other, have a conversation, and it was wonderful. Still is.

That was four years ago. I was doing better for myself and looking to settle a bit, move in behind a picket fence and start taking on responsibilities. Age was kind to Maria and when I met Molly, who I didn't even know existed, I regretted all those years of absence. It's made Molly stronger, I think, that she spent that time without her dad.

Even so, when we did finally get back together, when's the best time to mention that your new father is from a family of perverts and killers?

Today. Today was the time.

. . .

She didn't take it well.

"Dad! Who were those people?"

I told her that Claire was an old girlfriend of mine, from long before she was born, from Canada. I said Vivian is Claire's mother, and the young woman was somebody Claire thought might be our daughter, but she's mistaken.

"And the man you were pointing your gun at?"

"He's a police detective. Like a private investigator."

"Are you in trouble with the police, dad?"

Maria was looking worried. She knows I skirt a fine line around the law.

"Not at all, sweetie. They all just made a mistake, that's all."
"So who's Jess?"

I sat on the couch beside Molly, with Maria beside me, and told her the story of Jess. I told her about a happy little girl, with friends and dolls and a pet dog. A beautiful little girl who was taken at the mall on her fourth birthday and never found. I told her that Claire was always suspicious I took Jess myself, to keep her close in Florida and not have to fight for custody. I don't say anything about why Claire called me a sick fuck, which surprised me and upset me, but then, Molly was inside the house by then and didn't hear that.

Then I took a breath and carried on and told her about my other family: my father, my brother, my younger sister. I explained that they're the reason why some people, like Claire and Floyd Woods, point fingers at me. I told her that I've spent all my adult life trying to escape their stigma.

Turned out, she was okay with having a grandfather fried in the electric chair, and fine with an uncle waiting his turn on Death Row, but the news of a stolen half-sister was just too much.

"Dad!" she said. "I had a sister and you never told me. I might still have a sister! You have to find her! How could you just forget about her? How could you just leave her, like you left me when you ran away from Mom?"

This was rough, because I had all the reasons, all the excuses, but I didn't have any answers. I couldn't take it, this overwhelming oppression of failure. I left her crying with her mom, and I walked outside.

I didn't tell Maria about maybe having Covid. There wasn't much else to worry about. If I had it, they probably had it too. That's too bad. They'd be okay, though. Maria thought she had it last year but it only lasted a few days, before there was even time to get checked, and now she's probably immune anyway. Molly's too young to be hurt from it.

Maria came outside to find me, but I didn't know what else to say. Right then, I didn't want to lose the advantage I had of time. I got back in the car, drove up onto the main highway and headed north.

I was so tired. I just wanted to pull over and stop for a few minutes. Take a nap and try to breathe easy for a while. Breathe without straining. Close my eyes now the sun was starting to set. I couldn't though. I drove for a half hour until the next exit was New Port Richey. I was hoping time's on my side, for that night at least.

. . .

New Port Richey is an unremarkable, forgettable community close to the coast. I don't think I've ever been there without just driving past.

The address from Andrea Jackson's car registration, 176 Connecticut Avenue, was not far from the main highway. The trees were less lush than around my own neighborhood, and the houses were smaller and cheaper, but the lawns were well cut and most houses had American flags flying loud and proud from above the garage or beside the front window.

Some had front porches, kind of like my own, and there were handfuls of people outside on a few of them enjoying the breeze. I slowed down on Connecticut when I passed 176, and there was somebody sitting quietly there in a patio chair on the small veranda. That person probably knew who Andrea really is.

I parked the car just down the street and sat for a while, thinking. Thinking of any reason at all for knocking on the door, wanting to ask about Andrea Jackson. Finally, I swallowed hard and got out of the car, locking the door with a chirp.

The man sitting outside Number 176 was still there, with a blanket covering his lap. He looked about my age. I called hello from the sidewalk but he didn't reply. He looked at me without a word.

"Are you Mr. Jackson?"

The guy said nothing. Now I was closer, he seemed like a retard. His head lolled about and his eyes were moving constantly.

Somebody inside the house spoke up.

"Who's that? Somebody there?"

An older man came to the door, walking unsteady, holding a cane. Thin white hair, big swollen nose. Watery eyes. "Who are you? What do you want?"

I was still standing down on the sidewalk and my mind went blank. I'd thought up a pretty good story in the car, something about looking for Andrea Jackson because I manage a restaurant and she'd applied for a job, but that was all jumbled now and it wasn't coming together. I just spoke whatever words came into my head.

"Er, my name's Jim," I said. "Jim Jefferson." *Where did that come from?* "I moved in down the road a couple of weeks ago and I like to take an evening walk. I've often seen this gentleman out on the porch and I thought I'd say hello."

"Which house is yours?"

"The blue one around the corner, on Sycamore." I drove on Sycamore just before turning onto Connecticut. Here's hoping there was a blue house there.

The older man softened. "Tyler often sits out here, but there's not much else he can do. He was injured pretty bad years ago, at work. Brain damage. My son. But he likes the fresh air, even when it's not so fresh, and he likes the sound of the birds and the crickets. It helps keep him calm."

"*Cheep! Cheep!*" said the retard. I guessed that's his level of conversation.

"It is pleasant on a night like this, isn't it? I like it too," I answered, all neighborly. "I was thinking of getting a dog to come on these walks with me, but my wife's not so keen on dogs." The lie was coming easy now, and the old guy seemed less guarded.

"Nothing wrong with dogs," he said. "We used to have a Shepherd ourselves. Helps keep the house safe. Might keep your walks safe, too."

I smiled, as friendly as I could be.

"What's your name again?" asked the guy.

I had to think for a moment, but when I remembered 'Jim,' the 'Jefferson' just followed.

"Wes Jackson," said the man. "Nice to meet the neighbors."

We chatted for a couple minutes, talking about dogs while his kid's head flopped around. Bugs buzzed the 40-watt bulb that lit the porch from beside the front door. He told me a little about the town, too. Sounded boring as hell. Finally, I got to ask the question I'd been waiting for. The only question that mattered.

"Don't you have a young woman living here too? Red hair? My wife and I saw her the other day and I said, look at that woman's hair! I told her, I'll bet that woman's called Wendy, you know, after the burger place. Was that here?"

"You've gotta mean Andrea. She's at school in the city. You must have seen her when she came by last weekend." The man in the chair stirred when he heard the name and looked up at his father.

"*Andry!*" he said.

"Andrea will be home soon, Tyler." He looked back at me. "She has a son of her own now too, so we'll have four generations in the house. Can you believe it?"

Now my head was swirling with questions, but I got out of there while the going was still good. The old guy stood stiffly next to his son on the verandah while the cicadas buzzed from the trees all around.

. . .

When I got home, I could see Molly's bedroom light was on upstairs, but it turned off as soon as I pulled up to the garage. I knew what to expect, and sure enough, Maria was asleep on the couch with some Spanish-language show on the TV. It was late – after 11. Mentioning the Wendy's in that lame exchange with Wes Jackson put me in the mood for a Dave's Double with a root beer, but truth be told, I was in no hurry to get home. I took the long route back for some time to think, though most of the drive, my mind was blank. No radio. Just driving.

There was a half-empty wine glass on the table next to Maria. I turned off most of the lights and switched off the TV, but left her where she was for the moment. I took the glass into the kitchen and emptied it down the sink, then headed upstairs. Outside Molly's room, I tapped lightly on the closed door. When there was no answer, I turned the handle quietly and stepped inside.

Molly was in bed, breathing softly. I knew she wasn't sleeping because the light was on just a few minutes ago. Her head was in shadow, but the room was lit by a moonbeam through the window. She wasn't acknowledging me, which is usual whenever I come into her room this way, late at night, when her mother's asleep.

There were posters on the walls, probably like every other 12-year-old girl in Florida, in America. Billie Eilish. BadBunny. Taylor Swift. Half a dozen pictures of blond-haired bloggers printed off the Internet, still in their teens and probably millionaires already, probably living in bigger houses than this. They were watching from all around, protective, accusing, their eyes following me as I padded toward my daughter, her slim young body lit in the bed by the moonbeam.

I stopped at the head of the bed and squatted down so my face was close to the level of Molly's. Her eyes were closed. Her breathing was steady. She was pretending to be asleep because, well, I guess it's easier for her this way.

I whispered to her gently. "Sweetie?"

She didn't react. Her breathing barely changed. I knew she was listening to me.

She's so beautiful. Maria is beautiful too, but not in the clear, innocent way of our daughter. Smooth, lightly tan skin with not a wrinkle or a line. No makeup now she was washed for bed, just clean, pure features. Pale lips. Long lashes and thick, natural eyebrows. Dark hair like her mother and a few light freckles on her forehead and her nose. I could see them now my face was close to hers. Just a few inches away.

I whispered again. "Sweetie?"

This time she stirred. I knew she was listening. She was waiting me out.

I reached forward and touched her shoulder through the thin blanket then, with the back of my fingers, I brushed some strands of hair from her cheek.

"Sweetie?"

"No, Daddy," she murmured, then her eyes opened slowly and looked directly into mine.

"Please, Daddy. No."

BIRD ON A WIRE

Chapter 15

CLAIRE, Tampa

Poor Jess was a wreck from meeting her biological father after all this time, and from him shooting a gun at her. Mom and I took her home and Floyd followed in his car.

She told us that she'd worked briefly as an exotic dancer in a Tampa club and that she met John there and he'd assaulted her. Neither realized their relationship at the time, of course. She said she had him thrown out, but the whole thing was so traumatic that she'd never returned.

"I guess I owe him that," she said. "I was so worried about money at the time that I'd have done anything, but he made me see there are some lines that shouldn't be crossed, even if he was okay to cross them. I'm still close to broke, but at least I have my standards."

I'd have talked more with her but Howie was acting up, so Mom suggested we take the evening to clear our heads and we can regather tomorrow to work out the next steps. We offered to get her a room at the hotel with us to make sure she'll be safe tonight, just in case, but Floyd said he'd stay with her, sleeping on the couch with his gun at the ready, and she preferred that. Howie would be more settled in his own bed at home, she said.

In our two-queen-beds deluxe room, before we even sat down, Mom broke the seal on the minibar.

"We need this," she said. "I don't care how much the booze costs. It's been a rough day."

There was scotch and vodka and gin and mixers and beer, but we started with the wine. They were small bottles that cost more than the large bottles in the bar downstairs, but Mom said she was paying and she already had the top unscrewed from the Chardonnay, so there was no point holding back.

The bottle barely filled two glasses but the wine tasted good. Actually, it tasted great. I could have drank this whole minibar, and if Mom wasn't there, I just might.

"You want to talk about it?" said Mom.

I paused to swirl the wine in my mouth, just for a moment. The sweet chill on my tongue was so welcome.

"I always said he was a good-looking guy. Makes up for not being too smart. He's held up well over the years. He'll be 44 now, a year older than me. I wonder how he's made his money? Illegal, I'm sure."

"Probably. That was a nice house, on the outside at least."

"Why does he get to live in a nice house? What's wrong with this world that he can do the things he's done and it all works out for him? When I saw him, I wanted to slap him so hard. I wanted to slap his stupid wife, too, for going along with it all. And Molly – I feel so sorry for her."

"Did you see those birds? I thought it was like a Hitchcock film."

"Good thing they didn't attack us!"

Mom finished her glass, drinking it like water, and went back to the minibar to return with a little bottle of Riesling.

"This is all there is for white wine. I recommend we drink it."

She'd already unscrewed this one, too, so I finished off my glass and held it out for the refill.

"I wonder how he explained it to his wife and daughter," she said.

"I'd love to have been there when he did."

"I wouldn't. It must have been hard on his little girl."

Mom was right. Molly didn't ask for any of this. That was a sobering thought.

"I did love him once, you know. I was so young. I thought he'd be a good father, but I was so wrong. I looked at him today and all I could see was a monster."

We were both silent for a while. I was trying to get his face out of my mind but I was studying it closely: his brown eyes, his full mouth, his short beard with its greying hair; the little scar in his eyebrow. Then his face blurred away and I could see his new daughter come into focus, standing behind him on the step. His replacement daughter, with his replacement wife, at their comfortable Florida home.

I wanted the image gone, so it was me who spoke first.

"I hope Jess is okay. We shouldn't have gone over there like we did. John is a dangerous man and we should have left it to the police. Left it to Floyd."

"You think Floyd would have followed it up properly? He didn't seem to want to when it was first mentioned."

"Oh, I'm sure he would. Once a cop, always a cop."

"But you never thought he was a very good cop."

"No. So maybe you're right. He'd have done a crappy job. We did the best we could, under the circumstances."

The wine was kicking in – *that's quick!* – and my reasoning was starting to scramble. Neither of us had eaten since lunch and it was going to our heads.

"You know, I can't believe John," I said. "To be so dismissive of his own daughter after everything he's done to her."

"Well," said Mom, "I really do think he believes she is not his daughter."

"Yes, but he hasn't seen the DNA test from Floyd that proves it without a shadow of doubt."

"And perhaps, neither have we."

She just threw that out there and let it lie for a while. It stopped me cold. Cold.

"*The fuck?* What are you saying, Mom?"

"I'm saying that we should just be a little cautious here. A man who you agree was a bad cop, who we hired to find Jess, now says he's found Jess and we have only his word for it. There was a letter from the police laboratory with the results of the DNA test, but he could have written that himself. It was on photocopied letterhead. It wouldn't be difficult."

"Why would you say this? And why would he lie to us? He gets paid the same either way."

"But maybe he gets paid better if he finds Jess, and so does she. She's already been very clear, a few times, that she's low on cash, and she may be just building up to ask us for money."

"I don't believe this! How does he get paid better?"

"Maybe he gets a cut of whatever she takes from us. John seemed to think that was what was happening, and it could be that he has a point. He lives here. He's wise to these things. We're in a foreign country, Claire, and we're vulnerable – two women who both let their emotions get the better of them. I think we owe it to ourselves to be more careful than we've been."

"Whose fucking side are you on, Mom?"

"Yours, dear. Only yours."

"Well, then how do we get to be more careful?"

"Maybe we get a DNA test of our own, just to set our minds to rest."

Mom reached into her purse and pulled out a clear plastic sandwich bag. I could see it held a tangle of hair.

"I went to the bathroom at Jess's house, and I took the time to liberate this from her brush. It's very red – it's definitely her hair. There are four or five private DNA clinics here in Tampa, I've already checked, and we can get this tested for ourselves, just for our peace of mind. For *my* peace of mind. And when the test comes back to prove she's Jess, then we know we can trust Floyd, and we can take the results to John, and we can take that to court."

. . .

Mom meant well, I know she did. There was no harm in us doing this private test, and as she said, it would be peace of mind. It may even be something necessary for Jess to prove to the authorities that she's my daughter, for when she moves north and starts preparing for Canadian residency and citizenship. We probably need to do the same for Howie as well. It might even help us to find out more about Brian Hunter, his father. Only good can come from this.

It was very clear Mom didn't think much of Floyd. That's no surprise – he was the antithesis of everything she appreciates in a man. He's fat, he's a slob, and he's American. She likes suave Europeans, men who don't wear socks with their shoes and who leave their shirt cuffs unbuttoned. Me, I don't really think about guys anymore.

Since I went home to Toronto, I've not been in a relationship with a man. I've screwed a few, but nothing more than that, and there's never any real intimacy. I'm careful to not hook up with anyone who works with me, and only one time did I see a guy who'd been a patient, but that was after he was out of the hospital and so it was all quite legitimate. Some guys want to take it further but I'm just not interested.

Even now, men still hit on me – not so often these days, it's true – and I just can't let them in. I don't want to go there; I refuse to go there; I don't feel there's anything missing. I have some female friends and I own two vibrators and if I want to get laid, I can go to a bar and I can get laid, though I rarely do. No guy ever, *ever*, comes back to my place. That's all I need to be happy in my life. I doubt I'll ever bother with men for more than just basic sex now and that's few and far between. Sometimes, I wish I was a lesbian and I did try once, to see if it might work, but it didn't work. It very clearly didn't work.

I knew Mom worried about me. I knew she'd been sad, too, that she's not been able to be a grandmother, but now that we'd found Jess, I hoped that missing part of her life would be restored. She deserves happiness as much as anyone. She was happy with Daddy, but he was taken from her and that was my fault, I know. Then she was happy with Lex for almost 10 years, but he was also taken from her. That was not my fault that time – that was cancer. Now she's been dating the German guy back in Toronto and she seemed to be happy again.

Mom's always happiest when she's into a project, and the DNA proof would be her project for this weekend.

Me? I thought I'd be happier than I am. I guess there were still some loose ends to tie up before I could finally feel complete again. Mom must prove to herself that Jess is legitimate, and that will let her become a grandmother again, and maybe that's when I'll finally get to be a true mom myself. And when I'm 1,000 miles from here, and John's behind bars with a faded tan and a sore ass – well, then our family will be complete and I can live happily ever after.

I wondered what John was doing then in that fancy house of his, with his bought-and-paid-for family? I wondered if he was taking out his frustration, his anger, on Maria? On Molly?

As soon as I thought of it, I imagined the possibilities and the thoughts made me shudder.

BIRD ON A WIRE

Chapter 16

JON, Tampa

I was lying in my Texas King while the morning sun filled the room with light and warmth. It's one of the best features of this house: there's a switch on each side of the bed that opens and closes the drapes, so I can roll over and flip the switch and the drapes will glide quietly open to let the morning begin. I've stayed in a few hotel rooms with drapes like this and when I saw they were fitted in this house, I think that's what sold me on the property. Maria likes it too.

There's a switch on my side but I like to wake up and roll over and across Maria to use the switch on her side to open the drapes. That way, when the light comes into the room and she wakes groggily from the night, I'm already right there with her, ready for whatever might happen. When it goes as I hope, it's the best time of the day.

This morning, though, I opened the drapes from my side and left Maria alone to sleep a little longer. It was Sunday and neither of us needed to be anywhere. She used to attend church, something her sister got her into, but I pulled her away from that nonsense. I didn't stop her, not at all. She can be religious if she wants. It's just a waste of time, and I think she recognizes that now.

I'd get up in a while and make some coffee, which I'd bring to her in bed, but for now, I left her alone so I could think over my time last night with Molly.

Poor Molly. She couldn't forgive me for not telling her about her half-sister.

"Daddy, how could you keep her from me?" she asked, when I wouldn't take no for an answer and made her sit up in bed to talk to me. "You know I've always wanted a sister."

"But sweetie," I said. "Your sister died a long time ago, just as my sister died too. Both my sisters. Aunt Tammy, and Aunt Kelly. Both of them died before you were born."

"It was Aunt Kelly who died when she was a little girl, right?"

"Yes. She died in an accident. It was my father who killed her, accidentally." That had been a tough one to explain. A poor white lie. A very poor white trash lie.

"When he choked her to death."

"Yes."

"But the judge said he did it on purpose, and he was executed."

"Yes."

"And then your brother did the same thing with two other girls."

"Yes. And this is why you must never, ever, let a man touch you in anger, or in any way you don't like. Never let *anyone* do *anything* to you that you don't want. You know this. Mom and me have told you this. School's told you this. Sometimes it's an accident and sometimes it's bad people who do this on purpose, but it's all the same. You know this."

"Daddy, I'm 12 years old. Don't talk to me like I'm a baby."

"I'm sorry, sweetie – I'm your dad. I'm the only man allowed to talk to you like you're a baby. It's in the Constitution. It's the 28th Amendment. It's in the Dad Bill of Rights."

She was awake now, and getting into this. She switched on her bedside lamp and the watchers in the posters on the walls suddenly became more friendly, sympathetic.

"How do you know my sister's dead?"

"I just do."

"No you don't. Did you see her dead body? Claire thinks she's alive, even if she's not that other woman who came here yesterday."

"I just know that she's dead. It's a feeling I have. I'm her father. Fathers know these things."

"No you don't."

"Yes I do."

"No you don't, and it's in the Dad Constitution that if your daughter goes missing, you must look for her and never ever give up until you find her. Would you give up looking for me?"

"Of course not!"

"Then why did you give up looking for her?"

There was no answer to that.

Because I didn't know where to look? *Not good enough!*

Because I had to get on with my life? *Not good enough!*

Because I believed she was dead? *Not fucking good enough!*

"You're right, sweetie. I need to look for her, don't I?"

"Yes, you do. Because you're the only person who will."

So I made Molly a promise last night that I would look for her sister Jess, and that I would never, ever give up until she was found. Now I was laying there in bed, in the reality of the daylight, wondering where to start.

. . .

"Hey Jon! *Wassup?*"

"Grant, you want to come over to the house for lunch today? I've got something I want to ask you."

"Well that depends. Are you going to ask if I want to drive the new Corvette?"

"No, it's a bit more involved than that. Can you make it for noon? We're having burgers."

. . .

The black Challenger was still in the driveway, parked in the exact same place Grant left it yesterday morning.

"You haven't even moved it! I could have kept it an extra day!"

"Sucks to be you, bud."

We walked through the garage to the backyard, where the barbecue was set up on the patio beside the pool. I always like taking Grant through the three-car garage so he can appreciate the smooth, lacquered floor and the tidy red tool chests that rarely get used. The Harley in the corner that I never ride. The empty workspaces, so clean and uncluttered.

"All I have in my life are women!" I always tell him. "One day, all this will be yours!"

This time though, Molly was on the patio as we walked through and I was expounding my promise of Grant's inheritance and she staked her claim.

"I'm having it first," she says. "Girls can like cars too, you know. And I'm having that motorcycle."

"Maybe Grant will take you for a ride on the back, sweetie."

"Forget that!" says Molly, in a one-of-the-guys way.

"Hey," says Grant – "You can ride bitch!"

That's too much. Molly gave him a raised-eyebrow-tipped-head look, while I caught his eye with a fatherly frown and he realized his error. He looked mortified.

Maria walked out, stunning in a red one-piece and robe, and saved the day. Saved by the belle.

"Grant – so glad you could join us!"

The conversation was light and easy and comfortable. Grant knew not to raise any subjects that weren't safe subjects, and certainly not to mention the red Mazda we were discussing just yesterday. We talked about his YouTube channel and websites and social media as if he was Uncle Grant, one of the family. I think Molly had a bit of a crush on him but that's okay because Grant would never do anything with that. Maybe that's why I liked him, because he's a regular guy who's not a perv or a criminal or a cracker. Just a regular guy.

After lunch, a little too heavy a meal for such a warm, sunny day, with thick burgers but salad on the side and a couple of beers, I excused myself to go to the bathroom but actually used the time behind the locked door to take a second Covid test, shoving the Q-Tip up my nose, dunking it in the fluid and dripping the fluid onto the paper strip. Those tests take a while to show their results, so I left it under the sink to process and went back out to rejoin everyone. Right away, it was Molly who got the real conversation going.

"Dad, are you going to ask Grant about what we talked about last night?"

Maria knew all about this, too. The three of us were cornering Grant here.

"Why don't you ask him, Molly?"

"Grant, Dad says you know about my half-sister, Jess."

Grant stopped grinning. Stopped looking curious. Started looking like the spotlight was on him.

"Your dad told me he had a daughter, Jessica, who died a long time ago, yes."

"She was abducted by somebody from the Fairfield Mall on her fourth birthday."

Grant could see Molly was up to speed on this. He looked concerned, but he also looked a little relieved that he might not accidentally say something he shouldn't.

"Yes, he told me about that."

"Well, Dad's going to look for her and he's not going to stop looking for her until she's found, dead or alive."

"Okay, that's great."

"And he wants you to help him, because you're a journalist and you know how to investigate stuff."

"Hey, slow down!" He started coughing and had to hold up a hand for a moment while he hacked down whatever it was. "I make videos about cars and I *create content*" – he air-quoted those last two words – "for Tampa's Hometown Homepage. I don't investigate missing people. I investigate missing horsepower!"

He tried to laugh at his joke and looked over at Maria and myself. Both of us were looking back at him and we weren't laughing.

I told him, briefly, about Claire and her mother and the stripper and Floyd coming over to the house yesterday. I told him that Claire thought I took Jess myself, to keep her in Florida. I didn't tell him she also thought I'm a sick fuck who molested my daughter. That still upset me. Nobody needs to hear that. I knew he had questions about me, but he listened without saying a word.

"Grant, I don't expect you to be Woodward and Einstein, but I'm serious about this promise I've made. I've left the memory of Jessica to eat away at me for too long. I'm just looking to bounce some ideas off somebody, maybe point me in a couple of directions. And you did study journalism, right?"

"Well, I took a course in high school. Enough to learn the difference between Einstein and Bernstein."

"So maybe there's something you can suggest, some rock I can look under? Would you help with this, if you're able to?"

Grant could see we were all of us serious and there was no easy getting out of this.

"Well, hell yeah. Whatever you need, Jon."

Great!

We chatted some more. Grant mentioned some document tracing that he might be able to do. Maybe he could help find her by just checking addresses, or something. He sounded more enthusiastic than five minutes earlier.

I got up to go get a couple more beers, and a glass of wine for Maria. First though, I went back to the bathroom and pulled out the Covid test strip from under the sink. There was just the one stripe on the paper. Negative. Still negative.

Hey, that's great! I don't have the virus! I was worried all this time over nothing. That's good, right?

Right?

Chapter 17

CLAIRE, Tampa

Mom dropped off the hair samples at the public DNA lab first thing in the morning. It was Sunday but there was an office near the hotel that was open, and they could get us results within 24 hours. It would cost extra and it would be worth it just to put our minds at rest because she'd got me thinking now. Even so, everything Jess told us checked out for me; she even knew about spraining her ankle that time when she fell from the swing. How could she have known that if she wasn't Jess?

After some breakfast, we went back to the house at Orient Park. The night had been quiet and Floyd left before we arrived. He called and told us he still had somebody keeping eyes on John, and he wasn't charging us for it, so we shouldn't worry about any unexpected visit, which was a huge relief. Mom and I were happy to spend time with Jess and Howie. It helped that I took a couple of extra pills just to calm myself, to take off the edge and reduce any suspicion. Mom made me promise not to mention the DNA test, but I couldn't stop thinking about it. The pills helped like they always do.

I'd wondered if she colours her hair, but no, when I looked closely I could see it's all natural. I visited the bathroom and picked up her hairbrush to examine the bristles, rubbing between my fingers the hair that was caught there. I don't know why, I just did. And it was okay, because everything I saw, everything I questioned, checked out every time. It should have reassured me that I was with my daughter and my grandson.

But I kept hearing John's words: *She has you suckered. She's not Jess.* Why was he so convinced when the proof was right there in front of him, looking at him with her green eyes? Surely he was just trying to cover himself, intimidate us with that story about the dance club, because he knew what would happen to him if Jess goes to the police. *When* Jess and Mom and I go to the police.

It was good to spend time with Howie, too. He's an adorable little boy. I'd already begun to knit him a pair of socks, in yellow. It's difficult to think that he's the son of the man Jess called her father, but Brian was only an adoptive father so at least there's no shared blood there. Even so, we talked over coffee about how we might introduce Jess to life in Canada, and how her child should be explained. We decided the best thing was to not try to explain any of it, since John and I were on Jess's birth certificate as her parents, and Brian Hunter was on Howie's certificate as his father. Jess said nobody questioned him at the hospital as being the father, since his adoption of Jess was never official and their relationship was never made clear.

I wondered how John knew Brian and Robin, and whether his plan had always been to pass her along to them. I wondered if he sold her or gave her to them, and if he followed her as she grew up, watching her in some way. Now Jess knew what he looks like and she said she had no earlier recollection of him at all, so he probably never came to visit. I think maybe he stayed in touch with them for a while and then just moved on, as assholes do. Maybe he lost touch when they moved out to the house she's in now. If Brian and Robin were drug dealers, they probably didn't tell too many people their forwarding address.

We talked of when Jess would like to come to Canada, to restart her new life with us, flying to her true home like a swallow to Capistrano. Mom and I both wanted her to come right away, since there was nothing left in Florida to tie her down, but Jess asked to wait a while because she'd never been outside the state in wintertime. In Toronto, February is the coldest month of the year.

"I've heard Toronto's really chill," she said, "but it's also *really chill*, right?" We all had a little laugh at that. It's true. It was 10-below when we left and none of us were in a hurry to leave the warm weather.

She took another sip of coffee. It was quite weak, the coffee from her machine; we should have bought some over from a store.

"I'll have to buy all new clothes for up there!" she continued, but there was another option, too: maybe we should invest in a home in Florida for all of us to spend the winters, to split her time for better weather, at least while she sorts out citizenship for herself and Howie. I don't like Florida and its politics but the warmth is welcome and the idea does make a lot of sense. If Mom sold her place and moved into a smaller apartment, as she'd been thinking, or if she sold and she and I moved in to a rental together, that would free up a ton of money to buy a winter home for all four of us in Florida. We'd put it in Jess's name to make it easier with taxes, since Jess is the American citizen. Not Tampa, though – too many memories. Maybe Miami. Maybe the Keys.

We spent all afternoon thinking about the options, then we went out to an early dinner and kept talking about them. Sometimes, I was almost able to forget the worries that Mom put in my head about the DNA, but then something was said, or something was intimated, and it was like the moment juddered to a pause while I fought back another claw of suspicion: "Are private schools expensive in Canada?" asked Jess. "I really do need a new car." "Are there background checks for becoming a Canadian citizen?" It was foolish though. Perhaps the pills were over-compensating. I took a couple more after lunch, and again before dinner, and that was really too much. I'll need to hold back another couple in case I can't sleep later.

. . .

No, I didn't sleep well. Far too anxious, I guess, but I don't think you can blame me. I was thinking about John turning up at the house in Orient Park, so I decided to try to persuade Jess to move into the hotel with us. Mostly, though, I just wanted that independent DNA proof so we could all move on with this next wonderful stage of our lives.

Mom got back from the DNA clinic soon after 10 am. I was still upstairs in the hotel room and I'd asked her to phone me so we could meet downstairs in the lobby and then head out, but she didn't phone me. I was sitting on the bed, reading stuff on my phone, when I heard the door unlock and open.

Mom walked in. I smiled at her, a little annoyed because she didn't call to meet downstairs, but she just looked stern and walked straight over to me without even kicking off her shoes.

She handed me the piece of paper, which was folded from being placed in an envelope. I took the sheet, unfolded it and saw all kinds of bar charts and graphs, and beneath the letterhead of the clinic, there was an outlined graphic box and I read the bold-font words within it.

Sample 1 and Sample 2: Possibility of biological relationship - 99.99 per cent.

Thank God!

But there were more lines beneath it.

Sample 1 and Sample 3: Possibility of biological relationship - 0.00 per cent.

Sample 2 and Sample 3: Possibility of biological relationship - 0.00 per cent.

I looked up at Mom.

"I'm Sample 1, and you're Sample 2," she said. "That young woman is Sample 3."

Chapter 18

VIVIAN, Tampa

I don't think I was ever really fooled. I tried to be, tried really hard for Claire's sake, but it just never all clicked into place. My daughter so wanted to believe it was true. She needed to believe it was true. But it was not. It was a lie. Of course it was a lie.

If Claire wasn't already on the bed when she read the results, she would have collapsed. She looked up at me as if I'd just pointed a gun to her face, then she read and re-read and re-read again the paper, flipping it over, trying to make sense of it. It was very clear. Whoever Becky Hunter is, or whatever her name is, she's not related to us in any direct way at all, and she is most certainly not my grand-daughter.

Eventually, Claire slumped back against the pillow, then with her eyes tight shut, she screamed at the ceiling. So loud. So *primal*. It was horrible, just horrible. I felt as if I'd stabbed my own daughter through the heart. When she realized she was still holding the paper with the results of the testing, she shrieked and ripped it to pieces, throwing the shreds to the floor. Then she lay back and moaned, a deep guttural moan, covering her eyes with her hands.

I remember that moan. I've heard it only once before, when it came from my own mouth. It's the sound I made when they told me Patrick's body was found, washed up on the rocks of the bay in Nova Scotia. It was the moan of resignation that all hope was now lost. I could hear it then in my ears and it scared me, as if it was coming from someplace else, something in me hiding in a deep, dark place I'd never known was there. Claire stood with me when I collapsed onto the sand, just as I stood with her today as she lay on the bed. I tried to take her hands, to hold them and offer some comfort, but she slapped away my touch.

Eventually, I pulled the cover from my bed and spread it over her, then turned out the lights and drew the drapes. I sat for a long time on the room's single chair, beside my daughter on her bed, thinking through what must happen next. Please bear with me while I take her turn with this story. She needs time to rest.

. . .

"Hello, Jess? Sorry, Becky? This is Vivian. I don't think your mom and I should come over to see you today. Claire thinks she may have the Covid virus. Yes, she's running a temperature and she's short of breath. I'm going to get her tested, but until we're in the clear, I think we should isolate ourselves here at the hotel. It's for everybody's good. If she has it, then I probably have it already and we don't want to take any chances for anyone else.

"Yes, I'll call you as soon as I know anything. We're both going to rest up today. I'll call you soon. Love to Howie. Take care."

Chapter 19

JON, Tampa

Another day, another million bucks, *know what I mean?*

I did feel good about opening up to Grant about Jess's disappearance. He's going to see what he can come up with, just look at whatever he can with a fresh pair of eyes, a new perspective. I didn't feel good, though, that I still felt like shit, really drained, really short of breath. If it wasn't Covid, I didn't know what it was, so I gave in and called my doctor. For $400, he'd see me that morning, but when I said I might have Covid, the woman on the phone told me to wait in the car when I arrived and then put on a damn mask. It's too bad. He used to have a cute receptionist who could lift your spirits. More than just your spirits. Mind you, you don't want to be fighting down a stiffy while your doctor's examining you, so I guess it was all for the best.

My phone rang. The doctor's assistant asked me to come in. She told me to be sure to be wearing the mask. When I got to reception, I saw she wasn't the cutie at all but a kinda gruesome *fräulein* I'd never seen before. No worries about a stiffy now!

I never visited this doctor much. Doctor Patel, an Indian guy. This was maybe the second time I've ever seen him. He was our family doctor but it's Maria and Molly who use him, not me. Even so, I was on the books, so I headed where I was pointed into his office and he rose from his desk to come around and greet me with a firm handshake. He was wearing a paper mask too, which didn't hide that he's a bit older than me. That's all that matters with a doctor.

He pointed to a pair of easy chairs and invited me to take a seat.

"I took the tests and they showed I don't have Covid," I told him. "Why do I still have to wear this mask?"

"Just an abundance of caution," he said. "We'll take another test here but I've seen the list of symptoms you outlined to the nurse and that's why I have a concern. Have they changed at all in the last couple of days, your symptoms?"

"Not really. I'm still tired. I still get a bit short of breath. I should work out more. Otherwise, I'm okay."

I coughed, just a little cough into my mask against the back of my hand. Patel frowned.

"You have a cough?"

"No more than the usual. It's just a cough."

The doctor took a plastic thing from his desk. "May I?" he asked. It was a thermometer, one of those gun-like ones they point at your forehead. Before I could even answer, he leaned across and turned over my wrist, then aimed the thermometer at it and clicks the trigger.

"No fever," he said. "You probably don't have Covid-19." He didn't take off his mask. "Even so, I'll retest you – the results from the home tests are often inaccurate. And I'd like to take some blood too. We just want to see if there's anything else that might be going on we should know about."

"Anything else like what?"

"I really can't say without some testing. Probably, you're just a bit run down, for any number of reasons. But if there's a cause for concern, it's much better to find out early. Do you still smoke?"

"Yes."

"Since you were young?"

"Yes."

"We'd better do an X-Ray then. Again, no need for any concern, but we can do that next door right now and it's best to get it out of the way."

Before I could say anything else, he pressed a button on his desk phone and called in his nurse. It was the warden woman who pointed me in here. She looked even more fearsome than before, despite her mask, and while I sat there in the comfortable chair, listening to the doctor make small talk about his golf game and his sail boat, she checked my blood pressure then poked a needle in my arm and started filling a handful of vials with my blood. I watched it flow red into the small glass tubes and thought about inviting her to take a couple of extras, for her lunch, but reined myself in and stayed silent.

. . .

I wouldn't tell Maria about going to the doctor. I'd do it the same as the Covid test – I wouldn't say anything unless it came back bad. Patel said he'd call the next day. There was no point in her worrying and she does worry about health. Molly's never had any issues to concern us, but that didn't mean Maria doesn't get worried. I have good insurance through the dealership that I've topped up to make sure they get only the best treatment. Don't let yourself think the doctor didn't know this. Patel knew exactly how much he can get away with billing for each visit. That was the real reason for all the tests – he can bill the insurance company for every one of them.

Normally, by Monday lunchtime, I'd have called in at the wreckers already to say hello but I was avoiding the place. I hadn't been back since Saturday morning when Uncle Luis gave me the smack. He'll call when he needs me, but until then, I didn't need him. There was way too much happening with everything else, anyway.

I was going to go back into work and sit there and pretend to try to sell somebody a car, but I thought the doctor might be right. I was kinda run down. So instead, I drove out to the farm for a few hours of R&R. That used to mean "rough and rowdy" for me, but I'd take the rest and relaxation this time. I was back to driving my own truck for a while, so I stopped on the way out and picked up a new queen-size mattress for the trailer's bed. The old one hadn't seen much action in the last few years. It was too soft for me.

I hauled out the old mattress, carried in the new one, lay on it for a while and ended up sleeping for a couple of hours before I even put the sheets on. Then I sat outside in the easy chair with a book, a Stephen King I found at Cindy's place in Orlando, and swatted at bugs for a couple hours more.

I couldn't get into the book. I kept thinking about the visit from Claire and Vivian, and seeing the stripper and just wondering, could she be Jess? I didn't think so, and I hoped to God no, after she started on that blow job at the club, but Jess would surely look a lot like her if she was still alive. Probably not so tall, probably closer to Claire's height, but both of us held our weight well so she'd probably be slim.

If she'd have lived, if she'd never been taken from us, what would have happened?

Back then, I thought Claire was fixing to move back north and take Jess with her to Toronto. She kept talking about Canada like it was the Promised Land, but for me, it was just another country with too many liberals. She wanted me to go with her and really make a try of it, but I never planned to. I don't like snow for more than a day or two. And why should I have gone? To run away from what I have here? What I had here wasn't so bad, though it wasn't looking so great right now, working for an uncle who spied on me and treated me like shit.

If Claire wanted to move north with Jess, I'd have let her go. I could still visit there, and she could still visit down here. I wouldn't have to pay any support in a foreign country, but I'd have paid it anyway and I'd have been freed up to get on with my life. Claire was a good mom. Like a helicopter with Jess, always there hovering over her, but I never had to worry about them.

I used to tell Claire I loved her but I never did. Nothing against her – I really liked her and we had fun and the sex was great in the beginning, but that final click-into-place never quite clicked into place. Don't know why not, but it never did. Nobody's fault.

So Jess would have grown up a happy Canadian with Spring Break every year down here in Tampa, calling some other guy Dad and probably protesting for Black Lives Matter and against gun rights. That's okay. She'd have been her own person, making her own choices, just like Molly is learning to do.

Molly.

Would I be okay if Maria wants to move home to Cuba this year and take Molly with her? *Fuck no!* Have some Spanish guy take over as her dad? Protest in Havana against American imperialism? *No fucking way!*

So why the difference? I've known Molly now for four years, just as I knew Jess for four years, but Molly's age means she knows how to get to me. How to relate to me. She can communicate with me, and that helps me love her and respect her and appreciate her as a thinking, thoughtful person. It was the same for Maria – as soon as she cleaned up her English and could communicate properly with me, I was able to love her and appreciate her. I owe the same to Jess.

Maybe Molly's right. Maybe Jess isn't dead. None of us know for sure either way. I would never stop searching for Molly, so I can never stop searching for Jess.

Of course, I don't know where to even fucking start.

. . .

I was back in the truck, headed home, and I called Grant. The signal was so crappy at the farm it's not worth bothering, and I would always turn off the phone anyway so I can't be located, but I turned it back on when I got closer to the city and it showed five bars.

"Grant! How you doing?"

"Pretty good. I've been reading up all the old news stories about Jessica's disappearance. Those cops didn't like you, did they?"

No they didn't. It was tough to make the first move on this, to start telling Grant about the snatching, which meant I had to tell him about my family, but he listened well and it got easier. I told him everything I told you at the beginning of all this, so he's up to speed now. It felt okay. He's a good friend.

"Was there ever even a theory about how she just vaporized at the mall?" he asked. "Sorry – that's harsh. I mean, how she was taken?"

"That's okay, bud. It's been a long time for me to deal with all this. But no. I wasn't there and the cops could never explain it. All those cameras did fuck all for her. Literally, she looked up at one of them, smiled, and then vanished. Gone like a puff of smoke. It's the biggest mystery of all."

"I'm going to go to the mall tomorrow and take a look for myself."

"That's a good idea."

"Also, I want to go to the police tomorrow and see if they'll tell me anything. I have a friend on the force, not a detective but I'm sure he knows some people, and maybe somebody there will speak to me. Are you okay with that?"

No, I was *not* okay with that, but I didn't think I had that choice any more.

"Sure, but can you keep me out of it? Don't tell them you know me?"

"That won't be a problem, Jon. I'll just be a Hometown Homepage reporter looking to dig into a cold case. People love cold cases, and if somebody can help solve one, the cops are usually happy to help."

He seemed to be getting into this now and that was good, because I'd need all the help I can get if I was to keep my promise.

I drove the rest of the way in silence as the sun set off to the left, stopping on the way at the dealership to throw the old mattress into the dumpster out back. When I finally got home, I parked in front of the garage, locked the truck, and I was walking to the front door when a voice called out from behind.

"Excuse me! Jon?"

I turned, a little too quick. I was jumpy.

What the fuck is *she* doing here?

Chapter 20

VIVIAN, Tampa

John looked startled when he saw me back at his home. I'm sure he didn't expect me to return so soon, if ever, after shooting a gun into the air to shoo us away.

"I'm alone. It's just me," I told him. "I'm hoping you're a man of your word, and you're not going to shoot me."

"Why are you here?" he asked. "Why are you harassing me and my family? Did Floyd send you over?"

"Nobody sent me. I haven't seen Floyd in two days. Claire is at the hotel, sleeping. She doesn't know I'm here. But I want to tell you that we know we were wrong. We know that young woman is not Jessica. I want to apologize to you, and I want to perhaps put your mind at rest, too. I'm sorry. Both Claire and I are sorry."

None of this was easy for me to say to the man who hurt my daughter so deeply and who may have stolen my grandchild, but it needed to be said and at that moment he held all the cards. He didn't look to soften at all. He wasn't letting up. His hands were by his side. I wondered if he had the gun under his shirt.

"Why did you tell me she was Jess if you knew she wasn't? Why this change of heart?"

"We thought she was. She told us she was. Floyd Woods told us he'd found her. But we did our own DNA test and realized she was lying to us. She's a charlatan, and probably Woods is too. I thought you should know this."

"You thought so? Or Claire thought so?"

"Claire is under sedation at the hotel. She's taking this very badly. She had really thought Jessica was found, and she's crushed by this. There's no reason why you should be hurt too."

There were many reasons why he should be hurt and these words were like ashes in my mouth – he's a criminal, after all – but I bit my tongue and waited.

"Okay."

He was still on his guard, just looking at me. I needed to go all out.

"John, as Claire's mother, and as somebody who only ever knew of you through Claire, I want you to know that I think you've been treated very badly. There's a monster out there and Claire always thought it was you, but I think that's because she had to believe it was somebody tangible and she lashed out at the closest person to her, at least at the time. But I think she got it wrong. I'm sorry about that."

"Well, okay," said John. And then, "Would you like to tell that to my family?"

. . .

John opened the front door and gestured me inside. He called out – "Maria! Molly! Can you come meet our visitor?" – and the mother walked through from the back and the daughter appeared on the central staircase. It was a wide, well-lit, double-height hallway. My shoes slipped a little on the faux-marble floor and I could see myself in the mirrors to each side, clutching my purse like the Queen of England. This was one of those grand foyers for a grand entrance that suggests the rest of the house is also large and luxurious. Normally, I'd be unimpressed by such an ostentatious display, but I wasn't feeling in any mood to judge anybody.

The two young women were clearly surprised to see me, and they slowed to a more cautious walk when they realized who I am. Both were well-dressed in jeans and Ts and could almost be sisters, one trying to be older than her years and the other holding onto her youth. I was like both of them once. Neither said anything. Both looked at John.

"You met Vivian yesterday. We were just talking outside and I asked her to come in and speak with you. Vivian?"

Everyone looked at me, so to hell with it, and I started speaking.

I told them what I told John outside: that the woman who we thought was Jessica had deceived us and is somebody else, and that Floyd Woods was in on the deceit. I said that Claire is unwell at the hotel, but both she and I want to apologize for the upset we caused on Saturday. I said that Claire has never known who took Jess, but in her emotion, she thought it might have been John. And I said that we both knew now that this was obviously not true, and that we were very, very sorry.

"You deceived us too, coming here and claiming to be neighbours," said the mother.

"*Lo siento*," I said.

Maria tried to look serious, but failed at the absurd memory of not speaking English and spat a little laugh, between closed lips. She seemed a little tipsy, just a bit. She looked down and tried to cover her smile with her hand, but Molly called her out on it.

"Mom," she said – "you're hopeless at being Cuban!"

"Well, I guess that breaks the ice," said John. "Vivian, can I put some in a drink for you? Or some olives?"

. . .

In the sitting room off the hallway, which was just as airy and well-appointed as the entrance suggested, John brought me a martini and Maria and Molly started peppering me with questions about Jess. I didn't want to stay long because I really wasn't comfortable and I was worried for Claire back at the hotel, but Molly never knew she had a sister and she wanted to know if I think Jess might still be alive. She'd told John to look for her, and John said he had a friend who is an investigative reporter who'll try to reopen the case. It's because we came over on Saturday. Maybe there'll be some good from that visit after all. If he did take Jess then he was very good at denying it, though I suppose he would be after all these years.

I knew I should leave, but I told them the story Becky Hunter told us, of being adopted by Brian and Robbie, and of mothering Brian's child. I didn't mention her working as an exotic dancer, or that John said he had met her last year. These two women didn't need to hear that from me.

For all I knew, Becky's account was actually true. It was Floyd who connected her to us. And she said she couldn't remember any of the During time, if such a thing ever happened. Claire, in her anger, had taken it on herself to say that Becky knew more than she did.

"But Brian and Robbie are now dead," said John. "That's convenient. Do you believe they even existed?"

"I don't know. There was a photograph of them on Becky's fridge, but that could have been a picture of anyone, downloaded from Google."

"Well, none of this helps us find Jess."

"No, it doesn't. I'm sorry, but I really must be going. I'm concerned for Claire."

"I heard Canadians are always apologizing," said Maria, "but I think you've apologized enough for one evening. Please, let's just move on."

"You're parked on the road?" asked John. "I'll walk you to your car."

I told him that wouldn't be necessary but he insisted. When we got to the car, parked under a streetlight near John's gate, he opened the driver's door for me, and then asked if he could sit with me for a moment inside. There's something else, he said.

John got into the passenger seat and let the car's inside light fade to darkness. My heart was in my mouth. I was alone in a dark car with the man my daughter believed to be a monster, and yet, he didn't seem so monstrous. He seemed, well, *normal*.

"Vivian, I think I know who Becky Hunter really is," he said. "Thank you for not mentioning what I said in the driveway, but I met her a few months ago at a strip joint. Long story short, I took a photo back then of her car. I've traced her licence plate to a house north of here. She's a Business student at college in the city, and her name is Andrea Jackson. Her real dad is a guy named Tyler, and he's got some kind of mental handicap, real serious. She was living with him and her grandfather, too. That whole story about Brian and Robbie has got to be bullshit."

Really? John and the investigative reporter must have been onto this already.

"If it helps," I said, "I can give you her address and phone number in Orient Park. Floyd's phone number too, if you like, though I don't know where he lives."

"Sure. This was all pretty elaborate. Those two put a lot of thought into this. I've got to ask – are you a wealthy woman?"

"I'm comfortable, yes. Probably not like you, but I do have investments."

I was surprised at how easily I told him that. The man was a charmer, that's for certain.

"Floyd would know that. He'd have an idea of it, anyway. There's not much that stays hidden from detectives, especially when they're retired on a crappy pension with time on their hands."

I was thinking of how we'd talked about buying a winter house down here, and how Becky had suggested it be put in her name. To avoid foreign taxes, she said. How would she even know about foreign taxes?

"And I'd like your phone number too, Vivian. I'd like to stay in touch."

I thought we'd have more to gain than to lose with this, and as I said before, John held all the cards now, so we swapped numbers and he put mine into his phone. I started the engine, but he wasn't moving out of the passenger seat just yet.

"Vivian, can I ask something else?"

Okay.

"Why did Claire hate me so much? And why was she so convinced I would steal away our little girl and harm her? I just don't understand that at all. I thought she knew I'm nothing like my brother, or my dad. In all our time together, I never did anything, or said anything, to make her think I was."

How to put this carefully? We were past that stage now. Long past. It was dark in the car but I could see him searching my eyes when he asked the question, and I was thinking that maybe he really was a man who'd been misjudged.

"Claire didn't hate you until Jess was taken. But your alibi was that you were with another woman. And that night, you left her alone until late. Her imagination ran wild. Something switched in her. What else could she think? She thought you'd taken Jess, because of your family's history, which she'd always tried to deny. Because the police always said Jess must have been taken by somebody she knew, to slip away so easily. And because she thought that when she was alone that night, you'd been with Jess, wherever it was you would have taken her."

"But you don't believe this now."

This is tricky.

"I don't know what to believe, John. But no, I don't believe you snatched away your own daughter. I don't believe you killed her, or that you sold her on to somebody, as Claire thinks. I don't believe that now."

In truth, it's not so much that I don't believe it, as much as I don't *want* to believe it. Right then, with him sat beside me in a parked car in the darkness in an unfamiliar neighbourhood in a foreign country, I didn't see that I had a choice.

"Vivian, my mistake was that I didn't trust the police, and then I trusted them too much. That evening, when I thought Claire was asleep, I went over to my uncle's place because I thought he was involved and could help. That same week, somebody had threatened him and his family, a real serious threat, and his only family was me, and Claire and Jessica. We thought that person took Jess as a ransom thing, or a punishment. We never thought it was a sex thing. My uncle is a wealthy man with plenty of people envious of his success, who would do him harm if they could, and we had to deal with that. I told Claire I was with Luis but she didn't believe me."

"You should never have left her alone."

"No, I shouldn't. When Luis and me came up with nothing and the cops took me in to question, we realized this had to be a sex thing after all. That's when I trusted the police to find the guy. I left them to do their job. There wasn't much else I could do. They'd found my dad, and my brother. I thought they'd rule me out and then they'd find Jess, alive or dead. But they didn't. They weren't good enough. Floyd Woods wasn't good enough."

"You know, Floyd told us last year he'd found that woman Kim, and she said she was never with you that morning. She said nobody knew where you were for at least three hours when Jessica was taken."

John looked genuinely shocked. If he was faking that reaction, he deserved an Oscar.

"*What*? I *was* with Kim! I'm not proud of it, but I was. Why would she say I wasn't?"

"Floyd said you blackmailed her into it, to cover yourself."

John sank into the seat and looked forward through the windshield, but I didn't think he was looking at anything at all. I wasn't scared any more that he was there beside me. I remembered how Floyd told us he was watching John, and had people watching John, to make sure Jess would be safe in her little house, and I realized then that must have been a lie. There was never a need to watch John. I'm sure Floyd never even stayed over on the couch that night. I thought about mentioning that but decided against it. John had too much else to worry about.

He paused a long time before he spoke again, still looking ahead.

"Vivian, I can't prove to you one way or the other that Kim was lying to Floyd, if he even found her to speak with him. I think she's in California now. But I promise you, on Maria's life and Molly's life, that *I'm* not lying to you. I was with Kim when Jess was taken and I was with Luis that night until I came home. I did not take Jess from the mall, and I don't know who did. I've promised Molly that I'm going to work to find her, and I'll make you that same promise too."

Now he turned to look at me.

"If Floyd is capable of telling you all this, then he's a very dangerous man. He's an ex-cop – they're the worst, because they've got reasons to hate people and they've got friends who feel the same way. If Floyd thinks you're onto him now, you've got a lot to lose. He can't just walk away from this. He's in too deep. Please, take Claire and get home to Canada, as soon as you can. Leave this to me. Let me handle it."

Now he was frightening me.

Okay.

I started the engine and he got out, walked around the front of the car, and then tapped on my window. I slid it down, scared again. Not so much by him anymore, but by everything.

"Vivian, go home. Look after yourself, and look after Claire. She deserves better than all this."

I pulled out and drove away down the quiet road. Just beyond the next streetlight, there was another car parked in the shadow. I could see through its dark glass that there was somebody in the driver's seat, just sitting there, and as I passed, they turned their head from me so I couldn't make out their face.

Maybe Floyd already knew I was there. Maybe it's *me* he was watching. I drove more quickly back to the hotel, my stomach in a knot and the taste of fear on my tongue.

BIRD ON A WIRE

Chapter 21

JON, Tampa

This is what Grant told me he did this morning, after I told him about meeting with Vivian last night:

First, he drove out to Orient Park to take a look at the house where Andrea Jackson is staying. There was a Chevy in the driveway with a different license plate from the Hyundai I saw at the club, so he took a photo of it to trace the ownership. He didn't see anyone at home.

Next, he went to the Tampa PD station downtown. He has a friend on the force, a patrolman, and that guy gave him a recommendation to speak with someone in the cops' PR department.

"They were happy to talk with me," said Grant. "They introduced me to the head of their cold case squad. She wanted to know why I had an interest in this story and I told her it had just always haunted me – that picture of Jessica in the papers, looking up at the camera and smiling. I said I used to shop at the Fairfield Mall all the time, which is true. I said I have some time on my hands right now for developing content. She said she'd check into what evidence I'm allowed to see, and I can come back later and look at it."

It's not easy for him to trace a license plate, so I did that through the account at the wreckers. I can't just sign in from home, though. Luis doesn't allow that. Everything, legit or not-so-legit, is on an internal intranet account and doesn't leave the building. I could probably get away with it from outside if I knew the password that's built into the desktops at the yard, but I don't.

So I had to drive over to the wreckers and sign in from there, and of course, Luis's Benz was parked in its usual place under the sun canopy at the back.

Normally, I'd go in to see my uncle, my much-beloved and trusted uncle, and I'd tell him all about this scam of Floyd's, and we'd figure out how to deal with it. Pretty straightforward. But I don't trust Luis as much as I did last week, and he sure as shit isn't much-beloved with me right now.

I walked in the side door, straight into the chop bay, and there was Luis, talking with Domingo. They both looked over when I entered, then went back to their conversation. I wasn't going to stand there waiting for them, so just gave a nod and headed toward the offices.

"Hey Jon – wait up!"

That was Uncle Luis. I stopped, and I waited.

He finished the conversation quickly, then walked up to me and took my hand.

"Here, come with me," he said.

We walked together to his office, hand-in-hand in his Puerto Rican way. Once I was inside, he turned and shut the door.

"Sit down," he said. I sat down.

He sat at his desk and lit a cigarette, so I lit a cigarette for myself. Neither of us spoke while we took those first drags, enjoying the taste of the tobacco, savoring the feel of the warm smoke in our lungs. I was waiting him out.

"Jon, maybe I shouldn't have smacked you the other day. You're family. You shouldn't get smacked."

"Okay."

He wasn't going to apologize, but he was acknowledging it. This was as much as I could expect.

"Thing is, this whole Covid thing has me thinking about priorities, and I'm thinking I want to take it a little easier. Not work so hard, you know?"

"Okay."

"If I don't work so hard, it means somebody else has to work a little harder. Somebody I can trust. Family. And I need to know if I can trust you to make smart decisions. Can I do that?"

Is he saying what I think he's saying?

"Sure. What about Gary?"

"Gary does what he's fucking told. He's not blood."

"Okay."

"This is why I had somebody keep an eye on you. There was nothing wrong, no reason to doubt you at all, but I just had to know for certain. Being *careful*. Gary was more suspicious than me, but he's probably just jealous. He knows you're family."

If this was supposed to make me feel better, it wasn't helping.

"Jon, is everything alright? You seem a bit – *different,* these days."

"It's fine. I've just been tired. I went to the doctor yesterday for a checkup and he said I was good, just a little run down. Long days. So I went to bed early and I'm feeling better already."

He probably knew I was at the doctor, probably had somebody follow me there. Maybe that's what this was really about. Better to volunteer the information first than have him grill me on it, *know what I mean?*

"Everything else okay, Jon?"

Why was he asking? What did he know? Did somebody see the meeting in the driveway on Saturday? Did somebody hear the gunshot? Did somebody see Vivian come over last night?

If we were a normal family, I'd open up and tell him about Floyd Woods and the stripper leaning on me and my old girlfriend – them making up a story against us about my abducted daughter, trying to extort money from anyone with a guilty conscience. He would assure me that he'd use his considerable resources to help in any way he can. He'd pull the spy off my ass and put it on those two. That would end my problems overnight, thank you, Uncle. I'd slide into his chair to assume my rightful role in his empire. Gary would start taking his orders from me.

That's if we were a normal family, and we're pretty fucking far from being a normal family. I just didn't know how much of this was a fishing expedition, so I wasn't taking any bait.

"Everything's fine."

He looked at me for what seemed a long time before he spoke again.

"Well, that's good. I have another run for you tonight, just up to Jacksonville. You okay with that?"

I guess I was. I always am, right?

. . .

Before I left, I ran the Chevy's license plate through the FDOT computer in the main office. It came back as registered to a numbered company, with a post office box address in Ocala. I wrote the numbers on a scrap of paper, not too big in case I have to eat it after rhyming the numbers off to Grant – *yeah, that's going to happen* – then drove a few blocks to a Micky D's and called him from the parking lot on the encrypted work phone.

"The car's owned by a numbered company," I told him.

"Of course it is," he said. "Do you have those numbers?"

I did and I started reciting them to him. Near the end, he took over and recited the last few numbers back to me.

"It's the same company that owns the house in Orient Park, which was bought two years ago," he says. "I already checked it out at City Records. And guess who the president is? Your friend and mine…"

"Floyd Woods."

"*Ka-ching*! You win – a new car! Check under your seat now."

"So why'd he move Andrea into his house and give her his car?"

"So she could pull off this whole Becky Hunter thing, I expect. It's a home base for her to be convincing, where nothing's registered to her real name."

"Do you know where Floyd is?"

"No – I can't find an address anywhere, except for this PO box in Ocala, which probably means nothing."

"You think they know we're onto them?"

"I don't know. Depends how convincing Vivian is with the claiming-to-have-Covid thing. But I think I should go up to New Port Richey tonight and just take a look at the house there for myself. Want to come?"

I couldn't that day, if I was driving up to Jacksonville that night. I told him, maybe tomorrow.

"Sounds good. Tomorrow then. I haven't heard back from the cops yet, to look at the evidence file, but I'm sure I will soon. It's all on now, Jon!"

. . .

Since I was already at McDonald's, I ordered a Big Mac meal and sat in the truck to eat it, so I could have a smoke too. Just as I bit into the burger, my phone buzzed. It was the doctor.

"Jon, this is Doctor Patel. How are you?"

"I think I'm fine, but aren't you supposed to tell me that?"

Always a smart ass, they say.

"Ha! We have the results of your tests. Can you come in so I can go over them with you?"

"Can't you just tell me over the phone?"

"No, we never like to do that. It can be confusing, and we also like to ensure confidentiality. You can never be certain if somebody else might be listening in, these days."

Sounded plausible, but I knew the real reason: if I'm there in person, he can bill for a personal consultation.

"Sure – when are you thinking of?"

"Are you free this afternoon? How about two o'clock?"

That was just an hour from then, but sure, I told him. Two's just fine.

. . .

It was still the gruesome *fräulein* doing guard-tower duty at Patel's office, but she didn't make me wait in the car or wear a mask, and she pointed me in to where he was seated behind his desk. He wasn't wearing his mask, either.

"Jon, hello," he said. "The follow-up tests confirmed you don't have Covid."

"Well, that's great. Thanks!" He brought me all the way in here just to tell me this? Fucking doctors.

"Any change in your symptoms?"

"No. I think you're right that I'm a bit run down. There's been a lot going on recently."

"It's more than that, I'm afraid," said the doctor.

Uh-oh.

BIRD ON A WIRE

Chapter 22

VIVIAN, Tampa

It was a simple decision to go home. Florida is usually nice to visit in February, but it has its share of shadows and demons too. The thought of being watched by Floyd, and why he'd do so, was too much to bear. Long before I reached the hotel, my mind was made up to get Claire back to Canada just as soon as possible.

She was awake when I stepped into the room, watching a television show with the lights out, a rerun of *Everybody Loves Raymond*, but not really watching it. Just laying in bed with the TV on for company. She didn't ask where I've been. I wasn't sure she really knew where she was. Her own prescriptions didn't seem to make a difference, so I'd given her some of my Valium to help soothe her nerves and it was acting like a sedative. She'd hardly spoken, hardly eaten, since I showed her those test results.

I told her I think we should go home, kept it light as if we were just a little weary from a day of shopping, and she didn't respond. I took that as approval and opened up the Air Canada app on my iPad, then bought two tickets for the noon flight the next day, Tuesday. *Done,* less than 10 minutes from walking in. I didn't even bother trying to change the tickets we already had for the return flight on the weekend. Maybe I'd get a refund when we're back in Toronto, if I remembered.

It was a restless night for both of us. I took a Valium as well to help me sleep, to just keep me under, and I managed four hours before waking in the dark. I could hear soft moans coming from Claire in the bed alongside.

"My love, it's okay," I said, still resting my head on the pillow, but she didn't seem to notice. After a while, the moaning ended and I could hear her breathing, steady, safe. I thought about getting into bed with her to hold her and make sure she knows she's secure, but I fell asleep again.

Then I woke with the first sunlight and packed for both of us. There was a half-finished baby sock that Claire had been knitting, and I cleared the yellow wool from the needles and carried it out to the garbage near the ice machine so she wouldn't see it. It was all I could do to wake Claire and dress her; she was like an automaton, barely conscious.

Before leaving, around nine, I called Becky or Andrea or whoever she is. I was relieved to just get her voice mail. I tried to sound as upbeat on the phone as I could.

"Hi, it's Vivian. Bad news – Claire tested positive for Covid. I'm going to take her home to Canada right now. We don't have good health insurance for the virus here in Florida and I want her safe and near a hospital just as fast as possible. I'm hoping they let us on the flight. I'll call you this evening. Take care!"

And yes, of course they let her on the flight. I let them know Claire was just a bit hung over from last night's leaving party. I'd become as deceptive as everyone else. She was in the window seat beside me, half asleep, hiding behind her mask, and we taxied out to the runway and should be safe in Canada by the afternoon.

How ironic. They thought it was great that we'd been at a party. It doesn't matter. I think it will be a long while before either of us goes anywhere.

Chapter 23

JON, Tampa

Driving up to Jacksonville last night gave me plenty of time to think about the conversation with Doctor Patel.

He showed me the X-Ray of my lungs and he pointed to the pale patches. He showed me the numbers from my blood tests and he tried to translate them into English. He did a lot of talking, a lot of looking sympathetic. He never mentioned golf or his stupid sail boat. All I remember is: lung cancer.

I have to go back this afternoon for the next check, a tube down my throat and into my lungs. He wants a proper look in there and to remove some tissue for more testing. I'm not allowed to eat anything or drink anything before it, which is too bad because I'd really like a coffee right now. When I got back in last night, I poured myself a scotch – *what does it matter?* – and just carried on thinking about all the things Patel said, and they always came back to the same two words: lung cancer.

He didn't know the state of it, but it's bad. Apparently, it's not usually so obvious in an X-Ray but mine was like a big flashing warning sign. Small cell carcinoma, he called it. Patel said the poking with the tube would answer everything and then they'd know what to do next. "We'll have a better idea of how much time we have," he said. This is a pretty fucking big bullet coming right at me that it's too late to dodge. Fuck – it's already inside me. *Fuck!*

So I spent the whole drive and the rest of the night thinking about my life, and what I've done and what I still want to do and wondering if I'll get to do any of it. There I was, worried about Covid, worried about people following me, and all this time the real killer was right inside me, getting comfortable, spreading slowly and steadily through my lungs and my blood and everywhere else it could crawl into and find a quiet little home.

I should have quit smoking back when Claire tried to get me to stop. Patel said this is probably because of the pack-a-day cigarettes. I'm not supposed to smoke in a shop car but fuck that, and I worked through almost two packs on that seven-hour Jacksonville run, lighting the next one from the still-smoldering butt of the last one. It doesn't matter how much I smoke now. Might as well enjoy it while I can.

I won't tell anybody until I have to. Maria worries too easy and Molly's too young for crap like this. I'll wait till Patel knows more, and then we'll see. Maybe it's not so bad – he said he couldn't confirm anything with just the X-Ray and the blood. I don't know what this tube exam will show, but I know I'm not going to end up bald in hospital, shitting into a bag and gasping for breath through a hole in my throat. That's just not going to happen.

So there's a few things to be done while I still can, and finding Jess, alive or dead, is at the top of the list. Right under it is nailing that stripper and that fat fucking detective, Floyd Woods, which is why I was driving up to New Port Richey with Grant. He was chatting away in the passenger seat but I wasn't listening to what he said. I could only hear two words: lung cancer.

. . .

We parked at the corner of Connecticut and Sycamore and walked the half-block to Number 176. It was cooler that morning than it'd been recently, and it looked like it might rain, but even so, Tyler was sitting outside on the porch just as he was last time, his legs covered with a red tartan blanket.

Me and Grant walked straight up onto the porch. There were some white plastic chairs and we made ourselves comfortable. Tyler looked at us without saying anything, his head tipping from one side to the next. His arms and hands started waving slowly in small circles in the air.

"How you doing, Tyler?" I said. He didn't reply, just tipped his head around some more.

I called out toward the door, loudly this time: "Hey – anyone inside?"

"Just a moment," called back a woman's voice.

And sure enough, in just a moment, the screen door opened and out walked Andrea Becky Cherie Jessica. Her long red hair was pulled up into a tight bun and she was wearing sweatpants and a T-shirt with no make-up. She looked good for it too. When she saw us sitting with her dad, she froze. For a second there, I thought she was going to run, but then she slumped and just stood at the door, wordless.

"Hi Andrea," I said. "We've gotta stop meeting like this."

Always the smart ass.

She clearly didn't know what to say, so I said it for her.

"Andrea, this is Grant. He's a journalist. I thought he might be interested to meet you. I'm sure there's a story here, don't you think so?"

"Hi Andrea," said Grant, and gave her a little wave.

She was still silent, so back to me.

"It wasn't difficult to find you. Are you moving back here now, or were you going to stay at Floyd's house a while longer? I guess you don't need to now, right? Claire and Vivian are back in Canada and you can take a break from that whole Brian and Robbie storyline crap."

"Get the fuck off my fucking porch," said Andrea.

"Now that's not very charitable. We're just getting to know your dad here. You think I should phone Vivian and Claire to let them know we're here? We're friends again, you know. United against you."

Andrea leaned back toward the screen door and hollered inside.

"Grandpa! Get out here now!"

"Coming!" called a voice from inside, and soon after, as we were all just staring at each other, Wes Jackson came to the door, holding his cane.

"Andrea, what is it?" he said, and then looked at me and Grant. "Hey – you're the new neighbor."

"He's not a neighbor," said Andrea. "This is John Morgan. This other guy is a reporter."

Wes's face, friendly and welcoming, froze over as he took in the situation. I could almost see his jaw clench.

"Then get the fuck off my porch," he said. "Both you assholes. I know my rights. You're trespassing. Don't make me get my gun."

"Do you know Andrea's rights too?" I said, not moving from the chair. "Her right to go to prison for fraud and extortion and impersonation? There's probably 50 charges the cops could lay right now. She pretended to be my dead daughter. I have home security video of her doing it. That'll look good on YouTube, won't it? Do you know who your grand-daughter really is?"

"Of course I do, you two-bit cracker punk," said Wes. *Ouch!* "I know who you are too, and who your goddamn family is. You're a piece-of-shit sidekick to Luis Lopez, and you're a Morgan. I heard your daddy screamed when they fried him. Knocked out the power to the prison with all those volts. Carl was still screaming when his face melted. Wasn't so brave with other men as he was with your sister, right?"

How the hell does he know all this?

"And the same's going to happen to your piece-of-shit brother, and you know what? I'm going to watch it when it does. I'm going to spend my last dime on a limo ride up to Raiford so I can sit in that room with what's left of the Cooper family, and I can watch Mike Morgan fry. I'll smell his hair burn and see his blisters explode. I hope it's gonna be a real long time he's strapped in that chair. I want to savor every second."

What the fuck? Who is this guy?

I wasn't expecting this, and I didn't know what to say.

"You can't watch something like that," I told him, lame. "They don't let you in unless you're a victim."

And in the corner of my eye, I saw Tyler sitting there in his chair. He was waving his arms more quickly now, and he'd pushed the blanket from his lap. He was looking at me as his head knocked around and he was hissing – *hissing!* – through his teeth. Something clicked in my head.

"Grandpa, you're upsetting Daddy," said Andrea.

Wes took a step back, literally, and regathered himself.

"We're all victims of Mike Morgan," he said. "Tyler might be the one he attacked, but all of us live with it, every day."

. . .

It was Grant who intervened and settled us all down. The story came out there on the porch, Wes leaning against his cane as he spoke, and Andrea hunched down beside Tyler, holding his hand to calm him.

When Tyler went in to arrest Mike, more than 20 years ago, he was the first patrolman through the front door and he was the cop that Mike hit in the head with a baseball bat, crumpling him to the ground. The three other cops came in guns blazing but Mike had Tyler's service revolver by then and held them back, shooting into their bulletproof vests. It gave him enough time to get his own shotgun from someplace else in the room and he used it to blow Tyler's feet clear off at the ankles.

JON - Tampa

That was the last time, Wes told us, that a Tampa arrest team ever came in through only one doorway. They were supposed to come in through the back and the windows, too, but somebody was lazy and it was late at night and they didn't expect Mike to be crazed on pills and ready to fight back. So when Tyler was lying on the ground behind the sofa, where Mike was holding off the patrolmen, Mike got to stomp him in the head, over and over while shooting back at the cops. Blinded him in one eye. Clear kicked his jaw right off before they got across the room and took him down.

Those cops gave Mike as good as Tyler got, but like Tyler, he survived. My brother got his health care paid by the state so he'll look good when they execute him.

"Your brother's an ugly man in so many ways, but he's still alive and my tax dollars are feeding him three meals a day," said Wes. "Most everything about my son died that night and there's no insurance left to take care of what we still have. So I've got no problem making his white-trash brother pay us what we're due."

Wes had been a desk sergeant and his best buddy was Floyd Woods. When Floyd told him over beer late last year that Mike's brother's old girlfriend was looking for her lost daughter, who was just three years younger than his granddaughter Andrea, and who had the same color hair and eyes, they figured out a way to make some money off it. They thought Claire would be good for buying a house in Florida for her daughter, and when she went back to Canada, Andrea would sell the house, pocket the money and disappear. If there was some way to hurt me too, that'd be gravy, but I live down here and I know people so they'd better be cautious, as they found out this morning.

"Andrea, Claire doesn't have Covid," I told her. "She and Vivian are on to you, so they've gone home to Canada just to get away from you. It's me in charge now. We know who you are and where you live. You need to be very careful what you do next."

Grant, always the mediator, stood and suggested we leave.

"Both of us have places to be," he said, "but we'll be back."

"Don't bother," said Wes. "You can just go straight to hell with the rest of the Morgans, and stay there and rot."

In the car, it was Grant who spoke first.

"You know, don't take this the wrong way, but I can kinda see where they're coming from."

So could I. For them, I'm just a name in a newspaper, and the name is Morgan. Maybe that's what I really have to do with the time that's left me. I've got to find Jess, alive or dead, and I've got to prove that I'm not my brother, and I'm not my dad. I'm Jonathan Morgan, and this apple fell a mile from that tree.

Chapter 24

CLAIRE, Toronto

I don't remember much about that flight home, but I do remember stepping out of the terminal with Mom and into the bite of the winter air, and feeling my breath freeze in my lungs when I gasped at the cold. It was only a moment before we got into the Uber, but it was enough. Twenty below, said the driver. Coldest day of the year.

The cold reminded us we were in another country: we were back home where we belong.

It's not a pretty winter wonderland in Toronto in February. The city's not a ski resort with manicured white snow and horse-drawn sleigh rides. It's millions of people trying to stay warm, with oily, frozen sludge at the sides of the streets and chill drafts finding their way through every crack.

When the Uber pulled off the expressway and waited at the lights to crawl its way into the city, I saw a woman walk down the line of cars holding a cardboard sign. "Homeless and Helpless. God Bless," it said. She was heavily wrapped against the cold and she wore pink gloves. When she passed our car, she looked in and tried to catch our glance, but then looked away again and continued walking. I could only see her eyes, which were green eyes, deep set with no make-up. Her face was hidden by a dark blue scarf, her head covered in a pink hat and her parka's hood. She walked slowly and looked very cold. She looked very alone.

Across the junction, at every road coming to this four-way, there was somebody out walking each line of cars, all of us meeting here.

Everyone was wrapped up and it was already dark before six o'clock. We got to Mom's and she bustled about, turning up the heat and making a bed for me, and I just wanted to sleep. Maybe it was the Ambien, maybe it was the early darkness, but when my eyes were open I could see only a place without Jess. When my eyes were closed, I saw Jess, far away, trying to call for me, her voice muffled as if she's masked in a scarf, walking in the cold past lines of cars, their drivers all looking away, shunning her world.

. . .

I stayed three days, maybe four, with Mom. The weather stayed cold, no better than 10 below. We hunkered inside and I watched TV and slept. That's all I really wanted to do.

Yesterday, though, I think it was Saturday, I told Mom I wanted to go home to my own place. It's her constant optimism that was getting to me, her constant "it'll all be okay," and "when this is over" blather. This won't be over anytime soon.

"I spoke to John," she told me yesterday. "He thinks we shouldn't press any charges against Andrea Jackson. He spoke to his lawyer and he said we have no evidence against her. When she was pretending to be Jess, we didn't record any of those conversations, so it's our word against hers. When we went to John's house, she didn't even speak. And in the end, we didn't give her any money. She didn't take anything from us."

She took everything.

Whatever.

"He said he's not going to press any charges against us, either. I think I showed him that we meant no harm, and we were deceived."

I meant every harm in the world.

But sure, whatever.

"He also said Floyd Woods is nowhere to be found."

Disappeared. Laying low. Maybe he was dead. Death by misadventure. Death by suicide. Dead, like Jess.

It really didn't matter. All those people were a long way away, stuck in their endless summer. Stuck in their fake news, fake smile, Disney world. Stuck, like Jess.

So I told Mom I wanted to go back to my own place. She didn't argue too much. I'd made a point of getting up, getting dressed. I looked as perky as I could. I told her I felt better for cutting back on the Effexor and the Ambien, which was a lie because I'm on about triple the dosage, and I told her that just a few Valium would be enough for me. I promised her that I'd go see my therapist and get myself sorted out properly.

"Okay, my love," she said. "This cold weather is making us all a bit stir-crazy. Just promise me you'll call every morning and every evening until this is done."

Of course, I promised her. Phone calls are easy. She packed me a bag of groceries and some basics and I took a cab back home. The sun hadn't yet set when I arrived, but I walked in, drew the curtains, put the groceries away and went to bed. Maybe, when I wake up, this will all be over. If I wake up.

. . .

But it's not over, of course. It's another fucking day, a wasted day, a cold Sunday in hell.

It's more than that, too. It's a public holiday weekend here in Toronto: "Family Day," for families to get together and spend time together.

Where's my family? It's only Mom, and we were together non-stop for a week. I called her when I woke this morning to get it over with, and she went on about everything we've been through and she asked me to come back to her house, but I told her I was fine and I was staying put.

It's also Jess. We all know how that's been.

And I guess it's John, because he's the father of my child, but I could not care less about that asshole. He's got himself his own family now anyway, and he's welcome to them.

Is that enough? No, there's more, just to lay it all on. *Give it to me, you fucker!* Today is February 14, Valentine's Day. My Facebook and my Instagram is nothing but red roses and *love love love*. You know what I'd love? For everyone to just fuck off. Everyone.

Even you.

But it's not that easy. Everyone doesn't just fuck off. Life goes on, though it shouldn't have to. Life ticks by, and Mom makes tea, and John makes love to his trophy wife, and Andrea Jackson makes cookies or whatever she does, and the patients in my ward at the hospital get better or get worse and get discharged or die and nothing ever changes. Jess still calls to me. Jess still walks that line of cars, looking in from the cold, through the sealed, darkened glass, walking on, searching for me.

. . .

BIRD ON A WIRE

Mom said I needed a project; I couldn't bring myself to start any knitting, so I'm going to make some soup for lunch. There was a bag of carrots in the groceries she gave me, so I'm going to make some carrot soup, from scratch. I'm not hungry but I can manage that. I've got some butter, some vegetable broth, a couple of onions, some garlic.

At least there's finally some sunshine today. Still cold, but there's fresh snow on the ground and in the trees. I can look out at it through the window in my kitchen, three floors above the building's front door, near the tops of the trees on the lawn. I'm chopping the garlic when I see a cardinal fly to one of the topmost branches. He stands out with his bright red feathers, red as roses, red as blood, against the green of the tree's needles and the white of the snow.

He's the most beautiful bird. His crest is up and he starts to sing, *cheer cheer cheer!* My window is open, just a crack, and I can hear his song. How can I be sad when there's such beauty? I swear, he's looking straight at me, his black eyes meeting mine, and now he's trilling, just for me.

Beyond him, down on the ground, a grey shape bundled in a parka hustles along the sidewalk and turns onto the pathway to the building's front door. Pink gloves. At the last moment, she hears the bird's song and looks up, looks toward the cardinal, looks toward me, pauses for just a heartbeat.

Jess! It's Jess!

She looks down, enters the building. The bird flies off to settle on another tree out of sight.

It wasn't Jess. I know this. It's just my mind, wanting to believe there's hope.

I push the garlic to one side, gather it up, drop it in the broth that's simmering on the stove. I start chopping carrots, very fine, but my mind is elsewhere and the knife slices into my finger. Just a little slice. It doesn't even hurt, and I watch the blood drip slowly onto the cutting board, onto the cut-up carrots.

Who did I used to be? His *cutie carrot*? Daddy would have loved to see that cardinal just now, hear his song.

"Only the male cardinals have the red feathers," he'd say. "They want to look handsome for their partners."

For Valentine's Day.

There's more blood dripping on the cutting board but the Band-Aids are in the bathroom. I'm about to go get them when the cardinal returns, back to the same branch on the same tree. Again, he looks at me and again, he trills.

Cheer cheer cheer!

I pull a Kleenex from a box on the kitchen counter and wrap it around my finger to staunch the blood. The white tissue slowly turns red, red as roses. The cardinal sings again, and as I'm watching, a man below walks toward the door. He's lightly dressed in shorts and sandals. There's no snow. He looks up at me. He smiles.

Daddy!

Claire! Come join me! Let's go look for shells.

I put down the knife and walk out to the corridor to find Daddy. Where would he be looking for shells? The back garden? The sea?

I walk down the stairs, three flights to the ground.

He's standing at the open door to the pool, off the lobby.

Daddy!

I can hear the cardinal, but there are other birds gathering now, beginning to drown out the song.

Claire – I missed you! Why did you let me go?

I didn't let you go, Daddy. I've always been here.

But you left me, like you left Jess.

I didn't mean to, Daddy! I didn't want to!

It's okay, Claire. Come, bring me some shells. Some beautiful shells. They're under the water. Collect them all.

Yes, let me bring you some shells.

Now bring them to me. Bring them to Jess. We're here for you.

I don't feel the bite of the cold water; I don't feel anything at all. On the second step, the water laps against my feet, then a step farther, against my knees. When I move off the final step, it comes to my hips and I keep walking forward. I trail my fingers against the surface of the water and the tissue floats off and the blood from the rose's thorn leaves a trail, like a wake of red with seabirds shrieking overhead.

The depth of the water drops off sharply, past my chest, past my chin, and when my head goes below the surface, I can hear the sound of all the birds in the world calling to me, crying and shrieking and wailing. I look up through the water and can see them flying overhead in the green sky, swooping and soaring, free of the earth. When I open my mouth to gasp at the wonderment of it all, the water rushes in to fill my lungs and I hear the owl, screeching, screeching, screeching.

PART THREE

BIRD ON A WIRE

Chapter 25

JON, Miami

Vivian phoned last night to tell me Claire drowned herself. She's not dead, she's sort-of-alive in hospital, being kept in a medically induced coma, but she might as well be dead. Technically, she died in the swimming pool of her apartment building and was found by the super who'd been changing the water but left for lunch. He saw her floating face down, fully clothed, and jumped in to haul her out. He knew how to revive people and he worked on her till the ambulance came. He said he'd been gone for 20 minutes. Nobody can say how long she was in there.

Vivian was in tears, of course. Barely able to speak. She'd been at the hospital all day and called me from Claire's room there. It's the same hospital where she's a nurse.

"It makes no sense," she said. "I mean, she was clearly depressed. Very clearly depressed. To go from such a high of thinking she'd found Jess, to such a low of feeling so betrayed, that's a huge emotional fall. But she seemed to be coping with it…"

She paused, taking a moment to compose herself like she'd done a dozen times already, just five minutes into this call.

"She's talked of suicide before but she was a rational woman, you know? She knew that there's always a solution, and it doesn't have to be final. She's told me, many times, that when she's at her lowest, that's when she stops to step out of herself for a moment, just to think things through a little more clearly. There's a psychiatrist the hospital provides and he's been great. She's seen him a few times over the years and he's always helped her take the next few steps."

There was nothing I could say, so I just listened.

"The doctor today, he said he didn't think this was a conscious decision to kill herself. He did blood tests and found she had far too many prescription drugs in her system and he thought they may have made her hallucinate. She probably didn't know what she was doing. That I can understand. She was always terrified of drowning, after what happened down east to Patrick, to her father, when she was a little girl.

"The cruel thing is, the pool was closed. It was due for some repairs to the room's floor. The door was supposed to be locked. They'd been in to change the water while it was closed but they weren't heating it. The superintendent went for lunch and forgot to lock the door. The doctor said the cold water might actually have helped. He said the sudden shock of the cold slows the heart and when that happens, the body sends whatever oxygen there is straight to the brain and the heart to keep them going."

"But we don't know how long her heart was stopped, do we?"

"No. It could have been a minute or it could have been almost 20 minutes. They only know the time she was pulled out of the water. 12:17 pm."

What goes around comes around. 12:17 pm – the exact same time Jess went missing. I stayed silent and listened some more to Vivian as she beat herself up, sobbing, letting it out, sitting at Claire's bedside in the hospital, holding her phone in one hand and her daughter's still fingers in the other.

. . .

One last run. Uncle Luis wanted me to drive over to Miami tonight and I'll doing it, but this'll be the last one. I've taken some extra precautions too, just to play it safe. I'll run the errand, make a quick 10 grand, be back in the morning and then I'll go in and quit. I'll tell him why, too – because I don't know what time I have left and there are other priorities that should, that must, come first. Jess. Molly. Maria. He'll understand. He shouldn't trust an errand to somebody who's not in peak shape anyway. I'm family, he said so himself. He'll let me go.

This time, my car was at the Bayshore Motel and I'd return to the Sunset. It was a Ford Focus at the Bayshore, very nondescript and just a basic model. No automatic lane-keeping or automatic headlights, but everything worked as it should and there was nothing to attract attention. In a way, that's too bad. For my final run, this should have been a Cadillac or a Lincoln, with a high-end sound system and a massaging seat. It should have been a friggin' Rolls-Royce. There are enough of them in Naples and Miami that nobody would look twice. Maybe the car I'll swap into will be more upmarket, but I'll take what I'm given. It'll come with 10 grand – that's the most important thing.

The drive south and east was as boring as ever, which meant more time to sit and think about lung cancer. The news from Dr. Patel was every bit as bad as he'd said it might be: Stage Four, with the cancer already spread into most of the rest of my body. The word he used was "rampant." "It's everywhere, Jon," he said. "At this point, whatever treatment we can give you is about controlling the movement and perhaps slowing the spread, but it's not about curing you. Once the cancer gets to this stage, it's too late to cure you. It's palliative. We only have time to make you comfortable and ensure your dignity." And how much time is that? "A month, or a few months. Maybe a year," he said. "The human body is always full of surprises, but we need to be realistic. Small cell lung cancer is quick. I wouldn't expect much more than a year."

The shitty thing is that I don't feel like I'm about to die. I feel tired, and I feel older than I should in my 40s, but you wouldn't look at me and think I have a year to live. "The deterioration will be fairly rapid once it begins," said Patel. "From now on, you should make the most of every day that you can, because it could literally be your last day of feeling strong, and feeling healthy."

I've still not told Maria, or Molly. I'm dreading that, but it has to be done. I don't want sympathy. I just want them to be prepared when the time comes. Patel was urging me to get chemotherapy and radiation and all the rest of it, but from everything I've been reading, that's only going to stretch out the inevitable and it'll make me look and feel like crap. He wanted me to quit smoking too – like that's going to happen if I'm dying anyway.

On this drive to Miami, back now on Alligator Alley, maybe headed east for the last time, I've been working out how many cartons of cigarettes I'll need to last me through to the end. Let's say a carton a week, that's 10 packs for seven days, multiply that by 50, we're looking at 50 cartons at around 70 bucks each, so about another $3,500 to finish funding my lifetime habit. That's less than a dirt bike. When I get back to Tampa, I should go to Costco and buy those 50 cartons, then hide them around the house in case Maria or Molly get all holy and try to stop me smoking. Take some out to the farm. I've got to have some pleasure in life, don't I?

It was clear and dark the whole way, as it normally is this time of year, and I got to Miami around 11 o'clock, as I usually do. I sent a text from a few blocks out and when I pulled in front of the garage door, it slid up in a shaft of light on the dim road. I drove in to see Mateo wave at me from the back of the shop. There was just one other guy inside though, not the usual handful, and he closed the door.

Mateo strode up and offered me a "Hey Captain Morgan!" and a fist pump before I was even out of the car. "Where is everyone?" I asked, and he shrugged. "They got the Kung Flu!" he said. "Just me and Danny tonight."

I was more concerned that the only other vehicle on the polished floor of this shop was a bright green Dodge Dart. Not the almost-cool Dodge Dart from the '70s, but the little sedan that Dodge stopped making a few years back because it was so crap.

I pointed to it as Danny walked up. "That's not..." I started, but Mateo was already nodding and grinning so much his silver tooth might pop out.

"Sorry Captain – that's your ship tonight! Gary called and told us to give it to you. Don't ask me why. All I know is they call that green 'sub-lime.' It's gonna be sublime for your drive home!" He pulled the word out – *subliiiiiiiimme* – just to make his point, and it would be pretty funny if it wasn't me who had to drive it out of here. So much for living my last days with dignity.

"I only like lime in my margaritas. You sure I have to drive that piece of shit?"

"Hey man – Gary said so, and Gary's the boss, you know."

Gary's the boss. Yes, he was. If Luis wasn't shitting me, though, then it could be me who's the boss, except I'm fixing to quit the business. Maybe I should stick around to take over as Luis wants, get rid of Gary, then die happy. There'd be plenty of time to think this through on the drive home.

I headed into the back for my customary piss, then came back out to get the Dart's key from Mateo and move over my stuff from the Focus: M&Ms, Gatorade, Glock.

"We can't follow you out," said Mateo. "Not with just the two of us here. But you'll be okay. It's only four blocks up to the interstate."

This had never happened. I know exactly how far it is up to the fucking interstate because I've made the drive a hundred times, and a hundred times

JON - Miami

before this, I had an escort up to the highway. The roads there are dark; it's an industrial area; a lot can happen that would never be witnessed.

"Can't you just send Danny out to drive behind? It'll only be for a couple of minutes."

"No – there must always be at least two people in here, or there are no people in here. Rules are rules, Captain."

"Then both of you come out with me."

"Can't do it, man. It takes a while to lock this place up and you'd be outside on the street like a sitting duck."

"A *sublime* sitting duck," said Danny, beside him. He screwed up his face grinning at his joke and the flame tattoos on his neck wrinkled into half their size.

Asshole.

I didn't like it, but there was nothing I could do. I shrugged.

"That's okay. Just trying to stick to protocol. I can take care of myself pretty good."

"I know, man. If anyone can, it's you. You'll be fine. Miami's mean streets ain't so mean."

Yeah, right.

I got in the Dart and slid the driver's seat way back, and turned the key in the ignition. The exhaust sounded like a farting muppet.

"Hey, it kinda suits you," laughed Mateo, and slapped the roof of the car while Danny went to open the garage door. "See you soon, Captain, and stay *subliiiime!*"

. . .

I really didn't like this. I don't like change at all. Even so, I slid the car through the door and onto the street. There was light from the door, but everything darkened quickly when it closed. The headlights on the Dart were okay but nothing special and when I turned right onto the street to head west to the interstate, I could see the traffic on the overhead highway in the distance, white lights heading north, where I'd be in just a minute.

There was a wind up tonight, enough to blow the taller palms around, and the small car felt none too solid on the ground. That was just me and my nerves though. Like I said, I don't like change and when just one small thing changes, everything feels very different. The wind seemed stronger. The dark shadows in the side streets seemed darker. The road, quiet of cars and people, seemed emptier.

It was four blocks to the interstate, where I'd be safe in the tumult of traffic and lights. That's four stop signs, and the roads weren't so wide in there. The three- and four-story shop-fronts and warehouses blocked my view down the alleys and side streets, so I didn't stop at the first stop sign, but I did slow down and roll through. I've heard there are some cities where people never stop at stop signs after dark, or even red lights, because it's just too dangerous to sit there and have someone run over from the shadows and point a gun through the window. If I was just a regular driver, there's no way I'd have been stopping or even slowing down at those four stop signs, but I was not a regular driver. For all I knew, I was carrying a half-million dollars of crank in the trunk, or a private army of Uzis under the floor, or the plans for a nuclear bomb in the glovebox. Or nothing. God only knew. Well, God and Gary and Luis, I guess. And all this in a bright green friggin' Dodge Dart. There was no way I wanted to break any laws and give the cops the excuse to search this car.

I was probably running empty, anyway. Like I told you, I never know, and this wasn't a big enough car to carry that much stuff. Maybe somebody in Tampa, somebody with no taste whatsoever, wanted to buy a green 2016 Dodge Dart and Gary realized I was headed home anyway so I might as well deliver it from where he found it at some dealership there. Maybe that was it. It was such an absurd thought that I allowed myself a little smile when I paused at the second stop sign, all law-abiding, and moved ahead, just a couple more blocks to go, the traffic up on the highway only 30 seconds away.

I was smiling as the little Dart gathered speed through the four-way intersection, and I was still smiling when I saw the dark smudge in the road on my left suddenly become a huge, blacked-out pickup truck grill, which smashed so hard from the side street into my driver's door that the little car lifted clear off all four wheels and was slammed like a cue ball into the street on the right. *FUCK!* My head snapped to the left, hard, real hard, into the side window. My left arm crumpled against the buckling door. The airbag powered into me and held me against the seat, and I could smell the stink of its powder when it deflated. When the car fell back to the ground, one of its wheels caught against the sidewalk curb and the entire thing flipped right over itself, once, twice, a thousand times as it tumbled over and over down the dark side street. The roof caved in and I tried to raise my hands to protect my head, but my left arm didn't move and was useless. *Fuck.*

I was still conscious when the car stopped moving, right side up and a hundred yards into the shadows of the side street. It was spun right around so it was on the sidewalk, facing back the way I came. That was when the adrenaline kicked in and I knew exactly what to do. Out of the seat belt, over to the passenger seat, got the gun from the glovebox and dragged myself through the smashed passenger window, where I could squat with my back to a warehouse wall, shielded by the car.

The pickup truck was alongside on the street and two guys stretched out through the windows on each side. Their gunshots started almost immediately – semi-automatic gunfire directly at the driver's door. I'd already moved down to the back of the car and I had a clear shot at the guy leaning out of the passenger window, but when I readied the Glock's trigger safety, it didn't move. It was jammed. The tab wouldn't release. *Fuck!*

If these two guys were smart, they'd never have started firing, attracting attention to a deserted place like this. They'd have just driven their big blacked-out pickup truck, a super-duty Ram, into the side of the Dart again and crushed me against the warehouse wall. They'd have also turned on their lights to see what they were doing – there were no lights at all on the truck, which is how it stayed hidden before driving into me, but now they were just shooting into darkness.

Idiots. But idiots with guns.

They'd not seen me. They stopped shooting and both of them got out of the truck to check on my slug-riddled corpse in the driver's seat. Except I wasn't there, I was back behind the trunk, and when they approached, I stood up, pulled Maria's little Glock 19 from underneath my belt, and popped two rounds into each of them. They both just sagged to the ground. Hollow points will do that, especially with no body armor, only jeans and T-shirts and ball caps. All that time at the range just paid off for me, as did carrying a spare gun this time around, those precautions I mentioned, just in case. I was shooting for body mass, and it would've been hard to miss these fat fuckers.

Damn that felt good!

Both were groaning on the ground. The passenger guy, he was moving and trying to reach for his gun, so he got another two rounds in the head to put an end to that. It was messy when the slugs went in and they just smacked against the asphalt on the other side. I couldn't help but wince at the splash. The driver guy, he was moaning but not moving. I wanted to ask him who he was and what he wanted from me, but I could hear sirens already, attracted by the gunfire like flies to shit. Besides, I knew who he was, now I was looking down at him. He was one of the guys who works with Mateo just a couple of blocks away. Covid my ass. The passenger guy probably was too, but I couldn't look at him again to check because there was no face to recognize.

I shot the driver in the chest, two more rounds right in the heart, because I didn't want to see that splash again.

As the sirens grew louder, I put Maria's Glock back under my belt beside my own jammed gun, picked up the driver's AR-15, then ran across the street and into the shadows of an alley. My left arm was not working properly, but my legs were just fine and I was a long way yet from dead.

. . .

I hid for a while behind some garbage in another alley a few blocks over, just to catch my breath and let the cops settle down. They came by and took a look with their cruiser lights, but they'd not try real hard to catch anyone. Down here, they leave gangs to settle their own scores. They'd wait for more backup before they even got out of their cars. It stank in the alley, which meant it helped keep people away and I needed some time to rest up and think things through. My left arm was throbbing and I was itching from the powder on the airbags, and I had a headache from hitting my head on the side window, but everything else moved okay. Nothing was bleeding.

I still had both my phones and when it seemed safe, and the sounds of the commotion over at the crash are a little quieter, I used the light on one of them to take a glance at my Glock. The trigger safety looked okay but it was still jammed, and there was a small glint from the metal beside it. Some clear substance. Glue! The tab was super-glued open. I checked the gun before I left Tampa, when I told Maria it wasn't working right and borrowed her handbag Glock for the night, and it was working just fine then. Extra precautions. That fucker Mateo must have glued it when I was in the can. They were all in on it. So there was no point going back there unless it was just to get in another gunfight, and one was enough for tonight.

But what was the point? If they wanted to steal whatever was in the car, they could have done it in the garage. If they wanted to kill me, they could have done that in the garage too, a lot more easily.

I let another hour pass hiding in the garbage, crouched down and listening to the rats, shaking them off whenever they scurried over my legs. Every few minutes, I tried to suppress a cough – I'd never noticed how often I cough, and how bad it had become, and after a while, I figured out how to just loosen the phlegm from the back of my throat and hawk it over to the rats. My left arm hurt like fuck but it didn't seem to be broken. I had to get out of there and find someplace safer, and right then, any place was safer.

When dark clouds began to spread across the sky and the moon dulled into the night, I stood up at last, stretched, and started moving off up the alley. A few blocks north would do it, then a few blocks west, underneath the interstate to the sanity of the residential area on the other side of the tracks. I left the bulky AR-15 in the garbage with the rats. Where I was going, I wouldn't need it.

BIRD ON A WIRE

Chapter 26

GRANT, Tampa

Well, this is cool. Jon wanted to know how I was doing with looking for his daughter Jessica, who was abducted from the Fairfield Mall 19 years ago on her fourth birthday. He was betting big I could come up with something but he was being way too optimistic. He thinks I'm some kind of trained investigative reporter, which is pretty much the opposite of what I do for TampaToday.com, Your Hometown Homepage.

At Tampa Today, they're all about the clicks. I get $30,000 a year to produce a minimum two stories a day, and a bonus for any story that gets more than 10,000 hits. It's the bonus that I work for every day, and it's on a sliding scale so it's not quick to describe, but the best I ever saw was an extra $500 for a story on the cars of sports celebrities. Top Ten Sports Cars For Sports Stars it was called, to solidly hit the SEO rankings. I started it with the Fisker Karma that Steven Stamkos drives, the captain of the Tampa Bay Lightning, to give it the home town connection, then just scraped around on Google for a while to dig up the others, with pictures. That's the kind of investigative reporting I'm good at – scraping around on Google for a while.

I met Jon years ago when I was still in school and I had a job cleaning cars at his dealership. I've always liked cars, and he and me just hit it off. He didn't have any friends at the dealership because they all knew he was only there because his uncle owned the place. More important, there were stories about him coming from a bad family, the kind of people you don't want to piss off, so people stayed well clear of him to not piss him off. It didn't worry me any – I thought he was an okay guy, and he let me drive some of the good cars that came in. He let me take a couple home, then I filmed myself with my phone, and next thing you know, I had my own YouTube car show,

Grant's Garage. Some weeks now, it makes more for me than the job at Tampa Today, and it's pretty easy money.

Once, years ago, when we'd both had too much to drink, he opened up a bit about his family. Told me about his dad and his shit-for-a-brother. I told him he should change his name and run away from it all. I remember I said he should change his name to Johnnie Walker because, well, that's what we were drinking at the time. Then we finished the bottle and he was going to change his name to Jim Beam. In the end, he woke up the next day with a hangover, remembered nothing except the change-the-name part, and next thing I knew, he was Jonathan Morgan. I don't think anyone noticed, but he did and he said it was good for him to make the break.

I never mentioned the bad family again, but you'd better believe I Googled the crap out of his name and I've known the story of his dad and his brother for a long time now. I knew about his missing daughter, too, because those stories were the first to come up in any search. For years, I wanted to ask him all about it because I'm just curious. Curiosity can be dangerous though, and I always just left it for him to bring it up. Which he never, ever did until that Sunday a week ago beside his pool.

Now everything's in the open between us. Well, kind of, about his missing daughter anyway. I still don't know how he makes his money and *that*, I really don't want to know. He's not just a car salesman, I know that much. I assume he works with his uncle in some way, Luis Lopez, and I make sure Luis's name never gets published in Tampa Today. What would the story be? Top 10 gruesome murders believed ordered by Luis Lopez? Seven reasons to never visit Tampa? Fentanyl – five fun facts? Luis Lopez has a reputation in this town and I never want to meet the guy. Jon, though – he's always been straight up and a good friend, and we appreciate each other as lovers of fine automobiles.

Today, I'm in a little deeper, but it's still cool. I was headed back now to the police station. They're going to let me look at Jessica Morgan's missing person file.

. . .

Last week, I was still waiting for permission to see the file – the Superintendent who gives the okay was away on vacation, and none of those cops dare do anything that might get them in trouble – so I took a visit to the

Fairfield Mall, where Jessica disappeared. It's a big place, with at least a hundred stores on two levels. I've been there enough times, and I was hoping I'd see something to jump out at me.

Of course, I didn't. It's just a mall. There's the main floor, laid out like a cross or a crucifix, and on the second floor, the higher-end stores have a wide floor in front of them like a balcony, so you can look down over the railing at the main floor. The food court is where the cross intersects and there's a big glass dome over it. It's probably just like a thousand other malls.

Jon told me his girlfriend back then, Claire, was shopping with Jessica and another kid in a stroller, and she was distracted by the other kid when she was in front of a stationery store, and that's the last she saw of Jessica. There was a photo in the paper from a security camera that showed Jessica standing at a cookie booth not far away, and then she just vanished. Not much to go on, and it doesn't help that there's no stationery store there now, or even a cookie booth. I walked the length of the mall but I just couldn't picture it. If the trained detectives could find nothing at the time, I don't know how I'm going to do any better, 21 years later.

. . .

At the station, Det. Sgt. Beth Anderson met me in the lobby and right off the top, she insisted I call her Beth, or Sgt. Beth if I really want to be formal. She was an attractive woman who knew how to wear makeup and a pair of pants, and I'm sure she'd look good in uniform if she wasn't wearing jeans and a shirt and a red leather jacket. I'm not sure if she was African-American or just deeply tanned, but I think, from her dark eyes, that she's Black. Probably a mixture of a whole lot of good things, like Halle Berry. She was old enough to be my mom, which didn't seem to slow her down any.

"Remind me, Grant," she said in the lobby, asking with a kind of sultry drawl. "Why the interest in this old case?"

"It's just always bugged me," I told her. "I remember that picture of the little girl looking up at the camera and it's always stayed with me."

She nodded. She knew the picture I was talking about. Probably, everyone in Tampa back then remembers that picture.

"Have you talked to anyone involved with the case?" she asked. "Have you talked with the parents?"

I told Jon I wouldn't bring him into this, but I didn't want to lie, and especially not to a cop right there in Cop Central.

"I've talked to Jessica's father and he's told me his side of the story. Her mother is up in Toronto but I don't know how to reach her. I don't need to anyway. I'm not looking to solve this case myself, but maybe it'll ring some bells for somebody and someone will come forward."

"You spoke to John Morgan?" she said. She sounded surprised. "How was he to talk to you? You know we brought him in for questioning, and he was a suspect for a while?"

Oh yes, I'm well aware.

"He was okay. He says this still tears him up. He said he'll help me any way he can. He seemed an okay guy."

"Maybe you got him on a good day," she said. "Come – follow me."

She flashed a pass key at a door off the lobby and I followed her through a half-empty labyrinth of desks and cubicles to a small meeting room on the other side of the building. If I didn't know this was a cop station, I'd have thought it was an insurance office. In the room, there was a brown file box on a table and a desktop computer.

"Here's your office for this morning," she said. "Please don't leave this room. The officers' notes are in this box and all the pictures from the mall cameras, all on CDs that you can see on the computer. We had to take out some of the statements from the time – privacy. Take a look through it all and I'll come check back on you in an hour. If you want copies of anything, ask me. If you need anything, call me on my cell. I won't be far away."

She left and I took a look in the file box. There wasn't much. Some photocopied notes that must have been from the police notebooks, and some school books that were labelled as coming from Jessica's room at home. Some printed photographs of Jessica and her parents. She was really young, just two or three years old according to the labels on the backs. More than that – Jon and his girlfriend were really young, too. Everyone had long hair. There was a picture at a picnic in some park, with little Jessica sitting on a blanket, holding a cup and seeming to look for something. Her red, shoulder-length hair stood out even against the red blanket. In the photos with her mother, Claire, I could see where she got those Irish looks. It all seemed so normal. So commonplace. So mundane. So tragic. More than 20 years later and I was peeking into those lives through pictures from inside an evidence box.

I felt like an imposter.

There were several stacks of CD-ROM discs, and those were the photographs from the security cameras at the mall. There were more than 50 cameras both inside and outside, and the note with the discs said these were all from a three-hour period, beginning before Claire arrived with the children and continuing through until two hours after the disappearance. There were more than 2,000 color photographs from each camera, as well as a separate disc of photos from several of the cameras later in the day that had Jon punching out the fat detective.

Most of the pictures just showed anonymous shoppers seen from overhead, going about their day, but somebody put the most relevant photos separately on the disc that shows Woods being punched. The computer in the room had a CD-ROM drive so I could feed in the discs to look at them, and it had a software program that let me watch long successions of pictures, like a stop-action movie.

There's Claire on Camera 6, realizing Jessica was not there. There's Claire on Camera 19, running through the mall, people watching her and avoiding her. There's Claire on Camera 28, surrounded by mall cops, frantic. The photographs were silent, of course, but I could see her face and feel her panic.

And there's Jessica on Camera 5, walking away from her mother and the little boy in the stroller. And there's Jessica on Camera 7, walking north through the mall, just the back of her head visible. And there's Jessica on Camera 10, standing by the cookie booth, looking up, the little red-haired girl with the infectious smile, about to disappear into God knows where.

I checked the time on the photograph – 12:17:00 – and then started looking through each of the other discs to see if there might be any evidence at all of Jessica walking, running, being chased, being dragged, anything, but there was nothing. Not a single other image of her after that time. According to all these cameras, Jessica stopped, looked up, smiled, and disappeared.

"There's got to be an explanation," I said to myself, and I was surely not the first person to say this. "There's just got to be."

BIRD ON A WIRE

Chapter 27

JON, Fort Lauderdale

It was a half-hour ride in the Uber, and the driver had his foot down. I didn't blame him. I stank. I looked like I was homeless, too, because I found some pants and a shirt in a bag beside a used-clothing drop box, one of those metal bins where you leave stuff for charities. They didn't fit too bad, and I left behind the rat-piss-covered clothes I'd been wearing that were a damn sight better quality, so I guess the Diabetes people came out ahead, *know what I mean?* The Uber guy tried to kick me out when I first got in his Camry, but I told him I wasn't going anywhere except the address in Lauderdale and that was that. Not sure I'll keep my five-star passenger rating, though.

I was lucky to get a ride at 3:30 am, but I was luckier to still have my wallet and my phones. And my guns. And my life, of course. In the back of that Toyota, my whole body went into little spasms of shaking and it must have been the adrenaline wearing off. The driver kept glancing at me in the mirror and he probably thought I was tweaking, which is why he didn't slow down.

It'd been a long time since I killed anyone, and it bothered me that I took such pleasure in it tonight. I killed a dealer once who ripped me off but I took no satisfaction in that. It was an exhausting fight at his home, or at least the place where he was living, and I killed him with a kitchen knife. We were arguing and he'd come at me and we fought without weapons and made a hell of a mess of the room, which was already a fucking pigsty. Then he found the knife, came at me with it, and I got it off him and stabbed him right in the neck. Lots of blood. It was disgusting. I watched him die then just walked away, feeling like God, sure, but not a good God. The cops never investigated much – just another druggie off the streets.

Sometimes, awake at night, I still see that guy's face as the blood drained away. He must have realized it was all over and his eyes looked amazed to know this was the end, finally catching up to him after 30 or 40 years of keeping it all together. Sometimes, I'd wonder what he was seeing then. Was it me? Was it the hand of God? Was it nothing at all? Probably nothing at all. His eyes just kind of glazed over and that was that and I got the fuck out of there. Never told anyone. Just walked away from it, victorious and empowered but no pleasure. Now I'm telling you, because I'll be dead like him soon, and what does it matter anymore?

Part of me thought I should have gone back to the garage and taken care of business there while I was still pumped. The smarter part of me knew that would have been suicide, even with the more powerful gun, and I don't need to die till I have to. Those guys in the Miami crew wanted to make the hit on the car look like somebody else, otherwise they'd have just taken the Dart from the garage before I got there, or the drugs or the guns or whatever it was. They needed to shrug it off to Gary and Luis and they'd have made backup plans to be sure I wasn't coming away alive.

I was still thinking this through in the Uber when we pulled up to the building and, just as we were slowing down, I started to cough again. It was only a smoker's cough, nothing I'm not used to, but the driver looked in the mirror and screwed up his eyes. I was wearing a mask because I didn't want him to see my face – it was a white paper one I found on the ground near the clothes, and it was mostly clean – but the driver looked disgusted.

"Fuck, man!" he said, when the car stopped at the door and the catches unlocked. "Please, go clean yourself up!"

"Fuck you asshole," I told him and got out onto the sidewalk, ripping off the mask as soon as I was outside the car. The white paper was splashed with blood, dark on the outside through the filter, thick and bright on the inside.

. . .

There was still at least three hours before sunrise but Jodi wouldn't mind. She's a horny little minx. I'd take a hot shower and check myself over or, better, she could check me over, then we could fuck away the last of the adrenaline. Really, I needed to sleep, but not yet. I'd clean up, text Luis, get myself back to Tampa and sleep in my own bed.

JON – Fort Lauderdale

There was a pass card in my wallet for the building – I own the condo, after all – and I got myself inside quickly, then rode the elevator up to the 18th floor. This was a nice place, higher end, and when I saw myself in the elevator mirror, I ran my fingers through my hair and licked them to wipe away the worst of the grime from my face. I still looked like shit, but I've looked worse.

I phoned Jodi from the corridor outside the condo door. It took three separate calls before she answered.

"Yeah?"

"Hey baby. What's up?"

"What?"

"I've got a surprise for you."

"Fuck you."

And she hung up. Probably woke her up, but I like doing that.

I was still standing outside the door. I called back.

"Hey baby – it's Jon."

"I know. Call display. What is it?"

"Come to the door and I'll show you."

"What? You're here? It's 4:13 in the middle of the night."

"I'm here! Come to the door and see for yourself."

There was a pause. I could hear the rustling of bed sheets.

"Jon – I'm not alone."

I didn't expect that. Of course she wasn't not alone. Why would she sleep alone? Like I said, she's a horny little minx. We've made no promises to each other. No exclusivity. But she'd never mentioned other guys, while she knew all about Maria. Well, Maria in Tampa, not Maria in Orlando. *Shit.* Guess this adrenaline would have to work itself off then. Unless, maybe, it was another woman, another horny little minx. Oh, wouldn't that be something?

I switched to landlord mode.

"That's okay, Jodi." *Like I have a choice.* "But can I come in and just use the shower? I won't stick around, but I do need to clean up."

She hung up without saying anything, and a minute later, the door unlocked and she was standing there, looking sexy as hell in a creamy silk robe. Her short red hair, trimmed back since I last saw her, was messy and had that just-fucked look. I know that look.

Please let it be another woman.

"What the hell?" she said. "You look like shit. Why are you here? Why didn't you call? You're supposed to call."

"I sent you a text. I said I was coming over."

She looked at her phone.

"You sent it at 3:31. I was asleep. That's what people do at night – they sleep."

"I know. I didn't expect to be coming over. I was in Miami and got cut off on the road and wrecked my car" – which in a way, I did. "Look, can I please just use the shower? Clean up?"

"I guess," she said. "And what the fuck are you wearing? You look like a bum!"

"Yeah – these aren't my usual. Long story."

"Maybe you can take some of Dustin's spare clothes. You can't stay here. They're in the closet. He's still asleep."

Damn. This night was such a *tease*.

. . .

Before I hit the shower, I sat on the can and sent Luis a text from the encrypted phone.

Big trouble tonight. Got hit in Miami. Lost the car. Need a ride home. Will explain in person.

I don't know why text messages sound like old-time cable messages, but they always do. Luis would reply when he woke up and he'd send somebody over to come get me, bring me home safe.

Just as I was in the shower, shampoo in my hair and starting to feel clean, I heard the phone buzz beside the sink. He was awake? I finished up more quickly than I'd planned – I was going to jerk off to finally get that adrenaline out, and it wouldn't be the first time I've gotten jacked off in this shower – and yup, there was a text message waiting from Luis. No voice mail.

Send address. Help on the way. Be ready at 5:30 am.

Five-thirty? That was barely an hour. He must be sending somebody from Miami.

Oh shit.

I wrote back quick, not ready yet to send the condo's address.

Miami crew is compromised. DO NOT send anyone from Miami crew.

Luis replied right away.

Relax – it's Gary. Visiting his mom. What's the address?

I sent Luis the address, and I should have been relieved it was Gary, but I didn't feel relaxed at all.

. . .

I was ready outside the building at 5:15, clean and wearing fresh clothes: a pair of baggy blue jeans that were snug around the waist, and a red hoodie. Jodi brought out some clothes to me in the main room and those were the only ones that fit. I'd have taken a T-shirt but they were all too tight. I never did meet the Dustin guy. Jodi hustled me out of there fast. She didn't ask again why I was there and such a mess, just wanted me gone.

I took some Tylenol in the bathroom to deal with my headache, and my left arm stopped aching and started working. I took the time in there, too, to chip away at the safety tab on the trigger of my Glock. It was definitely glued shut, but I scraped around it and under it with a metal nail file and got it to move open. Only problem was, it stayed gummed and if it's used again, it might stick as it did before. So there was nothing in the barrel and the gun was tucked into the front pocket of the hoodie. Better that than a useless two pounds of steel. Maria's gun was tucked under my belt beneath the hoodie. My wallet was in one front pocket of the jeans and both my phones filled the other front pocket. I'd not be comfortable sitting in the car, but that was just the way it'd have to be.

I was waiting on a little bench off to the side, underneath a low sidewalk lamp. This was where the condo residents walk their dogs. There was nobody around, of course, and the place was quiet. Even so, I was nervous. Nervous!

What if Gary was involved with this? What if he arranged the hit, to claim the drugs for himself, or just to kill me off? What if the target wasn't the package, but *me?* Luis seemed to say that Gary knew I was being moved into line to take over the business, and maybe now he wanted me out of the picture. Suddenly, that made sense.

At 5:30, a black Nissan pulled off the road and into the driveway for the condo building. It slid in toward me and parked outside the front door and I just watched for a while from where I'd moved to in the shadows, cupping my hand around the glowing end of my cigarette. The car windows were heavily tinted. I didn't recognize the Nissan at all, but I walked out, took a drag and waved with my left hand. My right hand was in the hoodie pocket, holding the gun. The passenger window slid down and I saw Gary lean across the seat, looking up at me.

"Hey Jon – get in! Let's get you out of here."

"Gary – good to see you!"

My left arm was working fine now and I took the cigarette from my lips.

"Just let me get rid of this."

I walked over past the car to the trash and stubbed out the cigarette in the sand bowl. When I walked back to the passenger door, I caught a glimpse of the license plate and I recognized it right away. I guess Brenda Bradley wasn't using this car tonight.

. . .

"You want to tell me what happened?" said Gary, after we were out of the residential streets and up on the interstate, headed west at the speed limit toward the Alley. The road was a little bumpy along here.

"I got hit, that's what fucking happened. It's not like they could miss me in that green piece of shit."

"What green piece of shit? What are you talking about?"

"Mateo gave me a Dodge Dart, green piece of shit, to drive home. Said it was orders from you."

"Not from me. You were supposed to be in a black Chrysler 300. Big trunk, you know?"

"Well, it was a Dodge Dart, and Mateo was in on it. Glued my trigger safety, then got two of his guys to ram me off the road two blocks away."

"I heard there was a shoot-out. How'd you do that with a glued gun?"

"I carry a spare. Always carry a spare. Used the whole magazine, though. I just fired off everything I had. I was lucky to get out of there."

Neither of those statements about the gun were true – I rarely carry a spare, and there were still seven rounds in Maria's magazine, but Gary didn't need to know that. And he definitely didn't need to know I freed up my own gun, and it was sitting loaded in my hoodie pocket, aimed straight at his crotch in the driver's seat. There was a round in the barrel now, too. I prepped it while I was waiting outside, just in case. Like I said, I was nervous.

"Can you put those rounds from your jammed gun into your spare gun?" asked Gary.

"Yeah, I think so. It's still glued. I'll do it when the pavement smooths out."

Which I wouldn't, because my big Glock now worked just fine.

"Well, I'm sorry that happened," said Gary. "I've been wondering about those assholes for a while. Guess you just proved me right."

This fucked me off.

"Next time you're wondering, let me know first, will you?"

"Of course," said Gary. "Can't have something happen to you. You're family."

And then he slid the car over into the right lane and signaled right for the exit that was coming up.

Huh?

"I gotta piss. There's a place here, before we get to the tolls. I always piss against this tree when I'm headed back from Miami, when I've been visiting my girlfriend. It's my lucky tree."

"I thought you were seeing your mom?"

Gary blinked a couple of times. It's a nervous thing he does. Maybe he was nervous like me.

"Mom, girlfriend – she's somebody's girlfriend now." Then he seemed to regather himself. "My mom's in Miami, my girlfriend's in Miami Beach. I was visiting them both. Got out of bed early just for you."

This was a quiet area, residential with widely spaced houses and duplexes and low-rise apartments and small parks, and it was still dark. Dark enough for me to see in the side mirror there was something driving behind us, a couple hundred yards back. Sure enough, when Gary pulled into a small park to the right – "There's my lucky tree!" – the lights shuttered out on the vehicle behind. So this was how it was going to happen. As we drove in, I lowered my passenger window. The air from outside had a chill to it.

Gary parked over in the corner of the small lot, under the branches of a live oak and away from the single overhead lamp in the center. When he turned off the ignition, the car lights went out and the tree went dark.

"You should take a piss yourself," he said. "It's another three hours and I don't want to stop again."

"Oh, I'm good."

"No, really – now's the time. We can cross swords."

I couldn't see the vehicle that was behind us, but I knew it was there somewhere. There was only that one central light in this little parking lot and it left all the edges dark, and I was weighing my options.

"Maybe you're right," I said, though I waited till Gary started to make a move to open his door before I began to leave the car. It was a bit awkward and maybe he was on to me but he got out all the same. No going back now.

When I got out, I glanced around and could see there was a small pickup truck stopped near the entrance to the lot, on my side. As fast as I could, I suddenly threw open my door all the way and ran around it, crouching down behind its metal.

"Gary – there's a truck over there! He's waiting for us!"

Gary hardly flinched, standing on his side of the car.

"Waiting for *you*, I think, Jon," he said, and then called over toward the truck. "No rounds – empty mag!"

The driver got out of the truck. He was carrying a short shotgun and started walking slowly toward us. When he moved closer to the edge of the light, I could see the glint off his silver tooth.

"Gary! *What the fuck?*" But I knew exactly what was happening.

"I'm family too, Jon! I might not have your blood, but I'm fucking family too."

And for the second time on the night that never seemed to end, I rose up from behind the shield of the car door and fired two nine-millimeter hollow-points through the Nissan's open window into Mateo's chest before he even realized I had a gun. He cried out and dropped his shotgun, and he was already spinning when I sank two more rounds into him, the slugs expanding like mushrooms through his heart and lungs. There were plenty more in the magazine – this was the first time it was fired that night. Gary, who thought I was running empty, looked astonished when I switched around and aimed the big Glock directly at his head.

"Don't fucking move, you asshole," I said, but he dropped anyway, crouching behind the car. I fired off a round and it missed – he was too fast. His door was still open and I could hear him reaching into the car.

"Not quick enough, Jon!"

I was plenty quick enough. Before he knew it, I'd scrambled around the back of the car and he was in front of me beside it, stretching his arm under the driver's seat. That'd be where he kept his gun.

"Don't bother, Gary. I've got you now."

He knew my barrel was pointed straight at him and his own gun was caught in the mechanism under the seat. He was fighting to free it.

"Fuck you, Jon." He was still working at it, but slowing down. It looked like his hand was caught under there.

"Was it you following me all this time, Gary, or someone else?"

"All kinds of people, Jon. Nobody wants you in charge."

He stopped reaching for the gun. Must have slid back too far.

"Your girlfriend ride along too?"

He looked surprised at that, still squatting on the ground beside the open driver's door.

"Yeah, sometimes."

"What did you tell them about me, Gary?"

He didn't care anymore. He was a brave man, I'll give him that.

"I told them you're no Lopez. I told them you're a fucking Morgan. I told them what you did to your little girl, and I told them you're no different from your loser cracker brother and your loser cracker daddy."

What?

"What do you think I did to my little girl, Gary?"

"You think I don't know? Your brother told me, a long time ago. Your brother told me everything."

"Told you what?"

"Go fuck yourself, crackerjack."

I shot Gary in the kneecap first. That made him yell and buckle over, and then I shot him in the balls, which made him yell more. Then, as he was laying there on the ground, clutching at himself, I shot him in the chest, the stomach, the legs, everywhere but the head. I paused for just a few seconds to watch the throes of pain, his mouth opening and closing in shock and confusion and fury. He thrashed around at first, then squirmed for a while, then lay still.

Lay still, like Mateo there in the lot, and those two guys on the street back in Miami.

Like Claire.

I wasn't wasting any time there. I loaded his tattered body into the Nissan's trunk – it was empty, no bags from visiting Mom – and picked up the shell casings, too. I fired off the whole magazine. *Damn it felt good.*

I'd leave him for somebody to find when the sun came up in an hour, but he's a Tampa name, not a Miami thug like Mateo. I was keeping my gun because it's registered to me and besides, I liked it and I thought I'd want to fire it some more, sometime soon. I was in charge.

The car was untouched – no ricochets, no scratches. I walked over to the nearby tree and took a piss. It'd be three hours and I wouldn't want to stop. When I got into the car, started it up and turned it around, the headlights shone directly onto Mateo's body, lying there useless in the middle of the lot. I had the power.

I gunned the engine and aimed the left front wheel directly at his legs, feeling them bump and jump when the front tire drove over them, and then crush and sink when the back tire struck the cracked bones, like hitting a broken tree branch in the road. In the side mirror, I saw the body lurch and then lie limp again in the edge of the light. Not so sublime now.

I was headed back to Tampa. I had the power of life and death, over everyone but myself.

Chapter 28

CLAIRE, Toronto

I should have done this long ago, but I think I did do this long ago, just floating, no push, no pull, suspended like a bird in the wind, like a fish on the ocean current, watching everything that's above and below and all around, looking down at my bed on the sea floor, watching my mother, my father, my daughter, my son, my lover, watching me, watching everyone, seeing everything, feeling everything, being everything, floating, soaring, diving, aiming high, aiming low, under the arch, through the cave, out to the sky, over the desert, leading the flock, following the lead, swooping, soaring, slowing, waiting, turning and turning again, tracing circles through the air, through the water, into the empty, over nothing, toward the light, away from the shadow, up to the height, into the sun, then floating again, suspended above it all, lying below it all, out to the edge and looping, looping, looping back to the centre, hearing, listening, pausing to remember, lost names, lost faces, lost touch, lost taste, then out to the edge and through, almost to the other side, but turning back, and falling, dropping, down, down, down to the bed.

Claire.

Touch the blanket, so brief, so there, so gone, so nothing, so soft, so lost, just searching, looking, wanting, needing, loving, hating, lusting, taking, faking, shaking, waking, waking, waking.

Claire.

Then off again, into the air, high in the room, into the void, back to the empty, back to the sea, back to the ocean, back to the sand, looking for shells, looking for birds, looking for love, looking for Jess.

BIRD ON A WIRE

Chapter 29

GRANT, Tampa

Jon was away, doing whatever it is Jon does, and I'd made a couple more trips to the mall. Now I'd seen the photographs, I could place everything a bit better. The stationery store was now a clothes store, and the cookie booth was a jewelry booth. There was an extension at the north end but that didn't matter. I spent my whole time there imagining how it was 19 years ago, when I was still in high school and little Jessica was four years old, visiting the mall with her mom and her friend on her birthday.

I went back in there today, another visit. There was something missing in this puzzle and I didn't know what it was, but I'd not find it sitting at home. I parked close to where I knew Claire parked on December 20, 2004, and then went inside to the cooler air. I was trying to imagine her walking right in front of me, pushing that stroller with the little boy and Jessica holding tight to it. There would have been Christmas decorations everywhere, and now, there were still Valentine posters left over, and even a giant inflatable heart near the main doors, which looked kind of weird. The three of them walked in, then through the food court – which would have been a lot busier than it was today – and turned left toward the Macy's at the end. All the photos that included Claire were copied onto that separate CD, so I could follow the three of them through the mall, and I paused with them outside the same stores where they stopped.

Most of those stores have different names now, and some are bigger and some smaller. It's easy to put up walls in malls like this, take them down, move them around so the interior stores are constantly changing in size, accommodate the whims of this year's shoppers.

Like Claire, I walked down to the former stationery store where she stopped to fix something with the little boy in the stroller, and where Jess walked away. I didn't need to go inside the store, which is just as well because it sells women's fashion and it's exactly the kind of place I never go into. Was there a guy watching them from the center of the floor, maybe over by the benches, signaling to Jessica to leave her mom? Then I walked back up to the jewelry booth that once sold cookies. I looked up at the camera there, but I didn't smile.

Then I went up to the second floor and walked the entire mall from up there, looking down at the shoppers. I came back to being above the jewelry booth, and I stopped for a while to lean on the railing and watch all the people below: families, couples, mothers with strollers and children. There was nobody with red hair, and there were no little girls walking on their own, looking into storefronts, smiling up at cameras. From up there, it was almost like being a camera myself, looking down on Claire running through the mall, calling, yelling, screaming. It wasn't too busy, nothing like that December, but it didn't take much imagination to put Claire in there with the throngs of Christmas shoppers from the photos, and to feel her panic.

I had pictures on my phone of some of the original mall security photographs. I just snapped them off the computer screen when I was looking at them at the police station – it was easier than asking Sgt. Beth for copies. They're just a reminder, anyway; I know the 2004 layout from memory. There was a shoe store across from the cookie booth on the opposite side from the jewelry booth, with boutique clothes stores to each side. Where I ended up standing up was a video store. Beneath me, in 2004, there was a bookstore and another clothes store and a store under renovation behind boards, about to reopen as a luggage store. There was another store I could see halfway down the mall today that was similarly boarded for renovation. Like I said, the place is constantly morphing itself to cater to changing tastes. I watched a construction worker with a yellow hard hat walk into it through a door in the center of the boards. When the door in the boards closed behind him, it was as if there was no door there at all, just a blank board. I kept watching as the door opened and closed for workers to come and go, carrying tools, pushing a dolly.

Whatever it was, I couldn't put my finger on it.

I went back down the escalator and over to the store under renovation. If there'd been a door in the boards of the luggage store 19 years ago, then that would have been the fastest way out of the mall for Jess. But the cameras watched every inch and were set to take a photograph every 10 seconds, and even if some guy had picked her up and run to the door with the screaming child under his arm, like a wide receiver headed for the touchdown, he couldn't have made it in 10 seconds without being caught on camera. It made no sense at all.

. . .

I went back to the police station and drank my second coffee of the morning, still hot. I brought it over from the mall. Sgt. Beth let me back in the meeting room with the evidence box, which was just sitting on the floor in a corner of her office. She said she was leaving for much of the day and introduced me to another cop, a gruff guy called Sgt. Jones, no first name I guess, who had a desk just outside the door and could help me if I needed it. Which means, he was the guy who'd make sure I stay in the meeting room and would escort me out when it was time to go.

The answer had to be in those photos, flashing up on the computer screen as I clicked through the compilations from each camera. Every image had a time stamp on it and I already checked there were none missing. Everything was there. I could see the entire mall in 10-second increments. It was a crappy, cheaped-out system to have not recorded video, but every picture was there, all present and accounted for, and each one overlapped so every single part of the mall was covered. Two cameras, Numbers 1 and 2, were in the two corners at the south end, looking north, then three cameras each in about a dozen lines of coverage up the mall, one to each side looking in and a third overhead, looking down. Not a tile on the floor ws missing.

Here was Jessica, looking up from the cookie booth at Camera 10. Here she was from the left side on Camera 9, with the shoe store behind, and here she was from the right in the distance on Camera 11, with the bookstore behind and, to the north, the boarded-over luggage store. "Opening this spring," it said on the boards in red letters. I looked for the workers' door in the boards but it was just out of range on the right side of the frame. It'd be in the picture on Camera 14, which would overlap to show the door.

Except, when I loaded the disc and found the photograph, it didn't. It showed the boards at the north end of the luggage store – "The new Louie's Luggage" written on them in large red letters – but the frame stopped short of showing any possible door to the left. There was no door visible in the boards, no way for workers to access the store, and because the door was probably just another blank white board, there was nothing obviously missing in the photograph. There must have been a door somewhere. Above on the second floor was the railing and a video store. Between the two photos, the end of the video store was missing.

I was alone in the room, so I took a photo with my phone of the picture on the monitor. I loaded the other disc and took a picture of its image, too. Then I loaded the disc for Camera 2 and tried to zoom in, far enough up the mall to see the boarded store, but it was too distant to be clear. I loaded the discs for some other cameras to see if any showed the luggage store in their periphery but none did.

I put everything back in the evidence box and sent a text through to Sgt. Beth to let her know I was done but want to come back soon. Then I waved at Sgt. Jones and he escorted me almost at a run down the corridor and out the door to my car.

. . .

At the mall, standing beside the jewelry booth, I took another look at the photos on my phone and compared them to the storefronts now. I looked up at the second floor with its wide balcony in front of the stores up there. There were planted flower beds in long troughs against the protective railing. In the 2004 picture from Camera 11, I could see the beginning of a flower bed trough in front of the video store, which was now a phone store; on the picture from the next camera to the right, there was no trough and no right side of the store. It began at the next store to the right. I flipped back and forth on my phone between the two old pictures, comparing them to the current stores.

Then I went south to the store that was being renovated with its own boards in front. On the left, they were painted to read, "You're going to love the new Smiths" and on the right, "Coming in July!" The access door – just another white board between the painted boards to each side – was blank. While I was looking at it, the door opened and a worker stepped out, pushing a large cardboard box on a dolly. Behind it, I could see all kinds of construction going on, shielded from the main mall itself.

I turned on my heel and looked back toward the luggage store. I could picture the boards from 2004 in my mind. "You bastard," I whispered. "That's where you took her."

. . .

I really wanted to tell Sgt. Beth about all this – to impress her, I admit – and I wanted to recheck those original photos. She'd gone for the day, though, and besides, Jon should know first.

It was clear now that Cameras 11 and 14 did not overlap, as they should have done, and there was a strip of six or eight feet left unseen between them. More to the point, that missing strip probably included a workers' access door to the luggage store under renovation.

There were some other scenarios to think through, too.

One is that Jessica walked away from the moment in that final photo where she's looking up at the camera and into the missing black-hole area, then walked on her own through the door and away. But that's just not realistic, so let's assume somebody lured Jessica from the final photo place and into the black hole. Maybe he was somebody she knew, since she went along so willingly, or at least somebody who knew her name to call her over.

Second, the abductor would have been incredibly lucky to lure Jessica into literally the only place in the mall where cameras couldn't see her. That's just not realistic, either. I don't much believe in luck. This means the abductor *knew* about this area, probably even created it by adjusting the cameras. If it's that, the abductor was somebody who worked at the mall, or somebody with access to the cameras.

Then, once Jessica was behind that door, how did he get her away from the mall? All these stores have back doors to the parking lot. It must have been through there, somehow. Maybe there were no workmen behind the boards in the store because it was Christmas week. I hadn't looked at the pictures from those outside cameras to study them properly, and I didn't see hard hats in the crowd inside. Now I knew what to watch for, I should get back to the police station as soon as I could.

But first, I tried Jon. He didn't pick up earlier, but maybe he would now.

"Yeah?"

"Jon, it's Grant."

He sounded like I woke him up, though he was in his truck somewhere.

"Okay."

"I've got news on Jessica. You ready for this?"

And I told him everything, and he woke right up, and when I finished, he said he wanted me to text him all the pictures on my phone.

"But I've gotta ask, Grant – how good are your contacts with the cops?"

"Pretty good, I guess."

"Good, because I have a huge favor to ask. I think only a cop can make this happen."

"Okay."

And he told me what he wanted, and I could feel my eyes widen, and my stomach knot up, and suddenly, I was really, really scared.

Chapter 30

JON, Tampa

It didn't go so good this morning. Once I was through the tollbooths and headed back to the Gulf, I sent Uncle Luis a text to say all was well, and me and Gary would see him in a few hours. Then I turned off both my phones and when I got closer, I took a detour over to the farm. That's Gary's final resting place. I never liked the guy, and I cut off his stupid ponytail from his dead balding head and tossed those stringy, greasy strands of hair into the mangroves. I threw his body in the water near where I blew away the gator and I don't expect there'll be much left of him by tomorrow. Not gonna lie – I enjoyed doing that.

Then I drove direct to the wreckers and spilled my guts to Luis. That's the part that didn't go so good.

I thought about playing dumb and telling Luis that Gary drove me home, then I'd just let him disappear, but I knew I couldn't keep that story going. I can lie pretty good when I have to, but not to Luis. He'd catch me out. Besides, he should be on my side. He should sympathize, back me up. He should – unless he was in on it, and that's where I had to roll the dice.

I sat in Luis's office, him at his desk and me in the chair opposite, and I told him to trust me.

He nodded, impatient.

"Luis, Gary is dead," I told him. "He tried to have me killed, and when that didn't work, he tried to kill me himself. So I killed him. It was self-defense."

Uncle Luis just stared at me, didn't blink, but his lips were pushed together so tight they lost all their color. He'd picked up a rubber band from his desk and was pulling on it without noticing it, stretching it, twisting it. He stayed silent, didn't take his eyes off my eyes, forced me to fill the empty air.

"He told me he knew you wanted me to take over here, but he said he was family too, just like me, and it should be him taking over. He pulled into a parking lot while it was still dark and Mateo followed us in, and he thought I didn't have any rounds in my gun and he told Mateo it was empty, and Mateo was going to blow me away with a shotgun, but I did have a full magazine and I shot Mateo first and then I pinned down Gary while he was trying to get his gun from under the seat and Gary told me he should have the job and he told me to go fuck myself, and that's when I shot him…"

I tailed off the story, not sure what to say next. Luis still hadn't blinked. His face was expressionless. His hands were on his lap now, hidden behind the desk, and I hoped he was still pulling on the rubber band. For all I knew, he was pointing a rifle at me between his knees and about to shoot me in the gut because Gary was only following orders. I didn't know if honesty was the best policy, but I knew there was no going back now.

I stayed silent, and eventually Luis spoke.

"You killed Gary there in the parking lot? And Mateo too?"

"Yes."

"And what did you do with the bodies?"

"I put Gary in the trunk and took him away. He was dead already. I left Mateo there."

"You sure Mateo was dead?"

"I drove over him."

Luis didn't even flinch. I thought he might wince to that, at least. No reaction.

"Were there any cameras? Anybody around? Anybody drive by?"

"No cameras, and it was before six in the morning. Still dark and nobody was there to see anything. It was Gary that chose the place, for me."

"Where's Gary now? Where's your gun?"

"I dropped his body in the swamp at this place I have. It's private land. My land. Nobody goes there and there'll be no trace tomorrow. The gun's there too." Which it was, reloaded and locked away in the trailer, but Luis didn't need to know that.

Luis closed his eyes. He stayed silent for a long time, then he opened his eyes and looked at me.

"Tell me about the hit in Miami."

JON – Tampa

I described what went down. I told him about my gun's trigger safety being glued shut, about the bright green Dodge Dart, about the shootout and how I got out of there. He listened impassive, without reaction of any sort. I imagined his hands beneath the desk, twisting and twisting on the rubber band, stretching it tighter and tighter and tighter, his stubby manicured fingers white against the thin elastic. I told him about taking the Uber to Fort Lauderdale, and about how I changed my clothes at the condo there. I told him about Jodi being my tenant, but I didn't mention the boyfriend visiting.

"So this Jodi – she knows you were in Miami, and that you got into trouble?"

"I told her I wrecked my car. That's all."

"But she can place you there."

"Yes, but she's cool."

And that's when the band must have snapped and Luis lost it. He stood up, knocked over his heavy chair, and I thought he was going to throw something at me.

"I'll tell you what's fucking cool and what's so fucking far from cool it's on the fucking sun!" he yelled, his whole bald head turning red. "Gary worked for me more than 30 years! You did not have the right to kill him and throw him in a fucking swamp!"

"He tried to kill me, Uncle. It was him or me. I had no choice."

"*Aaaaagh!*" screamed Luis. This time, he picked up one of the model cars from his desk and threw it at the side wall. It was solid metal and heavy, a custom T-Bird that he once told me was the same model and year as his first car. It smashed into a framed certificate on the wall and shattered the glass, real loud. Luis scarcely seemed to notice.

I stayed silent. Luis knew I was right.

He stood a while longer, panting and wheezing with a hand resting on the desk, then sat down again. Slumped, more like. We both just sat there while he recovered his composure.

"So," he said eventually, and he spoke quietly and steadily, as if he was a judge pronouncing a sentence, which in a way, he was. "You killed Gary and you killed Mateo, and you killed two other guys from the Miami crew. That means there's one other guy left, Danny. We'll have a word with Danny – a *persuasive* word – and if his story bears out your story, then we'll move on and I'll grieve the painful loss of my friend. But if his story does not exonerate you in every single fucking way possible, doesn't paint you to be Jesus Christ himself and his twelve fucking apostles, then we'll move on and I'll grieve the painful loss of my nephew. With the emphasis on 'painful'. You understand?"

I nodded. I understood completely.

"Now get the fuck out of here. And don't leave town."

"Thank you," I said, and rose to leave.

"One more thing," said Luis. "I'll need the number of your unit at the condo building in Lauderdale."

. . .

Grant called me when I was in the truck, headed home. He said he'd found a gap in the security photos from the mall, and it looked like there was an area the cameras couldn't see that might have had a door in it: a workers' temporary door for a store under construction. He said it was likely that's where Jess was taken from the cookie booth, and that she would have left the mall from the store's freight door out to the parking lot.

Floyd Woods must have been a lousy detective to miss that. Lousy and lazy. Jess had to leave the mall somehow, and there must be camera footage of the parking lot, and the police must have scoured it all. Why wouldn't they see a little girl being led outside, or being carried somehow? Grant said he'll go back to look at the exterior photos, but probably can't get into the station again till tomorrow.

That's when I asked him for a real big favor. I asked him to get me, or get him and me, a visit with Mike up on Death Row at Raiford. He was a part of this puzzle too. I wanted to ask Uncle Luis about what Gary said, about how "your brother told me, a long time ago, what you did to Jess. Your brother told me everything." Obviously, today was not the time, but maybe Luis didn't even know. Him and me were together for most of that night 14 years ago, chasing down the Jacksonville crew that had threatened him and his family, and who we thought had taken Jess. It wouldn't surprise me if Gary never spoke of it with him, but was happy to tell it to anyone who he wanted to hate me.

Grant asked if he had to come along to Raiford, or if he could maybe just wait outside. I knew it takes a month to get a visit approved, and the cops would never speed things up to let me see Mike on my own. This couldn't go by the book. In Florida, the prisoner doesn't have to see anybody he doesn't want to see – murderers and pedo perverts have rights in this state, and even if Mike should agree to see me, maybe because he's just bored, it'd take a month and I didn't know if I even have a month. I was trying to live each day as if it's my last healthy day on Earth, and at this rate, it wasn't going so good.

If Grant makes the request for himself, and if he's a golden boy for the cops who'll take credit for his work in solving the cold case, and if the warden's in a happy mood, then maybe he can get the pass to see Mike soon, and maybe I can go in there with him. I won't say a word to Uncle Luis – he didn't want me leaving town.

Grant said he'd try, but he didn't sound too pleased about it. I don't blame him. The last place I want to be is in a windowless room across from Mike. But it was time. Time to go see big brother.

. . .

Before anything else though, I had to go home and get some rest. I was exhausted, but also, I think all the slaughter was catching up with me. Before that day, I think I mentioned already that I've killed two people in my life, but now that's up to six. It might even be seven or eight, but I called Jodi after I left Uncle Luis and told her to get the fuck away and stay away for a while, like *right now*. I said not to ask questions and I'd make it up to her, and I hope she understood. Even so, I was already a mass murderer and the buzz was wearing off fast. I'd crash hard. I can't keep it up like I used to, in so many ways.

"Hi handsome!" said Maria when I walked through the front door and into the living room. She looked beautiful with her fresh, smiling face, perfect eyebrows, and carefully brushed dark hair. "Everything okay? I thought I'd be waking up next to you."

I texted her earlier when I got into town to let her know I'd be home right after meeting Luis. I wanted her to know where I was, in case Luis turned real bad with the news about Gary.

"Sorry, honey. I was out of town for Uncle Luis and I've been up most of the night. I've got to lie down for a while."

"You want to go to bed, or just stay here on the couch with me?"

If I went to bed, I'd be asleep in minutes and then I wouldn't sleep tonight. More than that, I wanted – I *needed* – a little closeness right then.

The couch sounds pretty good, I told her, and once I was settled at one end of it with a couple of cushions, Maria stretched out next to me and rested her head on my shoulder. I put my arm around her and she snugged into me, and we were like a real married couple making the most of each other.

"You've been pushing yourself hard these last few days, baby," she said. "Why don't you take a couple days here, get up late, swim in the pool? Can you do that? It'll be good for you, and it'll be good for us, too. I like spending time with you."

There was a full glass of white wine on the side table. It was noon. That'd be her first of the day. It was good to know she was sober and this was coming from the heart, not from the bottle.

"I like spending time with you too, honey. Maybe you're right. Maybe I do need a couple days just to rest up."

Was this the time to tell her? Oh by the way, since Molly's at school and we've got the house to ourselves, I should let you know that I'm about to die. I won't be living much longer past today. The doctor gave me just a few more months, and once I start to decline, it'll be real quick. I've already been coughing up blood. Lung cancer.

I wanted to tell her so bad, but even more, I didn't want to tell her. I didn't know where to begin. She'd listen and she'd cry and she'd be supportive and then what? We'll never go to the carnival in Brazil. We'll never go to Europe. I'll never go to Cuba with her to meet her family. She'll travel there with Molly and she'll take photographs of me to show her parents. This is Jon. He was a good man. He wanted to be here, but he's dead. Lung cancer.

There's just no way to begin a conversation like that, so I stayed quiet, blinking back the wetness in my eyes as Maria lay against me, comfortable and safe, her hand gently stroking my hip.

"This is nice, isn't it, baby?" she said. "I could stay like this forever."

. . .

I fell asleep on the couch like that. I don't know how much longer Maria stayed with me, but it was Molly who woke me when she came in from school.

"Hey Dad! How are you doing with looking for Jess?"

I opened my eyes and there was my daughter in front of me, and for just a moment, left over from a dream that's already gone, I thought she was Jess.

JON – Tampa

I thought I was on the couch back in my little two-bedroom, and Claire was in the kitchen fixing supper, and Rags was on the rug and Jess was home from school and waking me from a fitful sleep. But the image went as quickly as it came. I never knew Jess at 12 years old, and this was Molly, who has dark brown hair and is on the cusp of becoming a woman, and my wife Maria was somewhere nearby, and Rags was long dead, and I was in a million-dollar home with glass walls and marble floors and a swimming pool.

And I'm a mass killer, and I'm on the final lap.

I blinked a few times and yawned, then stretched. I'd slept for three hours, maybe four.

"It's going good, sweetie. Grant's been looking at the old photographs and making some trips to the mall, and he thinks he knows how Jess was taken."

Maria walked in to see her daughter home from school, and I told them both about Grant's investigation. He told me once that every news story should answer five Ws and an H: what, when, where, why, who, and how. We've always known the first three Ws – Jess was taken in 2004 from the Fairfield Mall – and now we probably knew how it was done. The why didn't really matter, not any more. All we had to figure out now was who did it. If we knew who, maybe we can find that person and find some resolution to the mystery, maybe even find Jess herself.

"I knew he could figure it out," said Molly. "Grant's smart, you know. He's smarter than those detectives, anyway."

"I think you're right, sweetie, but there's a way to go yet."

I thought about mentioning that I was wanting to go up to Raiford to talk with Monster Mike, but that was best left alone for now. I didn't want Molly reminded of him, and I wasn't sure how to explain why I needed to visit him.

"Dad – just imagine if Grant finds Jess. We'll all be together as a family at last. She can come to my graduation. She can be my maid of honor when I get married. Maybe I can be her maid of honor if she's not married yet. You can walk us both down the aisle and we'll look beautiful and Mom will cry and it will be just like it's always supposed to be. You'll have brought more love into the world."

She paused, and the happiness on her face turned to concern. She could see the tears beginning in my eyes. She watched them form and when they gathered enough to move onto my cheeks, she smiled and reached across with her gentle hands and wiped them each away.

BIRD ON A WIRE

Chapter 31

CLAIRE, Toronto

The wind's gathered and I can hear it now around me, picking me up like a feather on the breeze, a gull on the thermals, a handful of sand in a storm, no, just a grain of sand, a single grain, blowing across the dunes, flying through the air toward the sea. I can hear the waves against the shore, against the cliffs, against the rocks, against the pebbles on the beach, against my legs, my feet, my toes. I can smell the salt, smell the water, smell the air, and hear the word,

Claire!

I'm pollen in the still air, hovering in the layer between earth and sky, slipping down to the ground, to the room, to the bed, to the place where I belong, and I hear the word,

Claire!

And I feel the touch, the squeeze, the caress, the gentle pressure of a loving friend, a loving parent, a loving mother, someone who reaches up toward me to hold me to the ground before I float away, dust in the air, nothing there, someone to care, and I hear the word,

Claire!

And I'm so close, so close to something, I can hear it, hear its song, hear its call, it's right here, here beneath me, here inside me, a part of me, growing, expanding, filling, and I hear my name,

Claire!

BIRD ON A WIRE

Chapter 32

VIVIAN, Toronto

Claire first saw me this evening at 6:35, two days after she was pulled from the pool. Her eyes had been open for some while, open or closed, awake or sleeping, but not properly registering anything. A doctor shone a light into her eyes this morning and she blinked, which he said was a good thing. It showed her brain was reacting to the stimulus of the light, which it hadn't done the day before.

We can expect this, he said. She's doing what she's supposed to do. We're cutting back the drugs to bring her out of the coma, he said, but it's a careful process. Do it too fast and she'll overreact and her body won't be able to cope. Leave it too long and she can stay trapped wherever it is she is, and while her body may recover physically, her mind will never find itself again.

The doctors all told me to encourage her brain's activity by talking to her and providing familiar sounds. She's always loved listening to the birds – when she was young, Patrick taught her to identify many different birds by their calls and their son – so I've been playing her clips on my phone from bird websites and reading her the descriptions.

I played her the wood thrush. "It says this is the prettiest of the song birds," I told her, and I played the thrush's song, an *ee-oh-lay* that repeated each time in the middle of the tune. "The wood thrush has more than 50 songs, it says. It sounds like a flute, doesn't it?"

And after that: "Here's a warbler. It has a falling pitch. Listen!"

And next: "Remember the loons when we went to Muskoka, you and me and Lex, that summer after high school before you started at York? We'd wake to this every morning, remember?" I played the slow call of a loon, swimming on a northern lake. "Let's go back there this summer. Maybe we can rent a cottage. Maybe we can go with Jess." I played it again, a long, mournful call that seemed to echo softly around the room. Claire moaned, gently. I wasn't sure, but she seemed to smile, just the ends of her mouth curled slightly in that way she has. This made me smile too.

When the doctor returned this afternoon, her eyes were already open, staring up at the ceiling, and he shone his little flashlight into each of them and she closed her eyelids right away. Very good! he said. It shouldn't be much longer now.

There must have been a hundred birds I played for her from the websites, softly calling and cooing and singing their individual songs. Her eyes were open and now moving around but looking always at the ceiling. Her head was still, her body immobile, but the fingers on both her hands would twitch.

I pressed Play for another call.

"This is the mourning dove, Claire. It's cooing for its mate." I played the long, low call of the gentle dove and slowly, Claire moved her head to one side toward me. Her eyes caught mine, and finally, she saw me there.

Chapter 33

JON, Tampa

I didn't sleep much last night, even though I was still so tired. I was up in the night, coughing in the bathroom, trying to get rid of all the thick phlegm in my throat, and the crap that's down deeper than that. All the hacking made me throw up, too. Maria heard me and called out. I locked the door. I didn't want her to come in and check on me, because I didn't want her to see all the blood on the toilet paper. I flushed everything away to make sure there was no evidence. I'll tell her, and I'll tell Molly, but not just yet. I want to get past visiting Mike first.

"You should see the doctor about that cough," she said when I came back to bed. "It sounds bad. You know you should quit smoking. It's not healthy. I'm not losing you to cancer or nothing, not just yet. We've got a lot of living to do first."

I'll go see the doctor, I promised her. Soon, I promised her. And I'll tell her, soon, that it's a done deal and I'll probably be gone before Christmas.

So I didn't sleep much last night, even though I was still so tired.

I did sleep a bit later than usual, at least. Maria brought me some coffee while I was still in bed, but even so, I was up and dressed before eight. I've never been much good at lying in bed on a morning and today was no different. I had a dream that I couldn't remember, but I know Gary was in it, and he was out at the trailer, and I became concerned for what was out there and I wanted to go check on the swamp, just to be sure.

"You said you wouldn't go in to work!" said Maria, when I told her I needed to head out. It'll just be for the morning, I said, and I need to make sure everything's cleared so I can take a few days free, turn off the phone, enjoy some Florida sun. She thought I meant tidying my desk at the dealership, tying off some leads, maybe some local stuff for Luis. Of course, what I actually meant was heading out to the trailer she doesn't know exists to see if the corpse of the man I murdered yesterday had been eaten entirely by alligators. I didn't think she needed to know those details.

I took the truck and headed direct to the farm, detouring through a drive-thru Starbucks for a latte before leaving the city limits. The dream was coming back to me, or at least I think it was. I was in the trailer and chewed-up Gary was at the door, wanting to know where his pony tail was. That was pretty funny when I thought about it, but it wasn't funny at the time and when I woke I did so with a little gasp for breath. That got me coughing again. I was able to get up and hawk it out into the toilet bowl before Maria came through with the coffee, and yes, the phlegm was red and brown and thick and gross and I flushed it away, but I got back into bed and she never knew I'd already been awake.

My latte was cool by the time I pulled off the interstate, and when I reached the farm, it was finished. There's never traffic on that narrow road that runs along the edge of the swamp, with wire fencing to each side along the ditches. If you didn't know where to look, you'd probably never notice the chain that runs across the entrance to my property, but I knew exactly where it is and I pulled up, jumped out of the truck, looked up and down the empty road from force of habit, then unlocked the padlock and lowered the chain to drive in. I wouldn't stay long, but even so, I pulled the chain back into place and re-locked it. Force of habit again.

I've never cleared the path because I like it to look unused. The truck had no problem making its way through the high grass and past the low trees to the trailer, twisting around a couple of stands of sugar maple along the way just to keep things obscured and help muffle any sounds from the road. Maybe I should clear the path so whoever takes this place on after me can find it. Maybe I should give it to Grant. Maria would want nothing to do with it, and I don't like the idea of Molly visiting a place where corpses get eaten by alligators. This is a guy's hang-out, anyway. Maybe I'll bring Grant here sometime and we'll have some beer and if it seems he likes the place, I'll just hand him the key to the trailer and tell him it's his. That would be a cool thing to do.

I parked outside the trailer and went inside to get my gun, because it belongs in the glovebox of my truck. Also, I don't like walking down to the swamp without a weapon, just in case I meet something predatory on the path. It's never happened, but you never know. It was dark and hot inside and I thought about turning on the air before dismissing the idea – I wouldn't be sticking around. I left the easy chair where it was. I really did want to get home and lie beside the pool with my wife.

The gun was behind the wall panel beside the sofa, where I left it, and I took it outside to clean it and get rid of the last of the glue. I'd brought a fine chisel from home to scrape properly beneath and behind the trigger, as well as some Goop to dissolve the last of the residue. All the rest of the tools I needed to clean it were there in the bottom kitchen drawer. It's a relaxing thing to do on a warm day: clean my gun then shoot it at some cans or any birds that fly past, then clean it some more. Clean, shoot, repeat – doesn't get much better, *know what I mean?*

There's a coffee machine in the trailer too, so I made myself an espresso. That was the third cup of the day and it was barely 10 o'clock. "Gotta cut back," I muttered as the water poured. "This stuff will kill me."

I drank the coffee while I cleaned the gun, sitting outside on my white plastic lawn chair and just enjoying the heat. This was what February should be like: cool in the morning but when the sun comes out, warming up to 70 degrees or more. Half of America was freezing its fat ass in blizzards and snowstorms and here was me, Florida Man, making the most of what I had.

It couldn't be put off though, and when the gun was clean and the coffee was gone, I headed out down the narrow footpath through the knee-high grass toward the swamp.

There was no ghost behind the trees. No hand reaching up from the water. It was just a quiet pool with mangroves hanging over it, their thick roots rising from the dark surface and the buzz of cicadas in the warm air. I looked around for any sign of any part of Gary but there was nothing to be seen at all. Not even the shadow of a gator, or a ripple from a submerged tail, moving slowly, quietly, through the muddy depth. All was peaceful, all was as it should be in this remote graveyard.

Even so, I felt I was being watched.

Of course I was. This place was full of creatures that call it home, and you'd better believe there were dozens, maybe hundreds of eyes watching me from behind trees, under water, beneath the grass. I was king of this land, but it started to feel uncomfortable. Then I heard a noise behind me, just a gentle crack, and I spun around, expecting to see Gary standing there, grinning through the holes in his cheeks, no eyes, and slugs crawling from his nose.

"You think I don't know? Go fuck yourself, crackerjack!"

There was nothing, of course. Just nerves.

I walked back toward the trailer, more quickly than I came in, but before I left the cover of the trees, I stopped and turned once more, just to be sure there was nothing behind me. There wasn't, but when I turned back, there was a flash of red through the last of the bushes. It could have been a bird, but I was jittery, so I waited it out and sure enough, there it was again, in the clearing over by the trailer.

I was frozen in the warm morning. Slowly, I reached behind my back, pulled the Glock from my belt.

It was a man, a big man, an intruder in a red shirt, somebody who'd walked down the path from the road. I couldn't see him properly through the overhang of the trees, but he was at the door of the trailer. I didn't lock it. I left the door open so the heat could get out. *Fuck!* He was moving slowly, carefully. He wasn't just walking about like a casual trespasser or a lost tourist – he was taking his time, feeling his way around. He was holding a handgun. He stepped up to the door and when he paused, framed in the entrance, and he looked around once last time before committing to go inside, I caught a glimpse of his face and realized what was going on.

As soon as he stepped in, I ran silently to the trailer and crouched down beside it to catch my breath. I could hear him inside, moving quiet, checking the bedroom. He'd stay there long when he knew I was out there.

And then, of course, I started to cough.

The movement inside stopped. I tried not to cough again, but I couldn't help it and my throat spasmed and I tried to shield my mouth with my elbow but it was no good and I coughed some more.

"Jon – that you?" he called from inside. I knew that voice.

"Sure is!" I called back. I hawked a giant loogie onto the ground and my throat settled.

"You wanna talk?"

"Why, you fat fucker? You got something to say?"

"We've gotta clear this up, Jon. You know we do."

And Floyd Woods stepped out of the trailer. He wasn't holding the gun anymore – it must have been under his shirt, tucked into his belt. I stepped out from around the side and I had my gun in my hand, but I wasn't pointing it at him, not yet.

"Why you here, Floyd?"

"To talk to you. Make it good." He was looking at my gun.

"I'm good already."

"Didn't sound like it from that cough. Cigarettes will do that to you."

He was acting real friendly, but that might have worked at home, not here.

"How'd you find this place, Floyd?"

He laughed.

"I'm a detective! That's what we do. We find people."

He must have followed me from the house. Damn. Wasn't thinking. Not on my game.

"You're not much fucking good at it though, are you? You never found my little girl."

"No. No we didn't. Hey – can we sit down, talk? Be civilized?"

He was still standing in the doorway, and sweating like a bitch.

"You can sit, Floyd. Take a seat. I'm good to stand."

And Floyd Woods took a seat in the white plastic chair, made his fat ass comfortable, and looked up at me and smiled.

"Nice place you got here," he said.

. . .

Floyd seemed relaxed, far more than me. He said he already knew about my trailer, and he wanted a chance to talk to me away from Maria, away from home, *mano a mano*. He said he came out here hoping to find me and hey, here I was!

It's bullshit of course. I didn't believe a word of it. Nobody knows about this place. He followed me this morning, parked up beside the road and walked in so he could get the surprise on me, then came up with a cover story when his surprise fell through. I expect he planned to kill me here, somewhere out of the city. I'm not stupid. If I'm dead, then he'll be okay and there's no threat against his buddy Wes and his family. They knew that Claire and Vivian can't do much up in Canada but I sure as fuck can, and I was a loose cannon. Get rid of me and it might just all go away. I'll listen to his story, though. No sense being hot-headed. I wanted to hear what he had to say.

I made nice, still holding my Glock, and me and Floyd danced around the conversation, feeling each other out. Right away, he admitted he and Wes made up the story about Andrea being Jess because Wes needed money for his son's care. He did his research and prepared Andrea, who he said was real timid to do it – right, that's something else I didn't believe. He had access to the investigations file through his friends at the station and even found a hospital record of Jessica twisting her ankle when she fell out of our tree swing. They spent a couple of months, off and on, turning Andrea into Jessica and figuring out the back story of how she got to be living in Floyd's little house, driving his little car. She even stayed out of the sun the whole time to let her tan fade and pale up her skin. And while she hadn't yet legally changed her name, that was going to be the next step.

Apparently, says Floyd, I was never going to be included in all this and he advised against it, but Claire really wanted to get at me, and Andrea thought there might be a way to shake me down for something. She figured that if I really had raped my own daughter, maybe I'd be more likely to cave. That was before she realized I was the guy at the strip joint. I really shook her up that afternoon at my house, when I fired the gun in the air. That was their big mistake: they didn't think that one through, about including me. They went for double-or-nothing and they ended up with nothing.

Even so, Floyd was clearly pleased with himself but tried to downplay it all. He said the deception was wrong and he was sorry and if I wanted to prosecute him for fraud, he deserved it and please leave Wes and the family alone. I'm sure he knew there was no evidence that would stand up against him, not in this state.

"In the end," said Floyd, "I made a few thousand bucks off your ex and her mom. I got a game of golf out of it when I went up to Atlanta and told them I met that woman you were fooling around with. I already gave the money to Wes, but if you want me to give it back to them, I will. I just want to put this behind us now, and leave you all be, and move on."

That offer was about as hollow as his apology. He asked for a bottle of water and I fetched one from the truck, but I never turned my back on him. That gun wouldn't be coming out of his belt quickly while he was sitting in that chair, and that's just the way I wanted it.

I changed the subject.

"Floyd, why did you never find my little girl? Why did you never find Jessica?"

"I felt bad about that, Jon, I really did."

Like fuck you did, you asshole.

"We were stretched real thin in those days," he carried on. "I'll be honest with you – we thought it was you. By the time we realized it wasn't, any trail there might have been was cold. I had a good record for finding people and it's always bothered me we didn't find her."

"You think she might still be alive?"

"I don't think so. I'm sorry, I just don't know, but I don't think so. If the abductor followed the usual pattern, she'd have been killed before the end of the day. Maybe he brought her out to a place like this. I reckon there are plenty of places round here to dispose of a body."

Was he scouting me out? Trying to get an answer, even now, to a long unsolved mystery? Was he recording this? It didn't matter. I wasn't taking the bait.

"How do you think the killer took her, Floyd?"

"Damned if I know. We could never figure how he got her past the cameras. For days, weeks I guess, I looked at all those photos from the mall, but it stayed away from me. We questioned everybody – *everybody* – who was seen leaving the mall with anything suspicious, or loading boxes onto trucks, anything like that, and everybody checked out."

I was keeping my cards close to my chest. I was listening to his words, but I was waiting for him to move around in the plastic chair, squirm his fat ass and grab for the gun under his shirt, and that was not going to happen.

A thought came to me.

"You think my brother had anything to do with it?"

"What? No. He was in prison already. What could he have done from there?"

"I don't know," I said. "Just putting it out."

"We thought it was you, because of your family. And then we thought it was somebody who knew your daughter, because that's the way it usually is, a neighbor or a family friend, but you didn't have any friends who fit the profile. You had a bad rep, but you stayed away from people like that. And like I said, the trail grew cold, fast. When we pulled you in the very next day? It was already cold."

"Did you ever look for her again? Like, when Claire called and asked you to?"

"No. What was the point? What was I going to find? I thought about it, but it would just be going back over those photos and reading the old reports and I'd already done so much of that. There was nothing new I was going to find. I figured if Claire thought there was some hope of finding her, that might give her a good Christmas, at least. And like I said, I was trying to help out Wes, and Tyler. Was that a good idea? I don't know. Would I do it again? Definitely not. No way. That's why I came here now, to try to make good."

Bullshit!

"You know Claire tried to kill herself this week?"

"What? No – I had no idea. How come?"

"Just sadness. Sadness you caused. False hope. That's on you."

He looked genuinely surprised. Not sure if he looked sorry for her.

"I'm so sorry," he said. "I never thought that would happen. We should never have done this."

"No. Can't be helped now."

"So where does this leave us, Jon?" He was looking at my gun again.

"I think we all just walk away. You and me, we never see each other again. You leave Claire and her mom alone. Keep the fucking money – it's from me. This never happened."

Floyd nodded. He looked thoughtful. He put down the plastic bottle, stood with some effort – I was watching his hands, my finger on my trigger – and offered me a sweaty handshake.

"You want to make good on this, Jon?"

"No. I want you to fuck off, and never bother me again."

"Okay," he said. "Sounds reasonable. Thank you. You take it easy."

And he walked away, past my truck, up through the grass toward the road. He got about 20 yards before he paused. Just stood there. Then he said, "Just one more thing!" and he started to turn back toward me and he raised his hand from beneath his shirt, and he moved his arm across to brace his firing arm, but I was ready for this and my gun was already pointed directly at his body mass and I fired, again and again and again, and he looked astonished, and he threw both arms into the air and spun over backwards into the long grass, and I kept on firing, again and again and again and again.

I felt the adrenaline surge with every round, through my face, through my arm, through my chest, through my groin. My gun was heavy in my hand but now felt light, just an extension of me as if it's always been there. I was panting from holding back the recoil, trembling from watching the death, fixed still to the ground like one of those mangroves, rooted through the water to the graveyard.

Eventually, I freed myself from the killing's hold and walked toward Floyd's body. He was lying face up, eyes open and looking direct into the overhead sun, blood leaking from his mouth, still that expression of astonishment. Dark red stains on his red shirt. I kicked around in the grass to look for the gun he dropped when his arms went up in the air, but it was nowhere to be seen. Surely, it would glint off the sunlight, but it did not.

And then, after a minute of searching the overgrown ground, a thought occurred to me and I went back to Floyd's body and kicked with my boot to nudge his loose shirt up and past his gut. And there was the gun, tucked securely into a strapped-down holster on his belt, where he left it when he came out of the trailer to reason with me.

BIRD ON A WIRE

Chapter 34

GRANT, Tampa

I couldn't wait to get to the police station this morning to look at the mall photos, but Sgt. Beth was out of town. I had to phone her from the lobby, and she got Sgt. Jones – the guy with no first name – to let me in and bring the evidence box back through from her office. He didn't start work till 10 am, so I had to go sit in a Krispy Kreme around the corner and be patient till he turned up. I think he's the kind of cop who only turns on the cherries when he's driving to a donut shop.

Yesterday, I told Sgt. Beth on the phone that I might have found something with the pictures to explain how Jessica Morgan was snatched. She listened quietly when I explained about the gap between the cameras. She told me she was away for a couple of days in Nashville and she'd look at them when she got back. And then, since she seemed in a good mood, I asked if she could help me get approval to visit Mike Morgan up at Florida State Prison. That made her curious why I'd want to talk with him, so I pulled out all the stops and said that if the department could actually solve this cold case now – not me of course, you understand, but the hard-working detectives from the Tampa PD – then I wanted to interview all the players in the story before anything major might change.

"And, here's an idea," I said on the phone, as if I'd only just thought of it, spit-balling a suggestion. "How about if I can convince Jon Morgan to come with me? I don't know if he will, but you never know, and then there'll really be a story! Who knows what could come out?"

"You trying for a Pulitzer there, hot-shot?" she asked.

"Hey, if they want to give me one, I won't say no!"

"It would be quite the story if it all comes together," she said. "I might be able to help. I know the warden at FSP and he owes me a couple favors. Let me see and I'll get back to you."

When I called her this morning, she said she'd not heard back from the warden but she'd let me know. If you don't ask, you don't get, right?

. . .

The CD-ROMs were all in their plastic sleeves, and I went straight to the disc for Camera 44. I knew the layout now, and that was the camera that showed the parking lot outside the luggage store, halfway down the mall on the west side. None of these pictures were on the separate disc of photos the police thought were relevant. I spun it to the time stamp at noon and then started cycling through the images.

There was a lot of stuff going on. Every picture, 10 seconds apart, showed cars moving, people moving, stuff happening. The back door to the luggage store stayed closed until right there, at 12:18 pm, when there were four fuzzy images of a man in a yellow hard-hat leaving the store, pushing a dolly with a large cardboard box. The first two showed him pushing the box over toward a blue van; the second two showed him loading the box into the van. In the next picture of the sequence, the van was already driving away and it wasn't in any further photos.

I went back in time to see if I could watch the van arrive, but in every photo, it was parked still in its space while all the movement happened around it. The earliest photo saved on the disc was from 11 am and the blue van was there already. It stood out because every other vehicle around it was parked ass-in but the van was nose-in, prepared for easier loading through its back doors.

I scrolled forward again to the images of the guy pushing the dolly. He was too fuzzy to be easily recognized and besides, he was wearing the hat and his head was down, looking toward the ground. He knew where the camera was and he was avoiding it, hiding in plain sight.

It's clear what I was witnessing. I don't know why Floyd Woods didn't see this. He was there on the day itself. I don't know why he didn't look over from inside at the cookie booth and see the service door and hustle through it to follow this guy out. I don't know why he didn't see this photo and realize what happened. Maybe, if I could find Woods, I could ask him.

My phone buzzed and it was Jonathan. I was about to call him.

"Hey Grant," he said. "I'm at a McDonalds. I don't have my truck here and I need to get somewhere. If I buy you a Big Mac, can you give me a ride?"

Of course. I'll never say no to a free Big Mac!

. . .

When we met up, it turned out Jonathan needed a ride out of town to some place where he left his truck. He looked like shit, but he's my friend and he bought me a Big Mac meal, and besides, I was happy to have the time to tell him what I just saw on Camera 44.

I had photos on my phone of the mall pictures that I took from the police computer screen, and I showed them to Jon while we were still at the restaurant. He tried to zoom right in on the worker's face, pinching his fingers apart on the image, but it was blurry to start with and just turned into more blur.

"This has got to be the guy," he said. "She's in the box, right?"

It was a cardboard box for some kind of air-conditioning unit, but I couldn't read the writing on it.

"Maybe she's unconscious inside; maybe she thinks she's playing hide-and-go-seek," I said. "I don't know why Floyd Woods wouldn't have picked up on this. If we can find him, we can ask him."

Jon didn't answer, just pursed his lips and nodded. He looked angry. Don't blame him.

"Let's go," he said. "Bring your burger. There's a place I want you to see."

On the drive south out of town in my Toyota, he seemed distracted. To be honest, he didn't look well, and when he coughed, the hacking went on for a long time. I should have said something, but I was his friend and I'm sure he didn't need to hear from me about it. Even so, when he coughed up something that sounded really wet, and he wound down the window to hawk it out onto the interstate, I had to comment.

"That cough sounds nasty," I said. "You should maybe go see someone. It could be bronchitis or something."

"Yeah," he said. "I went to the doctor. I've got some meds for it."

That was it. That was all that needed to be said. Soon after, he told me to take the next exit and we ended up on a side road headed to the swamp.

"I have a place down here. I use it to get away sometimes, you know what I mean?" he said. "I had to leave my truck here. You should see the place."

We drove probably for 10 minutes, past swampland and scrub and trees, and then he pointed to just up ahead and told me to pull over. I thought there was nothing there, but when I pulled up, I could see a chain stretched between two metal posts. There was no driveway or anything, but the grass on the other side looked beaten down.

Jon got out and unlocked a padlock to release the chain. I drove over it on the ground and waited while he locked the chain back into place and then got back in the car.

"The ground's quite firm and it's just grass," he said. "Welcome to the farm."

I followed a kind-of track through some trees and then we came out into a clearing. Jon's truck was there next to a beaten-up trailer with tin-foil on the windows. This was Jon's place? This was so far removed from his home in town, I could scarcely believe it. Welcome to Deliverance! There was a plastic lawn chair by the trailer door and an old rusted barbecue. Is this where he plays the banjo? Let's cook some blue meth!

Jon got out of the car.

"It's not much, but I like it," he said. "This is a guy's place. No women come here. Maria doesn't even know about it."

Lucky Maria!

He went to the trailer door and poked in a key and tugged on the latch to make it swing open. I thought a good kick would have done the same thing.

"Come on in – let me show you around!"

Inside, it was exactly what I expected. Dark and hot. A cracked leatherette La-Z-Boy, with a kitchenette to the side. In the back, a closet bathroom and a queen-size bed with a new-looking mattress, no sheets. It was all fairly clean, though. There were probably fleas in a place like this but I couldn't see any signs of them in the dim light. Against the walls in the main room, and in the bedroom, were shelf units piled with paperback books and magazines. More magazines on a little dining table: car mags and some porn, by the look of them. *Road & Track. Hustler.* Something was missing though, and it took a while to realize it was the TV. There was no television. No screens at all.

"This your man-cave, huh? This where you get away from it all?"

I noticed a box of Kleenex next to the easy chair. *Ewww!*

"Yeah. I can unwind here. Sometimes I spend the night, but usually I just visit for a few hours, read something, kick back. I do target shooting outside, too."

This gave me the excuse to look interested and get the hell outside of the trailer. I knew Jon came from white trash, but I didn't realize he was still so nostalgic for it.

"There's 22 acres," he said, following me out. "It's mostly swamp but I like it this way. Nobody bothers me here."

There was a narrow pathway that went down to some trees that looked well-trodden.

"This go somewhere?" I asked, and started off along it.

"I wouldn't go down there just now," said Jon. "That goes into the mangroves. This isn't a good time of day to head in there."

I'd have thought lunchtime would be the best time, the sleepiest time, but I didn't bother debating it.

"You like it here?" asked Jon.

"Sure! It's a great place," I lied. "Really cool. Really…" I was searching for a word here. "Really *inspirational*."

"Good," he said, and handed me a pair of keys. "If anything ever happens to me, this place is yours."

. . .

We didn't stay much longer. John locked up, got into his truck and led the way out to the road. We were back on the interstate headed home, me following behind in my car. I was lost in thought about taking a flame-thrower to the trailer and the swampland when my phone rang and I answered it on the hands-free.

It was Sgt. Beth. The warden got back to her. Both Jon and I could go see his brother Mike up at Florida State Prison in Raiford. The visit was already booked for tomorrow morning at 10 am. *That was quick!*

"Don't be late," she said. "Make sure you pass on my warmest regards to the warden, and turn this into that Pulitzer!"

I phoned Jon up ahead to tell him and I saw his truck veer across the line when he heard the news. Then it settled again in the center of the lane headed north, straight and true.

BIRD ON A WIRE

Chapter 35

JON, Raiford

You know, I felt pretty good about this visit. I felt pretty good about a few things, all things considered, despite the obvious. Yesterday, I took Grant to the farm, showed him the trailer, gave him the keys and he looked real happy. He's the guy to have it and I'm glad he'll enjoy it. It's not the kind of place where you want to build property, but he'll probably move another trailer onto the lot and it can be a getaway for him like it's been for me.

He started walking down to the swamp and I had to stop that. If he'd made it to the water, he'd have seen Floyd Woods in there, joining Gary in the mangroves, in the gators. I felt bad about shooting Floyd, but the guy was a lazy fucker when it came down to it, and Claire was in the hospital because of him. I'm sure that after Jess was taken and he scouted out the mall, he never went back there again. He just sat in the station lunchroom, or in some bar, and looked at the security photos and shrugged off the mystery. Grant couldn't understand that part, but Floyd said it himself: when he couldn't get an easy answer out of me, he was already too late. I think he gave up fast on Jess and moved on to the next case. In his head, she was just some cracker's kid, Mike Morgan's family and a waste of his time.

Well, that came back to bite him in the ass, didn't it? Literally, there in the swamp. I'll never tell Grant what's in there, who's in there. No need for him to get spooked by the place.

My tally was up to seven now: five dead just this week, and two in the lifetime before that. It might even be up to eight or more. Luis told me my story checked out with Danny in Miami, and I'm sure that's when Danny got checked out, too. And Luis said I'd need to find another tenant for the condo in Lauderdale. No details, just one more thing, one more person to be checked off his honey-do list. Maybe the boyfriend too. I think Jodi got away, though

I'm sure the place was still being watched, ready for when she comes back. If she listened to me, heard the urgency in what I told her in that real quick phone call, she won't go back. I hope so. I feel real bad for her but I guess she'd moved on already. Fortunately for the Uber driver, Luis never took an Uber in his life, so he doesn't know the ride details are saved on some Big Tech server somewhere. I'm not going to tell him. Lucky break for that guy.

This is a lot of people, a lot of collective lives lived, and if it wasn't for me, they'd all still be living. I really don't care, though. We're all going to die sometime. I'll be joining them soon enough and maybe I'm turning into one of those Egyptian pharaohs or Chinese emperors, the rulers who took their entourages with them when they died. Buried alive to serve them in the afterlife. Is that what I've been doing?

I was settling some scores before I go – that's what this is. Some people got sucked along in my wake who really didn't deserve it, but I don't deserve it, either. I didn't ask for lung cancer. Cigarettes don't kill everyone who smokes.

Maybe now I was turning into the guy Luis always wanted me to be. "I didn't think you were cut out for what I do," he said to me yesterday, when I drove in with Floyd's Cadillac and told him what I'd done. "I didn't think you were hard enough. You didn't have the edge. But I sold you short. I think you'll do just fine." Bit late, of course. I didn't tell him I'm on a clock, not yet.

We watched the crusher take care of the Caddy. I put Floyd's gun in the car too, and his phone – I couldn't break into it and it wasn't recording when we met. Luis told me I should have left Floyd in the trunk, like in that Tarantino movie, but I told him I wasn't going back to fish that fat fucker's ass out of my swamp and he saw the reason in that. Then one of the guys dropped me at a McDonald's and I ate a double-quarter-pounder meal with a Coke. Death builds an appetite.

Me and Grant went through the drive-through for breakfast sandwiches and now I was hungry again. I'd be eating better than Brother Mike this morning and I'd make sure he knew it. He always loved McDonald's. It's funny – a week ago, before any of this, I'd have been real nervous to go meet the monster, scared even, but now I'd got more notches on my gun than he'll ever have.

. . .

It took about three hours to drive up to Florida State Prison, just short of Jacksonville. When we got close, we could see the low buildings from the road, behind miles of razor-wire fencing. There were guard towers at the corners with flat, treeless land all around. Nowhere to hide. We drove under the arch at the entrance and it was like that arch at Auschwitz, where "Work will set you free."

I'd been to prisons before but never this place. Grant said he'd never been to a prison, period. We checked in a half-hour early at the gate, parked and walked through another check-point with a turnstile and metal detector. A guard patted us down, and another guard got a dog to sniff us. Grant handed over some papers Sgt. Beth sent him and he'd printed off. We left our phones in the truck but I had to give up the keys, then we waited in a small room off to the side. No one else was around; regular visiting hours are in the afternoons. We sat there on hard plastic chairs, looking at posters on the white-washed walls that listed the rules for visiting prisoners: no drugs, no skin-tight clothing, no weapons, no touching. I don't think Mike would care if my T-shirt was too tight.

I was sitting there, and I was thinking: seven down, I should be on the other side here. Even then, I'd never do more than a few months before the devil checks me out.

After maybe 20 minutes, a sharp-looking guy in a black suit walked in. He's a black guy – there was a lot of black going on. He introduced himself as the warden, Warden Al Baines, stocky with short thinning hair and a gray goatee to cover his jowls. Like the room, he's very serious.

"Which of you is Michael Morgan's brother?"

"That's me, sir," I said, very humble, very respectful.

"He didn't want to talk to you. He didn't really want to talk to *you*, either," he said to Grant, "but we let him know it would be good for him if he did. Is Beth Anderson here?"

"No sir," said Grant. "She couldn't get away. She asked me to pass on her very warmest regards."

The warden was clearly disappointed.

"That's too bad. I've known Beth Anderson for years. She's brought me a lot of business," he said. "I was kind of hoping she'd be up here with you to talk to him. She's quite the woman – I'm sure you know that."

Grant agreed and I just nodded. I could see now why we got the quick access.

"What is it you think Morgan might be able to tell you?"

"I'll be honest, sir – I really don't know," said Grant. "This is a bit of a crapshoot. But Jon here had his daughter stolen from a shopping mall years ago, after Mike was already in custody, and we're sure he knows *something*."

"I see. Well, let's find out, shall we?" Baines led the way out of the room and down a wide, well-lit corridor. No windows. A guard in a crisp white shirt, wearing a leather holster with pepper spray and shiny chrome handcuffs, walked with us.

"For this, I thought it best for you to have an interview room," said Baines. "Morgan's been trouble so he's in shackles, just in case, but there'll be an officer in the room with you. I can assume there'll be no trouble from either of you. This isn't the place for that."

He was looking at me when he said this. Grant and me both nodded our heads.

"Of course not," I said. "This is only words."

"Words start wars," said Baines. "Choose yours carefully."

We came to an iron-barred gate and a sentry guard let us through, then we turned off into another hallway with another gate, and then Baines paused outside a door on the left.

"I'll leave you here," he said. "Good luck, and say hello to Beth for me. Tell her she's always welcome to visit." He opened the door and motioned us to enter.

. . .

The room was small and bright, maybe 12 by 12, barely more than a storage locker, with white walls and a brown polished floor. There was a large paned window on one side that looked out onto another room, and to the other side, a painted-over window that was now just part of the blank, white wall. A broad-chested guard stood in one corner, legs apart and hands crossed in front of his waist. A handlebar moustache dominated his face. He nodded to the other guard in the hallway as the door closed behind us.

My brother was sitting on a chair under the window. His hands were shackled together with a short chain; his ankles were shackled by a longer chain, fastened to the chair. This was the first time I'd seen him in more than

20 years. What's left of his gray hair was close cropped and his face was now very wrinkled – he looked like one of those hairless dogs. His right eye had a droop to it and seemed to look away to one side; his left eye was focused on me when I took a seat in the chair opposite, the regulation six feet away against the wall, maybe a couple more. He didn't even acknowledge Grant, who sat beside me. There was no other furniture, and the white walls were bare. I wished there was a table, or a clear screen at least. Something between me and him. Something bolted down.

Mike was dressed in a short-sleeve orange V-necked shirt over a white T-shirt, a pair of shapeless blue pants and white running shoes. There was a plastic name badge clipped to his shirt with his headshot and his name and inmate number, as well as some physical details: height, weight, color of his hair and eyes, and his race, "white." I took all this in with a glance, but it was the tattoos that jumped out, of course. Many more than I remembered. Snakes, dragons, faces, demons on both arms, crudely drawn in blue and green; flames of some kind reaching up from under his shirt to circle his neck; round designs on the backs of his hands and letters on the fingers; beneath the outside corner of each eye, a dark teardrop. I didn't recall those from before.

"What the fuck?" said Mike.

"How you doing, Mike?"

"How the fuck does it look like I'm doing?"

"This is my friend Grant. He's a journalist."

He turned and looked at Grant for the first time, just stared at him with that left eye while the right eye lolled off somewhere toward the wall. Grant nodded at him and for a moment I thought he was going to do okay, but then Grant backed down and looked over at me. He really didn't want to be there.

"He one of your faggot boyfriends?" said Mike, looking back at me. I heard a quick sniff from the guard, who was standing near my shoulder. Shouldn't he have been between us? Mike was wearing chains, but it's not like he was bolted to the floor or anything.

"Nope. He's a friend of mine who's a journalist. He's helping me look for my daughter, Jessica."

"So? What's this got to do with me? I've been in here 24 fucking years, asshole. I've got the Death Row record! Ain't that right?"

He called that over to the guard, who ignored him.

"I thought I'd come ask you if you knew anything about who might have taken her."

"What? Go fuck yourself! This is why you're here? Leave me to rot and then come up here and make nice and ask, all polite, if I 'know anything about who took her?' Go fuck yourself!"

This wasn't going well. I should have gone over this a few more times in my head. I didn't know what I was expecting. Mike was laughing at us now, and it was not a good feeling. I wasn't sure where to go with this. I'd planned to just wing it and see where that went, but it looked like it was headed nowhere. My brother was so unpredictable that anything could bring results, but anything could set him off, too.

Grant stayed quiet, leaving the talking to me.

"We never found her," I said. "We know *how* she was taken – we've seen pictures of it on the mall cameras. What we don't know is *where* she was taken."

"Why you asking me? I was here! You think I'm keeping her in my fucking cell, under the bunk? How would I know this shit? I've got enough going on without your fucking dead kid as well. Have you noticed this is a fucking prison? I'm on fucking *Death Row*!"

He lifted his hands and made his point by shaking the shackles that were chained to the belt around his waist. The guard beside us sniffed again, loudly, and Mike dropped his hands to his knees, started drumming his fingers, looked down at last. On his left hand, I could see a clock tattooed on the back, and on each finger, the symbols from a deck of cards: spade, club, diamond, heart. The clock seemed to move as the fingers drummed up and down but it had no hands. The cards seemed to shuffle. On his right hand, there was a compass with no directions and there, on the knuckle of each finger, there was a letter: EWMN. I wonder what all that crap means, I was thinking, but then Mike looked up, met my eye, and brought me back to the moment.

"Look, Mike..." I said.

"Don't fucking 'Look Mike' me. Not a letter, not a call, not a visit. You're not my brother any more. You want me dead as much as everyone else. Well, it's gonna happen soon. No more options here."

"Look" – and this was Grant speaking now. *Good for him!* "There's one more option for you, that I see, anyway. It's possible there's something you know, something you've heard, that can help us find whatever happened to Jessica. If that's the case, it can only do you good."

Mike looked genuinely bewildered. It was the most human he'd been so far.

"Listen, faggot. It's too late for me for anything good. Believe me, if I could get some smokes out of this, a fucking burger and fries with a Cherry Coke, I'd tell you whatever you want to know. You don't even have to say please. How's that for a deal?"

"I can talk to the warden," I said.

"Fuck you."

"Hey – I've got some pull. I got in here in 24 hours, didn't I? Wouldn't you like McDonald's? We went there this morning."

I couldn't resist, but that shut him up. He looked down again, started drumming his fingers again, started shuffling again. So I hit him with my only card.

"Gary Richards told me you know something."

Mike looked up, sharply. He glanced over at Grant, then back to me.

"What did fucking Gary say?"

"Gary said you told him a story about me and Jessica."

That was it. The hand was dealt. There was nothing to back that up. Just sit and wait and see what happens.

"Gary's not been here for years. He visited a few times. Last time, he said it was my birthday visit, but nowhere near my birthday. It was Gary told me your kid was taken. He's an asshole. What's he doing these days? He your boss now?"

I didn't know where this was going, but it might be somewhere. I realized I did have another card to play – the 'I don't give a fuck anymore because I'm dying' card. There was a guard beside us listening to everything and normally, I'd have to choose my words carefully, but what the fuck? I'm dying!

"Gary's dead, Mike. Somebody killed him and threw him in the swamp, fed him to the gators."

I knew Grant was looking at me, but I was careful not to look back at him. He had no idea who Gary was, anyway.

"No shit!" said Mike. "For real? How come I didn't hear? Gary's a name! News like that travels quick in here."

"It's recent," I said. "I only just heard about it myself. How come Gary used to visit you? What was the story you told him about me and Jessica?"

"You gonna get me that Big Mac?"

"Yes. I'll talk to the warden when we leave, but you have to talk to me now. They won't let us back in anytime soon."

I had no idea if I could send in a burger, or speak to Mike again, but I wasn't letting this go.

"What the hell. One time when he came here to visit, I told him you were fucking your kid. It was the last time he was here. He was going at me because I'd fucked those two Cooper girls on a hit he'd ordered, and I was supposed to just kill everyone but I took some time for myself while I was doing it. I told him you're worse than me. I fuck teenagers, or I do when I'm not in this fucking place" – and he looked at the guard again – "but you fuck babies. That's what I said. That's what I told him. You're no better than me, John. You think you are, but it's only because you'll suck Luis's cock that it's me in here, not you."

Mike was such an asshole. I hated him. Always did.

Grant stayed very quiet. There was no sound from the guard, either.

"Why would Gary believe a story like that?" I asked. "Even if it was true, how would you have known? You've not even seen me since before Jessica was born."

Mike smirked. He was drumming his fingers again, shuffling the cards.

"I told him you came to visit one time. I told him you were boasting about it to me. How I don't get pussy in here, but you get all you want, even your baby girl. Of course he believed it. And you running around down there in Tampa, all free and living good, while I was here, waiting for Judgement Day. Well, fuck you Johnny Boy."

"I never visited you."

"No, you didn't. Because you think you're better than me. But you're not."

Grant was looking at the floor. I sat up on the chair, ready to stand. Ready to tell the guard we were leaving. Ready to admit this was a mistake.

"And I told him about you and Tammy, too."

Tammy! My little sister. That was a jolt.

"You told him I was fucking Tammy?"

"Sure did, asshole. And I told him you killed her."

What? All the air went out of the room. It's like in those sci-fi movies when everything just freezes, goes into slow motion, movement blurs. I could still hear Mike, but all I could see was his mouth moving, fleshy lips slapping around rotten teeth.

"You thought I didn't know? Billy told me. He came up and visited one time, years ago. He knew you killed her. He saw you do it. You thought he was passed out, but he saw you shoot her up. He heard you tell her, 'this is the last one, sis. I'm not giving you no more.' Your exact words, he said. And then you walked out on her laying on the couch, and she frothed up and her heart gave out, and she choked and that was it. He saw it all. He couldn't move because he was flying too high, but he saw it all. And he told me everything. Dad fucked and killed one sister but you fucked and killed the other, just as dead. You're a killer, Johnny Boy, no better than me, and you know it."

I didn't know what to say.

Mike was grinning now, rattling his chains. His few teeth were brown and stumped. The tattoos on his arms seemed to ebb and flow as the muscles tightened and loosened; it was as if the snakes and dragons there were writhing in their lair, waking up, looking for a way out. The faces of the demons scowled and grimaced. His mouth stretched tight and the flames leaped up around his neck. Finally, I'd walked into his trap and he'd got me.

"I... I..."

"Don't bother, little brother. You're gonna tell me it was an accident. You're gonna say it was just a little bump, and you wanted her to get off the smack, and you were trying to save her. But I know, because you're like me. You knew it was over the top. You knew you'd kill her. You knew she was the last of the Morgans for you to get rid of."

Yes. Yes, I knew that.

"I'm the one with the date with death, and you've got the good life going on. But you'll never get rid of me, little brother. Never."

Maybe, but he was in chains. I still had choices.

"Yes, I will, Mike. You're not the only one who's dying. Difference is, I'm trying to do some good here before I check out; you're just trying to drag everyone down with you."

Grant looked over at me, questioning with his eyes. Mike looked unimpressed.

"My date is August Third, asshole. Can you beat that?"

"Maybe. I have cancer. Lung cancer. Stage Four. I won't live past this year. The doctor says I could be dead in a month."

Grant didn't take his eyes off me, but I was watching my brother in the chair across the little room. He looked victorious.

"Only God can judge you, John. Guess you just learned that."

"So let's be clear here, Mike. You're going to die soon. I'm going to die soon. We're both guilty of being assholes. The world's going to keep turning. But if either of us can find *any* salvation, it'll be by doing one thing good before we go. Helping one innocent person, one person who's never done anything to deserve all this shit we've given them. I want to find what happened to Jessica, and maybe even find Jessica herself. If there's anything you can tell me, now's the time because we're not seeing each other again till we meet in hell."

Mike slumped in his chair. The snakes settled; the dragons went back to their slumber.

"Listen Dude – she's gonna be dead. This is bullshit. There's nothing I can tell you. But maybe go talk to Billy. He said he'd get you for what you did to his girlfriend, fucking her and killing her. Go find out if he ever did."

. . .

In the truck, it was Grant who spoke first.

"Was that true? About the cancer, I mean?"

"Yeah. It's true. Nobody knows except me and the doctors, and now Mike and you, and you're not going to tell anyone. I'll tell Maria and Molly soon. I just want this other crap out of the way first."

"I'm sorry, Jon. I had no idea. I feel really bad for you."

"Thank you. You'll be getting the trailer sooner than you thought."

"Guess so."

We drove back out, under the Auschwitz arch, and then Grant spoke again.

"Was it true what he said, about you and your sister? The way she died, I mean."

There was no point hiding anything now.

"Yeah. I never had sex with her or anything like that, that was just a dirty story Mike used to tell people when we were kids, but I gave her the fatal dose. And yeah, I knew it would kill her. She was a meth head, anything she could put in herself, and it was hopeless. I used to give her bumps and it was okay, but then she hooked up with this guy Billy and it got worse. He was as bad as she was. I'd give her some, but he'd give her more, you know? I should have just figured out how to deal with him, but it didn't take long for her till there was no going back."

Grant stayed silent and I told him about Tammy, how we grew up together with Luis, she and me against the world. She became the twin sister who my dad had taken from me, and we looked out for each other. Mike was jealous of that. But in that environment, where there were always drugs, always the offers of sex, always easy money, only the strongest survive and Tammy wasn't strong. She was good and kind and frail and trusting, and the wrong people got to her. I did what I could, but that wasn't enough. By the time Claire arrived, and then Jess, Tammy was just another scrawny cracked-up whore, living with a low-life and both of them begging for handouts for their habits. I couldn't help her, so I put an end to it and the guilt hung with me all my life. There's always hope. I know that now.

Billy was supposed to die too that day, overdosing from the overpure packet of smack in their little house, the place he'd inherited from his parents, the place they turned from home to hoard, cozy to condemned. But she died, unaware of anything, while he survived. Last I heard, 19 years back, he was in rehab. I had no idea he'd ever known my brother, or ever gone visit him in prison. And I had no idea he'd realized what I'd done, and what he thought I'd done, and vowed revenge for it.

"We're not going straight home," I said to Grant, who nodded an okay. "Let's take some advice and see if we can go find Billy first."

"Sure," said Grant, "but are we going to McDonald's?"

I never did speak to the warden about getting a Big Mac to Mike. I'm sure he'd say no, anyway. That's okay. I'd order one and eat it myself. It'll taste great.

BIRD ON A WIRE

Chapter 36

VIVIAN, Toronto

Claire was talking to me, but it was not conversation. They were just random words, spoken so softly I could barely make them out. I wrote them down, in case it might make a difference: "air," "face," "egg," "ice" – though maybe it wasn't "ice," maybe it was "Jess." I don't know. At least they were words, even if they made no sense.

The doctors said it was still too early to know how much of her will return. We don't know how long she was under water and we'll probably never know. There was no security camera, no entry code punched into the door. She just walked in and that was that. We'll also probably never know *why* – it'll just be conjecture. Some say that at this stage, it doesn't really matter, but it will be important if she ever returns to be anywhere near the person she was.

Listen to me. I should be more positive. She was making progress and it had only been four days. "This healing process cannot be rushed," the doctor told me this morning. "The first hundred hours are critical, but it's the first hundred days that will show us where we're headed."

I was lucky I was here at all, sitting by Claire's bedside. It was only Tuesday last week that we flew home, and now it's Thursday and so much has changed already.

The staff were all so kind. Of course, many of them knew Claire – she worked on the ward three floors above, and they came down on their breaks or after their shifts, just to check in. She was always like an angel to her patients, they said. Like a saint, even. They told stories about their times together on the ward and I smiled and laughed and looked over to see if there was a reaction from Claire, and sometimes there seemed to be. Sometimes, she acted just like she was listening and knew who was talking, and other times, she checked out for a while, went back to wherever she was resting up.

Came and went. There was no rhythm to it, no schedule. Sometimes she was with us and sometimes she was not.

I called Jon down in Florida last night, to tell him about Claire's progress. He sounded relieved to hear the news. He was at home with Maria and Molly and he put his phone on speaker for a while so I could say hello to them. They're both of them such nice young women – not the plastic mannequins I thought them to be, but so full of life! Claire never had a good thing to say about Jon, and I'm sure he's guilty of a few crimes, but maybe those two had set him straight, at least with the important values of family and compassion.

Jon told me he's getting somewhere with finding out what happened to Jess. He said the cameras at the mall were set up so they missed a small area of the floor, and Jess might have walked in that unseen space to a door that could have taken her outside. He said he's working on this with the journalist friend and with the police.

He also said he'd found Floyd Woods and told him to stay away from us. He said Woods had "got the message," whatever that means. To be honest, I don't care what that means, as long as he does stay away. I'm sure Jon can be very forceful when he needs to be. He's a smart man and I'm glad he was on our side, even if I'll never quite trust him. If anyone now can find what happened to Jess, I think it will be him.

Chapter 37

JON, Tampa

Grant got a call from his cop woman friend in the car on the way down to Tampa. She'd been away but got back early to her desk in the station, and she wanted to know how the visit went. Well, she wanted to hear his side of it, anyway – she'd already heard from the warden. Grant kept his phone up by his ear, but she spoke loud enough that I could hear it all.

"Did he say Gary Richards is dead?"

"Yes," said Grant. He was being vague so I wouldn't pick up on the question.

"Are you in the car with him now? Can he hear me?"

"Yes. And no."

"Okay. Can you come in so we can talk?"

"Sure."

"Come straight here, okay? Al said Jon might want to go find Billy Evans?"

"You know about Billy Evans?" Grant couldn't help himself. Evans – that was Billy's last name. I don't think I ever knew.

"I've been looking through the interview files, the ones we can't let you see because they're tied up by privacy. There was a Billy Evans that Floyd interviewed on the day. He worked at the mall as a maintenance guy. It looks like we had no idea he had a connection to the Morgans, but Al said he was the boyfriend of John Morgan's sister. In the interview notes" – and then it sounded like she was reading from them – "Evans said he packed up a faulty air-conditioning unit in the rear of the Louie's Luggage store, which he took from the building around noon and delivered to Frigidex Air on Phillip Street, Tampa. Evans said he stopped for lunch on the way to the delivery, then returned to the mall around 3 pm. That was a long lunch, huh?"

"Yes," said Grant, who wasn't bothering now to shield me from hearing the call. "I'm sure he's the guy we can see on Camera 44, leaving the store and loading a box into a blue van. Jessica must have been inside the box. The air-con unit he delivered must have been already in the van."

"I looked and I'm sure you're right," said the woman cop. "I expect he really did deliver an a/c unit to Frigidex. He had plenty of time. We got his home address that we'd have taken from his driver's license, and it's ticked off, so we would have verified he was legit. I've looked it up on Google and it's just an apartment over a store in East Ybor. I've sent a patrol car over anyway to check it out. There's no record in any Florida police or civic database of what happened to Evans after this time – he probably moved out of state."

"Okay," said Grant.

"Still, maybe it's an answer for you, huh? This Billy Evans would have known Jessica – enough to stand in the construction door of that luggage store and call her name, anyway. He worked in the mall, so he could have moved the cameras, even set them to blink when they took pictures, so he could have a 10-second countdown. If he's still alive somewhere, we're gonna want to talk to him again."

"Sounds good," said Grant, trying to be coy again.

"But first, we want to talk to you. Come straight here. Don't let John Morgan lead you off on some wild goose chase. You don't want to be part of his vendetta. He's a dangerous guy."

Grant ended the call and turned to me.

"You heard all that, right?"

"I did. You want me to drop you at Tampa PD?"

"Hell, no!" said Grant. "We're in this together!"

. . .

I don't remember much about where Tammy and Billy were living back in 2003, but it wasn't above a store in East Ybor. It was a shithole meth house in College Hill, ready to be condemned when I last saw it. Sure enough, when we pulled up outside, it was still a shithole house but somebody had put some TLC into it. Fresh paint, cut grass, new windows. There was a realtor's For Sale sign on the lawn. That explained it.

I could have knocked on the door but that'd get me nowhere. I wouldn't even recognize Billy if I met him now, and I was sure he wasn't living there. There might be some records with the realtor though, so we headed over to the realty office that was not so far away. I made a stop first at a bank machine. I'd need some cash for this to go smoothly.

At the office, Grant and me walked in and said hello to a woman at a desk near the door.

"Hi there," I said. "I'm hoping you might be able to give me some information on a house you're listing in College Hill."

"I can try," she said. What's the address?"

"320 Foster Crescent."

She looked disappointed.

"Right – that's Gord's listing." She pointed at a guy sitting at another desk near the back, who's already looking up at us. "That's Gord over there if you want to speak with him."

We headed back and said hello to Gord, real nice.

"I'm afraid I'm not here to buy a house," I told him, straight away, "but I did used to know the guy who lived at 320 Foster and I'm hoping you can tell me where he moved to. I'm guessing he's not the current seller. We're talking close to 20 years back."

Gord turned serious.

"I'm sorry," he said. "I can take a look, but there's probably nothing I can tell you. We're bound by privacy, you know."

I sat down, still real nice.

"Oh, I know. I don't want to get you into any trouble. But whatever you can tell me might really help me find my friend. His name's Billy."

Gord nodded. He tapped on his keyboard, though I couldn't see his screen.

"Hmm," he said. "There's more here than I thought there'd be. We had the listing for the place back in 2004. Sold for real cheap. Is that when your friend would have been living there?"

Maybe. Tammy died there in 2003, so the following year sounded about right.

"Like I said," said Gord, peering into the screen, "all this information about the seller and the buyer is bound by confidentiality. I can't divulge any of it to a non-realtor, I'm afraid."

This was bullshit, but I knew where it was going.

"Oh, I'm a realtor," I said. "Here's my documents."

I slid five hundred-dollar bills across the desk toward him. He looked around to see if anyone was watching, but it was only me and Grant paying him any attention. He picked up the bills and pocketed them quickly in his jacket.

"Glad to hear it," he said, and spun the screen around for us to see. It was a grid of information about septic systems and land transfers, and for a moment I thought it was completely worthless, but as I scanned the boxes I saw the name of the seller, Billy Evans, and a forwarding address. It was an apartment in East Ybor. It looked like the place was sold in April 2004 for $27,000 with no property inspection, and Billy used the money to move to the apartment. That matched what the cop already told us. Total waste of five hundred bucks.

"There's your forwarding address!" said Gord. "Maybe you can find your friend there."

"No – he moved from there long ago," I said. I was hoping there might still be something Gord could pull out of his ass to justify the cash.

"Hmm. Well, maybe he bought another place from us since. I can take a look."

Gord spun the monitor back around so it was hidden from us again, and tapped away at the keyboard.

"Hmm. There's no record of anything else with Billy Evans buying or selling. We have offices around the state, but he's not coming up on any of them."

An idea came. "Try William Evans."

"Sure." He tapped away again, shook his head again. "Nothing, I'm afraid."

Then, "Oh – wait a second."

He was scrolling on the screen, reading something, not showing us what it was.

"How about that?" he said, to himself.

Both Grant and me were staring at him, waiting.

Gord shrugged.

"I'm afraid I really can't tell you. It's privacy."

What an asshole. I'd play nice one more time, and then he gets my gun in his face. I reached into my pocket, pulled out five more C-notes and slid them across the desk. This time, I didn't care who was watching.

He picked them up real quick and put them in his jacket.

"There's a numbered company that bought a residential house from us a few months later, still in 2004, still in the Greater Bay area. William Evans is listed as the President and sole member of the board. It doesn't give any other information about him and it might not even be your guy, but here's the listing from back then."

He turned the monitor around and I could see a tidy little home in Northeast Tampa, listed as a two-bedroom bungalow, a quarter of an acre, 40 feet of frontage on Lincoln Avenue.

Gord tapped away some more.

"The place is still registered as being owned by the numbered company," he said. "There's no mortgage on it."

"Thanks – I'll go take a look."

"Sure. If I can help with anything else, I'll be pleased to do so. Always happy to assist a fellow realtor!"

But Gord's voice fell flat behind us. We were already half-out the door.

. . .

The address was listed as 4237 Lincoln Avenue. It didn't look like it had changed much: still an unassuming single-story white house set a little back from the road, two small windows at the front, surrounded by green sycamores, tall sugarberries and drooping live oaks. There was a short patch of grass for a lawn and it was newly trimmed to match the general tidiness of the home. There was no vehicle in the driveway or under the car port, but even so, I didn't slow down as we passed.

I drove through the stop sign, swung the truck around and parked facing the house. Gotta think. The road was narrow and leafy, almost an afterthought to the area's grid pattern, and the truck was not too obvious.

My plan was to bang on the front door, kick it down if I have to, and yell for Billy Evans. Even I knew that's a bad plan.

"Well, what do you think, Grant? This doesn't look like a business address to me."

"Nope," said Grant. I could tell he was nervous. This was all so far out of his comfort zone, but for me, the way this week was going, it was just Thursday.

"Maybe I'm putting two and two together and getting 22," I said, "but to me, it looks like Billy Evans went to rehab, sorted himself out, created a shell company, sold the shitty house he'd inherited from his parents and used the money for a down-payment on a nice little family home, just a few months before Jess was taken. And he kept the rental apartment to have an address for his driver's license."

It was all falling into place. The afternoon sun was still hot and I had the truck windows open so I could smoke, but I was getting chills as I worked through Billy's mind.

"He can live here anonymously, maybe even change his name, get a job, keep his nose clean. Stay off the radar. The cops check him out after the abduction but there's nothing to ring any bells and they don't really care anyway. Maybe they even went to his place in East Ybor. But he wasn't living there. He was living here. And they didn't know about this place."

"And if he was living here," said Grant, "then maybe he wasn't living alone. It seems a lot of trouble to change your residence and everything else if you're going to take somebody and kill them the same night. This sounds like he brought her here. And then he kept her here. This was a long-term plan."

As he said this, a red Silverado pickup drove past us from behind, and instinctively, I ducked my head. The truck paused at the stop sign, carried on up the street and pulled into the gravel drive of the little white house. I ducked again when the driver got out.

"Did he see us?" I asked.

"Yeah, I think so. He's heading in the house now."

"Well, I guess it's now or never."

I reached across and took my Glock from the glovebox. It'd been getting a workout this week, and we weren't done yet.

"Jon! Shouldn't we just call the cops? I can call Sgt. Beth now and she'll have cops here right away."

"Sure, give her a call," I said. "Tell her I'll meet her inside."

. . .

JON - Tampa

Is this one of the most stupid things I've ever done? I've done some stupid stuff, after all. I should be sitting back there in the truck, waiting for the cops to arrive, instead of standing here on the doorstep of 4237 Lincoln Avenue with a loaded gun in my belt. But the cops screwed this up from the start and I can't let them screw it up again. This is on me. This is my moment. I'm in charge.

I've knocked on the door. Chances are, some guy's about to come answer it and he'll be a tenant who's never heard of Billy Evans, and I'll apologize for wasting his time, and then I'll go back and tell Grant and I'll drop him at the police station and maybe they can do some forensic accounting or whatever and figure out what happened to Billy. Maybe.

Or could be, Jess will come to the door and I'll recognize her and Billy will be there and I'll shoot him in the face and I'll get my little girl back and fulfill my promise to Molly. We'll be a happy family, if only for a few months. Maybe.

Or, Billy will be here and I'll bluff my way in and then I'll put my gun to his head and force him to tell me what happened to Jessica, and I'll shoot the bastard and claim self-defense and still get to fulfill my promise to Molly. The mystery will be solved, and I'll be the one who solved it. I have the power.

I can hear footsteps coming to the door. Of course, there's another scenario that could play out here and so I reach under my shirt, but before I can think it through, the door opens and there's a guy standing there, a short guy about my age with a brown ball cap and a Hulk Hogan moustache.

"Yeah?" he says.

I should have a story ready, a ruse of some sort, but I don't. I just ran up here and now it's on. I have the power of life and death.

"Billy Evans?" I say.

And the guy gives a little nod and opens the door wider, and he's holding a shotgun, and he fires and I feel the hot burn spread through my chest and my stomach before I even hear the crack or feel the hammer of being knocked backwards off my feet. My hand's already on my gun and I pull it out and fire it at his chest and I don't know if it hits because I hear another crack and there's another burn that fills my whole body this time and I'm lying on my back and looking up and I want to close my eyes but they won't close and I hear the words: "That's from Tammy." And I fire my gun again and again

and I'm not aiming at anything, but I see his head drop away and down, and I just lie there on the grass and I realize what's happening, finally catching up to me after all these years, and I won't have to buy those smokes after all, and I beat lung cancer, and I beat Mike, and I can hear sirens, Grant must have called the police, and I hear screams and I feel somebody hold my head, and in the blur, in the blue, in the sun, there's a face, and I see red hair and green eyes and I hear the name,
    Jess.

Chapter 38

VIVIAN, Toronto

I was sorry not to attend Jon's funeral. His friend Grant told me it was a large affair and he said it was like those mafia funerals, with the police standing off to one side and taking photographs of people. Of course, I don't think Jon would have cared if I was there or not – funerals are for the living, not the dead – but I'd have liked to be there to be with Maria and their daughter Molly. And with Jess, of course.

Jess is living now with Maria and Molly. We've spoken by Messenger and we speak two or three times a week with Claire. She couldn't handle more than that. Jess, I mean, not Claire. Claire is keeping regular hours now, awake in the daytime and asleep at night, but her conversation is still not there. Like the doctor said, it's the first hundred days that will show us where she's headed, and we're well past that now.

They discharged Claire and she's come home to live with me. Already, I've been taking her outside, wheeling her along the footpaths now the snow is long gone. She loves listening to the birds and they've come home too and built their nests, starting the whole life cycle for another year. It's just turned summer but the weather's only now starting to warm. People are saying this year has to be better than the last and in so many ways, they're right.

Maria tells me it will take a long time for Jessica to readjust to life. It was very hard for poor Jess to see the man she thought was her father and her lover killed in front of her by the police. She has no memory of any life before she was taken, so she thought her whole experience was normal, what every little girl lives through. Billy Evans kept her out of school, kept her to himself, all this time. When she grew old enough, which is to say, when she showed the first signs of becoming a woman, they lived as man and wife, though she would rarely leave the house. He didn't tie her up or anything – she just didn't know any better.

Because of this, she's not been able to relate to Jon at all, to realize what he did for her. She's an intelligent woman, but still with the mind of a girl. To her, Jon is just the man who killed her lover, and I'm sure she loved Billy very much. She didn't know she had any other choice. She even carried a child by him, but she said Billy punched her in the stomach to kill the baby because 'it wasn't time.' I'm sad for that, but I'm so relieved. I don't think I could have loved that child as I should.

Now, at last, they're coming to visit, just for a few days. We're starting to get back to normal, or whatever it is that normal's become. Toronto is such a lovely city when the days are warm and the trees are in leaf. I know Molly's looking forward to it, and to sharing it with her new sister, and I'm sure Maria will be pleased for the break. These last few months have been very hard on her.

Grant is coming up too, more to help with their bags than anything. I've never met Grant in person but he seems a nice man. He's been doing well for himself down there since his story was published so prominently in *The New York Times* and he says he's had a few offers of journalism positions, including up here with the *Toronto Star*. Jon would be so pleased for him.

Of course, Grant's been busy enough sorting out Jonathan's affairs. Jon knew he was dying – lung cancer – and in his last few days he wrote a will that named Grant as the executor. He was worth quite a lot of money, several million dollars, plus his house. As Grant said so cryptically in his article for the *Times*, that was pretty good for a used-car salesman, but Jon was no ordinary used-car salesman. He even left money for the care of Tyler Jackson, the police officer injured by Jon's brother. Grant didn't say how much it was, but apparently it's enough to help look after Tyler and his father properly without leaving anything over for Andrea, the woman who tried to pass herself off as Jessica. I was pleased to hear that.

I've not heard from Floyd Woods, which is a surprise. I thought that once Jonathan was no longer around, Woods might come back to try to claim something but he's not done so. I asked Grant about him and he told me not to worry. "I don't think Floyd Woods will be coming back to bother us," he said, and then he added: "still waters run deep." I don't know that I want to think about that.

. . .

When the doorbell rings, it's just like any other visit. It reminds me of Claire ringing the bell and then fussing over locking her bicycle on the porch, but Claire's here now, sitting in the front room, washed and dressed and ready. I answer the door and the four of them are waiting outside, their cases already brought up the steps.

"Grandma!" says Molly. "We love your house!"

That's sweet of her. She's only seen the front door and my background on Messenger. It's even sweeter that she calls me Grandma. She has real grandparents of her own in Cuba, but she says I'm her honorary grandmother and there'll be no arguments, which there aren't.

I hug her and I hug Maria, but it's Jessica who stands back a little, unsure what to do. She has none of her father's impetuous nature and all of her mother's reservation, so I step out on to the porch and take her hand. I think she expects me to embrace her and she recoils a little, but I just hold her hands and give them a gentle squeeze and she relaxes.

"Jess – this is such a pleasure. Come in and meet your mother."

The three women walk in as Grant gathers their bags outside. They won't stay here tonight – they're at a hotel downtown – but they wanted to come directly over from the airport to see Claire.

Jessica's gained some weight since she was rescued. Back then, she was gaunt and pale. Her hair was long and like string, because she'd never been to a hairdresser. She would wear shorts and T-shirts or vests, never a dress, because she wore whatever Billy Evans provided. Molly's been teaching her about fashion and now she's wearing a long skirt and a pretty cream-coloured blouse that sets off her bright red hair, which is short, in a bob. Her eyes were deep set in the earlier photos but they seem more vibrant now. The clothes might be Molly's – they're both around the same height, not very tall. Molly's been showing her how to apply make-up, too.

Claire is knitting Jess a sweater. I joked once that it could be a Christmas sweater and Claire didn't know what I meant by that, but that's okay. She's as adept with her knitting needles as she ever was because knowing how to knit is like knowing how to ride a bicycle; even so, Claire is a long way from riding a bicycle again. Knitting is safe and it gives her satisfaction, and it gives me satisfaction, too, to see her able to accomplish something.

They walk in to the front room, where Claire is waiting in her chair, and they all slow as they approach, as if they're unsure. I guess they are. I'm nervous, in case Claire is asleep or resting or absorbed by her knitting, or just taking some time away, but she's there in the room with us and when Jess takes her hand and kneels down, she grasps her hand back and the two women, two generations, mother and daughter, hold on to each other for a very long time indeed. The photo of Jess as a three-year-old, sitting on the picnic blanket, is beside them on the glass table. Claire sobs but Jess stays composed. She'll be okay.

I have some tea ready in the kitchen and I ask Grant to help me bring it through, with some slices of carrot cake. And there's something else too. The letter. The letter from Jonathan that he wrote at home on the evening before he died, which he mailed directly to me and which I've never opened. It's addressed to Jessica, care of both Claire and myself. We all know it's here, and when the tea is poured and Maria and I are seated, I take the letter from the tray beside the teapot and give it to Jessica.

"Here, my dear," I say. "This is for you, from your father. He sent it to me to be sure it would reach you safely."

Jessica knows about the letter, the letter I've refused to open and saved for her. I offer her a small knife and she takes a seat then slices open the envelope carefully. She pulls the letter from inside and begins to look at it – it's written by hand, I can see, with a blue pen – but then she gives it to Molly.

"Please," she says. It's the first word I've heard her speak.

Molly takes the sheets of paper, unfolds them, and begins to read to us all. She speaks as a young girl, but it's as if the voice is her father.

My dear Jess:

I hope you're reading this, and I hope you're thinking kind thoughts about your mother and me. As I write this, I don't know if you're alive or not, but it almost doesn't matter. In our hearts, you'll always be alive, and you'll always be the Jessica we love so much.

I don't know when we'll find you, but my own time is running short. The doctor says I have lung cancer, so I'm writing this now in case it's the only way we'll get to meet. Don't smoke! Life's too valuable to let cancer take it from you before your time.

We didn't make it easy for you. I was not always there for you, and I was not there for Claire. I regret that now more than you know. Your sister Molly taught me that fatherhood is a sacred trust and I've tried to fulfill that with her, and to share a loving bond with her mother Maria. I've learned a lot in the last few days, but if nothing else, I hope I've learned that love is something you've got to earn. If you're reading this now, I hope it means I've earned your love. Nothing else matters more to me than the love of my family.

If you've not experienced this yet, I hope you will now. Please forgive us all for not finding you sooner. Please forgive your mother for despairing, and thank Molly for proving to me what's important. And please accept Maria as a mother, and Vivian as a grandmother. They're your family. In the end, you must dismiss the evils that delayed this meeting and embrace the overwhelming power of good.

I'm not a good man. I've been a bad man. I come from a bad family and I've done some bad things. But I've done some good things too, and in the end, I found love. Molly told me that the only thing that matters is to bring love into the world, and now I can say I've done that. It was the right thing to do. It's what makes me proud to call myself your father.

With all my love forever,

Your father,

Jonathan Morgan

Molly finishes reading and refolds the letter. Claire's eyes are closed, as if she's asleep. Maria and Grant are both looking down at the floor, and their eyes are wet. Outside on the porch, through the window, I can see a yellow hummingbird hovering at the feeder, sipping at the sugar water that Claire and I left there this morning.

Jessica takes the letter from her sister and holds it with both hands as she looks around the room at all of us. "Thank you," she says, and the corners of her mouth curl upward in the gentlest of smiles.

THE END

Acknowledgements

No book is created alone, and the full story of how *Bird on a Wire* came to be can be seen at my website, markrichardson.ca. Originally, Claire and Jonathan were happily married lottery winners, so they had quite the journey to result in this novel.

Much of that evolution was thanks to the perceptive advice of my editor, Nora Savage, who read the first manuscript and stuck with me through various iterations to publication. She shared my vision for this story, and she encouraged me when I needed encouragement most.

A number of people helped me get my facts straight. Paul W. Walker of the Florida Department of Corrections ensured I would not need to actually spend time at Florida State Prison to describe it properly. Gabrielle Calise at the Tampa Bay Times answered my questions patiently about Covid's restrictions during a period when I could not visit from my Canadian home to see for myself. And Dr. Sanjay Patel suggested various horrific cocktails of drugs and medical treatment to maintain the authenticity of Claire and John's health challenges.

Jackie Smith, Julia Sinclair-Smith, Neil Horner, Jacqueline Janelle, Scott Colby, and my son Tristan Richardson read various drafts of the manuscript and made essential suggestions. Special thanks must go to Norris McDonald, who set me straight by reading the first draft and saying, "Well, it'll make a good short story!" Keith Morgan was the first to suggest I self-publish this novel in order for it to appear without the constraints of traditional publishers, and James Wysotski, an accomplished author himself, gave me invaluable insights from his experience with his own novel, *After the Next Pandemic*.

My wife Wendy never lost faith in me during the considerable time it took in solitary confinement to create the story of Jonathan and Claire. Her suggestions after multiple readings also helped define their characters. For her support, I will always be indebted.

Finally, I must also give special thanks to my former agent who will remain unnamed, who read the final manuscript and declared it "unpublishable." That rankled so much with me that I determined to publish it myself with the car and attention it deserves, and to allow you, the reader, to make the ultimate judgement. Whatever your opinion, please consider leaving a review at either Amazon.com or at Goodreads, or wherever you prefer, to let others know about this story.

About the author

 Mark Richardson is a journalist and author, based in Cobourg, Ontario.

Mark is the former automotive editor of the *Toronto Star* and now contributes regularly to Canada's national newspaper, *The Globe and Mail*, among other publications.

He is the author of *The Drive Across Canada: The remarkable story of the Trans-Canada Highway* (Dundurn, 2025), and *Zen and Now: On the trail of Robert Pirsig and the art of motorcycle maintenance* (Knopf, 2008).

Bird on a Wire is Mark's first published novel.

His second novel, *Running on Empty*, is the story of Tampa's Grant Gibson in the summer of 2024, after taking Jon's Harley-Davidson to strike out to see America. Along the way, Grant meets Zack, who is looking for his wife and son, lost years ago to a horrific cult. Their ride becomes a quest for both discovery and resolution, but in turn, they're hunted every mile of the way. "Vivid and strong – engaging and satisfying." – *Don Butler*

www.markrichardson.ca

Manufactured by Amazon.ca
Bolton, ON

45026197R00169